EASILY
FOOLED

———

ESSENTIAL PROSE SERIES 185

Canada Council   Conseil des Arts
for the Arts   du Canada

ONTARIO ARTS COUNCIL
CONSEIL DES ARTS DE L'ONTARIO
an Ontario government agency
un organisme du gouvernement de l'Ontario

Canada

Guernica Editions Inc. acknowledges the support of the Canada Council
for the Arts and the Ontario Arts Council. The Ontario Arts Council
is an agency of the Government of Ontario.

We acknowledge the financial support of the Government of Canada.

EASILY FOOLED

No Safeguards 3—Millington's Story

H. NIGEL THOMAS

GUERNICA
EDITIONS
TORONTO • CHICAGO • BUFFALO • LANCASTER (U.K.)
2021

Michael Mirolla, general editor
Julie Roorda, editor
David Moratto, interior and cover design
Guernica Editions Inc.
287 Templemead Drive, Hamilton, ON L8W 2W4
2250 Military Road, Tonawanda, N.Y. 14150-6000 U.S.A.
www.guernicaeditions.com

Distributors:
Independent Publishers Group (IPG)
600 North Pulaski Road, Chicago IL 60624
University of Toronto Press Distribution,
5201 Dufferin Street, Toronto (ON), Canada M3H 5T8
Gazelle Book Services, White Cross Mills
High Town, Lancaster LA1 4XS U.K.

First edition.
Printed in Canada.

Legal Deposit—First Quarter
Library of Congress Catalog Card Number: 2020947076
Library and Archives Canada Cataloguing in Publication
Title: Easily fooled : No safeguards 3, Millington's story / H. Nigel Thomas
Names: Thomas, H. Nigel, 1947- author.
Series: Essential prose series ; 185.
Description: Series statement: Essential prose series ; 185
Identifiers: Canadiana (print) 20200354124 | Canadiana (ebook) 20200354140 |
ISBN 9781771835817 (softcover) | ISBN 9781771835824 (EPUB)
| ISBN 9781771835831 (Kindle)
Classification: LCC PS8589.H4578 E28 2021 | DDC C813/.54—dc23

For Caswell "Fatman" Grant

We are big and blunt and easily fooled and know few of the fine points of translation
—Don McKay "Meditation on a Small Bird's Skull"

1

H E HAS BEEN pacing the corridor backward and forward—from the main door, through the living room, to the dining area. His skin's tingling. It began as soon as he got into the elevator on the ground floor. Now sweat's coursing down his sides from his armpits. An hour and a half ago he received his permanent resident visa. Starting over at thirty-six. Tough.

He takes off the navy-blue blazer he wore to the Citizenship and Immigration office earlier and hangs it in the coat closet. He should change his damp shirt too. It reeks of the Paco Rabane he sprayed himself with. He moves to the couch, begins to sit, but hears the crows clamouring outside. They come around 11 a.m. on a Tuesday, garbage collection day. He walks to the dining area, unlocks the patio door, goes onto the balcony, and watches them. Twenty-one are feeding rowdily from atop the three overflowing dumpsters. On the ground below, five gulls, their white plumage contrasting with the crows' black, move around and eye the crows nervously. *The simple, instinctual life.* He sighs. *Do crows worry? If they're as intelligent as the biologists say, they probably do.*

He hums:

> *All things which live below the sky*
> *Or move within the sea*
> *Are creatures of the Lord most High*
> *And brothers unto me.*

One of the few hymns from his Methodist past that he's still comfortable singing (minus the third line).

On the metro on his way home from the immigration office, he vowed to start focusing on what's beautiful in his life. Took over three years, 2012 to 2015, to process his immigration application. Yesterday was Thanksgiving. Today he has something to be thankful for and one thing less to worry about.

He returns inside, walks back to the living room, and sits on the couch. His mind turns to Gladys, a parishioner back in Barbados now studying at McGill. This afternoon he's meeting her for the fourth time since she arrived in Montreal at the end of August. She insisted that she must see him urgently but wouldn't say why. He thinks she has found out something. Is she about to confront him? *No surprises, please. Not today.*

He wonders: Will his nightmares end now? Will he stop dreaming that he's back in St Vincent looking for a job and a purpose for his life? The feeling that his marriage to Jay is a mistake, will that too end? Suppose Jay says to him when he returns from Atlanta today: Millington, you are a permanent resident now, so let's annul this marriage.

That Friday evening: February 17, 2012. What came over him? Why did he uncork so easily? Why did he spill like that? He'd sealed it for a long time. Longer and he might have exploded, gone insane for real. If Jay's brother Paul hadn't stayed behind in the hotel lobby, he would have been more measured. But the stopper blew and he gushed like a geyser. The bar was deserted, just a man and a woman at a corner table at the far end from them and the bartender behind the counter.

He told Jay that he'd resigned from the Methodist ministry. Jay complimented him for doing so, "if that's what you wanted." And now I'm destitute, he resisted saying. He asked Jay about the possibility of immigrating to Canada. Jay said he'd heard that the easiest way was to marry a Canadian citizen ... That the government had launched a campaign to discourage Canadians from marrying people they meet while holidaying abroad. A long pause. "I'll check out the Citizenship and Immigration website and let you know," Jay said, his head turned away.

Millington took a deep breath, held fiercely onto the sides of the table—his hands slippery with sweat—closed his eyes, and said: "Did you ever suspect that I'm gay?"

"No."

He wanted to take back the question.

"That's why you left the ministry?"

Millington nodded.

Jay put his hand under the table, tapped him on the knee, nodded slowly, and said without even glancing at him that he understood.

What did he understand? He was silent, his head down as if contemplating the table, pensive, for a long time afterwards. Was he recalling the rumour he'd heard from someone he'd met at the Vincy Thousand-Islands Picnic in 2011? "That fellow from Havre, Millington, AMC Methodist minister, heard he went through the looking glass." Took four months after they'd been married for Jay to tell him.

Back home. Sitting up in bed. Unable to sleep. Angry over his poor self-control. His cell beeping. A text message from Paul: "Millington, Jay is gay. Was in love with u while u2 were in h-school. Can u meet us at the airport no later than 7 a.m. tomorrow?" A tearful meeting next morning. And Jay and he were married four months later. If a parishioner had presented him with such a scenario, he would have discouraged it.

In the nightmares in which he's back in St Vincent and penniless, Melvin, his ex-superintendent, and the other ministers laugh at him. One time he dreamt that he met his dad Edward coming up Pasture Road toward their house, and Edward glared at him and spat as he walked past. Another time, near the bottom of the hill, Neil Charles, in the soiled white gloves and white soutane that he took to wearing after he returned crazed from a Catholic seminary in Trinidad, accosted him. Neil, now skeletal, no longer sensual and desirable: crimped beige skin, eyes dark and feverish in their hollow sockets, mouth agape as if wanting to swallow him, arms extended in a semi-circle to embrace him—rushed out from his father's house onto the road and blocked his path. "Still have eyes for Jay only, huh"—exactly as he'd done on two occasions back in 2011. When Mem's present in the nightmares, she screams "Disgrace," and wags a finger at Millington.

These dreams? Perhaps no more than the fluff that fills our heads when we're unfocused. Not the one in which he's on his belly pushing himself through a narrow tunnel and gets to the tunnel's end and can't go back. That one's definitely not fluff. In the last month before he left his ministry in Barbados, it occurred almost every night.

The nightmare in which his godfather Elijah first points a handgun at him, then shoots himself on Millington's parents' porch, and a finger-wagging Reverend Hennessy shouts over and over at Millington: "You caused it"—that's definitely not fluff. That one goes back to when he was fifteen. Elijah had sent him to Ma Kirton's shop to buy a tin of sardines and a packet of crackers. Upon his return he called to Elijah to come onto the porch for the items. Elijah told him to bring them into the house. Millington met him seated at his dining table. On it a bottle of rum, a half-filled tumbler, and a handgun.

"That's a real gun?"

Elijah nodded. "Don't look so frighten. I not going shoot you. Might shoot meself though ... Only joking." He picked up the handgun, turned it over in his hands three or four times, then put it back down. "Buy this from a sailor in Kingstown ... Sit down." He pointed to the dining chair opposite him.

Millington hesitated. He had never sat in Elijah's house before, had never gone beyond the porch.

"Sit. What's your hurry? Your mother know you running a errand for me." His eyes glazed, his speech slurred, his breath rummy.

He sat. It would have been impolite not to. A long silence. In one gulp Elijah downed the rum in his glass and refilled it. Millington didn't know his godfather drank. He started getting up to go, but Elijah waved him back down. "What's your hurry? ... Heard about my wife? Yes?"

Millington nodded. Haverites knew that his wife had left him, had fled with their two daughters to the U.S.

"I want to see my two girls. What they look like. I don't have even a photo of them." He stared at the handgun for several seconds. "I buy this when I find out Thelma been butting me. Been butting me coming and going ... With Smallboy." He snorted. "No-count Rasta scum! Live in bush like wild beast. Thelma use to leave here, not a care what anybody think. I been the last one to know. When I find out, I buy this gun, and the next day I head for Smallboy shack. I did plan to kill the two o' them and meself. But half-way there, I start wondering what going become o' my two daughters, and I change my mind. Two days later I go out to the kitchen where Thelma been cooking, and I cock the gun, and I push the nozzle 'gainst her chest, and I say: 'Thelma, I know you is horning me. You is horning me with Smallboy. I will blow your brains out if you don't stop.' Then I go back inside and lock away the gun. She run away a week later. First to Trinidad, then New York. Three years later she send me divorce papers, then she send for Smallboy and the girls ... I ain't see my daughters since. Irene and Ophelia. They was eight and six when they leave. Now they is twenty-three and twenty-one. Ain't see them since." He wiped his eyes with his shirt sleeve.

Millington felt sorry for him and was about to say so when he heard Mem's voice calling: "Brother Elijah, Millington by you?"

Millington answered her, got up, and left the house.

Two months later, it was Millington's life that he threatened, and his speech wasn't slurred, and alcohol wasn't on his breath.

He's not to dwell on such things today. He should cancel the meeting with Gladys too. Put it off until next week. No. She said it was urgent.

What's her situation with Horton now? Some nights, while Jay's snoring away, Millington stays propped up with pillows for hours, wondering how his relationship with Horton would have evolved, if he hadn't fled Barbados and Methodism.

He wants to be candid with Gladys ... So much he cannot tell her. So much. If he does and she leaves Horton, they'd blame him for the breakup.

He likes Gladys. Most people pretend to be good. She's genuine. The little masquerading she does is beneficent; done for smoother relationships. Too trusting though. But distrust causes worry. Physician, heal yourself. His suspicions about how much she knows are probably unfounded. That or she dissembles well. Maybe she has decided that today she'll tell him all. Maybe that's what *urgent* means.

Horton. Con-man Horton. Can't blame him for his double life. People do what they must to blend in. Attention seekers of every ilk are on the prowl for outliers, to make scapegoats of them.

Why did Horton plant suspicions in Gladys's mind about him? … Horton set him on the path toward honesty, but he doesn't relish how he did it.

Would his situation be different today if they'd been in contact less often? Less dramatic for sure. But he might have dragged out his ministry and found rationalisations not to leave. The womb of faith is a comfortable place, says Matthew Arnold. Too comfortable. Or he might have done something stupid—something truly disgraceful. Or turn cynical and become a hypocrite. Takes unusually powerful storms to topple deep-rooted trees. He got out of Methodist soil dirtier but wiser than when he entered.

Not overly soiled.

Untainted?

I'll need a therapist to confirm or dispute that. Left with my sanity too—contrary opinions notwithstanding.

And left many tongues wagging. Even Neil Charles'.

Yes, Neil, theology has been bad for both of us. Let the tongues wag.

Might have lost my sanity for real if Jay hadn't intervened.

And when the full facts of his intervention become known there'll be venomous tongues.

We're staying away from that today. Remember?

2

HE REMEMBERS A sandbar in Havre's bay that bathers used to stand on safely year after year, then one day he walked out to it and dropped into deep, dangerous water. Gladys invited him, her pathetic bachelor minister—he was sure it was how she saw him—for supper almost every week. Most times he declined. Their two boys—Len, six at the time and Alex, four—called him Uncle Millington. He was Alex's godfather.

As the junior minister in the Authentic Methodist Church (AMC) Christchurch Circuit, it fell on him to chair the planning committee of the South Caribbean District for the synod that was to take place in Barbados in 2009. As steward of the circuit, Horton was automatically part of the committee. One Wednesday morning Horton came to the manse for them to go over the programme before sending it to be printed.

At various points in their discussion, Horton paused and fixed his cow-like, usually sleepy eyes intensely on Millington. He felt uneasy and probed his memory to see whether he'd left something undone. When he dined at Horton's house, Horton rarely looked at him, even when speaking to him.

They finished synod business an hour early. Doris, Millington's domestic helper, brought them a pot of tea. Horton poured himself a cup and held it suspended half-way between his lap and lips for several seconds while he stared into Millington's eyes. He was certain then that some item he'd overlooked was bothering Horton. Horton took a sip of tea and looked guiltily at Millington. Millington felt his palms moistening. Less than a metre and a half, the width of the desk, separated them.

The silence lengthened. Millington wanted to break it but knew there'd be a quaver in his voice. He might have said that he had another appointment, but they'd planned to meet from nine till noon, and it was 11:10.

"Reverend," Horton said, quite loud, startling him. Church officials used his title only when several people were present. Otherwise they used first names. Millington waited, tense, for the rebuke he thought was coming. "You look puzzled. Aren't you my reverend pastor, my shepherd who vowed at your ordination to lead me to watering holes and *suc-suc-cu-lent green* pastures and protect me from wolves?" Said with a wink and a slurp.

Didn't know you were a sheep. Millington chuckled nervously. His parishioners certainly expected him to beg God to grant them special favours. One had asked him to plead—her word—with God to send her a decent husband, "cause Reverend, these-here children too much to care for by muhself." John Wesley, Methodism's founder and Millington's de facto boss (though more than two centuries dead), had ordered Millington, in number twelve of his rules for ministers, to engage in prayers; at Millington's ordination ceremony, he had vowed to obey Wesley's rules and teachings. He'd been told too—ordered rather—by Melvin, his superintendent, to heed St Paul and feed milk to the ninety percent of his congregation who couldn't digest meat. Paying the ministers' stipends and keeping the churches in repair required lots of money—lots; every lost member was lost revenue, facts Melvin hammered on incessantly, facts he used to push his ministers to imitate the fundamentalists.

"Okay, Millington. This is hard to say." Horton's eyes, now two honey-coloured glowing marbles, were fixed on Millington. "Don't look so rattled. Millington, I believe you're gay."

A wave of spasms crisscrossed Millington's gut. *How dare you!* The demeanour drilled into him to deal with prickly parishioners kicked in. He inhaled deeply, deliberately, and said, in carefully paced words: "Horton, my sexual orientation is none of your business." He expected

Horton to stumble out some sort of stuttering apology and drop the subject.

"Millington, get serious."

"Get *serious*. I *am* serious. In Jamaica—"

"We're *not* in Jamaica. You're my minister. You're to get to the bottom of my troubles and commiserate with me and comfort me … Maybe more." He moistened his lips.

Millington had complimented him on his cologne when he arrived. A mistake perhaps. Caribbean men who wear cologne are sometimes asked why they smell like women. Horton was wearing a close-fitting peach tank-top that outlined his paunch and love handles (he's about six centimetres shorter than Millington and has a smallish frame with about five kilos of extra weight), and tight dark brown three-quarter shorts that accentuated his very round buttocks. Until the "maybe more," his clothes and cologne had meant nothing to Millington.

Moving his head like a cat appraising the mouse in its paws, Horton said: "Millington … Oh, Millington … You're thirty … Unmarried … Need I say more? … Eligible young women—more than a few—have their eyes trained on your every move, shower you with smiles, flirt with you at every opportunity. Do you acknowledge them? Never. Not the faintest hint of encouragement do you give them." He stopped, puffed his cheeks, and let out the air with a pop. "You're a minister in the Authentic Methodist Church; you're not a Catholic priest. Get real."

At fifteen, Millington did wish he were Catholic, so he could enter a monastery *and escape from this disgusting world*. And when Neil Charles left Havre for training to become a priest—Millington had just begun to work in the St Vincent and Grenadines civil service—he'd envied him.

"Horton, my mother's financially dependent on me. I can't start a family."

"Lame, Rev, lame. You're not *inclined* to want a family." His stare was intense, his eyes still glowing.

Millington stared at the door.

Horton swivelled his head, glanced at the door, and shook his head. "Not yet, Rev, not so soon. We're supposed to be here till midday. There's more than half an hour remaining. Enough time to accomplish a *great* deal." He winked and glanced at his crotch. "What I want to say is ..." He stopped, frowned, bloated his cheeks again, let out the air, without amusement this time.

"Is, is ...?"

"Since you're *that way* inclined, you shouldn't start a family."

Millington would have asked him to leave then, but he feared making him his enemy. Customer satisfaction. "Never forget that the congregation pays your stipend"—Melvin's words.

"I'm speaking from personal experience." Horton stood up.

A long silence. Millington's fingers dripping sweat. His face burning.

Horton grinned. "There's sweat on your brow. Gorblimey, Rev! I'm sweating the truth out of you. And, Rev! ... You're violent! Setting to cuff me down?"

Millington looked at his fists on the desk. They were balled. He breathed deeply and straightened my fingers.

"Seriously, Millington ... I am being ... shall we say, honest with you. Have you been honest with yourself?"

Horton continued to stare at him. Millington stayed silent.

"A life of lies. The life you're forced to live in Barbados when you're gay ... In all the West Indies ... Did you know that in Barbados you could get life imprisonment for buggery? Of course they don't enforce it. They harass you and hope you'll jump into the sea ... Good riddance. If you disappoint them, then they hound you and insult you coming and going. Make it clear that you'll pay a high price for existing."

Millington felt cold. The day was sunny. A breeze came in through the open window and occasionally rattled the wooden slats of the venetian blind. He glanced at the goose bumps on his arms. He looked up at Horton, who was staring at the desktop, at the sweat dripping from Millington's fingers. A small pool was already there. Millington put his hands under the desk and wiped them on his trousers.

The faces of Gladys, Len, and Alex paraded across his mind. He'd had supper at their house five days earlier. Alex had come running to him with a word game, which he played sitting beside Millington on the sofa. Len was the quieter one, was already a bookworm, and a year ahead of his grade. Millington felt that they adored their children, that they were a happy family.

Horton and he fell into a long silence. Just as it became overbearing, they heard Doris's footsteps coming toward the study. Millington stood, put his wet left hand in his pocket, wiped the right on his trousers and extended it to Horton just as Doris entered the doorway. She knew Horton well. Their parents had been neighbours in Eagle Hall. She still lives there.

"You ain't leaving, Bro Horton? I put a place setten for you too."

Horton looked at his watch and shook his head. "Doris girl, I gotter take a rain cheque. I already late for a meeten. Rev"—he turned to face Millington—"think over that matter we were discussing, and if you have any further thoughts on it, call me on my cell. Doris, girl, I gotter be running. I know is delicious Bajan coo-coo you gi'ing the reverend today. I done smell it. Like you scheming to turn he into a real Bajan."

She smiled broadly.

He left.

The rest of that Wednesday was ruined. Wednesday afternoon, 2–5 p.m., was time he set aside for his parishioners' visits. The three who came that afternoon did so to chitchat. Doris was off. She had a half day off on Wednesdays and Saturdays and a full day on Sunday. That night he fell asleep after 2 a.m. and dreamed that Horton and he were naked in bed and Gladys and Elijah stormed in on them. He awoke around 5 a.m., frightened.

If he still believed in prayer, he would have prayed, as he'd done many times before, to be cleansed of such desire. Gladys was his treasurer at AMC Hastings. There was such selflessness in her, a desire "to give and give and give again," as the hymn says. Always willing—always —to perform any task, from chauffeuring members around to coordinating fundraising activities to visiting shut-in members. She taught math at Combermere. And her effusive warmth showed that she was a fine, caring person. Her face—caramel, rotund, with a dimpled smile, slight buck teeth, and sparkling hazel eyes—held a childlike innocence.

She told him that her favourite hymns were "All Things Bright and Beautiful" and "Will There Be Any Stars in My Crown?" When a fundraiser they'd done to repair the church roof fell short of what they'd expected, her response was: "Behind every cloud there's a silver lining. We'll look hard and find it. We'll have other activities and we'll work harder." (She knows now that what sometimes looks like silver is often tin.) There wasn't an iota of malice in her smiling, bouncing, butterball body. To wrong her would have been unpardonable.

The second time Horton and Millington met to plan synod business five persons were present. At the end of the meeting, he tickled Millington's palm in their goodbye handshake. Slowly he came around to accepting what his dreams were already telling him: that he desired Horton. Did Horton awaken his sexuality? ... No. More like that coal fire that's burning below ground in Pennsylvania. Give it air and it will conflagrate. Horton had merely set ablaze what had long been smouldering.

He found himself repeating in his sleep: "Thou shalt not covet thy neighbour's wife." At breakfast the next day, he'd remember the dream and mutter: "Do not desire your church treasurer's husband."

And so a war ensued between his sexual desire and the ethical behaviour he'd vowed to exemplify. During the day he imposed a truce, but at night desire laid siege to his psyche. He'd awaken, his pyjamas damp with semen, relieved that he'd only been dreaming, and console himself with the thought that he wasn't responsible for what happened while he was asleep. But on those occasions when he supped with them, he returned home guilt-laden.

3

THERE IS AN election commercial on the television set on the wall separating the study from the living room. He changes the channel to BBC World. It comes on in the middle of a news broadcast about barrel bombs being dropped on Syrian civilians. He turns the television off. Not today. Hume's views that human misery contradicts the concept of a benevolent God come into his mind. He nixes those too.

The decisions we make. That others make for us. That fate forces us to make. Why did he become a minister?

He's thirsty. He heads to the kitchen in search of water, stands in front of the drainboard intending to take a glass but doesn't. Instead his mind wanders back to the first time he began wondering about God. (He had been parroting the Lord's Prayer and the Apostles' Creed since he was four. Woe to the mother whose child couldn't.) It was an evening when he was around six and in the first year of elementary school, a year behind his peers because he couldn't go when he was five. At five he was in and out of hospital. The doctors told his parents that he'd contracted typhus, and it had stayed untreated for too long. His parents had put too much faith in the folk remedies that his godfather Elijah made and sold. During the last of those hospital stays, Edward asked the doctor if he thought Millington would die, and the doctor said maybe. The same afternoon, Mem, Edward, and Reverend Hennessy came to the hospital, kneeled around his bed, and prayed, asking God to spare his life.

Manny, the boy in the bed beside him, was South Asian. The day after the prayer, Manny did an imitation of what Millington said in his sleep. "Me nah want fo' dead. Aah! Aah! Me nah want fo' dead! Ahh Ooh! Ahh Ooh!" And laughed. Then they both became quiet until Manny said: "You think me going dead too?"

"Nah, you no going dead. You and me going live and we going be good friends."

Manny was from Calder. He was eight years old. When his parents and his two sisters visited, they brought him food, and he told them to give Millington a share. Millington shared with him the fudge and coconut cakes that Mem brought. On occasion Manny shrieked, and the nurse would come and give him an injection, after which he'd go to sleep.

"How come you don' bawl out fo' pain?" Manny asked him one morning.

"Cause I tough."

Manny steupsed. "Crap! Me does hear you bawling for pain in your sleep. Aah! Ooh!"

Manny died three nights later. The nurses behind the curtain preparing the body must have thought Millington was asleep. They spoke in whispers. One nurse gave instructions to the other: to close his eyelids, bandage his jaw, straighten his arms and legs, put cotton wool ... Millington wondered if Manny could hear them. When they left wheeling out the body, he became afraid that he would see Manny's jumbie, and had trouble falling asleep for a couple of nights until a new patient occupied the bed.

Millington lived, felt that God had spared his life, and wondered if God would have spared Manny's too if his parents had prayed and asked God to. For a long time after he got better, he'd stare at the dark spots where the typhus rashes had covered his skin, and wonder about death and heaven and hell. He was sure Manny went to heaven because Manny had been a good boy.

That evening when he was six, Pastor Bowles—his son Brinsley was in class with Millington—who lived at the very bottom of the hill from Millington in a big wall house behind the church with the huge lit-up green letters SAVED AND SANCTIFIED BAPTIST CHURCH, had come to hold services at the junction where Millington's street, Pasture Road, met Hill Road, some fifty metres up from their house. Pastor Bowles used a megaphone. Lying in bed, Millington listened to everything he said.

Millington already knew that, when Mem and he went to church on Sundays, it was to worship God: that they were "in the presence" of the person who had made everything, and who was powerful and invisible, and who knew and heard and saw everything, even people's thoughts—and he wrote it all down in a big book, and sent people to heaven or hell depending on what was in his book. And they asked this powerful man to do all sorts of things and to grant all sorts of wishes, and sometimes he did and sometimes he didn't. When he didn't it was because he knew that the thing they asked for was bad for them. That's what Jay's neighbour, Teacher Morrison, taught Millington in Sunday school. Teacher Morrison was scrawny, fast-talking, with eyes so bold that Millington trembled whenever Teacher Morrison looked angrily at him. Some adults and the ne'er-do-wells on the Anglican Church patio called him Twiggy, but most kids and Haverites called him Teacher Morrison.

God had granted his parents' wish that he live. Millington didn't know the word awe then, but it was what he felt. Mem told him often that God loved him and that, if he loved God by being a good boy, God would let one of his angels protect him all the time, and if he got sick again and ... she couldn't bring herself to say *died*, so he said it for her. She paused long before adding: "You will go to heaven, where you go have plenty nice things; you will have nice white clothes that never get dirty and plenty to eat." While poring over the description of heaven in Revelations, during his time at Ecumenical Theological College, he recalled that conversation with her: He sitting on a makeshift bench Edward had made with scraps of wood brought from his workplace; she standing facing the wood fire blazing under the tripod cast-iron pot that was bubbling away, her back leaning against the stand where the washed, turned down dishes were; she smiling and tiny wrinkles appearing at the outer corners of her eyes. "And God go make you one of his angels."

"And I go have wings?"

"Of course, you go have wings. You can't be a' angel without wings."

He loved it and imagined himself flying around heaven and taking trips down to earth to visit his parents, and he wondered if he would be allowed to bring down goodies for them. How much time would it take to fly from heaven to earth and back up? Birds do it, and angels are more powerful than birds ... And then he felt sad because he would be having fun all the time and his parents would be on earth working hard. He loved talking with Mem about heaven and angels. Brinsley told him that the stars were light coming through holes in the floor of heaven. Shaking his head, Millington told him: "No way. God no go want to live in a house with worm-eaten floor." Brinsley said: "No. Those is glass tiles so people on earth go see the light shining through and remember that God up there." Millington couldn't look up at the sky without thinking it was where God lived and that one day he would be living there too. And when Mem bought him new clothes, he was happy when they were blue. She knew that he liked blue and always made sure that at least one of his two church shirts was sky blue. Later, because of his love for flowers, he was torn between blue and green. (When he checked out gay symbols, he discovered that wearing a green tie was at one time a covert gay code.)

That night when Millington was six, Pastor Bowles and his people sang many of the tunes that Mem sometimes sang, and Millington sang along too where he knew the words, and hummed where he didn't. Mem was on the porch grating coconuts and singing along as well. The sound of the grating and her voice came in through his open window. Two days before—it had been a holiday and he didn't have school—two Jehovah Witness women from Barrouallie had come to the house and told Mem she was in the wrong religion. Mem replied that she had been born Authentic Methodist and would die Authentic Methodist. And a week before that Miss Collins had tried to convert her. Miss Collins had left the Methodist Church to become a Seventh Day Adventist: "The only true church." She'd walked down the short stretch to their house and said to Mem: "Sister Samuels, I loves you dearly, and I wants to meet you in heaven." She'd met Mem trimming the hibiscus hedge with a cutlass.

"And you don't think you going to meet me there?" Mem said, her back turned. Miss Collins was standing in the road and was wearing a black dress. She was in mourning for her mother, who'd died a few weeks before. It had been a next-day burial in a casket that Edward had made. Mem had bathed and dressed Miss Collins' mother and made most of the wreaths from flowers that the neighbours had brought. Angelita Pebbles, who lived one house up from them and whose pigs were often loose and rooting up the neighbours' land, had helped Mem and was all the while asking her if she thought Miss Collins' mother would go to heaven, and Mem kept answering that it was only God who had the answer.

"Now, Sister," Miss Collins said, shaking her head, "if that cutlass what you swinging there like a man was to slip and slice you and all your blood drain out, you think you will go to heaven?"

Mem paused from her trimming and glared at her.

Miss Collins continued, still shaking her head. "No, Sister, no. You ain't going there. And you know how I know, Sister Samuels? Right now, right this selfsame moment, the Holy Spirit whispering to me that you is not saved; if you was you would be a Adventist."

"Honey," Mem said, "me is a sinner all right. Me think you telling me that you is a saint, and me glad to hear it. I is very glad, Sister Collins." Mem glanced over at Millington. He was observing them from the doorway of the kitchen. "Keep up the good work, Sister Collins. I sure the good Lord will reward you. I will listen to your preaching another time, you hear. I have to go cook. I think Mill already hungry." She winked at him. She had already cooked.

That evening Pastor Bowles' voice blasted away through his megaphone. It was a calm, windless, silent evening—not even the sound of the surf, so quiet it was—until Pastor Bowles began. Everyone in Havre, over in Laird's, in Esperance too, must have heard the blasting. "You must be born again. Christ blood must wash you clean. Make no mistake about it ... Let the Holy Spirit enter you ... Sinner, plunge into the fountain of blood and cleanse your soul of foul sin. Plunge in or die and go to hell and burn forever in the pit of fire. There will be wailing, and there will be *gashing* of teeth." He must have said *gnashing*, but *gashing* made sense to Millington. Then they sang "Jesus Is Tenderly Calling." There was a pause between stanzas for Pastor Bowles to tell his listeners to, "Come, sinner, come and dive into the fountain of Jesus' blood and cleanse your soul of foul sin." His words terrified Millington. He had trouble falling asleep after. When he did, he saw a tub like Mem's washtub and it was full of blood, and there were headless fowls on the ground everywhere around it, and Pastor Bowles stood over the tub and pointed a finger at him and shouted: "Jump in, Millington, or you will die and go to hell." And Millington shook his head and tried to run as Pastor Bowles moved towards him with outstretched arms to catch and dunk him.

The next morning as soon as Edward left for work, Millington asked Mem what it felt like to be in a tub of blood. She looked surprised. "You said you going to heaven when you die, so you did jump into a tub of blood one time. Fowl blood." She frowned, wide-eyed. She probably thought he meant *foul*. He told her what Bowles had said the night before. She replied that God was a God of love, and that, yes, there was a place called hell for very bad people. But he wasn't interested in that. He wanted to know how it felt to be in a tub of fowls' blood. "Okay then, did you dive into a pool of blood, blood from fowls?"

She frowned and shook her head slowly, confused.

"How many fowls did they kill?" He had just learned to count and found numbers magical, and had seen Mem chop off enough heads of roosters to know that one fowl produced very little blood.

"Dive into a pool of fowl blood! Mill, what you is talking 'bout?" She began to wring her apron, then she came to the kitchen bench where he sat and felt his forehead the way she always did when she wanted to know if he had fever.

He shook his head. "I don't have fever."

"Mill"—it was only she who called him that, and he didn't let anyone else use it—"you's too young to be thinking 'bout such things. Be a good boy, that is what important. The Lord going take care o' the rest."

"But Pastor Bowles said we have to dive into blood or we will go to hell."

She frowned, her face was flushed, had been for a while. "These *wayfarian* preachers that go 'bout the place frightening people. Mill"— she put her arm around him, a rare act, a protective gesture; she was loving but not cuddly— "you don' mind what Pastor Bowles say. You is a good boy; God knows that, and I knows that. You don' have to jump into no pool o' blood. Leave that to Pastor Bowles and his followers. These *Wayfarians*. Some of them belong in the madhouse. Hurry up else you going be late for school."

4

IT WAS AT Ecumenical Theological College (ETC) that he first heard about the Jonestown massacre. The tutor, Dr. Sloan, mentioned the creation of the commune to illustrate what he called "that imperious drive, that deep need, for self-perfection that all humans feel." Millington laughs now and wishes he had laughed then too. Divinity professors, even those with doctorates, can be deluded. Maybe Sloan wasn't deluded. Maybe he performed like soldiers who enter the military enthusiastically and discover that killing people isn't fun but that their contracts oblige them to. The number killed at Jonestown: 914, its gruesomeness, defeated Sloan's purpose. Upon hearing it, Millington's breath choked and a searing pain traversed his gut. He bolted from the lecture hall and ran back to his room for cimetidine to cool his gut. Now he understands why Jones's followers—most were African Americans—accepted suicide. Some say they were coerced. Their last filament of faith in human transcendence had been shredded: evil was unconquerable; regaining Eden was an illusion; and they couldn't re-embrace the sordid reality they'd fled. At least they died believing there'd be an after-death bliss: "No more sorrow, no more weeping, no more pain."

What is humanity? His brother-in-law Paul insists that because humans are at the apex of evolution, their genes encode—and their behaviour reflects—all that is despicable in other species, further amplified by human reason, but that humans are cursed and blessed with illusions that prevent them from seeing this.

End this, Millington. Prepare for your meeting with Gladys later.

That's what you should focus on. There might be surprises waiting for you. How would I prepare?

He notices the drainboard on the kitchen counter and remembers why he's standing there. He takes the water pitcher from the fridge, fills a glass, takes it to the dining table, and sits down.

What a surprise that phone call from Gladys was! He didn't need to ask her how she'd got the number. She'd most likely called Reverend Somerset in St Vincent, and he'd got it from Mem.

"Millington, I long to see you. What a pleasure to hear your voice! Now I want to see you in person. When can we meet? I'm staying at Royal Victoria College until I can make some other arrangement."

"When did you arrive?"

"Two days ago."

"How long are you staying?"

"I leave in early December and come back again in early January. I'm at McGill for a year. Let's meet soon. I can't wait to see you. What are you doing tomorrow?"

He tried to think up a lie but his brain wouldn't cooperate. He'd fled Barbados and Methodism to put her and Horton and other issues behind him.

"Hope I'm not intruding."

"No. No. I was just searching my memory to see if there's anything I have planned."

"Then why don't we meet for coffee? Besides I have a letter for you."

He tensed. "From whom?"

"Horton."

He was relieved that it wasn't from Melvin. He waited several seconds before saying: "I'll come only if you've forgiven me."

"Forgiven you! Why?"

"For the way I left. For my crude manners. No goodbyes. Nothing. You were a sister to me in everything but biology. You were, Gladys, and ..."

"Millington, all I want to know is that you're well, happy and well. My only worry has been over your health."

"So you *have* forgiven me."

"I never felt wronged, Millington. Never."

"Well, I feel that I've wronged you …"

"You mustn't think that way. You mustn't."

She said she didn't yet know her way around and inquired how far he lived from the McGill campus. She knew how to get to Paragraphe Bookstore, so they agreed to meet there.

When they hung up, he wondered what he'd say to her. He knew she'd know that he'd come to Canada. A year earlier, Jay and he had gone to shop at the Atwater Market. Standing beside them, in a loose dark-green dress, was a portly woman who looked vaguely familiar. She was staring at a basket of buttercup squash. She turned to look at them, frowned, then smiled. "You must be Jay, Ma Kirton's grandson. And … Reverend Samuels! Reverend! How wonderful to see you! Bless my eyesight."

Millington didn't know who she was and he saw Jay's frown.

"I know. I know." She pointed to her stomach. "In the thirteen months I've been here, I've put on seven kilos … Youth League? Charles Wesley Trophy? *Reverend Samuels, still don't remember me!*" She glared at him for a few more seconds, then steupsed, and turned to Jay.

Jay saved the day. "Oh, I remember you. You lived in the second-to-last house on Valley Road. I used to pass by your house on the way to my grandmother's land. Your brother. Wait. Don't tell me. He went to Esperance Secondary and you went to St Joseph's Convent." He snapped his fingers and smiled. "You're Mathilda. Your brother's name is Randolph."

She smiled and nodded. "And to think I used to hop a minibus to Hastings and skip going to Broad Street just to hear this one preach, and he doesn't remember me."

She told Jay that she'd married a Canadian and had come to live here. "When I was leaving Barbados, the Broad Street Women's League threw a going-away party for me, and they invited his friend Gladys"— she pointed at him with an out-turned thumb but didn't look at him. "Gladys told me she'd heard he was now living in Canada, but she thought it might have been Toronto. Oh, Gladys will be *so* happy to know I've run into him." Then her hand slapped her forehead and she closed her eyes tightly for a second. "Sorry, Reverend. I think I got carried away there. How's your health?"

"Fine. Fine."

She took a notepad and pen from her purse and wrote down her phone number and gave the paper to Jay. Jay didn't give her theirs. Millington uses every ruse he can invent to avoid contact with West Indians living here. His aunt Pearl, who lives in New York, is the only family member who knows he's married to Jay, and he made her promise not to tell Mem or anyone else.

Not surprising then that Gladys knew he was in Montreal. She could have got the info as well from Reverend Somerset, the AMC minister in Havre, who'd replaced Reverend Hennessy, the minister who'd been there throughout Millington's adolescence. Somerset would have told Melvin, and Melvin would have told Gladys. Back home that Saturday evening, Jay won all four Scrabble games that they played. Usually they were even. Jay sensed his disquiet and said: "Mathilda seemed upset that you forgot who she was."

"I'm upset too." How could he have forgotten Mathilda? By then he'd remembered who she was.

It still strikes him as something of a miracle that he's here in Montreal. He and Jay hadn't seen each other since July 1997 and had been out of touch since 1999. When Jay mentioned the word marriage in the first phone call two days after he left St Vincent in 2011, Millington's body went limp. He wanted to say no. But Jay had already told him that marriage to a Canadian was the only easy way to immigrate to Canada. Several times he came close to telling Jay that the marriage should be kept a secret. Two phone calls later he asked Jay if he had mentioned it to anyone else. Yes. To Paul, and Paul had started teasing him about it when their friends were present.

The full implications of marrying Jay sank in when the plane lifted off for Montreal. He was about to make himself a pariah in the entire Caribbean. He imagined the headlines in the Barbadian and Vincentian newspapers: ***Male Vincentian AMC Minister Marries Boyfriend***.

Could Mem withstand that scandal? Would she ever talk to him again? Bits of Bea and Mem's conversations on the porch came back to him. They were members of Havre's AMC Women's League, and, for as long as Millington can remember, Bea operated a snack booth outside of Esperance Secondary. Mem made the fudge and coconut cakes that Bea sold there. Bea had cut short a vacation in Montreal. Gasping for breath, rocking from side to side, and pausing every couple of minutes to wipe sweat from her forehead, full-moon face, and pendulous jowls, she came up the hill the day after her return to tell Mem why she had returned ahead of time. Loud, as if calling to the neighbours, and effusing a clove-and-nutmeg smell, her jowls jiggling, she told Mem that she'd never thought there could be a country like Canada. "Mem, them put you in jail if you try to teach your children manners. Mem, imagine: my grandpickney, five years old, ordering me away from the television so he can watch his programme. 'Mommy and Daddy set aside this time for me. Gran'mama, you're home all day. Why don't you record your programme and watch it when I'm not here?'" She imitated her grandson's voice. "Fire and brimstone, Mem! This hand"—she shook her open right palm—"did done raise to slap the saucy brat, when the bitch Sonia, his mother, show up, eyes like blowtorch, ready to scorch me. 'What are you doing? Are you threatening my son? You can go to jail for this.' Mem, I could feel my blood pressure mounting by the second. I say, Father God, don't let me have a stroke, and I go to my bedroom and lie down. When Carleton come home from work and I tell him, he don't say a word. Not a word, Mem. That son o' mine give Sonia right over *me*—me his mother, that carry him nine months in this belly." She patted her stomach. "But I did already see that was she that wearing the pants. So I tell Carleton, before I end up in jail or get a stroke, just change my flight so I can go back to my own house. What a country! Mem, up there man married to man, you know; man does hold man hand in the street and hug up and kiss up. All kind o' thing. Sometimes you see pretty, pretty woman, dress up nice-nice in high heel and purse, and when you watch close, you see them narrow hips and you realize is man in woman clothes. I see it with me own two eyes. Mem, up there is Sodom and Gomorrah. Is not a place for the righteous. Is a sure sign the Second Coming is at hand. A sure sign, Mem. I glad my Carleton not into that. Your Millington neither. We stick with we husbands through thick and thin, and, Mem, we raise we children to fear the Lord and to walk in the ways o' the righteous."

"'Train up a child in the way he ought to grow, and when he is old he will not depart from it,'" Mem said.

"Amen," Bea said.

"But, Bea, tell me something: how two man does do that? Two man no make for that."

"Why you don' ask Job?"

Mem laughed. "Easter gone I go to the Anglican fair, and thirst been killing me. But Job was the one manning the mauby stand: *'Herney, come and get yer delicious mauby,'* in his woman voice, hand-them flapping like if he going fly, his bottom cockout behind him as usual. Bea, I couldn' drink that mauby. I only had to think 'bout what he does do, and my stomach turn."

"The wutlissboy-them right for beat him up. Me hear he does pay them for leave him alone."

Job was in his early seventies. In 2011 he was still carrying the cross and leading the processionals at the Anglican Church. Millington has never known him to work. Haverites claimed that he'd found gold coins dating back to when the area was first inhabited by the French buried on his mother's land. He occasionally made short trips overseas. They were cause for much speculation.

Yeah, he was about to become another of Havre's pariahs, Millington thought as he looked out at the clouds below him. He doesn't remember much more about that plane trip. He's certain he wouldn't have come to Canada and married Jay if he'd found a job when he returned to St Vincent.

During the year that elapsed since running into Mathilda, he was tempted many times to call or write to Gladys. He felt he'd treated her unfairly. But he feared that Horton might have told her some or all of what happened the last time they'd met. On occasion he wondered what Mathilda had told her about meeting him and Jay. Wouldn't be bad if she'd mentioned that he hadn't remembered her. It would strengthen the belief that he'd had a nervous breakdown. But why hadn't he remembered her?

Might well be that Gladys and Mathilda know the score already. Jay and Paul's friend Lionel— he's one cocky ... –is a blabber mouth. He's constantly asking Jay and him if they know this or that Vincentian. Six weeks ago at Christchurch Cathedral, he, his parents, and his sister Muriel—she and the mother are social workers—took part in a symposium on West Indian families and same-sex reality. Lucky fellow to have an enlightened family. Maybe that's why he's so damn arrogant.

That symposium couldn't happen in St Vincent. In 1998, shortly after Millington began working in the civil service, a Vincentian living in Canada informed *The News* that he was gay, and asked the Anglican bishop whether he would implement the recommendations on homosexuality that came out of the 1998 Lambeth Conference. For weeks it was the only topic of the talk shows. The day after the article appeared, the chatter from Millington's all-male office colleagues turned from sports, drinking marathons, and sexual boasts.

"You all read the letter that bullerman in Canada send to the papers?"

"Boy, some people don't have no shame. And sign his own name to it! He wouldn't o' do that if he did live here."

"If was my brother, I would fly up to Canada and beat that shit outta him. Purge him. Turn him straight."

From Bucky, who was from Langley Park, and knew the letter writer's family: "When his relatives in the road, boy, shame weighing down their head."

Two years before that, no one had prayed when Haverites broke down Brady's door and almost killed him and his boyfriend Jack. Later flames engulfed the house. They fled to Trinidad. Around the same time too, a male teenager in Marriaqua, who was taunted with gay slurs, drank poison, and "the onlookers laughed while they gazed at his dead body." Millington settled for celibacy and deflected suspicion with hyper-religiosity. He didn't fool Horton. Definitely not Neil. Whom else? Stilford?

5

JAY WAS AT his CEGEP office that August afternoon when Gladys called. The school year had started two days before. Millington didn't tell him about the call. Jay brought home work that evening, so he was too occupied to note Millington's nervousness and question him about it. An icy sensation enveloped Millington— when it happens his body temperature drops and his fingers turn blue; it first came upon him during his last year at ETC—as he wondered what excuse Horton had given Gladys for staying out past 2 a.m. the last time he and Millington met.

He kept a journal account of his August meeting with Gladys. He got to Paragraphe at 5:25 p.m. To burn off some of the tension, he went on foot, along De Maisonneuve and up McGill College, to the bookstore. She was at the door waiting for him, her smile beaming, the dimples he loves so much unchanged. Her hair was now in an Afro, and had a few strands of grey. She seemed to have gained a few more kilos, but it might have been the effect of the loose grey fall coat she had on. She didn't really need it; it was a warm afternoon. They hugged, and she exclaimed, quite sincerely he felt, how glad she was to see him. The same Gladys, even wearing the lily-of-the-valley perfume that he'd come to associate with her.

"Let's get something to munch on. It's on me," he said. "You're now a poor student."

They headed to the counter of the Second Cup. She stared at the pastry in the display case. "It's tempting, but I shouldn't."

"Go ahead. I'm having an oatmeal cookie."

"You could have three-four. Won't make any difference. I look at food ..."

At their supper table, back in Barbados, usually after urging Millington to take a second helping, she sometimes remarked that he needed to gain weight and she and Horton to lose it. She sometimes lamented not being able to join a gym. Her domestic helper began work at 6 a.m., so she felt obliged to relieve her no later than 4 p.m.

In the end she took tea and rusk and he coffee and an oatmeal cookie. They sat at the back of the café, among several students working on their laptops.

"Millington. Finally. I'm so happy to see you. And you look healthy."

"It's alright. We can talk about it. I should tell you up front that I didn't have a mental breakdown, not the kind you folks were led to believe."

He noted her wary look and pursed lips. "It's the truth. I wasn't seeing things that weren't there. For sure I was anxious, but it was about my future, not about my health ... So you're on study leave."

"No. Long leave. A year's vacation. I put it off for two years, hoping Horton and I would travel, but his work got in the way, so I decided to use the time to pursue one of my goals: get a master's degree in mathematics."

"Very wise. How are Horton, Len, and Alex?"

Her face twitched slightly. "Everyone's doing fine." She picked up her purse, took out a plain white envelope, and handed it to him. "Horton says I'm not to worry. Of course, I've just arrived. I have full confidence in Louisa, and Mommy promised to help out and to get Doris' sister Maggie to fill in for her when she can't be there. All of them, even Len—can you believe it, at his age—encouraged me to go away and study. Of course, Alex doesn't understand why I couldn't bring him with me. We all laughed when he said he needed to be there to protect me. He said I should give you a big hug for him. He hasn't forgotten you."

She took a bite from her rusk. She chewed it quickly and

swallowed. "So how you like being in Canada? Here seems to be all about French ..."

"I'm trying to learn it."

"Stop me if I'm getting too personal. Are you landed?"

"Not yet. The paperwork's completed. I have a work permit but not much of a job." He didn't tell her what he was doing. He wasn't sure how discreet she'd be.

"Do you plan to do any further studies? I should say: are you doing any further studies?"

"I've done a few courses in sociology. Tuition's not cheap. I have an open acceptance into social work at McGill. Can't go before I'm landed. Too costly."

"Don't I know! My worry is whether I'll be able to keep up with the work. I've not done any serious studying in seventeen years."

"You will, especially when it gets cold. You won't be tempted to go out as much. In any event you'll push yourself to have something to show for the suffering winter will inflict on you; you'll want to make it worthwhile."

"We'll see. One thing at a time."

"You didn't say much about the kids."

"Not much to say. Alex. Let's see. He'll begin junior five in a week. They put him a year ahead, to junior one, when he entered public school at five. Like they did for Len. He's every bit a bookworm as Len, only more talkative. As to Len, he's his same, quiet, bookworm self. He'll enter secondary school next year. Usually that's when the trouble starts—bullying, peer pressure, raging hormones. I'll see if I can get him into Combermere where I can keep an eye on him. From personal experience I know I have to do this."

He nodded.

"Millington, how's your mother?"

"Mem's managing okay, I think. Has arthritis in both knees and some trouble climbing the hill to our house. She still insists on going to the land to collect whatever she can find there that's saleable. I urge her to sell the land, but she pretends not to hear me. She's probably sentimental about it. Inherited it—fifteen acres—from her mother who'd inherited it from her parents."

She said nothing. Seemed to be in another space. When next she looked at him, her face was taut. "I want to ask you a couple of questions. You don't have to answer them."

"Go ahead. Ask." He felt his body tensing.

"The first is easy. I wrote you two letters, and I know Reverend Somerset delivered them. Why didn't you reply?"

The honest answer would have been, because he hadn't read them. He realized he was scratching his right cheek and quickly lowered his hand. "I wanted to, Gladys. I'm not sure ..." His palms moistened. The icy feeling was coming on. *Please don't let my teeth chatter.* "You want to know why I left the ministry, right?"

"Yes, that too."

"It was the wrong vocation for me, and I couldn't go on being dishonest with myself."

"But couldn't you have left differently—less abruptly?"

"Perhaps."

"Mommy was shocked the way you walked out on the congregation high and dry that Sunday morning. An hour later you cancelled your service at Hastings and stopped answering your phone. For several days Mommy kept phoning me, even at work, to find out if I'd had news of you. After we couldn't hear from you, we felt you might have checked yourself in at Black Rock. I phoned the hospital to find out. Eventually Doris told us you were home but not answering your phone. I phoned Melvin, and he said he too thought you'd had a nervous breakdown. You'd resigned your ministry without offering a credible explanation. 'Some nonsense about doctrine, Gladys. I don't believe a word of it. Has to be more serious than that. Did you hear anyone say he was hanging around any woman?' I told him no. 'Gladys, this is bizarre. In my thirty-eight years in the ministry, I have never come across a case like his. Never. And the way he walked out on the Speightstown congregation and didn't show up for services at his own church, I'm convinced now more than ever that he's gone mad.'" Her eyes were riveted on him.

He remembered Melvin asking him if he'd impregnated a member of his congregation. "Well, he certainly spread the rumour that I was mad. It travelled to St Vincent. It was what everyone there, including Mem, believed. No one, she felt, in his right mind would turn his back on the Christian ministry."

Gladys squeezed her lips and squinted.

"I didn't feel the need for tranquillizers or antidepressants, Gladys. That's what I'm saying. Never went to see a shrink. I had sleepless nights, but I knew what was causing them."

"What? What was causing them ... your sleepless nights?"

"Oh, forget it. It's not important."

"But you'll admit the way you treated the congregations..."

"... was bizarre. I'll concede that I was a little unbalanced then. But there are periods in our lives when we all are."

She frowned. "That last night ... you know that night when Horton took you home, what did the two of you ... talk about?"

His gut began to churn. He felt a generalized tremor beginning. "Let me go empty my bladder first." He went to the bathroom, ran hot water on his hands to thaw them, then rinsed his face.

He returned and sat down.

"Millington, what kept both of you talking past 2 a.m.?"

"It was so insignificant, I don't remember ... A little bit about his law practice. How stressful it was. The demands of his clients. What else? Most of it was so banal, I can't recall. In my case—it was mostly about me—about my role as a counsellor ..."

"Horton didn't confess anything to you?"

Appear nonchalant, Millington. "Let's see. I'm searching my memory." He shook his head. "No. He didn't. But, Gladys, if he had, I would be obliged to keep it confidential."

"You're no longer a minister."

"But I'm still ethically bound to respect the confidentiality that my ex-congregation entrusted me with. You *know that*, Gladys."

She fidgeted for a while but said nothing. "I guess you're right." She nodded grudgingly. "What I'm about to tell you must stay between us." She interlocked her fingers and brought her clasped hands to her chest twice before putting them on the table. "This is so hard to say. I haven't even told Mommy. The same week that we thought you were having a breakdown, Horton's personality changed. He became silent and spent very little time at home. Horton who always tried to be home for supper, who would even at times break off work and come home and return to the office after supper. Whenever he truly had to miss supper, he was apologetic. But, beginning that week, he left home early and returned at one, sometimes two, in the morning, and always smelling of liquor, and he started sleeping in the guest room. This went on for two weeks, and then one night, I sat on a stool in the kitchen, by the carport entrance, and waited for him. He came in staggering at seventeen past one. 'Horton,' I said, 'what is happening between us? What is happening to you?'

"'Leave me alone,' he screamed and tried to walk past me. I grabbed his shirt front. He wrenched my hands free, ripping off a couple of buttons, and shoved me away.

"'I won't leave you alone. I demand an explanation for your weird behaviour, this sudden change.'

"'Fuck off!' ... Millington, Horton said that to me and left me standing there. Never, never once, did I hear him say damn. Never heard him utter a swear word. It had the effect he wanted. I went into our bedroom and cried and then I knelt down and prayed. The following morning, he met me at the door as I was leaving for work and apologized: 'As you can see, I'm not my usual self.' He came home for supper that evening, and for about two months, apart from appearing restless, he resumed being the Horton I knew, and then the bizarre behaviour began all over again.

"Three weeks into it, I had Melvin over for supper. Harry was there too. By the way, he too has been quite distraught over your leaving. Horton was present of course. He wouldn't have wanted Melvin and Harry to know that things were awry in our home. Melvin knew that Horton was one of the last persons you'd interacted with. He asked Horton if he had seen anything unusual in your behaviour or whether you'd told him anything out of the ordinary. Horton said no, but he got fidgety and nervous. So, when Melvin left, I asked him:

'What passed between you and Millington that night? ... You left to take Millington home at 11:45 p.m. and got back here at 2:37 a.m.' He said: 'We were having one of those exchanges men have between themselves. If you want to know about what exactly, you should ask Millington. Most of the conversation was about him.' ... Millington," she was shaking her head slowly, sceptically, "that tremor in his voice, sweat beads popping out on his forehead, his roving eyes ... Millington, I knew he was lying. And there was that dead give-away: an acrid-sweat smell he gives off when he's overstressed." She stopped talking and stared at him, her eyes asquint.

He wondered if her letters to him had questions about Horton's behaviour. "I'm shocked, Gladys. Shocked and surprised." He truly was.

Her stare was fixed on him. She was waiting for him to say more. He didn't.

"That's how it's been, Millington, from 2011 until I left: a few months of the loving, gentle person I married, who'd promise to be always there for his kids and me, followed by a few months of the estranged Horton. After the first apology he never excused his behaviour. And whenever I mentioned it, he'd slice the air with his palms and snarl: 'DON'T. Don't you start. I'm doing the best I can. I love our children and I love you.'

"'Then stop your bizarre behaviour,' I'd say. One time it was so painful; I'd confronted him a short while after the kids went to bed. He said nothing, but when I went to see whether they had fallen asleep, I heard the car driving away. I didn't see him again until after supper the next day."

"Astonishing."

She nodded.

"So, Gladys, now that you are face to face with me, you are asking *me* what—whether you should leave him?"

She shook her head slowly. "No. I can't raise two boys alone. Help me understand what's going on, Millington. Help me." Her eyes got glassy. She swallowed.

He decided to steer the conversation in a different direction. "The last time he and I met, we spoke about a long illness I had when I was around five"—they didn't, but Horton had already conditioned her to believe the conversation had been mostly about Millington—"and about his own unhappy childhood and adolescence." That was true. "He seemed to have had some difficulty transitioning from childhood to adulthood. He said that meeting you gave a new purpose to his life." He paused to gauge how this was registering.

She exhaled loud, looked away, then at him sceptically. "That was *all*?"

"All that I can remember about him."

"You two spent three hours talking about *that*?"

"I didn't calculate the time. Didn't know it was that long. There were long bouts of silence. I understood that he was unhappy but I was taught not to pry information out of my parishioners, but rather to listen to what they say and, when possible, guide them to a better understanding of themselves. But, as Horton said, most of the conversation was about me."

Again, an air of expectancy. He pretended not to notice.

"I did think it strange that both of you began to behave oddly at the same time."

Now she stared at him intensely. His sweating hands were under the table and pressing hard on his thighs. "Gladys, what else are you trying to tell me?"

She looked away. Swallowed. Her fingers on the table opening and closing.

He recalled a nightmare he'd had back in Barbados, in which she'd invited him to dinner, pulled a shotgun on him, and shouted: "You and Batey are vermin. I'm going to exterminate you." Batey was the name Horton's age-mates had given him. She often switched from one to the other.

"Millington, yesterday, I found it quite odd that you needed my forgiveness." Said with a gotcha tone, her gaze fixed on his face.

"I gave you the reason: forgiveness for my crude manners. Remember?" He looked to his left and saw that some of the students working there on their laptops were listening to them. "Let's go for a walk, and I'll accompany you home afterwards." He had to get away.

Out on McGill College, he recalled parts of his last conversation with Horton. They were on the manse's living room sofa. Horton's head in Millington's lap. It was already past 2 a.m.

"You know, Millington, there are some days when I can't look Gladys in the face."

Silence.

Suddenly his hands began frantically smoothing his thighs.

"You're okay?"

He sat up and shook his head. "The dam's about to break … Any day now … I don't know what to do. It will end badly. Poor Gladys. Why did I ruin her life? She never had a boyfriend before me. And there are Len and Alex. I love my children. What will happen to them? Why didn't I defy her and have a vasectomy?"

"End badly. What do you mean?"

He put a finger on his lips. "Don't feel like talking about it."

Gladys and he were now at the corner of Sherbrooke. "Gladys, what are you hoping to find out from me?"

She stopped walking, pulled his shoulder around, and stared into his eyes. "You know, Millington, the members of the Women's League used to wonder if you're gay."

His legs almost buckled. Wesley's third rule came to his rescue. He quoted it: "Converse sparingly and cautiously with women, particularly with young women." He quoted the fourth too: "Take no step towards marriage without solemn prayer to God and consulting with your brethren."

"At least now you're not a practising minister, and I'm not so young." She chuckled.

She knows more than she's telling me. She's assessing my honesty. Should I tell her the truth? Not yet. Read Horton's letter first.

They headed west. "Gladys, you and Horton have some serious unresolved issues, and I can't help you with them." He remembered Horton saying that he'd married her to escape the harassment men without wives or girlfriends faced in Barbados. For some thirty seconds they walked on in silence.

"You're so silent," she said.

"Lost in my thoughts. That's all."

"Share them."

"They're insignificant. Just memories of my ministry."

Silence again. A long one. He decided to break it. "Gladys, my reason for breaking off contact with you was simple: I didn't know how to remain in touch with you while I distanced myself from the church. It was as simple as that." He almost added that it had nothing to do with Horton, but checked himself, in case Horton had told her more than she'd disclosed.

She didn't respond.

Again silence. At Drummond they turned left, down to De Maisonneuve, and continued westward. He wondered which of the young women had been speculating about his sexual orientation. Once he happened to be exiting the church as the choir was assembling for practice and he overheard a choir-woman say: "He got plenty milk in he, and I sure he want one with silk hair and marble skin."

Glenda was his only parishioner who overtly courted him. She broke into a sunrise smile and quickly turned her face away whenever she saw him. She had a contralto voice as good as Jessye Norman's and knew how to use it. She was in her mid-twenties, with skin like polished ebony. About five-five. Bold, dark, glowing eyes. Just enough fat on her curvy body to make her sexually enticing. Beautiful. She was a graduate nurse and worked on the surgical unit of the Queen E. On the Sundays when she worked, the Hastings choir sounded tired. All four circuits called on her often to sing in the fund-raising activities AMC congregations were always having. She never refused. Her response was always: "God gave me this voice, and I will use it for his greater glory."

Gladys broke into his recall. "So this is Concordia University."

They were on the sidewalk fronting the Hall Pavilion. "Yes. The downtown campus. These are a couple of the pavilions." He pointed to the library building on his left and the Hall Pavilion on his right. "I take the odd course here until I start at McGill."

Glenda, in a sleeveless, tight-fitting yellow dress, hair a fresh brush-cut, and effusing a perfume muskier than Gladys' lily-of-the-valley, visited him during his second year at Hastings. She glanced at him sitting at his desk across from her. She smiled most of the time, and in the brief moments when she didn't, her face became an unreadable mask.

Suddenly, she turned her head away, but not before he saw the glint in her eyes.

He cleared his throat.

"Rev," her face still turned away, "us girls think you're handsome. Do you know that?"

"Which: being handsome or knowing what you girls think?"

She giggled. "You're playing with me, Rev." She looked at him now, her eyelids fluttering. "You know perfectly well I mean both."

"No, I don't. Which girls?"

"I can't tell you that, Rev. You want people to call me Lickmouth Lou?"

He took a breath that was too deep and couldn't exhale it quietly.

"I guess you'll be settling down soon, Rev?"

"I guess so. How about you?"

She straightened with a sudden jolt and squinted. "A man gotta propose first. I can't marry myself, Rev."

He glanced at his watch.

A look of embarrassment crossed her face and she said it was time for her to go. She thanked him for listening to her "story that got neither head nor tail."

He told her any time.

"In which part of Montreal you live?" Gladys asked.

"East of McGill, a longish walk from the campus." He remembered that she'd done all her studies in Barbados and had never been away from family and friends. This was her first trip outside the Caribbean. "I have a roommate."

"I'm not asking to be invited."

"We should do something together one Saturday soon, before the blood-curdling cold comes, before your studies get heavy."

They walked on. At Atwater he pointed out the Alexis Nihon Plaza and suggested that it was where she could do low-cost shopping. "We should be heading back."

She nodded. They turned and began walking east.

"I guess you'll be going to church on Sundays."

"Yes, I inquired before I left home. Melvin suggested St James United. He knows the minister there, and it's within walking distance."

The silence got heavy. First hints of dusk.

"Where's your roommate from?"

"St Vincent. From the same town—if you can call it that. His grandmother, Ma Kirton, took more than a passing interest in me while I was growing up. Jay and I went to the same schools in St Vincent, up to our first year preparing for A levels. He left then to join his mother in Canada. He teaches history in a junior college."

"And you, *what* do you do?"

"I work two days a week in a banal, minimum-wage job."

"Couldn't you get a pastoral charge? The churches here are quite liberal, I hear; some even ordain gay ministers ... Melvin said you left over doctrine."

"You'll be attending one of the most liberal." He waited for her response. There was none.

He'd been present on occasions when she spoke of her faith in God's power and seemed transported to another sphere by what she (and Authentic Methodist doctrine) would have deemed the Holy Ghost. Once when Melvin was thanking her excessively for something or the other, she flicked her hand dismissively and said she'd be rewarded in heaven. She clings to the Old Rugged Cross and expects one day to exchange it for a crown. Hopefully not one of thorns.

They were now in front of her residence. The dusk had deepened. He stopped walking.

"Keep going. I have to get some fruit."

They walked in silence to Park Avenue, where she bought apples and plums, and they headed back to Royal Victoria College. He walked her to the door and pecked her on both cheeks. In the grey light, he recognised the dimpled smile, and it rekindled the fraternal feeling he has always felt for her from the first time they met.

He took the metro home. Jay hadn't yet arrived. He'd gone to the annual Vincentian barbecue at Angrignon Park, and afterwards for a drink with Dale, a colleague. That morning, he had told Jay that he was meeting a member of his ex-congregation later, but he didn't say that it was Gladys. In any case, the meeting with her saved him from having to lie to get out of accompanying Jay to the barbecue. In July Jay had wanted him to go with him to the Vincy Unity Picnic in Thousand Islands. He knew that a picnic of ten thousand people would be torture. Apart from the fear of Vincentians finding out that he's married to a man, he genuinely dislikes being in large crowds. Spending time with a few hundred at church fairs used to exhaust him. He told Jay that he needed time to work on a summer course he was taking. Jay responded with his ironic, pursed-lip smile. Paul too loathes West Indian functions. He calls West Indians "a tangle of sanctimonious, sclerotic, homophobic nuts, better suited for life in the Pentateuch."

Opening Horton's letter, he almost tore the pages. Two handwritten pages. He gets up from the dining table, goes in search of the letter, sits on the couch, and re-reads it.

> *Dear Millington,*
>
> *Gladys asked me if there was any message I wanted her to deliver to you, and rather than send a verbal one, I decided to write you instead.*
>
> *As usual I continue to find existence a challenge. I'm sure Gladys will tell you a great deal about that. Ah, these battles with the self. You know what I mean. You have them too in ways different from me. In my case, being an exemplary father, a first-rate husband (I'm not even third-rate), an upright citizen, and an honest human being.*
>
> *I spend much of my time thinking about forgiveness. "To understand all is to forgive all." I don't expect you to understand ALL but I know that you understand a great deal and I earnestly hope that you are able to forgive a great deal. Send me a confirmation of this. It's very important.*
>
> *Our most egregious offences are judged in the court of conscience, a court with little mercy. And whatever mercy one finds there one day is usually extinguished the next day, for the*

*trial and sentencing are daily, unending. In my case it is. I hope
not so in yours. John Wesley would have been proud of you.
Millington, you are a man of steel.*

*I hope you are enjoying your new life in your new
surroundings and restocking your mental wardrobe. It should be
easy to do so in Canada. Here I wear—will continue to wear
until death frees me—the uniform society has put on me.*

*Millington, you never appeared happy to me. I hope that is
changing—has changed. We have a right to happiness. We
shouldn't have to wait until we get to heaven.*

*The other day I ran into a young man, Stilford. I was his
class leader when he worshipped at AMC Hastings. You seem to
have influenced him immensely. Do you remember him? He
said you once gave him some excellent advice which he didn't
think much of at the time. He asked me for your contact
information, and his face fell when I told him I didn't have it.
You see, your ministry wasn't at all in vain.*

*Give me a call on my cell. Please. If you've lost the number,
contact me at Brown, Bates & Erskine. There's a great deal I
want to discuss and clarify with you. And I have a couple of
favours to ask you.*

Yours truly,

Horton

Now he's struck by the quality of the writing, but when he first read
the letter the coded messages were what intrigued him. Coded in case
Gladys were to read it. He's sure she was tempted.

*Stilford wants to get in touch with me! Quite a surprise. A hopeful
sign.* He'd left AMC and joined the Wesleyan Holiness because they'd
promised they could make him straight. He has probably now seen the
holes in holiness and stubbed his soul in quite a few. Nowadays the
Barbadian media are gently prodding the public to accept same-sex
reality. That should in some way lessen his burden.

He hasn't called Horton. What would he say to him? Contacting
him would be returning to what he'd fled. From what Gladys revealed,

he suspects that one of Horton's favours is asking him to stay mum about what happened the last time they met. Maybe he wants to know too what Gladys has told him, to gauge whether she's on his trail. *Horton thinks he was the cause of my resignation. It's what all that verbiage about forgiveness is about. The second favour is probably a request to help him emigrate. To restock his own mental wardrobe. Can't help you there, Horton. In August I had no residency papers. I couldn't even help myself.*

6

WITH A FREQUENCY that disquiets Millington, Paul says that Jay's been lucky to extract a gem from "the heaps of slag out there." In line with Paul's belief that Jay had married a virgin. He told Paul that humanity should never be reduced to slag. Grinning, Paul said that W.B. Yeats would disagree, that Yeats was depressed because the woman he'd wanted to marry had turned him down; and one of his friends told him to cheer up because there were lots more fish out there to be caught, and Yeats replied: "They're mostly mackerel." He wanted to ask Paul what was wrong with mackerel. Smoked mackerel is delicious. How does his partner Bernard feel when he talks like this? Bernard's the boniest being Millington has ever laid eyes on. Paul's gem talk makes Millington nervous, and he holds his breath and waits for Jay to debunk it. But Jay never does, never offers an opinion in favour or against. *Slag:* physical, psychical? Does Paul consider why it's produced? Metaphors can be traps.

Never a dull moment when one's in Paul's company. Three and a half years ago, when Millington saw him back in Havre at their adopted aunt's funeral, he recalled a chubby boy much younger and darker than Jay coming onto the back porch of Ma Kirton's, their grandmother's, house and glancing at Jay and him sitting back there reading or listening to music from a boom box. Fifteen years later that chubbiness is one step short of obesity. Paul preferred to spend his days in the store with his grandmother. Jay must have told him so. When Millington did errands for Mem and Elijah, he used to see him sitting at the counter, his head turning this way and that as he observed the shoppers. When Paul won the junior spelling bee, his picture was on the front of the newspapers, and he appeared on TV when he took one of the top three spots in the high school entrance exam. He's six years younger than Jay, so he was eleven when they left Havre for Montreal in 1997.

All through childhood Millington longed for a brother. Never a sister, and, until now, he'd never imagined how different his life would have been if he'd had a sister. Guess what he wanted only a brother could give. Someone to romp with and to share the chores—to share the chores especially. There was talk of one, Felix, but he didn't live with them. A good thing maybe, he later learned. Edward's priorities being what they were. Seems for Jay, having a younger brother was a burden. While he and Paul attended school in Kingstown, they boarded there during the week, and Jay had to take care of Paul. When they moved to Montreal, the responsibility was even greater, to the point where Jay had to abandon his PhD. That must have hurt. Not sure it's any comfort to Jay when Paul thanks him for having been "an excellent parent." At first Millington thought Paul was being ironic. In St Vincent Jay was relieved of his responsibility on weekends and in July and August. In Montreal it seemed to have been 24/7 365 days per year. Good God!

Jay and Paul are such confident beings. So sure of themselves. Never needed the crutch that religion was for him. They dismiss notions of hell and heaven with a wave of the hand. At least he's at the point now where he believes heaven and hell aren't real places, but rather existential states. Paul's the more strident, more dogmatic, one. Jay says it's because Paul never had to listen to their father's sermons on hell or endure his beatings—their mother got beaten too—to keep them from sinning.

Paul thinks that if humans have an eternal soul, then cows, horses, and mosquitoes do too, for "all living things must conform to the rules of biology. If God existed, we'd find his descendants."

"Perhaps they inhabit a planet called heaven," Millington said.

"Yes. In Dan Brown's overheated imagination and the brain stems of Methodists. At least Brown doesn't pretend that his stuff is anything other than fiction."

"Why don't you emulate your namesake and write an epistle to humanity?"

"That's what my novel is."

Such confidence. Fruit of his grandmother's nurturing. Throughout Millington's childhood he wished he'd lived in that household.

That discussion was at Paul's apartment one evening a few months ago. When he and Jay got back home, Jay went into his study to correct papers. Millington sat on the living room couch intending to read, but his mind was on what Paul had said earlier. After about fifteen minutes he got his journal and continued where his thoughts left off:

> When I unhooked my clerical collar and put aside my priestly vestments, I was more of an atheist (agnostic?) than I am now. Why? Perhaps because Christianity has given us hymns like "All Things that Live Below the Sky," and poets like John Greenleaf Whittier, whose hymns and poems urge us to be the neighbours Christ illustrates in the parable of the Good Samaritan.
>
> Paul's right. The intellectual energy required to create the universe would quickly immolate the human brain, for that matter the entire human body. Dr. Menzies would shoot my reasoning down. "Logic is no road to religion's truths; divine inspiration is." His voice and accent like Churchill's; looked like Churchill too: same sort of hair, top heavy torso, sloping back, bandy legs, scaly psoriasis patches on his face and neck. I know enough now about human deception not to be surprised if he got drunk too—in private, of course. "A lighted path, a body of light, that's what God is in this confusing world of darkness."
>
> In my dark moments my first impulse is to want to reach for this light, this God. But empirical evidence tells me it's a construct the rulers of primitive peoples forged millennia ago to justify their tyranny and palliate their own and their subjects' fear of the unknown. But "Train up a child in the way he ought to grow, and when he is old, he will not depart from it." So says

the Torah; so say Mem and Bea. Not altogether true today. At least not in the Occident. But there was a fallback position in Torah times: death by stoning for disobedient children. Train up a child … In my case definitely true, for at times my whole being is like an assemblage of religious blocks that won't unlock. Train up a child … Mem, you've flogged others with that whip and soon you'll be beaten with it. The likes of Miss Collins will wield it. "You didn't bring up Millington right. You and Edward spare the rod and spoil that boy. Look what happened. You parents around better take heed."

Superstition. So much of what's in the bible—in most religious tomes for that matter —is. Superstition that twisted and twined its tendrils into my psyche and flowered and fruited. And now as I expunge it, I feel like a hollowed-out trunk. Empty. Like bamboo. Makes sense. God is defined as spirit, wind. (I'm made in his image and Plato thinks I'm a shadow: a ghost.) Probably why some preachers are so windy.

Nowadays, on those occasions when he wonders what his life would be like had he remained a minister, he remembers Pastor Bowles. Not just the Wednesday blastings at the crossroad, but his Sunday homilies in his church on Main Street downhill from them. On their way home from church, they heard him thundering against drunkards with threats of hellfire, until one Sunday, while his congregation waited, restively wondering where their pastor was, some fishermen found Bowles comatose beside a stash of empty rum bottles in the bushes near Wallilabou Bay, brought him to Havre in their boat, and used an improvised stretcher of saplings and disused seine to carry him home.

Come to think of it, Caleb, Paul and Jay's father, a preacher too who battered his wife and children, became a drunkard when his wife left him.

Paul—he's something else though—asked Millington one evening while he and Jay were having supper at Paul and Bernard's place: "Do you cut Jay's backside sometimes? … I'm sure Jay yearns for some of that pain he got from Daddy." He extended his tongue, grinned, rubbed his chin with one hand, and put the other behind his neck. "They say people who got beaten in childhood like to inflict or endure pain when they're having sex … Don't preachers beat their spouses when they and God are on bad terms?"

"And writers, what do they do?" Millington said.

"Dump on their characters. Seriously, Millington, listen to me. Watch out for Jay's fist. What's in the billy goat is *always* passed down to the kid." He turned and winked at Jay.

"You're lucky you're wrong, or your backside would be scarred," Jay said.

They all laughed.

Millington never heard anyone say that Pastor Bowles used to beat Mrs. Bowles. But Brinsley and Beatrice sure got it. At eighteen Beatrice escaped straight into the arms of a man three times her age. Snagged him from his wife too. Paul said that Sefus Blucher, who used to hang around Ma Kirton's store pretending to court her, told Mrs. Bowles to tell the Reverend that the next time he feels like imbibing spirits, he should do ganja—"it don't drunk you"—or hook up with Mother Bernice, the leader of the Spiritual Baptists. The comedians on the Vincentian radio stations weren't as gentle. The one on Nice Radio said: "You all hear 'bout that Baptist minister in Wallibou, right" (he couldn't bother to get the name of the village right), "who been waiting for the Holy Spirit to give him a sermon, and when the Holy Spirit say: 'Naw, I not giving you nothing,' he turned to bottled spirits? Man, I agree with the reverend. Don't the bible say the apostles got drunk on the day o' Pentecost and preach to people in languages they never learned? Now you and I *know* nothing holy don't drunk you." Another, on NBC radio—he taught English at JP Eustace Secondary—said: "Why all you beating up on that poor Reverend from Havre 'cause he take a drink. Well, more than one. Now if you all ever read the poems o' Dylan Thomas, you all will know good things can come out of the bottle. And Reverend emptied more than a few. I bet you all he done start writing poetry and St Vincent going be the West Indies fourth

Nobel." Millington's pretty sure Bowles will show up in the novel Paul's writing.

By the time he became a minister in Barbados Millington had already reflected extensively on the importance of rum-drinking in defining Caribbean masculinity. He'd heard ad nauseam that "A man must be able to hold his liquor." Said in a way that made one think that men who didn't drink and men who got overly drunk were abnormal. During Millington's childhood and adolescence, the men who came to play dominoes on their porch boasted often about the copious amounts of liquor they could consume and the drinking contests they'd won. One said that, when he lived in Coulls Hill, he'd drunk so much one night that he couldn't walk uphill and so he slept on the side of the road at the bottom of the hill, and woke up next morning in a puddle. A lot of their chatter was about cures for hangovers. Millington found them stupid—why consume a substance that would make you sick? That could cause you to lose control and even endanger your life?—until he understood that the domino and checker games, rum-drinking, womanizing, and wife-beating were momentary escapes from the dreary lives they were trapped in. *Most men lead lives of quiet desperation.*

Edward was one of those who could hold their liquor. Millington used to think he didn't drink, until Mem told him otherwise. July 14, 2010, two days after Edward's funeral, a dusty, windy, late afternoon, the sun close to setting in the harbour, he asked Mem whether she'd loved Edward. He and she sat on the porch, across from each other, at the table where Edward and his cronies used to play dominoes.

She took a while to answer. "I didn' hate him, if that is what you mean." She bit her lower lip, looked away, and swallowed. "There's things you don't know 'bout your father." She stared downhill, in the direction of the sea, before she turned her face to him and resumed talking. "A week after we get married, Edward come home drunk one night. Next day, when he sober up, I remind him that his older brother, Jacob, did fall down drunk and roll over a cliff up in Fancy and kill heself, and I warn Edward: 'If ever you come back here drunk, I leaving you. As God is above, I leaving you.' He never come back drunk, but a day didn' pass that he didn' drink … He use to break off a sprig o' mint from the bed near the gate and chew it. That way if I tell him rum on his breath, he could say is mint." Millington remembered his mint-chewing habit. A sprig was always in his mouth each time he came in from work or from their farm at Hollow. Millington had thought it was one of those habits that some people have: always whittling or chewing drinking straws or toothpicks.

"Edward use to stop off at Henley's Bar and Grocery ... up there ... before he come home from work." She pointed left, toward the top of Havre's southern escarpment. "He use to drink more than he could' pay for. One time he did owe Henley plenty money, and Henley come here—to this selfsame gate—and cuss him out. I praise God you wasn' home ... I didn' want you to know them things 'bout your father. I didn' want you to disrespect him, and I didn' want you to copy him. To quiet Henley and prevent a scandal, I promise to pay him. And little by little I pay it off. After Henley cuss him out, Edward do his drinking at Boatswain's Bar, and he run up a big debt there too. Boatswain did threaten to bring a bailiff and seize what we have. I borrow the money from Celestina and pay him. And I sell three goats and pay back Celestina. And when Edward didn' have carpenter work and he working on the land in Hollow, he use to take the side road over into Esperance when he coming back home and drink down there too. He create debt down there too that I did have to pay. They tell me he use to buy rounds for everybody, even sweet drinks for the women and children. Your father did love to play bigshot. Your father was a damn fool."

He was too stunned to say anything.

After a long silence, she said: "That is one reason we been always short on money. You won' know the relief I did feel when I see you turn out God-fearing. Mill, you won' know the comfort it give me. I use to pray to God every night that my only child won' turn out a drunkard." He stretched his arm across the table and squeezed her hand gently.

Edward never earned the respect Millington had for their neighbour Presley Murray. Yet he'd hoped his father was more disciplined than most of the village men, could resist the vices of Havre's menfolk. Sitting on that porch, reflecting on the privation Mem and he endured while Edward squandered the family's income on rum, he felt his anger rising. Eventually he consoled himself with the thought that Edward didn't make a drunken spectacle of himself like Twine and Percy did.

Twine, whose real name was Hamilton Scrub, and Lynette, his common-law wife, and their five children lived down the slope directly across from them in a two-room unpainted wooden shack with a gable roof of corrugated galvanized steel. A muddy track hemmed in by elephant grass led to it. Twine was the driver of a work gang on Laird's plantation. Occasionally he joined the players at the domino table on their porch. When Twine was drunk, on average twice per week, the neighbours heard Lynette and the children bawling. If the breeze was blowing uphill, off the sea, they heard him say, as a prelude to the beating: "Woman, that is it. Now you done make me lose me head," followed by the sound of the blows. They listened, shook their heads, and said to one another: "One o' these days that man will kill that woman." But they did not intervene. Sometimes Edward said: "He lose his head in truth. He belong in the madhouse."

Presley Murray felt that Twine needed a woman like their neighbour Angelita Pebbles "to bring him to order." She was the tallest woman Millington had ever seen, about two metres. Her turned-out feet looked like flappers. She had a horsy face. Mem told her so in one of their cuss-outs. Sister Murray called her "that shit-colour moko jumbie of a woman." They saw her leave for her land in the morning, seated on her donkey, and return in the late afternoon, the donkey loaded with produce, and she, perched on the produce. She cultivated her land alone and boasted that she was stronger than "all them sickly half-man-round-here that want woman to mind them ... Presley you is the exception," her cat eyes lighting up and her nostrils flaring. "Celestina, girl, don't say I didn' warn you. Presley only have to say the word and is take—I taking him from you." As far as the neighbours knew he never took up her offer.

She had a big behind and substantial breasts in spite of her trim frame. When Bellingy, a man from Esperance, went to live with her, Sister Murray called out to her: "Angelita, I glad you putting that big backside o' yours to good use." She didn't for long. One evening, about two months into the affair, they heard her shouting: "Get out! Bellingy. Me say, get to hell out! Or, so help me God, I going chop you up! Get outta *my* house. Quick! What! Box me 'cause I ain't give you wife!" The neighbours gathered on the road in front of her house in time to see Bellingy stumbling down the stairs. Some said, she'd pushed him. Next came his suitcase, which opened in flight, and all the clothes scattered, some onto the balcony, some below, some onto the road. Next came Angelita, brandishing a cutlass. Two evenings later she was at the crossroad beating a tambourine with her Church of God brethren.

Sometimes Lynette would come up the path and call on Mem, and Millington would hear them taking their "troubles to the Lord in prayer," and singing "What a Friend We Have in Jesus." And troubles Lynette certainly had. One time Millington saw Twine hitting her head against the side of the house. Years later, around the time that Ivan, her oldest, was about eighteen, she began having epileptic seizures. By then Twine had abandoned her and the children and gone to live with another of his women in Esperance. Lynette died from a brain haemorrhage two days before Millington left for ETC.

Percy was a loveable drunk. He'd stagger up and down the streets of Havre, singing popular hymns, and breaking off to propose marriage to every woman he came upon, even those already married. Sometimes he bought sweets and gave them out to the children. He had twenty-five acres of some of the best land in Havre and a lovely house at the opposite end of Beach Road from Ma Kirton's. His sister Karen, older than he and a regular worshipper at Havre AMC, lived with him and took care of his house.

When sober, Percy was sheepishly silent with a hangdog look and would merely grin, staring at the ground, or with his eyes turned away from the women telling him to make good his offer of marriage. He came to church on Easter Sunday and occasionally on Covenant Sunday, always in a charcoal-grey suit, white shirt, and a sky-blue tie. Roughly a quarter of the fruits and vegetables sold at AMC Havre's annual harvest festival came from him. "Poor fellow," Mem would at times say. "He used to be such a' upright man." Mem said that he became alcoholic after his wife ran off to Trinidad with a lover. He'd spent many years in Aruba and "when he come home, he make the mistake o' marrying a gal less than half his age that all the fellows use to have their way with. The only thing pretty 'bout that one was her looks. Poor Percy."

At least Millington didn't know about Edward's drinking and so he couldn't feel ashamed. He never needed anyone's pity either, and for that he felt grateful.

Jay and Paul's friend Lionel says often that he'd like to see Millington and Jay drunk. "You two are stiff in all the wrong places. Need a little Bacchus in you. Change that to plenty." He says it in a different way each time they're at his place. He's just as obsessed with nakedness.

7

JAY MUST HAVE been bothered by Paul's jovial talk about beating, because a week after the conversation, while they were home having supper, he said: "Talking about violence, Bernard's the one to watch out. We endured a lot from Paul. He hated himself—he admitted it—and he *made* us pay. Didn't we pay! Drug pushing, shoplifting, skipping most of his high school classes, defacing buildings with graffiti, inviting a female teacher to have sex with him. Even threatened to blow us up once ... One spring he wanted Ma to pay his passage back to St Vincent to spend the summer. Ma said no, and he hurled the dishes from the drainboard at her, then he told us that one day he'll bring home a Uzi and blow us all to bits. Yes, our Paul did that when he was around fifteen. I wonder how he'd have reacted if I'd reminded him of it the other evening."

"Better not to," Millington said.

"Not long after he turned eighteen, Grama died, and he went into a depression. By then he'd given up drug-pushing and his other criminal pursuits, 'because after sixteen you get a criminal record.' He stayed depressed for almost year. When he got over it, he took a nineteen-month trip to Central America and didn't contact us for the last fourteen months. Ma became ill and died and he didn't know. He blamed his behaviour on his asthma, his weight, his being gay. Said that he deliberately courted death. Millington, that's what happened to Ma Kirton's Genius—remember that nickname?—after he left St Vincent. Who would have thought it? Came here and revolted all through high school. Now I think he's trying to make himself look worthy in

Grama's eyes. Too late. But I'm glad I won't have to spend my weekends visiting him in jail or putting flowers on his grave. A woman in my mother's church does both, for a son in jail and another son who Paul used to push drugs for and who was gunned down. Paul wouldn't want you to know any of this. I'm telling you so you'd know what topics to avoid when we're together."

Still talking, Jay got up from the dining table, took out the apple pie they were having for dessert from the toaster oven, and brought it to the table. "I think that trip he took to Central America changed him radically for the better. It made me abandon my PhD. I couldn't get any work done while I worried that he might be dead. It hastened Ma's death too, though I've never told him this."

"How?"

"She grieved over the fact that in his letters to me he never mentioned her: three letters and two postcards that he sent me during the first five months of his travel. She felt too that leaving him in St Vincent when he was two was in some way responsible for his destructive behaviour. I think, more than anything else, she blamed herself for the way he was wasting his intellect. She asked me to apologize to him on her behalf. I did it unwillingly. Honestly, I felt she had nothing to blame herself for. Maybe she might have spent more time with him when we first arrived, but she didn't know that, and as Grama used to say, people can't be held responsible for what they don't know."

"How did the trip change him?"

"The change had already started around the time he turned nineteen. Shortly after he came out of his depression, I introduced him to Bill, a gay professor of mine. Bill died a year before you arrived. Paul, who hid his homosexuality from me, went to see Bill secretly, and I think Bill became a kind of father figure to him. Seems that he got Paul to have a more positive image of himself and advised him to travel to break away from bad influences and change his perspective about what's essential in life. In Central America, he discovered what it was to be on his own. But he got caught buying drugs, paid half of the bribe not to go to jail, and went underground for over a year to avoid paying the other half. All of that because he felt he had to triumph over the cops. Part of his quixotic personality. He has to win at whatever the cost. It's why he didn't communicate with us for the last fourteen months. But he also found a boyfriend, Carlos." He took a forkful of apple pie.

"But Carlos started sleeping with other guys six months after he arrived here. When he and Paul broke up, he consulted a lawyer hoping to get half of the money Paul inherited from Grama and from Ma's insurance. When he didn't succeed, he tried to make back up with Paul. At any rate that's how I read it. Up until then Paul dominated everyone who came into his orbit. You see how charming he is. In Carlos he met his comeuppance.

"But it's in his relationship with Bernard that I see how much he has changed. Now he understands that you sacrifice lesser things for more important ones. He has turned over the second bedroom in their apartment to Bernard for his painting. They've put weather stripping on the door to make it airtight so the fumes from the paints won't trigger Paul's asthma. He has learned that, to have Bernard's love and companionship, he has to accommodate his interests and hobbies. The Paul that I knew up to the time he began travelling would never have thought of that, let alone do it."

Millington wondered then what Jay had sacrificed to have him in his life, and began looking for a discreet way to ask him. But before he found it, Jay resumed talking.

"Of course, the second blow, the one that knocked Paul flat, was when he was diagnosed with malignant meningioma. I think the fear that it might return before he finishes his doctorate is what keeps him fired up. When he complains about not having enough time for his studies I laugh, remembering the scorn he used to heap on me for going to university and even beginning a PhD."

Millington listened in silence. He remembered Mem's advice: "When you can't say anything good 'bout somebody, you say nothing … And, Mill, remember that every story got three sides: the side o' one party, the side o' the other party, and the truth."

Paul's experiences won't be wasted. He's putting some of them into fiction. Millington suspects that Paul and Jay might be secretly competing with each other. Won't surprise him if Jay announces sometime soon that he's resuming work on his PhD.

Paul's stories about Jay are never told behind Jay's back. "You're the first guy he's had sex with. Until you rescued him, this man of yours"—he winked at Jay—"was a confirmed old maid. Oops! *Vieux garcon.*" He rubbed his thighs. "Man, I had to drill deep, frigging deep, into that thick carapace to get him to admit that he was in love with you while you both were in high school. And, man, if I hadn't kicked the ball and him too, he'd be on his butt contemplating a sexless marriage to Jonathan. Jay, admit it. You're a tight ball o' twine. Hope you're unwinding him. Millington, I'm not kidding … Eight years with Daddy and religious gobbledygook turned this boy into a tightly spooled bobbin … You're smart, Millington. You refused to let dogma damage you the way it damaged Jay." He winked at Jay, who listened, head tilted to the left, his forehead pleated. "Jay's wounds are still raw. Help him heal, Millington."

Millington said nothing.

"Okay, let me be plain: Jay hides his feelings. He's afraid to show his anger. When we were growing up, no matter how much I pestered him, he ignored me. I used to want to strangle him or bop him with the first thing I got my hands on … His silence is because when Daddy was angry he got violent with him and Ma. Admit it, Jay?"

"I'm not listening to you, Paul. You're testing our reaction to material in your novel."

Paul gave Jay a dismissive hand flick. "Millington, you must push him to show his anger. Force him to see it's venom … venom that could poison both of you."

Millington laughs and recalls the Saturday Jay and he got married. The ceremony at City Hall, witnessed by Gina and Paul, was simple enough. A month later when Guícho, who was in Alberta at the time of the wedding, met Millington, he said: "Good thing I was in Lethbridge or, so help me God, I would o' screamed: 'No, you can't marry him. What about me?'"

Jay had wanted a low-key affair. Paul would have none of it. "I know my brother. He'll never marry more than once, so let's make a big deal of this." Between him and Gina, they invited forty of their friends, rented Apollon for the Saturday afternoon, and had a West Indian caterer bring in the food. When Jay found out what they were up to, he offered to pay. Paul told him to leave it to Gina. She ended up collecting enough money to cover the costs with about $200 extra. Jay told her to give it to the Stephen Lewis Foundation.

Paul's wedding toast: what was it about? A continuation of their sibling rivalry? He'd probably drunk too much that day. Because of his asthma drugs, he's not supposed to drink. At Les Friends get-togethers, Bernard often picks up his wine when he isn't looking or glares at him when he attempts to get a second drink. On the wedding day, Paul wobbled as he walked to the microphone. Before speaking he gave Jay a big wink. "Oh! Oh!" Jay whispered. "Trouble's ahead."

"Dear friends and colleagues, see this couple." He turned to look at Jay and Millington and nodded. "They're going where no man has gone before."

The odd chuckle. Frowns mostly.

"Bet you never thought you'd attend a gay wedding where both parties are virgins?"

He waited until the tittering ceased.

"I shouldn't be telling tales out of school."

He stared at Millington. "Now, Millington, when you settle in virgin territory, there's timber to fell, land to plough, and crops to decide on. Oh yes, and testing of the soil too. Here's a bit of advice, Millington: plant the crops that will grow in Jay's soil. For starters, check out Dan Savage's columns. I'll give you a few more tips … in private, of course."

The guests groaned.

"And keep your tools well-honed, Millington. You'll be ploughing difficult soil."

Millington held his head down during the roaring laughter.

"Banter aside, Jay, my dear, dear brother, and Millington, my unimpeachable brother-in-law, may this day begin for both of you a life of happiness that will endure until you die."

Until you die. And if it isn't exactly happiness, how long should it last? Dan Savage would say: not very.

Two weeks later Jay hosted Les Friends and Millington began to get a clearer picture of who they were.

With his grey eyes fixed on Millington, a glass of whiskey in his hand, Lionel called across the kitchen to him where he was leaning on the dining table, "Welcome to Les Friends, Millington. Hope you're good at throwing shit. We splatter one another with it and hug afterwards."

"Speak for yourself," Gina called to him from the living room.

"Agree, Gina," Tyrone, whose gawky seven-foot frame stood right beside Millington, said.

"What's this? You're all ganging up on me?" Lionel said.

Everyone laughed. Millington didn't get the joke. With Jay's friends, he rarely gets the joke.

These thoughts take him back to Mem's other revelations on July 14, 2010.

"Edward had other women too," she said, her voice tinged with sorrow.

"Yes, Felix's mother. I know about her."

She shook her head. "That is old story, Mill. Long-gone story. Mildred been with him before Edward married me, and she and he continue in secret until Felix born. He deny it. What a wicked man! He wait till last week, while he on his deathbed, to acknowledge Felix. He used to say: 'For argument sake, let's say I been having relations with Mildred, and have a child with she, you think it going be black like Felix? No way.' One time Celestina hear him, and she call out to him from over the fence: 'Edward, sometimes the looks show up in the colour and sometimes it does show up in the hair. Look at that boy hair. It straight like yours. Look at his nose and lips: they's yours. Felix black 'cause Mildred black. Your eyes been shut when you been on top her?' He tell her to mind her own business. 'How you know Mildred not been sleeping with a coolie man?'"

"Mill, I don' mean Mildred. The woman I talking 'bout name Dorothy, a two-bit whore that live in Barrouallie. Never work a day in her life. The only job that one ever do is lie on her back and spread her legs."

His jaw fell. He'd never heard Mem talk like that.

"She's who your father used to be with when he leave here on a Friday. Here and there he did have other women too. But those didn' last. Twenty-six years Edward keep Dorothy. She and the rum shop owners got every cent he worked for and plenty o' what I work for. You was five, Mill, when he take up with Dorothy. If I didn' have you I would o' leave him."

She wiped her eyes on her dress sleeve. "Dorothy come to his funeral. You didn' see her? She sit in the last row in the back, on the right-hand side. Black-black woman, blacker than a crow. Was wearing black too and a wig with hair down to her shoulders. She sneak out before they wheel out the casket."

He wouldn't have noticed her. There were several women from the surrounding communities; and busloads of women, members of the Women's League to which Mem belongs, had come from all over St Vincent.

The only hints he ever had of Dorothy's existence were the jute sacks of root vegetables that Edward, dressed in his Sunday best, would leave with on a late Friday afternoon. Sometimes he returned the Saturday morning, and Mem said it was because he'd missed the last bus back and had to overnight at Cousin Albert's place, or that he'd stayed over to help Cousin Albert repair his house. Beyond finding it strange that they never visited Cousin Albert in nearby Barrouallie, and that Cousin Albert never visited them, he never questioned her story.

More came from her the following day. "Something else I should tell you … that I didn' tell you yesterday." She fell silent for a couple of seconds, then broke it with a loud sob. He held her hand to comfort her. Again they were on the porch and dusk was approaching. She took a washcloth from the pocket of her apron and blew her nostrils and stared a long while down at the Caribbean Sea.

"Mem, what are you holding back?"

She pulled at the loose skin under her neck. "Your father wasn't a bad man. He was better than most ... You see, I been too set on want-ing to walk in the ways o' the righteous while Edward been like every-body else." She bit her lip. Paused. "When he start to carry on with Dorothy, I tell him: 'No more relations with me, Edward. No more. Not while you is with that woman' ... You was five at the time, Mill, and you was in and out o' hospital. That is why I didn' leave him ... When he see I serious, he complain to your grandmother. Mammy tell me to change my mind, that I have a duty to have relations with my husband. I ignore her. After you get better, I stay with him. Boy chil-dren need their father to show them how to be a man."

By then the porch light had come on. He searched her face for irony but saw none.

"Edward didn' leave Dorothy, so I keep my promise." She gulped and swallowed a few times. He got up from the opposite side of the table, went to sit beside her, and put an arm around her.

While he puzzled over her mostly sexless marriage, she stared in the direction of the sea. Without turning to face him, she said: "Your fath-er been a better man than the men-them 'round here. I been a blessed woman, you hear: a blessed woman." He didn't want to contradict her. Guess she was grateful that he didn't beat her. She turned her gaze from the sea and smiled. "We was in agreement over one thing." Her smile got bigger. "When you been fifteen days old, I take you in my arms down to Ma Kirton store to buy your baptism clothes, and she tell me to bring you closer so she can look at you good. She ask me your name, and I tell her Millington Ambrose and that they come from Edward grandfather, Edward mother Father. Ma Kirton say the names too long and they old-fashioned. And she tell me I mustn't do like the parents around here and beat you, that educated people say beating children not good, that it cause them to grow up stunted and confuse.

"I tell her that AMC teaching say never spare the rod, and John Wesley mother say when children do wrong, we must beat them. 'No, Mem,' she say, shaking her head. 'John Wesley's mother didn' know any better, but nowadays educated people know that it harmful to beat children.' I tell her that I will stick to the bible and Methodist teaching:

'You have to beat children to teach them discipline.' Ma Kirton shake her head again. 'Mem, you cook with fire, and in cold countries people use it to heat their houses, but you know the damage fire can cause; you don't put your hand in it, and wherever fire burn you it leave a scar.' And she stop talking. Just like I seeing her now, behind the counter, her eyes like flame burning into me. Then she start to talk again. 'Beating children is like burning them with fire. It scar them on their body, and it scar them in their mind. Think about it: the same hand that you hug your child with is the same hand that inflict pain!' She shake her head. 'No, Mem. When children do wrong, you sit them down and show them why it wrong and you make them promise not to do it again, and when they slip up, you remind them of that promise, and you let them see that their bad behaviour hurt you.'

"Mill, I go home and I pray over it, and I been 'fraid to talk to your father 'bout it. But I pray. I ask God what to do, and just like the Holy Spirit tell me to talk to your father. And to my surprise, Edward say that your uncle Jacob, who used to drink from the time he wake up in the morning until he go to bed at night, until he roll over the cliff in Fancy and kill himself—he been only twenty-eight, and Edward feel it wasn' no accident—use to get licks from their uncle almost every day, 'to beat the devil out o' him,' and Edward think that is why he turn alcoholic when he been only fifteen, that and because their father been in Aruba. And Edward say to me: 'Mem, we going hold off the beating and see how it go. Some children born evil, and you does have for beat it out o' them, but when children good most o' the time, if they go astray once in a while you don't have for beat them for that.' Mill, it do my heart good, real good, that we never beat you, and look how proud you make us."

A year later when he quit the AMC ministry those words must have haunted her. *Worse news is waiting, Mem. A lot worse.*

Whom did she confide in? Ma Kirton would have agreed with her decision not to have any more children. She might have shown her too that the fifteen acres of land she owned was enough to support her and Millington. It was possible. Angelita worked her land herself, and it gave her an independent, comfortable living. The ne'er-do-wells on the

Anglican Church patio never trifled with her the way they did with Miss Collins. *Manicou know wha' tree fo' climb 'pon.* Mem didn't want to leave Edward and found a rationalisation to stay with him. Edward too had good reason to remain with her.

Mem had no relatives in Havre. Occasionally Marcella and Robertha, two of her female cousins, visited from Sandy Bay. Edward had grown up there too. The cousins brought gifts of dried fish, farine, and arrowroot and cassava starch. When they came during the blackfish season Mem gave them bundles of it. They never stayed long, never more than a couple of hours, because they had to hurry back to Kingstown to catch the bus and re-circle two-thirds of the island to get back to Sandy Bay. They always threatened never to return unless Mem reciprocated. One time she went for the funeral of someone. She didn't take him along. Edward didn't go either.

How different would it have been if he'd had this conversation with both of his parents present? The one time he asked Edward about their Sandy Bay relatives, Edward remained silent a long time before saying: "I keep away from them and I want you to keep away too. Nothing good come from them." Edward found it difficult to forgive. Mem filled in some of the details: Millington's paternal grandfather's name was Raymond, but everyone called him Boss. Edward's rift with the family had come over Boss' will, which dispossessed his first wife's children and gave everything, even property that he'd inherited from Edward's mother, to his second wife, Lily, and her daughter, reputed not to be Boss's child. Lily was ten years younger than Jacob, Edward's older brother. Boss and Jacob had come to blows once, after Lily had accused Jacob of propositioning her. Boss threw Jacob out of the house then, and six months later Jacob died.

Their non-Kalinago relatives had all immigrated to England before Millington was born. Some of the Sandy Bay relatives knew Millington. Bertram, Jacob's grandson, attended Kingstown Secondary with him. Millington rebuffed his efforts to befriend him. The ignorance about his forbears leaves a void. He knows nothing about his mother's father and almost nothing about Boss.

He feels there were other things that Edward wanted to talk over with him. Edward was home on the day the letter announcing Millington's bursary for ETC arrived. Torrential rain that morning and part of the afternoon had made outdoor carpentering impossible. Millington was home on vacation. Around three, the rain let up, and Edward came down the porch steps and stood beside him silently for several seconds. Millington was cutting excess growth from a bougainvillea he'd planted there. He paused the cutting and waited.

"So you going away to study to become a parson ... Your mother talked you into it?"

"No."

Edward sighed.

Millington put the shears on the step and waited for him to continue.

"All these people talking 'bout God, I does wonder if they know what they talking 'bout." He shook his head slowly, gesturing doubt. "Anyway, is your choice." He moved a couple feet away from Millington, gave him a look of appraisal, and muttered something.

"Daddy, I didn't hear you," Millington said.

Edward shook his head again, gesturing pity, and began mounting the steps.

Why was he pitying him? He should have set aside the shears and followed him inside and questioned him further. What did Edward wish for him? That conversation might have given him the opening to ask him about other issues.

How were his parents able to sleep in the same bed five, six, occasionally seven nights per week and not have sex? He remembers a parishioner who'd come to seek his advice telling him that after sex with her husband, she'd bury her head in her pillow and cry. She cried in his office too. She promised to return to tell him why. She never did.

When Millington began to attend elementary school, Felix told him he was his brother. He was a couple years older than Millington and played the role of his guardian at school. Felix lived with his mother over in Laird's shanty, now Laird's Village.

Millington asked Mem if Felix was really his brother.

"You stupid? That is a question for your father."

Millington didn't ask Edward, but Mem told him, because about a week later, Edward said: "You been hearing rumours 'bout me. They not true. That boy not my child." At the time Millington believed him. But as Sister Murray remarked many times, "the looks don't always come in the colour; sometimes it does come in the hair and all sort o' other ways." Millington resembles Edward only in his skinniness. Felix was lanky until he began lifting weights. Millington's near-white complexion means nothing, since both of his parents were pale-skinned; Mem was sometimes mistaken for a white woman. His face is somewhat triangular like Mem's. At six-one—roughly the same height as Felix—Millington's a foot taller than Edward. A large globe could fit easily between Edward's curved legs. Felix and Millington have straight legs.

Felix went sailing three years after he finished elementary school. Millington was in sixth form when he last saw him. A late afternoon. He was at the Leeward Bus Terminal about to board a bus to Havre, and a muscular, very handsome, jet-black man with a thick head of what looked like Afro-Asian hair walked toward him, smiling. Felix would have been twenty-one then. "You don' remember me, eh. Who use to look out for you in school?" They hugged. Felix stepped back and stared at him. "Mammy tell me you is doing well in school."

Millington gestured so-so.

"My brother, learn plenty, you hear. Learn plenty. I glad you have the chances I didn' have." While saying so he pulled out his wallet and gave Millington a $50 note. "If you fail your exams you going have to give me that back with three hundred percent interest." He winked and gave Millington another big hug.

He too was his mother's only child. He hadn't made it to secondary school. Universal secondary education came ten years after he left.

Millington spent a long part of the night of July 15, 2010 recording and parsing Mem's revelations. He understood why she'd tried to hide Edward's failings. She hadn't wanted him to judge or despise Edward or, worse, copy his rum-drinking habit. Millington would have been anxious too that Edward might abandon them and go live with his mistress. Many of Havre's men did, almost always women younger than their wives, women who never worked and therefore relied financially on their lovers. Little or nothing was left for their in-wedlock families. There were frequent conversations about these relationships at the domino table. When it turned to the most recent man to do so, Presley Murray would say: "Men put their treasure where they get their pleasure." Millington wonders now how Mem felt when she heard this. Was this a message meant for her? Had Edward put Presley up to it? Mem was always within their hearing—grating coconuts on the ground below the porch or ironing in the living room, right beside the porch. Presley didn't have any mistresses or out-of-wedlock children that Millington knew of. When the domino players teased him about this, he said Celestina was worth more than ten women. To which the teaser replied: "Ah chut, man! Is cause you is weak, you not a real he-man."

Mem said that Dorothy was eighteen when Edward took up with her. Edward was thirty-five. How did Mem manage to contain her anger so well all those years?

It explains why there was always a quiet tension between his parents, but money was the only thing he ever heard them quarrelling over, usually in their bedroom at night. Edward insisted that because he and his friends ploughed the land at Hollow, he was entitled to part of the money from the produce. Mem resisted him at first but eventually gave in. One time Millington heard her pleading through sobs that she'd wanted "to save some money to repaint the house." From these quarrels he found out that none of Edward's earnings from carpentry came into the home. Once, sobbing, Mem told him: "I know what you do with your money. But God don't sleep, Edward. God don't sleep at all."

He replied: "Woman, what more you want from me? I don't beat you. I don't curse you. I don't run you down with other people. What more you want from me?"

"Shh. Not so loud. Millington going hear us."

She was always up at five to milk the goats. Sometimes while changing from his pyjamas, he would hear her exchanging goodbyes with the women or the children who'd come to buy milk. Did Edward claim any of that money too? She earned a pittance from the ginger fudge and coconut-sugar cakes that she supplied her friend Bea with. Her Mondays were given over to harvesting bananas, Fridays to gathering produce for sale in the market. The other days she spent weeding and moulding and light ploughing either at Hollow or on the land of Edward's farming partners, usually in the company of Sister Murray and Zelda Brown.

At ETC, his studies of the Hebrew scriptures—and myths and fables in general—showed him how societies reinforce their dominant practices. Other stories too—about women whose lives depended on being able to spin straw into gold or keeping drowsy emperors awake on pain of their lives—gave him a better understanding of his mother's oppressive marriage and an ambivalent admiration for cantankerous Miss Pebbles, who refused the yoke of Vincentian matrimony and was dissed by the neighbours for having done so.

For what it was worth, after the fling with Felix's mother, Edward chose to do his philandering far away, where Millington couldn't see it. He wants to think—maybe he needs to think—that Edward was better than the many irresponsible fathers found in St Vincent—and, as he later found out, across the Caribbean. Men who voluntarily become the studs their forefathers, slaves, had been forced to be. Today's men flaunt children as proof of their virility and see the children's needs as their mothers' responsibility.

As to virility there were always exceptions to reinforce the claim: Joyce Wiley's affair with "lowlife" Donovan. Joyce was Havre's postmistress and the principal organist at the Anglican Church. She'd expected Donovan to keep the affair discreet. But the point of the seduction was to brag about it. There could be no denial when the son she gave birth to inherited Donovan's extra diminutive fingers. Her husband Bromley, a short, broomstick of a man, taught at Father Crowley's. On his way to and from work, the gang of ne'er-do-wells on the patio of the Anglican Church, screamed m-e-e-e-r-r-r at him and put their wrists to their temples and stuck out their forefingers to suggest horns. Not long after the baby's birth, Castigator, the calypsonian in Esperance, composed a song about the relationship:

> Donovan, now you's the man.
> Joyce, she say,
> To hell with you Bromley;
> I need a village ram
> To put somethin' solid
> In me hot frying pan.
> I tired o' this toothpick man...
> I want something solid in me frying pan ...

Bromley went to teach in faraway Owia when the new school year started and was never again seen in Havre.

And when Lloyd kicked out his woman Loulou and their three children from the mud shack he'd inherited from his mother, and installed two women "he pick up 'pon the streets o' Kingstown," Sister Murray exclaimed: "I use to think there been nothing new in the world left to see ... Mem not one o' the three lifting a stroke nowhere." Castigator made a song about them too:

> Lloyd say, Lou-lou
> You is only barefoot bookoo
> Ah wants sophistication
> And two town woman
> For ample satisfaction
> You is country boileen
> I wants plenty goat meat
> A side dish 'o chicken stew
> And lots and lots o' lambi too.

There was no follow-up calypso when the women left. Castigator had emigrated, and Haverites wished he'd been there to immortalize their departure. One of Old Man Laird's nephews caught Lloyd chopping off a cow's tail and shot out his testes and shattered his right hip. Six months after the incident he died from sepsis.

Philandering in the Caribbean is, of course, not restricted to Black men. Pembroke, who was Ma Kirton's friend and the general overseer of Laird Estates, was one of about twenty-five children Old Man Laird had fathered with the house servants and field hands. Jay said he'd overheard Pembroke telling Ma Kirton and Teacher Morrison that whenever the old man's wife, who was childless, upbraided him for his womanizing he would say: "My dear Alice, don't scold me. Do like those bible women—Sarah, Rachel, and Rebecca. They helped their husbands multiply." Pembroke himself had a taste for very young, very black women. He was sixty when he married his third wife, who was seventeen, fourteen years younger than his oldest daughter. Two others not much older were his mistresses.

Grudgingly Millington accepts that he cannot blame Edward for being a product of his society. But he can't always control his anger each time he remembers that Edward used almost all of the household income to satisfy his lust and alcoholism. Yet Edward didn't feel it necessary to flog him when he made mistakes. He wasn't subjected to the violence Jay endured until he was eight. Jay never mentioned it while they were in St Vincent. Millington will never have Jay's kind of nightmares, in which he begs his father not to beat him or to stop hitting his ma. In Millington's nightmares members of his ex-congregation catch him in bed with Horton; or he's setting fire to Elijah's house while Elijah and Willy Green are still in it.

8

MILLINGTON FIRST MET Jay when he was in junior three. Elijah had sent him on an errand to Ma Kirton's store. From behind the counter, Ma Kirton stared at him with her honey-coloured eyes, her spectacles hanging from a silver chain, and told him that her grandson was in the same school as he. "Jay is a darling boy just like you. You must take an interest in him. He lives with me now. Come visit him sometimes." Millington had already seen the shy, skinny, brown-skin, bandy-legged boy daydreaming in class. He never raised his hand to answer, and as soon as the bell rang at three, he rushed home. After Ma Kirton's request, he waited for Jay to speak to him. A week passed and he didn't, so one recess Millington asked him if his grandmother hadn't told him she wanted them to be friends.

He shook his head. "Grama told you so?"

Millington nodded.

"I'll ask her."

He asked Jay where he'd lived before, and he said Georgetown. Over the first weeks Millington learned that his mother was in Canada and that his father used to be a preacher. "What work your father doing now?" Jay looked away and said he didn't know. After their marriage, Millington asked him why he hadn't wanted to talk about his father's occupation then. He pursed his lips and turned his head sideways, showing discomfort: a gesture Millington noticed the first time they met. "I don't remember," he said. "Perhaps it was because I knew Daddy was removing stones from the beach illegally and had paid a government inspector to keep quiet about it. I've never said this to anyone before."

The morning after Millington told him that Ma Kirton wanted them to be friends, Jay sat in class and daydreamed, and Miss Robinson had to dangle the strap in front of him so he'd snap out of it and do his work.

At one point that year he said that he was having a birthday party and Ma Kirton wanted Millington to come. Edward said no. "Leave rich people to their antics. When your birthday come round, you going want to celebrate it too. I don' want you to start hanging your hat where you can't reach it. You will stay right here and eat roast breadfruit and smoke herring, when we can afford smoke herring." He'd so wanted to see inside of that beautiful house with all those flowers outside. He asked Mem to plead with Edward. But she shook her head slowly from left to right and back again before saying: "Wouldn' make no difference, Mill. When your father make up his mind 'bout something, not even God can get him to change it."

During that first year, whenever he went to Ma Kirton's shop on errands for Mem or Elijah, she asked him if he was being a good friend to her darling Jay. One time when he and Jay were in junior four, Jay came down with ague in class and got his sums wrong and Mr. Branch flogged him, and Ma Kirton came up Pasture Road holding Paul's hand and asked Millington what had happened in class. When Jay came back to school, he said he hadn't wanted Ma Kirton to know about the beating because he liked Mr. Branch and he didn't want her to say hurtful things to him. Millington asked him what she had told Mr. Branch, but he said he wasn't present; Paul was. But he wouldn't tell Millington what Paul had told him. Jay thinks Ma Kirton didn't love him. That all her love was for Paul. It puzzles Millington that he feels that way.

He remembers that morning when he and Jay went on the bus to Chateaubelair to write the high school placement exam. Their seats were two rows apart in the exam room. Neil was three seats left of Jay. Neil was one of the first to finish the morning tests. Jay was the last to come out. The invigilator probably had to chase him out. Was in there reading over and over what he'd written. Always worried that he might have overlooked something. In Jay's backpack he had a lunch of codfish cakes and bakes, two slices of pound cake, and two oranges that Aunt Mercy had prepared for him. Ma Kirton had told him to share his lunch with Millington. They ate sitting under an almond tree on Chateaubelair's Beach Road. They combined the money Jay had to buy juice with the lunch money Mem had given Millington and bought ice cream and cake for both of them, then wrote the general paper in the afternoon, and took the bus back to Havre.

When their results came out a month later, of 2926 students, Neil placed 14th, Jay 28th and Millington 34th "See," Neil said, sneering at them both, "you all don't like me but I beat you. Put that in you all pipe and smoke it," and began walking to the other end of the schoolyard. Millington was tempted to yell: "Run along, Nella," but a promise he'd made to Edward two years earlier, never to embarrass him, held him back.

The Ministry of Education announced over the radio that Jay and he had been assigned to Kingstown Secondary and Neil to Grammar School. Their guardians had to confirm acceptance within a week or they would lose their places. Edward said they couldn't afford lunch money and the daily bus fare to Kingstown and that Millington should go to Esperance Secondary. It was a kilometre walk over the hill from Havre and was a second-rate school for students who didn't rank in the first hundred and fifty passes.

Millington wanted to be in the same school as Jay. In the kitchen outside Mem mumbled aloud that the money that flowed out of their home could pay for two students, never mind one. He asked her what she meant. She said: "Ask your father." He didn't. When, following Edward's death, she told him about Edward's drinking and womanizing, he felt that if he'd known that Edward valued maintaining a mistress—and for short periods mistresses—over funding his education, he might have come to despise him.

Three days after their placement was announced, Jay said he'd be attending Kingstown Secondary. Millington told him he'd have to go to Esperance Secondary. Jay told Ma Kirton. In the late afternoon the same day she came up the hill to see Mem. Edward was away working on a project at Lowman's Hill. She told Mem that Esperance was not a good enough school for Millington, and that they should make the sacrifice to send him to Kingstown Secondary. "When children want to learn, you mustn't stand in their way." She asked Mem to come down to the store the next morning. She dialled the Ministry of Education, handed the telephone to Mem, and made her reserve the spot for Millington. That evening Edward looked at him with a big smile—one of three Millington received from him over a life time—and said he would attend Kingstown Secondary. "You is a lucky boy." He said nothing more. He should ask Mem about this the next time he speaks to her. How was she able to convince him? Edward was right about his luck, because, later that year, Aunt Pearl offered to pay Millington's travel costs to and from school. She had already paid to wire their house for electricity and to bring running water to their yard—to ease the burden on Mem, she later told him. "Millington, your father was a wastrel. I don't know why Mem fell for him."

In Kingstown, Jay and Millington saw each other only in the classes they had together and at recess. Jay and Paul stayed in town on school days. On Monday mornings Millington, Paul, Jay and Neil travelled into town, but on different buses. On Friday afternoons Father Henderson brought Paul and Jay home in his car. Ma Kirton's princes, Miss Collins called them: Jay was Big Prince and Paul was Little Prince.

Neil and Millington took the same bus back to Havre every day, but he avoided Neil, who had switched to Saint Martin's. The Catholic Church had given him an all-expenses-paid scholarship, and he became an even bigger windbag. One time he sat beside Millington on the bus back to Havre. Millington took a book from his backpack and pretended to read. Neil leaned into him and whispered: "Like you 'fraid your husband will cut your backside if you talk to me. I sure Jay bulling you." Neil waited for Millington's response. There was none. Neil began twisting in his seat. "You should feel honoured that I notice you." That too Millington let pass without comment. In terms of social class Neil had more in common with Jay. They were the same age too; their birthdays were two days apart. But the resemblance ended there.

Neil had a high-pitched, girly voice, which never deepened, and a bottom that rippled when he walked. The ne'er-do-wells on the Anglican Church patio renamed him Nella and whistled at him whenever he walked by them.

Millington's chores: gathering and bringing home firewood and pasturing goats, complicated his school life. On rare occasions when Mem worked at Hollow until 4 p.m., she brought the goats home. In November, December, and January, when the days were shorter, it was invariably at dusk that he was tying them to the stilts on which their house stood. When he began school in town, Mem took over pasturing them on mornings, but it was only in the last three years—when he was in forms five and six—that Ma Kirton made Mem and Edward understand his need for extra study time, and they relieved him of those chores. Somewhat.

"God bless these goats," Mem often said. They were the family's bank account. Whenever extra cash was needed, she sold one or two of the goats. They paid for Millington's new clothes on Harvest Sunday, his Boys' Brigade uniform, his church shoes, and even his everyday sneakers; once too to restore the electricity when Vinlec cut the power to their house; and as he learned from Mem, his father's rum-drinking debts.

The lack of a stove. That rankled. Until Ma Kirton intervened, Millington spent every livelong Saturday collecting and bringing home three bundles of firewood—each bundle a separate trip—on his head from their woodlot at Hollow, a mile away. Ma Kirton confronted Mem shortly after he entered secondary five. He'd failed a math test that Jay had aced. Jay was surprised. He'd told Millington to come by the Saturday before so they could study together. Millington couldn't. Edward had taken him early that Saturday morning to help him finish repairing a balcony in Esperance. In the afternoon he had his firewood chore. The next day there was church in the morning, Sunday school at 3 p.m., and Evensong at 7 p.m.

Alarmed, Jay told Ma Kirton about the test Millington had failed and why. She confronted Mem. Mem relieved him from going to Sunday school and attending Evensong and told Edward Millington could no longer get the firewood. A day later, Edward, smiling tight-lipped and scratching his temple, something he did whenever he doubted himself, stared from below the porch up at Millington for a few seconds, before saying: "I go ask Bentley to get the firewood. For the sake o' your future. Nobody must say I stand in your way. Now you don' have no excuse to fail." Bentley was a mentally-challenged fellow who did odd jobs around Havre. Six weeks later Edward stopped paying Bentley, and getting the firewood became another of Mem's chores. During school holidays, guilt-ridden, Millington resumed doing it. (When Millington began working and bought a stove, after Mem drew the first match and the flame appeared, Edward turned to him, smiled broadly, and said: "Thanks, Millington"—the only thank-you he ever got from him and one of two times he ever addressed Millington by name; Millington was always you or boy. Millington wanted to say that he bought it to ease the burden on Mem. *You don't know what burdens are. You put them on the backs of others.*)

Jay certainly outperformed him in school. Ma Kirton freed him from chores on Saturdays and Sundays so he could study. She even got him a computer when he entered secondary four. Some afternoons, especially during the rainy season, when landslides often delayed the bus, Millington was too tired to do homework, and would wake up at 4 a.m., at times 3 a.m., to do it. Twice he didn't wake up and had to listen to the teachers calling him a slacker in front of the class and serve detentions during his lunch hour. He saved up part of his lunch money until he had enough to buy an alarm clock.

He envied Jay his leisure time, and would have liked to stay in town too, away from those chores. All that freedom. No bonanza, Jay says. In the first couple of years he had to rush off at lunchtime to meet Paul at his school and take him to Elma's Restaurant, where they ate their lunch. Millington lied when Jay asked him where he ate lunch; said he did so at a cousin's place. Neil ate his in Frenches, at an aunt's house. One time he invited Millington to come by for lunch, but Millington said no. Millington ate the fruits he took in his backpack: initially two ripe bananas that Mem put in a Tupperware container so they wouldn't be crushed: one for recess and one for lunch, along with another fruit, whatever was in season—mango, orange, golden apple, plumrose, or mamie apple. At lunch, he added a bun and a piece of fried chicken that he bought from the food vendors at the market. When jacks and skipjack were in season, he bought fish, for then it was cheaper, and he was left with a quarter or two that he could save up. When his parents harvested cassava and made cassava bread, he carried it for an entire week and had it with avocado. And there was always a coconut cake and a piece of fudge which he held back for much needed energy when the school day ended.

He ate in the general market building with workers and students from other schools. He met Alan there. Alan was from Green Hill. He attended JP Eustace Secondary. He had pepper-corn hair, satiny black skin, bright bulging eyes, lips that opened like nutmeg pods, straight even teeth, slightly bowed legs, and a flattish bottom. On Monday of the second week, he stared at Millington bug-eyed and asked him in his hill-and-valley town twang, why a boy from a high-class school was eating with the down-trodden. Millington laughed and said that it was because the boy attending the high-class school was down-trodden too. They quickly became friends. After that Millington carried extra fruit which he shared with him.

Two months after they wrote their CXC exams, Alan spent a week with him in Havre. Their results came out while he was there. They'd all done well in their exams.

Friday, the last full day Alan spent in Havre, he, Jay and Millington were together. They walked to Hollow to take Edward's lunch, after which they bathed in the sea behind Ma Kirton's house. When they got out of the water Aunt Mercy had ham sandwiches, cake, and ginger beer waiting for them. They ate sitting on the back porch. At some point the question about the type of girl they would want for a wife came up. Alan said his uncle Carlton told him to stay away from Marilyn, his next-door neighbour. "Woman like she does cut off man balls." Jay and Millington laughed. "Cut them off, dry them out, run string through them, and wear them round their neck." They hadn't heard Ma Kirton come in from the store. Her cackling laughter surprised them. She came onto the porch, smiled at Alan, and said: "Tell your uncle, some men should never have balls. Sonny, what's your name?" Alan told her. "Alan, women have to be bossy. Most men I know need the guidance of a strong intelligent woman."

Does Alan remember this? Has he gotten married?

Around 6 p.m., Alan accompanied him when Mem sent him to take fruits and vegetables to the AMC manse. Neil saw them descending Pasture Road and waited for them on the road just outside his house. He broke into a big smile and shouted: "Somebody getting butt." Millington ignored him. When they were out of earshot, Alan asked what that had been about.

"Foolishness. He's weird."

The next morning, while Millington and Alan were standing on Main Street waiting for a bus to take Alan back to Kingstown, Millington said they'd all be in sixth form in September and would meet in class.

Alan shook his head. On their way back from Hollow the day before, Jay and Millington were excited about being in sixth form. Millington thought Alan would be too—JP Eustace and Kingstown Secondary did not offer the sixth form curriculum and their sixth-form students switched to Boys Grammar School. Alan, who was usually a chatter-box, was quiet.

"Just two more years, Alan. *Two*."

A bus came, stopped. He didn't board it.

"I have to find a job. Mama needs the money." He stared at the ground and swallowed. "Mama has three of us to feed ... Mama works as a domestic when she can find work." Silence. He pulled the front of his T-shirt out of his pants and used its tail to dab his eyes. "Three weeks ago, Rodney, my baby brother, went into a neighbour's house ... and ate his food. Mama flogged him ... We had almost nothing to eat that day." He wiped his eyes again. "Forget it. I didn't come here to tell you our troubles."

"Please. Talk."

"Mama was sick with the flu the week before. No work, no money. Right? ... Country people can always find something to eat. Not so in town." He glanced at the two shopping bags of fruits and vegetables Mem had packed for him. Earlier his eyes had glowed when Mem put two small plastic containers, one with fudge and one with coconut sugar cakes, in one of the bags. "I want to be in sixth form. I want to go to university afterwards. More than you can imagine. But first me, Rodney, Emily, and Mama have to eat."

Millington nodded his sympathy and breathed deeply to keep back his own tears. They stood there in silence until the next bus to town began descending towards them.

"Keep what I just tell you to yourself. Promise?"

Millington nodded and they embraced.

A week later, as he passed by Neil's house, Neil said: "Milly, your new boyfriend kind o' cute. What's his name? Jay know another man bulling you? I hope he cut your arse when he find out and ditch you."

Now that would be a shocker if Alan too has turned out to be gay. They'd slept in the same bed. Those days he sometimes wondered what it would be like to spend time in Jay's arms, sleep in the same bed with him. Sometimes he dreamed they were having sex and he was awkward. Other times, it was Jay telling him he didn't want to be friends with a bullerman. He felt no such desire for Alan, although he found him attractive, and saw something vaguely, pleasantly spiritual in him that he liked.

Millington had wanted to visit his home, but Alan made excuses. He said his mother and her three children, his grandmother, and an aunt and her two children shared a two-bedroom house. "Your home quiet, man. The noise in mine going drive you crazy. You going have to walk over pickney spread out sleeping all over the damn floor and pissing it down. And, on top o' that, man, there ain't nothing special to see or do in Green Hill." Millington held back from saying that it could be just for a day, that he didn't have to sleep over.

He last saw Alan three days before leaving for ETC. Alan was walking along Lower Bay Street toward the police barracks and was dressed in a police constable uniform. He had applied to get into teaching, policing, or the civil service. The police responded first. They chatted about police work and Millington's job as the complaints clerk at the Ministry of Labour. When he told Alan he was leaving for Jamaica in three days to study theology, Alan's face became glum. After a brief silence he said: "Good luck with your studies, man. I sure you going succeed." He frowned. "Pardon me if you find me out of place ... How you paying for your studies?"

"The church gave me a bursary."

Alan whistled and a smile rippled his face. "Man, all the good things come your way. You must leave some for the rest of us. Stay in touch. Write me in care of the police barracks."

Millington nodded and they shook hands.

He didn't stay in touch.

Three years ago, when he read in the online *Searchlight* that the police and a convoy of journalists had surprised and humiliated two men having sex on a remote beach in St Vincent, he wondered if Alan was part of the squad. What would Alan think if he finds out that Millington and Jay are married? He wouldn't have visited Millington that August if he'd had the remotest suspicion of his sexuality, even if he himself had had homosexual urges.

What has become of him? He too probably had a father who didn't think he should support his children. When Millington left the AMC ministry and went back to St Vincent, he avoided his acquaintances, was afraid they'd see him as a failure, and would have asked him too many questions. He wanted no one's pity or condemnation. Alan was probably not home. Most of those fellows had moved to the United States. Some had joined the British military.

Good things didn't always come his way. He was bothered by his parents' poverty. Mem tried her best to shield him from the problems caused by a shortage of money. During his teenage years he did wonder on occasion if Jay looked down on him. Neil definitely did. Edward too was ashamed of their poverty though his habits worsened it. Mem warned Millington not to tell him about money that Ma Kirton gave him every August—initially $100 later increasing it until it reached $200—to help pay for his school supplies. "Your father full o' false pride. He will tell her we don't need her charity."

The evening before Jay and he got married, he jested: "Jay, Ma Kirton would think I'm too low-class for you."

Jay laughed long, then wiped his eyes. "And what class did my grandmother belong to? She would have rocked with laughter if she'd heard you. I'll let you read a couple of her journal entries."

A lot of blessings have come his way. Yes, Alan, was right. Alan too might have had them if he'd had an Aunt Pearl, or a Ma Kirton for a godmother. But Neil's blessings—intellect and a well-off family—were no match for the persecution he endured. In the end Fate held the gavel and sentenced him to insanity. And the villagers felt he'd brought it on himself. Even created a tale to justify their belief. When Millington told Jay of Neil's plight, Jay said: "If I'd known he was home, I would have visited him that time you and I reconnected. Did you reach out to him?"

"No."

Jay pressed his lips and said nothing. Millington saw then how much Jay had forgotten about the Caribbean. Millington had had enough problems to deal with; he didn't want the suspicion of being a bullerman added to the list. He no longer believes that God—if God exists—had singled him out for any blessings. He wouldn't want to serve a God who was guilty of such partiality. "God made the high and lowly / And ordered their estate" used to be part of the hymn "All Things Bright and Beautiful." Rubbish! From an early age, when the neighbours were discussing their favourite religious topic: predestination, it perplexed him that God had chosen to send most of humanity to hell even before they were born. The Jehovah's Witnesses, who constantly harangued Mem, claimed that there was room in heaven for 144,000, and hence for Jehovah's Witnesses only. He felt a sense of relief at ETC when he learned that "Authentic Methodists see predestination as a heritage from our chauvinistic tribal past." *Curses have come my way too, Alan. As the ancient Greeks astutely noted—King Midas comes to mind—blessings are often containers that hold curses.*

Jay too had his travail with predestination. His father preached about the 144,000 figure too, but reserved heaven for his denomination. It came up last year after they heard Nate Phelps recount his ordeal with his father, the Westboro Baptist Church pastor, who was notorious for his persecution of gays. When Jay was six, he believed he was one of those God had assigned to hell, and had even dreamt that he'd died and gone there. From as early as Jay could remember, Caleb flogged him to discourage him from having thoughts and deeds that would send him to hell. *Talk about being illogical!* By age eight Jay came to see his father as a fraud—bribing a government inspector so he could remove stones illegally from the beach, beating Anna and threatening to beat her even more severely if she let the neighbours know—so when Anna told him that hell didn't exist, he had no trouble believing her. Anna too was lucky to have had Ma Kirton for a mother. She had seen Ma Kirton end an abusive marriage, and it gave her the courage to end hers. More importantly, she knew that she and her two children would be housed and fed after she'd fled from Caleb's fists. Then and now most Caribbean women in abusive marriages do not have that option.

Jay showed him Ma Kirton's journal entry about a book on world religions that she'd read at a young age. What a lucky woman! The author advises everyone to search for the divinity within themselves, not outside, and to cultivate it. That book helped to set her on a path of religious self-sufficiency. Such a book might have steered him away from a career promoting denominational theology. It was probably written by a Unitarian. At ETC the tutors had trouble concealing their contempt for Unitarianism. Unitarian doctrine, whatever its flaws, was solider than theirs. Unitarians didn't need anyone's blood to cleanse them of sin or to frighten people with tales about burning in hell eternally.

It disgusts Paul and puzzles Jay that their mother went back to fundamentalist Christianity after coming to Canada. It doesn't puzzle Millington. When he became agnostic, the space belief once filled became excruciatingly empty. It's still empty. Of the three of them, Paul's the luckiest. His flaw is that he refuses to accept the human need for myth, to reassure humanity against the unknown and inexplicable, and he refuses to see religion as more than an opiate for the downtrodden and a tool for controlling the weak. He has read Jung, and Millington has been urging him to read Joseph Campbell and Mircea Eliade. Campbell especially, because Campbell himself didn't embrace the common concepts of God or an afterlife.

9

HIS EARLIEST MEMORY of Ma Kirton goes back to when he was around four. Grama Emma had taken him to her store, and he had pointed to the sweet jar on the counter and asked her to buy him one. She shook her head, and he began to cry, and she raised her arm to hit him, and Ma Kirton said: "Don't you hit that child." Then staring at him, she said: "I will give you something better." She bent down and opened the glass case under the counter, took out a chocolate bar, and gave it to him. "Unwrap it, eat it," she said, and her eyes shone like pieces of beige glass. The taste of that chocolate bar! The smell! None he has eaten since tasted as good. After that Grama Emma never took him back to the store, but one day she was holding his hand while they were walking down to the beach to collect seaweed and to let him bathe in the sea (she was convinced that it would improve his frail health); on the way they came upon a house surrounded with beautiful flowers. "Grama, you see how them flowers pretty?"

"Yes, they is pretty for true. They belongs to Ma Kirton."

What with his long hospitalization and long convalescence, the next time he saw Ma Kirton was at Grama Emma's funeral when he was around seven.

He started going back to the store, Kirton's Enterprise, when he was around eight, on errands for Mem and Elijah. Ma Kirton remembered him. "You're the little boy who loves sweets," she told him, but didn't give him any. "Are you as sweet yourself?" He held his head down. Couldn't look into her eyes. She asked him what class he was in, his teacher's name, his favourite subject, if he liked school, and told him to raise his head so she could "see that beautiful face you have." He looked up then and saw that she was smiling. He told her that he loved her flowers. The next time he went back to the store, she gave him two envelopes, one with zinnia seeds and one with sunflower seeds, and said that he should choose a spot where there was lots of sun and that he should plough the soil and wet the ground. "Give me your hand." He did, and she pointed off on his index finger how deep he should plant the seeds. He had trouble softening the tough soil and Edward asked him what he was planting. He showed him the seeds and told him the story. Edward took the hoe from him and ploughed the ground, and sent him to sweep up the goat droppings and bring them. He mixed them into the soil. The zinnias and sunflowers grew and blossomed abundantly. There was something magical, fascinating, about it all. The neighbours thought it was Mem's garden. Millington told Ma Kirton how beautiful the flowers were, and she promised she would come up the hill one day to look at them. He doesn't know if she ever did. He expanded the plot and added other flowers.

Thus began his love for flowers and gardening in general, a love that got him into the deepest trouble he ever had with Edward. He began to steal cuttings and seeds from people's gardens until he stole from Miss Collins's garden. In stark contrast to the rusty roof, broken jalousies, and rotting porch of her ramshackle board house, she had at the front a lovely bed of gerberas: salmon, peach, yellow, magenta. He breathed deeply every time he passed by them. One night when there was a full moon—said to be the best time to plant anything—he went to her garden intending to pull out a few slips, but the gerberas were more firmly rooted than he'd suspected. Handfuls of leaves came but no roots. With both hands he grabbed another set of gerberas. This time a few slips with roots came but mostly leaves. He took the slips and left the leaves. All of it undetected.

The next morning, he planted them before he took the goats over to Hollow. He didn't have school that day. It was probably during the August holidays. On his way back, while he was walking down the hill toward their house, he heard Miss Collins's voice begging God to rain down fire and brimstone "pon the wicked, bad-minded devil" who had pulled up her gerberas. "Why all yo' hate me so? Revelations say Satan will rule for a season. I call upon God to smite the criminal." Just as he entered their yard she passed by on her way down to the centre of Havre, still calling upon God to avenge her.

On her way back uphill, she passed in to preach to Mem and saw the gerbera slips. She pointed them out to Mem and shouted out to the community around that she had caught "the Devil."

"What a powerful woman you is! Keep him under lock and key. Don't let him get away," Presley Murray called out to her from inside his house.

"You better stop your blasphemy," she shouted back before returning her attention to Mem. "I wants satisfaction. I demands satisfaction. When Edward come I expects him to cut this boy backside good and proper. Right here—" she pointed to a spot a foot from where she was standing inside their gate—"where everybody going see. Edward have to give me satisfaction." She wagged her finger at Millington, standing on the porch. "You will bu'n in hellfire. Take my word for it. As God is above you will bu'n." She was about five metres below him. Their front yard sloped steeply and the house was almost at the top of the ridge. Her stick-like body was swallowed up in an ash-grey long-sleeve jersey several sizes too big and a dungaree skirt that reached down to her ankles, second-hand clothing her niece sent her from Toronto—God's reward for her righteousness, Miss Collins often said, pointing out the package to all she met on her way from the post office, and she backed it up with a quote from Deuteronomy. When the neighbours chided one another, even the born-again fundamentalists would say: "Aye-aye, like you getting more righteous than Miss Collins." And everyone would laugh.

He was around ten then and at no point had he ever been beaten by his parents; at school for sure, but never by his parents. He felt a deep shame. He saw Mem standing just outside the kitchen door wiping her eyes as she apologized to Miss Collins. He was close to his mother. He always took her side whenever she quarrelled with Edward. He waited, tense, for her to get a pigeon pea switch—when there wasn't a tamarind tree nearby, it was what women used when beating their children—and *"wale"* (welt) his "backside good and proper." Instead she stared at him with the silent question: How could you subject me to so much humiliation from this God-awful woman? For the rest of that morning Miss Collins continued to call down hellfire and damnation on him and to recount the story to everyone who came up or down the hill, on the way to or from their farms, or to or from Esperance in the valley behind the hill. Mem and Millington stood there and took it silently as people stopped to hear Miss Collins retell the story. Some of the listeners smiled at her and winked at Mem.

Around 2 p.m., Miss Collins, most likely exhausted and hungry, left. He hid away in his bedroom and wondered what Edward would do to him. He came out around four to bring the goats home, and returned to his bedroom as soon as he'd tethered them. He had seen fathers beat their children in ways that frightened him. The children might have been killed or disabled if the neighbours hadn't intervened. (He's sure now that many were, psychically. He saw it in the widespread theft, drug use, gun battles, and disrespect for the rights of others, when he returned to Havre four years ago.) He wondered if Edward would do the same thing to him and braced himself. It was what Miss Collins's good and proper meant.

She knew what time Edward would return from work. She was at their gate waiting for him. She accosted him. "Edward, before you go in I have a complaint to make and I demands satisfaction." Her back was to their yard and her body blocked Edward's entry. "Your t'iefing son come to me place last night and pull up me flowers, take what he want and leave the rest there on the ground." Millington observed the scene from his bedroom window. Edward glanced about the yard and at the side of the house until he saw him. With his thumb, he beckoned Millington to come to the gate. He went.

"Edward, I expects you to cut this boy arse good and proper so he going never do it again." Her arms were akimbo and her head aslant. No doubt about it: it was an order.

Edward said nothing. He glared at Millington.

"Take off your belt," Miss Collins ordered, "and cut his arse ... What you's waiting for? Cut his arse."

By now a small crowd had gathered. Edward looked down at his belt. It was leather, at least five centimetres wide and a centimetre thick. Edward unbuckled it. Millington could see that he was hesitating. Millington held his breath. Edward pulled the belt out of the loops and swung it lightly. He stared at Millington, bit his lower lip, and grimaced.

Miss Collins saw his hesitation. "Edward, 'Spare not the rod and spoil this child' ... Edward, 'he that knoweth the will and doeth it not shall be beaten with many stripes.' Those is God holy words." She snorted and folded her arms.

Edward turned to face her. "Can I pay you for the flowers?"

The crowd mumbled its objection.

Miss Collins didn't answer. Edward repeated the question, louder.

"But you all hearing my crosses?" She pivoted to take in the reaction of the crowd. She turned again to face Edward. "Five thousand dollars and not a penny less."

The crowd guffawed. Some commented indecipherably.

"I don' have five thousand dollars."

"Cut his arse; that will satisfy me. That is all I ask," Miss Collins said.

"I not beating him," Edward said and began reinserting the belt into the loops of his trousers.

The murmuring in the crowd grew, some saying that that wasn't right, that it was no way to train a child.

"How you's going to pay me? Tell me that. You don' have two copper pennies to rub together," Miss Collins said.

"You have any repair work to do on your house?"

"Yes, the jalousies have to change and some o' the doors rotten."

"Okay. Get the lumber, I will do it."

"And rebuild the balcony too."

"For the balcony you going have to pay me. Full rate—not a penny less." With that he walked past Miss Collins and entered the yard. Millington turned around then and saw Mem standing on the porch. She had been there observing the scene all along. He entered the living room, one of four rooms in their board house. Edward was already there. He turned to face Millington. "Millington, this evening you make me hang down me head in shame. Don' do this to me again. Promise me, you will never make me go through this again." That was all he said. He sounded weary. Mem came into the living room then. Millington began to cry, and through his hiccups he promised his father that he never would, and he never did. Whatever his age-mates did: stealing fruit, stoning coupling dogs, dissing teachers ... he never joined in. Whatever could result in a complaint against him he instinctively avoided. He deliberately shunned his peers to avoid getting into trouble. Quite possibly why he was so drawn to Jay, a loner too, though it seems that he wasn't before his mother went to Canada.

Now when Millington looks back on the gerbera incident, he knows that his parents were exceptional. He's pretty certain they and Ma Kirton were the only parents/guardians in Havre who didn't flog children. But he can't help thinking that the promise he made to Edward also inhibited him from telling Edward things that he should have known. That promise continues to haunt him, even as regards his marriage. It's probably why he dreams that Edward glares at him and spits.

The stolen slips of gerberas grew and, nurtured by goat dung, prospered. Eventually he had a bed healthier than Miss Collins's. She'd look at them and grumble: "But all you look on my crosses. All you see how wickedness does prosper?" It still surprises him that she hadn't gone to the garden and pulled up the slips and taken them with her. Mem became as interested in the garden as he. While he attended secondary school, it was mostly she who took care of it, and she has continued to care for it to this day.

In his sermons he referred to this bed of gerberas many times without ever identifying himself as the thief. What fascinated him—and what he emphasized—was how necessary dung, feces, was for life to blossom, to prosper.

Yes, Miss Collins, wickedness does indeed prosper, and when we talk about it, we exaggerate the wickedness of others and downplay or hide our own. Look into the history of most millionaires and you will find that on their way there they exploited, robbed, dispossessed, and in some cases slaughtered the defenceless. Yet in one form or another, they claim their wealth to be gifts from God. Jesus observed that it was easier for a camel to go through the eye of a needle than for the wealthy to enter the kingdom of heaven. Jesus' observation was a favourite quote of Haverites whenever they recounted their tales of woe and wickedness in their dealings with Vincentian plantocrats, the Lairds especially, who once owned all the land from the town border to the foothills of the volcano. Like their confreres elsewhere in St Vincent, they sometimes "sold" land without the necessary titles to illiterate Vincentians and later they or their children repossessed it.

Dives was Haverites' favourite bible story and the spiritual it inspired one of their best-loved: "Rich man, Dives, / He lived so well; / When he died / He had a home in hell."

Not an accident then that Haverites found a way to league Ma Kirton with the devil. The evidence? She was wealthy, and she never went to church. Won't surprise him if Miss Collins now feels that his supposed insanity was a punishment from God for his having stolen her gerberas and for that beating he never got. He imagines her muttering with satisfaction: "The wheels o' God grind slowly, but they grind fine."

In Barbados, a decade or so after the domino players' conversations on his parents' porch, Harry Matheson, his dentist and parishioner—renowned gardener too—challenged him to take a second look at Dives. Harry felt the story was unfairly biased against the wealthy. He knew that the word Dives was generic: Latin for rich. He was perhaps Millington's only parishioner with extensive knowledge about how the bible had been compiled. Harry wondered, based on all that was left out and tinkered with, why Lot's seduction by his daughters wasn't removed or rewritten. "Those fellows could write whatever they wanted. Look at how they rationalized Jacob's theft of Esau's birthright. And they executed anyone who opposed them, like the Catholics did centuries later. They reigned and had full rein." He chuckled. "Rev, a man on trial for incest here a few years ago told the judge: 'Your honour, wha' Oi did ain't no different from wha' Lot did do, and Oi been drunk too.'" Reflecting on Harry's question, Millington came to the conclusion that for the compilers of the bible—the patriarchs of patriarchy—it was more important to stress the belief that a woman's purpose was to bear children—to such a degree, that if no other men were around, it was acceptable for her to do so with her father.

Millington stares at the flowering peach bougainvillea suspended from the ceiling inside the window of the dining area. Before he left for Citizenship and Immigration, he watered the two oleanders on the balcony—one pink and one white—every branch weighted down with flowers. Jay should have already cut them back and brought them in, but so far, fall has been mild, allowing them to stay on the balcony longer. Jay too probably inherited a love for flowers from Ma Kirton. He said the bougainvillea had been his mother's. The oleanders and bougainvillea are enough for Jay, but they can't compensate for the gardening Millington left behind. He needs to stick his fingers into soil or let soil flow through them.

In Barbados, it was a struggle to grow the flowers he wanted at the Manse but he persisted. Apart from the weeds covering the few square feet of land at the back of the church, nothing grew on it. Shrubs would have helped to soften the building's moss-blackened exterior. (Maybe just as well. The church was shaded on three sides by hotels that blocked the sunlight—hotels that constantly sought to buy it, but whose guests sometimes attended and enriched the offertory.) The ground at the front, sides, and back was paved over. Done for easier maintenance, Biddles, the sexton, said, standing under the tympanum—his hair as bushy and black as any twenty-year-old's, his brown body lean and erect as an Olympic runner's, belying his 81 years. "Know what else they do, Rev?" The hand holding a dustpan waving defiantly. "They tear down the belfry the last time they repair the roof and scrap the bell to save a couple thousand dollars. Beautiful belfry, Rev. Gave the church character. Now, ef you don't know this was a church, you gon' think is quarters for the garrison. Bunch o' no-class people. Wait, you gon see. And Rev, the lovely mahogany railing round the altar with them trefoils linking the slats and that beautiful scroll work, they did wan' rip that out too. Wan' rip it out, I tells you." He shook his head in disgust. "I tell them, my grandfather carve it with he own two hands and never charge the church a cent. Ef you all rip that out, I gon leave forthwith and join the Anglicans. What next you all gon rip out? The stained glass wheel window behind the altar? Gracie Stone, she 'gree with me, else Rev, your pulpit would be just a slab o' cold concrete. I tells you, Rev, this congregation, they's a bunch o' yahoos. They ain't got no class." But the congregation was being pragmatic. Termites were slowly consuming the pews, stained almost black, their centuries-old varnish brittle and cracked. But Biddles too had a point. The slabs of tawdry limestone needed some sort of adorning.

He lived in the new manse built at Vauxhall ten years earlier with lots of land at the front and back. (The old one that was beside AMC Hastings had long been razed and a four-storey hotel built on it). When he moved in, his first project was to relieve the monotony of the crotons and replace the sick hibiscuses and bougainvillea with geraniums, dahlias, and zinnias. He needed flowers. Zinnias certainly. They along with sunflowers were the first flowers he'd planted.

His battle with Barbados's porous limestone soil was unrelenting. Harry said he'd had to bring in truckloads of soil before he could plant anything. Harry fed his flowers with compost and inorganic fertilizer. Directly in the soil, he grew oleanders, Ixora, hibiscuses of every shade, hydrangeas and canna lilies. The more delicate flowers, like gerberas and orchids, he grew in cement pots on his porch and fed them with manure tea. His house was indistinguishable from the others around: a one-story cement-block bungalow with a corrugated steel gable roof painted red, and outside walls painted beige. But an extra lot at the back that he gave over to trees and flowers set his property apart. His yard was an oasis of beauty. Millington told him so. He replied: "It's how I distract myself from the world's wickedness."

After St Vincent's green valleys, mountains, cataracts, and fast-flowing crystalline rivers, Millington found Barbados flat and sere, and, in the case of gardening, paltry. On each visit back to St Vincent, he'd walk along the Vermont Nature Trail, stare up at Richmond Peak, stroll through Spring Village to gaze at Mangareau's pink cliff, or stand at Richmond's shore admiring the lush vegetation, the shades of green altering with the clouding and unclouding of the sun, all the way up the slopes to la Soufrière, and feel an exultation he had no name for until he came to Canada and Paul introduced him to Longinus' essay on the sublime and Wordsworth's "Tintern Abbey."

He finds comfort in Montreal's greenness and its many wooded parks. A pity the green lasts only five months. It was only when he got here that he understood why he always disliked Kingstown and its suburbs: there's not a single park in that city. Nowhere to escape from the heat trapped by its semi-circling hills. Not a tree anywhere with a park bench under it, unless one makes the long walk up to the Botanical Gardens, and now, there's an entrance fee. What's called a park, Victoria Park, is a stadium. Some colonizer's sick joke. Paul blames the British for this, since it was they who laid out the city. (Yet the same cannot be said for Bridgetown.) Says he sensed the problem when he first visited Martinique at age seven and strolled with his classmates through *La savanne,* the park at the centre of Fort de France. Jay remembers Paul asking him, how come there wasn't a park in Kingstown and trees for people to stroll and sit under?

Here nature metamorphoses from one season to another—in fall the trees relieving themselves of useless leaves, re-growing them in spring. Particular species of flowers in each season fill the wild spaces: in spring, dandelions and white margaritas; in summer, golden rod; in fall, gentian and wild asters. Even the sounds alter: the lazy percussion of leaves in summer cedes to the hissing of twigs in winter. The stamp of the time of year is everywhere and on everything.

When he first saw the naked trees on Mont Royal, it was hard to believe they'd be green again, and when they were, he was spellbound like a child observing a magician's tricks for the first time. His first fall and winter, as the sun's zenith got lower and lower and the periods of darkness lengthened, he understood viscerally why the Druids rejoiced each year when the sun stopped descending lower on the horizon— understood that gods are shaped by geography—a concept he couldn't have understood while still living in the Caribbean, whose religions were all imported. Of necessity peoples in temperate and subtropical lands put the sun at the centre of their cosmogony. In St Vincent, Barbados, and Jamaica—the places he has lived—where the warm Caribbean Sea insulates the land and keeps the temperature uniform all year round, nature, except when it comes in droughts, floods, and hurricanes, remains largely unnoticed. Here the motto might well be: ignore nature and perish.

If his marriage survives and he completes his studies and finds a job in social work, he'll try to convince Jay to move to a semi-rural area. Gardening in pots doesn't do it for him. He needs soil that's still bound to the earth's body, soil that speaks up from the ground to him, soil that runs through his fingers back to the ground from which he first took it. Compromises. Exchanging the blue plain and sloshing sound of the Caribbean Sea for honking horns, ear-piercing sirens, and bricks and concrete. Some days it's too much. And he's glad he can at times escape to the greenery of Parc Lafontaine.

Many ifs before you get there, Millington. Many. Your marriage might not even survive. Not today, Millington. Leave that one alone.

10

THERE WERE THOSE eight late afternoons when he jumped off the return bus from Kingstown and rushed to the church for instruction in basic AMC doctrine as a prelude to confirmation. The Saturday before the confirmation, he told Ma Kirton about it. She responded with a cold nod. He'd expected her to compliment him. Everyone else was doing so. Besides, until then she'd complimented him for everything he'd done. For sure, he'd already heard Haverites, including Edward, call her godless and devil-dealing. Classmates at Father Crowley's sometimes told Jay that his grandmother was a *dealer*, and because Jay and he were always together, they asked him if his parents were devil dealers too. Neil sometimes shouted the question at them from the far end of the school yard.

Devil dealers were rich people, like the Lairds. By age six every Haverite had heard that Laird's forbears had sacrificed humans to the Devil and fed the livers of newborn Blacks to a racehorse that won all the races in Trinidad for several years. Because Pembroke, the eldest of Old Man Laird's twenty-five out-of-wedlock children, was Ma Kirton's close friend, Haverites sometimes muttered, with a knowing head-shake: "Hmm. A person is known by the company they keeps."

Ma Kirton's response to his confirmation made him wonder for the first time if she were truly *godless*. Then he was sure no one could be, though at age nine he did wonder, albeit briefly, whether she would one day sacrifice him to the Devil.

When, after his confirmation, he joined other AMC members in collecting missionary funds, she always gave him two dollars. He knows now that it was a business decision, that she probably gave a similar amount to scores of her Methodist clients, to avoid alienating them. By age sixteen he pitied Haverites for their superstitious views about her and the Lairds. But, at seventeen, he never doubted that multiple demons inhabited Jestina. Of course, Jestina was insane; he knows that now. Ma Kirton knew that then; he read what she wrote about it in her journal.

The same year he was received into the church, Mem pushed him to join the Boys' Brigade. He hated Brigades. He found the military drills stupid. They played sports sometimes, cricket and soccer mostly. He was average at both: a good fielder, zero as a bowler, but an average batsman; in soccer they made him the goalie. In the little spare time he had from chores, he would have preferred to be doing schoolwork because he didn't want Jay to outperform him. There was the fact too that all through high school he was haunted by a fear of failing and disgracing his parents and wasting Aunt Pearl's money. Night after night he dreamed that he failed his tests, and Neil was laughing at him.

Their BB troupe averaged thirty. Each year it gained a few boys and lost a few. Most were students at Esperance Secondary. He was probably the only member of the troupe who hadn't been taught in elementary school by the leader Zephaniah "Zeppie" Brown. In Zeppie's presence they were expected to stand straight—at attention. In front of his face they dared not call him anything but Mr. Brown or Sir. Behind his back, he was Zeppie or Chimp. Zeppie was gruff, short, coal black, with stooped shoulders, and a jowly Neanderthal sort of face. His torso was egg-shaped and his walk lumbering. The BB boys called it the Zeppie Bop. He had a lisp that turned his "sir" into "shir" and his "zed" into "ess." Allsop, who'd had issues with him in elementary school, mimicked him behind his back. Millington never joined in. The promise to his father.

Zeppie was in his forties. The year Millington should have been in his class at Father Crowley's, Zeppie ran his scooter into an oncoming car and spent a long time recuperating in hospital and at home. Allsop said he was sorry he'd survived. Zeppie flogged his students for everything—but mostly, Allsop said, for being brighter than he. It must have rankled Zeppie that he couldn't flog them at Boys' Brigade. Allsop thought so.

Zeppie had begun teaching at a time when the only qualification was to pass the elementary school leaving exam. No one knew how he'd passed it. It was designed to fail ninety-five percent of the students to assure that the successful candidates—the future nurses, police officers, elementary school teachers—were intellectually gifted. Some opined that the invigilator must have given him the answers. But pass it he did, and managed never to fail each pupil teacher grade more than once and so avoided expulsion. But at the pre-GCE level, he stalled. Year after year, more than a dozen of them, he wrote the O level exams—the O level certificate was obligatory for entry into teachers' college, the completion of which was necessary to get a decent salary—and year after year he failed. BB troupe members were sometimes present when the ne'er-do-wells liming on the Anglican Church patio called out to him to "stop paying all that money to Cambridge.".

Allsop was two years older than Millington and small for his age. He was freckle-faced and pale, paler than Millington. He had a flattish nose that flared when he was excited, thick pink lips, green eyes, and blond peppercorn hair. In the military drills, he turned left when it should be right and vice-versa. One afternoon, Zeppie brought two strips of ribbon, one yellow and one red. He pinned the yellow strip to the front of Allsop's right sleeve and the red to Allsop's left sleeve. "Now Mis(h)ter Clever B(l)onny Clabber," he said, grinning at Allsop and waiting for the troupe's laughter to die down (some of it was for his pronunciation), "now zhlis will help you tell your left hand f(l)rom your right?"

Allsop retorted: "And *what* will help *you* pass GCE?"

First there was silence, then the odd chuckle, then uproarious laughter. If this had been school they'd have all gone home with bleeding backs, and Allsop might have even been expelled. Today Brown would be too, for his racism. (St Vincent has progressed.) Allsop never returned to Boys' Brigade after that.

Clement, who was from Havre's wealthy Northside, told them the rest of the story. He and Allsop had been in Zeppie's class together. Clement didn't recall being beaten by Zeppie anymore than by the rest of the teachers, but he remembered that Allsop and Zeppie hated each other. It started when Zeppie had given them the wrong answer for a math problem, and Allsop corrected him, went to the blackboard, and solved the problem. Back in his seat, Allsop muttered that Zeppie should consult the answer key if he wasn't bright enough to work out the problem himself, and Zeppie heard him. But Allsop didn't stop there. For about a month after that, whenever Zeppie gave them answers for anything, Allsop would ask: "Are you sure?" Clement agreed that Zeppie flogged Allsop a lot, but it was mostly for his insolence.

Three weeks after giving Zeppie his comeuppance, Allsop got the best GCE A-level performance in the Eastern Caribbean. His photograph was on the front page of all the newspapers and for a couple of days his success dominated the newscast. A month later he went off to study medicine in London. Some of the troupe members wanted to ask Zeppie how he felt about Allsop's success, but were dissuaded by others.

Millington soldiered on for almost a year after this, when an ankle he twisted brought it to an end. A couple of years later, Zeppie collapsed at Father Crowley's front door—while beating a student, some said, but Millington thinks that was invented—and was pronounced dead when the ambulance took him to the clinic at Esperance. Zeppie had a huge funeral. The Boys Brigade troupes from all over St Vincent came. Millington felt that he didn't deserve it. He attended to please Mem, who said of Zeppie: "He walked in the ways of the righteous."

Millington's family and his godfather Elijah Bowman—whose house was five downhill from theirs—were the only Methodists on Pasture Road who didn't belong to a second religion. Elijah—he wanted everyone, children included, to call him by his first name, but they added Brother in front of it—was the usher at AMC Havre. He picked up the collection on Sunday mornings and at Evensong. Millington doesn't remember his ever being absent; he must have gone even when he was sick. In 2010, when Mem phoned Millington in Barbados to tell him of Elijah's death, she added: "He never once miss church. I hope his jumbie don't haunt the church." His apparent piety was probably why Mem had chosen him to be Millington's godfather.

From all parts of St Vincent people came to consult Elijah about their ailments, buy his concoctions—retail and wholesale—rent his leeches, or have him work on their sprains and backache. A medley of smells, sometimes of almond, vanilla, cinnamon and rosemary, sometimes of sulphur and rotten eggs, came from his outdoor kitchen on days when he was preparing his medicines. Miss Collins felt that feces was the main ingredient. Whatever the ingredients were, they hadn't cured Millington's typhus and would have eventually killed him, if his parents hadn't consulted a regular doctor.

Elijah was also a master teller of Anansi tales. He loved doing so on their porch while the domino games were going on. On moonlit nights there'd be as many as fifteen people sitting on the steps, on folding chairs they'd brought, on the ground, or just standing around listening to him. Some of the stories had parts which the audience sang.

Oo hoo ma eeda
One
Oo hoo ma eeda
Two ...

Mem didn't want Millington to hear that one. It was about a man who'd been bewitched into sexual arousal by a pretty woman whom he was vainly trying to catch up with to consummate the act. In the end the man came upon a pumpkin. "Now his *tolo* been hard like iron, and he let the pumpkin have it, and the pumpkin explode and the seeds scatter all over the world. That is why you find pumpkins growing wherever soever you go." From what Elijah told Millington about his wife's tryst with Smallboy, she couldn't have been impressed with his *tolo*. Sister Murray once called Mem a Methodist hypocrite because Mem had feigned ignorance of the calypso that recounted Elijah's marital troubles. On their porch, her arms akimbo, Sister Murray sang it for Mem:

Bedroom inadequacy
Go drive yo' woman
Into the arms o' yo' enemy.
It more than true,
Little axe does cut down big tree.
If the blade not sharp,
And you neglect the handle,
She go butt yo'.
Pardner, don't carp.
Don' wrangle;
Just keep yo' axe blade sharp.

Yes, just keep yo' axe blade sharp

When Millington's parents were children, belonging to two religions was forbidden. Those who did were told they couldn't serve two masters and were ex-communicated. In Barbados a quarter of Millington's parishioners were also Spiritual Baptists. Sister Stone, ninety-one, her still thick hair looking like a crown of wool, her nose like a petrel's beak, her watery-blue eyes magnified by the thick lenses she wore, would come, on average once per month—never on a Wednesday, his day for visiting members; she called to make sure he reserved an entire morning for her—holding her cane but never leaning on it, to inform him about such matters, keep him in her sights, on the right track, or both, and lament the passing of the good old days. "When I was a girl, the minister used to read out, excommunicate, the ones that trafficked with other religions. You can't serve two masters, Reverend. You cannot." He never knew how she got her news. Probably from her domestic helpers. Her late husband had been a prominent politician and businessman; she'd held the post of permanent secretary—the most senior civil service position—in various government ministries until she retired. She owned three office buildings in Bridgetown and lived in a mansion in Worthing. Her chauffeur dropped her off at the manse and returned to pick her up.

Up to age eighty-five, she ran the AMC Hastings Sunday school and therefore knew most of the parishioners. And what a memory! She recounted with relish the crises Millington's predecessors had dealt with or caused—with whom, what year, whether the resolution was just or unjust. Each character came with a sketch: a Guyanese who needed a course in grammar and elocution; a Grenadian who was jumpy and couldn't keep his hands still, "especially when he was near beautiful young women—had a wife, but that didn't matter—until he put his hands on the wrong woman. Mr. Stone and I told Reverend Henry—he was the superintendent minister at the time—that not a copper of ours will go into the collection plate until they remove him." Regarding another: Haliburton. "Oh, the appetite that one had! Eat off everything in sight and had the girth to prove it. He was big on being primitive." She chuckled. "'We must return to primitive Christianity, to the purity of primitive Methodism.' Wanted to reintroduce love feasts. No surprise. Know what those were?" Millington nodded but she didn't seem convinced. "They existed in the early days when Methodists weren't sure if they were Methodists or Moravians. A primitive glutton, that's what Haliburton was. My husband—he was the circuit steward at the time—told him: 'Stop all your talk about primitive this and primitive that. We live in the twentieth century. Get with the times, Reverend.' (Millington wanted to tell her that Wesley extolled primitive Christianity and had enslaved Methodists to it.) "Mrs. Haliburton, now she was the exact opposite: had the waist of a wasp and the arms of pea switch. And loved to wear yellow. Looked like a buttercup and displayed herself like a daisy that all and sundry, even the sun, were expected to admire."

Gracie told Melvin that Millington was too gentle with sinners, that he was failing in his duty to call out the fornicators and adulterers in the congregation "who were polluting the body of Christ. Call them out until their consciences ache and they repent." Melvin chuckled as he said this. Melvin had probably asked her what she thought of Millington's sermons, because to Millington directly she neither disparaged nor praised them. She gave generously. Along with her regular donations, every Christmas, she gave the Church five thousand dollars in memory of her husband. She never suspended it, so Millington assumed that he was in Gracie's good graces. When AMC Hastings became his primary church, Silas, his St Phillip colleague at the time, smiled and said: "You will never go astray. Gracie Stone will keep you in the straight and narrow way."

11

WHEN HE ARRIVED IN Montreal and met Les Friends, Jay told him that Lionel had organized the group to provide mutual support, a family of sorts, for its members. There are eleven members. Gina and Emilia are the only women. Lionel wants more women to join, but membership is closed to new males unless they're partners of existing members. They meet every couple of weeks in one another's apartments. Muriel, Lionel's sister, who shares his apartment, interacts with them when Lionel hosts. She's a social worker and a very shy poet. Millington spends a lot of his time chatting with her, mostly about her writing. Twice per year some of Les Friends meet naked. Sexless batching they call it. Beyond saying that Lionel proposed batching as a bonding ritual and to encourage the members to be comfortable with their bodies, Jay evaded Millington's questions about it. So he asked Paul.

"Why you ask?" Paul grinned widely. "Want to participate? It's liberating. You don't need Jay's permission."

"First tell me how it came about."

Paul's eyes brightened, reminding Millington of Ma Kirton's. He was sitting at the far end of his dining table from Millington. "Lionel called a meeting at his place to discuss creating some sort of ritual to cement the group. We'd already been in existence for about six months. Guícho said to count him out if it was anything like singing and praying in a church. 'No,' Lionel said, 'I'm thinking that a couple times a year we should meet in dishabille.'

"'What's dishabille?' Gina asked.

"'Meet naked,' Tyrone said.

"'Naked! The only people who see me naked are Emilia and my doctor. Get serious guys. I'm lesbian. Why would I want to see your dicks? Want to know something else? You all would look better with your clothes on.'

"'Looks have nothing to with it. There's truth in nakedness. You'll be naked too, Gina,' Lionel said.

"'Oh no, I w-o-n' t be. *So* like men. Emphasis always on the physical. The deepest truths are inside you, Lionel. Try to find them. In the meantime, keep your clothes on when you're not your boyfriends' plaything.'

"'Quiet, Gina,' Tyrone shouted.

"Lionel continued. 'One of the rules would be no touching.'

"'What's the point then?' Guícho said.

"'To teach *you* self-control,' I said. Lionel went on to say that nakedness inspired trust, and that he knew from things we'd said that we had issues with our bodies, that being naked with one another would help us overcome them." Paul stopped talking for a couple of seconds. "Tyrone has issues with his body. Big time ... Bernard too. Carlos. Me ... You won't understand, Millington. You and Jay are trim and handsome. You could be models." He lowered his head. "I used to hate Jay for his good looks and slim body." He paused, stared across the table at Millington, and waited for his reaction.

Millington said nothing.

"'Let's try it for a year. If it doesn't work, we'll abandon it,' Lionel said.

"'Time to vote and take our clothes off,' Guícho said. 'I'll vote yes if you drop the no-touching rule.'

"In the end, Gina, Emilia, and Jay voted no. Everyone else voted yes."

"'So you exhibitionists, you will be running around naked in here with Muriel present?' Gina said.

"We decided then that we'd do our batching at Tyrone's... How would you have voted?"

"Moot point. I wasn't present."

Paul laughed. "If the answer was yes, you'd have no trouble saying so."

The last time Les Friends met at Lionel's place, Lionel, his grey eyes blazing and fixed on Jay, said: "You two have been together now … lemme see … three years … Things must be stale in the bedroom. You need a unicorn to spice things up."

Millington had never heard unicorn used in this context but understood what Lionel was proposing. Lionel, Jay, and Millington were standing around the dining table. The others were in the living room—there's no partition between both rooms—listening intently. Jay stared into the plate in front of him. Eventually he lifted his head, grinned at Lionel, and said: "Your white sauce is delicious. You must give me the recipe."

"Ah, but first you must taste my living sauce."

Loud guffaws. Carlos's the loudest. He was standing in the open space between the living and dining area.

"Hey! Millington!" Lionel came toward him and tapped him on the shoulder. "No need to be in pain, man. I'm not like snatching your man. Just want to borrow him. You could join in too." He winked at Jay, then returned his stare to Millington and began to knead his shoulder. Millington removed his hand and pushed out his arms defensively. "Bet you want to," Lionel continued. "But afterwards you'll like want to divorce Jay and marry me, and I ain't marrying anybody."

These get-togethers. At Gina's and Paul's, they're not so bad. When they're at Tyrone's and Lionel's, he's always anxious before going and during and relieved when Jay and he are on their way home.

He has wanted to ask Jay how he feels about Lionel's proposition, which Millington knows was serious—tempered by levity, but serious. For more than a year now, Millington has dreams every few weeks in which Jay asks him for an open relationship. He doesn't reply, and Jay says they should separate.

Lionel talks freely about the orgies he participates in and his good and bad nights at the sauna. Once Gina asked him why he was so obsessed with telling them what he did with his pickups. He replied that it was because he wanted to cure them of their hang-ups about gay sex. "Let's face it, some of you are ashamed to admit that you're bottoms." Paul told Millington that eight years ago Lionel had had a three-year battle with meningioma. Paul was dealing with his own meningioma when he met Lionel. At the time Lionel headed a group of meningioma survivors. Jay feels that Lionel is worried that his meningioma might return and, in the interim, he's savouring all the pleasure he can. Lionel's antics don't seem to bother Jay in the least.

Not everyone overlooks Lionel's attempts at poaching. One evening, about a year ago, Tyrone caught him caressing Laurent's butt and flew into a rage. His hand still on Laurent's butt, a grinning Lionel replied: "Dude, chill. You white guys get the best-looking Blacks. I got to dart in and out of the nest when you're out." With a wide sweep of his arms, that took in everyone, he added: "Can't help it. A virile rooster must have a harem."

Laughter.

"Besides. Face the truth. We all want to sample Laurent." He gave Tyrone a coy smile. "I'm the only one daring enough to try it."

Millington has trouble believing Lionel teaches philosophy in a CEGEP. How do they manage to remain naked and calm for an entire evening?

Jay's friends. Six weeks ago. A Tuesday evening. They were at Gina's place. The invitation had puzzled Jay. It wasn't her turn to host, and hosting's usually done on a Friday or Saturday evening. It turned out to be in honour of Guícho. He was visiting from Lethbridge. Gina and Emilia have been lovers since high school, and Guícho was Gina's pretend boyfriend in high school. That much Paul had already told Millington. When Jay and Millington entered Gina's living room, Jay slapped his forehead and lowered his head when he saw Guícho and whispered in Millington's ear: "He's here. Dammit! I'm not up to his sort of foolishness tonight."

They'd arrived late. Lionel was already tanked. Swaying slightly, he said to Jay: "Man, your soul's in a sling, or what? Ah the perils of the ring."

Jay chuckled nervously.

While Millington and Jay were in the kitchen getting food, Lionel waddled to within a foot of them. He gave Jay a wobbly stare and blurted out: "I've a hunch you've never had a hot, sweet fuck." Droplets of his saliva glistened as they fell onto Jay's arms. Jay winced and moved back.

The room got silent.

Lionel turned his stare on Millington. "Cutie-here looks kind o' anemic. Tools! Gimme a break! Can't hone what you don't have."

Thunderous laughter.

Lionel returned to staring at Jay but pointed at Millington. "He can never shoot you into orbit and land you safe. Come by one evening. Bring cutie too. He can like benefit from a little space travel himself. We'll smoke a couple o' spliffs and t-r-a-v-e-l-l-l-l." He extended his arms wing-like, flapped them, whistled, and wobbled.

Jay silently stared at the tabletop. Millington's hands sweated.

Next it was Guícho sidling up to Millington and saying: "Don't bother with Lionel. You and Jay fit like needle and thread. Which of you is the needle?"

"No have needle, just thread," Carlos called out from the living room sofa where he was sitting on Marc-André's lap.

Staring at Millington, Guícho continued: "How come there are no scars on *your* neck?"

From the living room, Paul guffawed.

Coming uncomfortably close, his eyes still fixed on Millington, Guícho crinkled his nose and rotated his hands. "Too white for my taste. But you got it in the looks department: a Beulah all right. How about the meat department? That's what counts, ain't it? Bet it's a vegan souvlaki. Mushy too."

Laughter.

Now turning to face Jay and wagging a finger at him, Guícho said: "Never, never you measure a man by his height. I am *two hundred* percent red meat," his voice at a screeching high pitch. He tapped his chest. "Ask Austin."

"Good thing he's not here," Emilia said.

"*Red meat!* He means tripe," Paul said.

"Without condiments," Gina, bent looking for something at the bottom of the fridge, said.

They continued riling Guícho.

Gina: "Did you come in Austin's private jet?"

Guícho (wincing first): "Yes, me, the pilot, and the butler. They're staying at the Ritz."

Paul: "Doesn't Austin own an oilfield?"

Guícho (holding up four fingers): "An oilfield for Austin, an oilfield for the butler, and two oilfields for me."

Emilia: "Last time you said a ranch, and you were his Baby Crockett."

Gina: "Still in touch with your monk?"

Guícho (eyes closed, waist wiggling): "Meeting him at the sauna later. Szzzzz. Can't wait to make him sizzle."

Paul: "Wow. Getting ready to take holy orders?"

Guícho: "Spell that h-o-l-e-y. Watch out, cutie (winking at Millington). I never take no for an answer. When it comes to getting my man, I beat the Mounties hands down."

12

MILLINGTON LEFT THAT party feeling anxious. While Jay was in the bathroom brushing his teeth, he went to sit at the dining table. Paul's wedding-day speech replayed in his mind. It was the rare get-together where Lionel, Carlos, or Tyrone didn't trot out the words *tool* and *hone*. Jay came out of the bathroom, and Millington told him to go to bed without him. Jay came to stand behind him and pulled the light cord on the chandelier over the dining table. Millington wanted silence and darkness. Gently kneading Millington's shoulder, Jay said: "I wish we hadn't gone to Gina's tonight. Lionel drinks too much. He'll probably say it's because he doesn't know if his cancer will strike again."

Before they left the party, Paul told Jay that Gina had instructed them not to let Jay know that the get-together was to celebrate Guícho's visit and birthday. Still kneading Millington's shoulders, Jay said: "Gina's not one to hold grudges. Cusses you out and then hugs you. Guícho's like that too. Have to grant him that, whatever his shortcomings. Once heard him say that his mother will see the light and beg him to forgive her. *'Yo nunca cargue mi alma con odio. Es basura.* Me, I pardon always. Hate, man, that shit fucks up your soul.' His mother—Emilia's too—is a Jehovah Witness and won't have anything to do with him, unless he turns straight. Easier to raise the dead."

"Jay, that statement about scars, what was it about?"

He removed his hands from Millington's shoulders and was a while answering. "Let's see. The first time Paul took me to a gay bar, Guícho was there. He propositioned me and wanted to know if I was a bottom or a top. I answered: a vampire. As you've seen, he's obsessed with going to bed with me. Paul told him it won't happen, that he's too sluttish for my taste. I'd said no such thing. I'd told Paul to warn him about picking up strangers, because one of Ma's male nurse colleagues used to, and his body was found naked and covered with cigarette burns in a downtown parking lot." Jay fell silent for a few seconds and resumed kneading Millington's shoulders. "At first, I found Guícho comic and harmless. But when Paul and Carlos broke up, he began to hatch schemes with Carlos to get half of Paul's money. Nowadays none of that bothers Paul, but it bothers me."

He wonders what his reaction would have been if he'd found Jay batching when he got here. "A great way to bond. Just as well you two don't batch. You are too insecure," a drunk, grinning Tyrone, pulling on his billy-goat beard, told Jay one time. Jay thinks batching is good for Paul. Millington tries to visualize their naked bodies moving about. Tyrone's gaunt 2.2 metre frame; his sloping back; his bean-shaped head with thin, pale blond hair; each cheekbone semi-circled by a scythe-shaped furrow whose handle ends at the corner of his upper lip; his chin looking even more dagger-like because of his three-inch triangular beard; his ruddy lunar landscape face; his fear-filled blue eyes that brighten when he's mildly drunk and redden when he's wasted; bottom flat as a tabletop; his body dipping to the left with each step. Lionel said Tyrone's left foot resembles a balled fist and his left leg is shrivelled to about half the size of the right, that he wears a corrective prosthesis. Marc-André's naked body: his tree-trunk thighs; the ridges of his abdominal muscles always visible through the tight black T-shirts he wears. Lionel and Carlos looking like two blackfish cows. Paul like a stunted blackfish. He sees the cruelty in these comparisons, stops and feels guilty.

After listening to Jay talk about Guícho that night, Millington said: "You're *so* comfortable with them." Jay didn't respond.

"Do they have to be so vulgar?"

"Are they vulgar? ... Not sure. Maybe they're more honest than we are ... We live in a society where everything's described with hyperboles and superlatives ... In any event you put up with family because family puts up with you."

"Some family."

Jay stopped kneading Millington's shoulder, and sat down to his left.

"Your family, not mine. Will never be." He regretted saying it right after.

For a second or two, Jay said nothing. "In 2010, while I was travelling in Africa, I found out how vulnerable you feel when you're truly alone. I got sick and had to be hospitalized in Kinshasa. There it's family to bring you food, family to wash your sheets, family to go to the pharmacy and get your drugs, family to pool their pittances to pay for your treatment, school fees, books, and uniform ... and a whole lot more. Without family you might as well be dead."

"But that's Africa."

"You're kidding. There's a social contract in place everywhere. Implemented differently that's all. Difficult to explain. It's why my mother returned to fundamentalist Christianity when she came here. She had us, but we weren't enough. She needed a community."

"But Jonathan used to be your only friend?"

"True. But the night Aunt Mercy died—the same night Paul met Bernard—I saw that my only remaining family, family in the sense of blood relatives I could count on, was Paul. I joined the Vincentian association and began attending its events, and, thanks to Paul, I'm now part of Les Friends."

And you brought me from St Vincent and married me.

"Guícho comes back to visit every chance he gets. No accident there. He needs to belong ... and to affirm his belonging. In Africa it used to be that people without a tribe were as good as dead. Alone they were defenceless, easy prey for slave-catchers."

Family, it was what Gladys and Horton were to him in Barbados. In small ways, his congregation too. The group of ministers who met at Silas's place every Monday. "Still I think your friends could tone it down some."

"To please whom? That's your Methodist programming ... whatever—speaking."

"Why's …?"

"Why's what?"

Why's …" He was trembling and had to press his elbows onto the table to steady himself.

"Your question?"

"Forget it."

Jay snorted.

Why is Lionel always implying that something's missing in our sex life? What have you told them?

"I guess you're pressing me to say why I associate with them. Look … when your status is settled and you begin studying full-time, you'll have lots of opportunities to create your own circle of friends. For the time being, if you don't want to mingle with mine, you don't have to. When they are here, find something to do outside, and stay home when they are hosting. Already you refuse to accompany me to community events."

"Go off to bed. You're tired. This is turning into a quarrel."

"I'll say one thing more: Stop judging people. You must know that what we are is a matter of luck or ill luck … Jestina's academic brilliance on the one hand, her insanity on the other. Remember? You were her neighbour. You witnessed it all. Paul's elite schooling in St Vincent turned out to be a handicap when he entered high school here. Luckily he bounced back, partly because of the confidence Grama's nurturing had given him before he left St Vincent, partly because he met Bill … A lot of accidents."

"And you've been the luckiest of us all."

"Really?"

"I'm serious." *Well, maybe not in love.*

"When you say vulgar, I think you have Lionel, Tyrone, and Guícho in mind. Guícho has to be louder than everyone else for the same reason that Laurent physically abuses Tyrone."

"Meaning?"

"We're university grads, professionals … Tyrone has an MSc in biology, is a CEGEP prof, and his parents own millions in real estate."

"So why does he put up with Laurent's violence?"

"Ah, that's human complexity for you. Laurent's illiterate. Expresses himself in Creole only. It's why he converses only with Gina, and rarely says more than *oui* or *non* to the rest of us. Tyrone's been pushing him to enrol in an adult literacy program, but he resists. Ah, but he has a beautiful body—although his gut's beginning to bulge. One night—you hadn't arrived yet—a drunk Tyrone blurted out that he'd married Laurent for his big dick. It was like he had to justify why he was in a relationship with him. Oh boy. Gina went after him. Both fists balled. Marc-André shielded him. Tyrone told her she was venting on the wrong guy. 'I've seen big dicks on White men, Black men, Latin Americans. Chill! Rushton didn't interview me. It's Black guys who misinformed him ... I've seen dicks this tiny on Black men.' He showed his little finger. Then he smiled broadly, placed his hand on his groin, traced his own penis and said: 'And my dick is the biggest most people will ever see.' There were guffaws all around. Lionel said it was the truth, that Tyrone had walked into his cubicle at the sauna one night and shoved it in his face. 'I could barely palm it. And long. Think of the longest, fattest plantain you ever saw and add inches. I said, "Man, how come you don't faint when you have a hard on? The blood that thing needs must leave your brain oxygen deprived." Folks, take it from me, it's monstrous, and it was half limp when I saw it.'

"'You pass up!' Carlos said.

"'Not a platter to be sampled,' Lionel said, shaking his head. 'I respect the limits of my anatomy. I shooed him out. Besides, I didn't want him passing out in there. And he only came in there to shake it in my face, to show off, to make me jealous.'

"Paul told Gina to ask Laurent what role Tyrone plays in bed. She said she didn't want to know. But Lionel pointed to Laurent and waved his right hand over his left. Marc-André began to titter. Others followed. Tyrone turned beet red.

"'You guys are disgusting,' Gina said.

Maybe, Jay, you regret that you chose not to batch.

"You were there the night when a drunk, morose Tyrone said nature wounded him in the womb, meaning the clubfoot he was born with and his withered leg, then played a joke on him, referring to his dick, and eventually took pity on him and gave him intellect. He forgot to mention, or deliberately omitted, that he was born to millionaire parents. We've been many times to his penthouse condo: three bedrooms, two bathrooms, humungous living and dining room, large kitchen, balconies with views onto downtown on one side and the Saint Lawrence and the South Shore on the other, on Rue de la Commune— the Old Port, one of Montreal's most expensive areas—worth well over a million. You know what? It's a gift from his parents." He sighed. "That's fate, Millington ... I read somewhere that Mahalia Jackson— famous Mahalia Jackson—was illiterate. Paul told me that Guícho barely scraped through high school. Now he has trouble keeping a job. He's lewd and loud. It's how he claims his space. He's certain he'll be dead by age thirty-five. But he's charming and lucky. As long as Gina's around he won't suffer. Those two cuss, then hug, then cuss again, and waltz right after. In a way I can't fathom they need each other."

"So, how do you account for Lionel's remarks tonight?"

"He drinks too much. Don't hold it against him. First find out why he gets drunk."

"No need to lecture me on drunken behaviour."

"You're testy. Relax. Lionel convinced Paul that having meningi-oma wasn't the end of his life. At the time Paul was on the verge of abandoning his undergrad studies. Now he's working on a PhD ... People are complex ... A mix of pleasing and disgusting ... Lionel's definitely sex-obsessed. He's probably hypersexed, in which case blame his hormones. It doesn't take much to see that Tyrone's angry and cyn-ical. And don't let Guícho's bluster fool you. Remember: his mother has rejected him ... You want our marriage to stay hidden ... from your mother ... from Vincentians ... the whole world ... You should under-stand how his mother's rejection is affecting him." He paused, a long one. "Fundamentalist parents. Ah yes—Fundamentalist parents ... Emilia's mother hangs up the phone on her when she calls. I too had to lay it on the line for Ma one time."

"Lay it on the line. How?"

"Over Paul's friendship with Bill. She'd overheard Paul and me talk-ing about Bill's gay art. It was around the time here that the court ruled in favour of gay marriage, and her church was telling her that gays were pedophiles bent on seducing children and making them gay. They had her primed. She asked me if I thought Paul was gay. I told her I didn't know, which was true, but that he was nineteen, and if there was anything going on between him and Bill, there was absolutely nothing she could do about it. 'And what about you?' she said. I told her I didn't know. At the time I felt I was bisexual. She wanted a definite answer. I didn't have one. Instead I told her that any religion that urged parents to reject their children for whatever reason wasn't worth belonging to. On her death bed I found out that she believed that her leaving us behind when she came to Canada had made us gay. A Pentecostal she'd worked for when she arrived here had planted that idea in her head."

Jay stopped talking for several seconds. "Guícho has toned down a lot. That sixty-year-old man he's with in Lethbridge is probably what he needs. The other day Paul mentioned that in high school Guícho never spoke to them about his father, that the one time that Gina asked him about his dad, he told her to change the topic ... In St Vincent, Paul barely noticed Daddy when he visited us. But Bill became the most important person in Paul's life when he met him. It was as if he transferred his worshipful admiration for Grama to Bill. Bill's death affected him as much, if not more, than Grama's did. Go figure."

Millington understood what Jay said about Paul and Bill. He always wished Presley Murray was his dad. It was because Presley was a responsible father and husband that Sister Murray had money that Mem could borrow to pay off Edward's rum-drinking debts. As for Guícho and Lionel, he could have said most of what Jay said himself, using other examples from the single-parent mothers and their children who had been members of his congregation, but he disliked Jay's get-over-it tone and the smothered anger that sufficed for what he wouldn't say outright: that their marriage has been a disappointment. He also wanted Jay to say categorically that he would never take up Lionel's offers. And he learned something new: that Jay once identified as bisexual. So why didn't he opt for a relationship with a woman? That's certainly more socially acceptable. And he began to wonder whether Jay might get the urge to be a father and ditch him.

"Did you read *Huxley in Hollywood*?" Jay broke the silence.

"No."

He'd asked Millington to read it following a discussion Les Friends had had at Gina's place about an interview in *Fugue* with a fellow whose husband was a porn star. Almost all of the guys, Paul and Bernard included, said they'd have no problem marrying a porn star. Emilia, Jay, Gina, and Millington stayed silent.

"Would you?" he asked Jay when they got home.

"I don't know. Every relationship comes down to what's acceptable to both parties."

"Do you take a stand on anything?"

"Yes. Against abusive power, cruelty, suffering, greed, dishonesty, injustice."

"I'm relieved."

During their talk the television was on mute. Jay reached for the remote on the coffee table and turned the sound on. It was after midnight and the *National* was on. After about fifteen minutes he got up from the couch where they were sitting, went into his study and returned holding *Huxley in Hollywood*. He pushed it toward Millington and said: "Read it."

"Why?"

"You'll meet a philandering man: Aldous, and a lesbian: Maria, his wife, who remained married to each other for life ... It just might clear your brain of all that theological debris and help you understand that marriages have to do with the needs of the parties in them—their needs, not ours."

When Jay went off to bed, Millington turned off the light and remained seated at the dining table thinking. Eventually he got his journal and wrote:

> *I wonder what Jay really wanted to say to me tonight. There's no doubt that at the erotic level our relationship is in trouble. Has he told Paul about it? Has Paul told Lionel?*

He went to bed after 3 a.m. and awakened with a start, just after five, from a dream that Jay and he were at a batch in Tyrone's apartment, and Jay, Lionel, and he ended up in bed, and Lionel took turns sodomizing Jay and him. The dream made no sense at all. He's not attracted to Lionel.

Two weeks later at Paul's place, they watched *Kinsey* and *A Dangerous Method*. In the discussion afterward, Paul said that satisfactory sex requires the sort of surrender that obliterates the ego, and that some men must go to extremes to do so. Like CEOs who frequent dominatrices, macho men who wear women's clothing as a prelude to having sex, or men who ask their partners to piss on them. Paul's convinced too that if the roughly thirty-five percent of humans that Kinsey says are repressed bisexuals could gratify their urges, the divorce rate would be halved and life would be less unhappy for the many people who're stuck in unfulfilling relationships.

His opinions left Millington uneasy. Why did he rent those films? Given the discussions Jay and Millington had been having, did Jay ask Paul to rent them? Why that dream about Lionel, Jay, and him? In bed with Jay, just hinting at sodomy causes Millington to sweat and his penis to go limp.

Maybe now that he's a bona fide immigrant he should focus on repairing his damaged sexuality. How would he do that? Marriage shouldn't be a burden. He said so to his parishioners who sought his advice about their marital problems. Paul had jested that they should: "Check out Dan Savage's columns." Had Jay told him about their first failed attempt to have sex? *Well-honed tools. Ploughing difficult soil.* They're not metaphors that pop up spontaneously.

Last year when all of Canada was agog over Jian Gomeshi's sexual "misconduct," Millington spent a long time wondering how the erotic drive could be so configured that pain becomes its engine. Some ask to be tied up. Others demand that their partners be tied up. There's another example Paul might have used. In their discussion over *A Dangerous*

Method, Paul said that Freud felt that sexuality includes a release of aggression. "Maybe, just as we humans vary in stature, so we vary in the degree and method of releasing aggression during sex. Ejaculating into someone's vagina, rectum, or mouth is clearly not enough for some. Jay, you remember that the man Ma worked for when she first came here told her that sex was sweetest right after a man had beaten his wife?" Jay nodded and Paul shook his head in puzzlement. "Go figure. It set me thinking about all those men in St Vincent who regularly beat their wives and girlfriends. Some of that beating might be from sexual frustration. And some o' that frustration's probably because West Indians fuck like farm animals and call it sex, afraid anything else would qualify them as freaks."

Is there something that Jay and he are yet to discover? Should he discuss it with him? And what if it's something that repels one of them? What would come to the fore if he got drunk? What in Jay's case? Jay's father regressed to infancy when he was drunk and Jay became the parent, sort of. Millington never saw Edward as much as stagger. Mem didn't say if he'd been violent that time he came home drunk. Compared to Twine—to a lesser extent Percy—Edward wasn't so bad after all. Except that his drinking debts kept them on the edge of poverty. Maybe one of these days he should get drunk and have Jay record the experience. Jay would have to agree to get drunk too and let him record it. *Stop kidding yourself, Millington. You're incapable of relinquishing self-control.* Why's human sexuality so complex? In Havre he saw all sorts of animals—cattle, hogs, goats, sheep, donkeys, chickens, doing it. It seemed so straightforward. Even the rams that mounted other rams did so with instinctual nonchalance.

In his high school biology class he learned that while mating the female mantis eats her partner, which could only mean that for the male mantis sex was more important than life ... *Ah, we naked apes who know so much and yet so little about our psyches!*

13

HIS DECISION TO leave the ministry, when did it crystallize? For a long time he stayed on based on what he calls survival need. One of his journal entries from 2010, right after he returned from his father's funeral, reads:

In childhood you sing, "All things bright and beautiful / All creatures great and small / All things wise and wonderful / The Lord God made them all"; and you wonder how they got ugly, why instead of wisdom there's ignorance, why cruelty and not kindness; and you are told that God's work has been perverted by the Devil; and to defy the Devil you should wear God's armour. You get older and observe your fellow humans searching for flaws in other humans and, in their absence, inventing them, as reasons to hate and oppress them—for pleasure or gain.

The few people on this earth who're attracted to justice and dignity look around them for exemplars and mostly find evil masquerading as good and a worldview that buttresses and rewards evil; in desperation they turn to God as the fountain of the humane values they long to see governing the world. But, as they examine the abstraction that's God, they discover that it too is tainted, that the masqueraders had shaped it. Maggie Thatcher, raised a Methodist, quoted St Paul—"If a man does not work neither shall he eat"—to justify, among other measures, reducing assistance to indigent children (I'm sure many pointed out to her that there's a difference between children and men, and that child labour was illegal in Britain), and earned herself the nickname "Thatcher-the-milk-snatcher." And those American evangelicals who call themselves Christian Reconstructionists advocate a return to slavery to keep the "idle poor" profitable and occupied, for Satan finds mischief for idle hands. And since the poor are poor because they're not of the elect, they must be God's de facto foes, who should be closely monitored. You wonder how and why Christ's commandment to feed the hungry, clothe the naked, and visit the incarcerated got perverted.

You come eventually to see the sorry state of Christianity, and you stop deluding yourself, and you understand that the more you delay your leaving the more of a tool and a parrot you become, and the battle between your authentic self and your public self intensifies. And you want the authentic self to win. But it is outmatched. What will others think? How will you make a living? Why give up all this security? You recall the story of Christ standing on a mountaintop contemplating the Devil's offer to make him landlord of the world. And you remind yourself that you aren't Christ, and that this is only allegory. Then you re-read Jung and see with certitude that your shadow is insidiously engulfing you, that your persona is displacing the authentic you, and fright overtakes you. But fear of the future paralyses you, and you put off your leaving for another day.

It was a long time before he could call himself atheist or agnostic. Now on some days he's one, on other days the other, and there are days when he wants to be neither. And when he read *The God Delusion*, he saw why. If he'd been an ambivalent believer, Dawkins's woolly arguments against God's existence wouldn't have convinced him. In a journal entry he has noted that:

Atheists rightly talk about spirituality because it's impossible to deny the constellation of psychic feelings in all of us that in part gave birth to religions. Expunging the so-called religious urge would be akin to expunging the psyche. The megaliths at

Stonehenge, our cathedrals, mosques, and temples exemplify that need to give substance in sublime form to this most insubstantial of needs. If only we could examine the "religious urge" like we can a liver, a kidney, or a femur.

Rationally, one can make the case against the existence of God. But doing so rarely bears fruit, because, as Freud rightly observes, humans invented God, and, as Voltaire before him opines, if God didn't exist, humanity would have to invent him. Well, they did. And the inventors understood the human desire to defeat death and to enjoy privileges denied the rest of living nature. Those needs make the task of the pro-God camp easy, especially when the defender's someone as formidable as Karen Armstrong. Who wouldn't want to live in bliss eternally! Christianity is one of humanity's best fairy tales.

Convincing others of what they want to hear has always been easy. Politicians who promise to make the wealthy wealthier and "put poverty into the dustbins of history" usually get elected. We embrace those delusions that make us feel good.

We enter these vocations fervently, confidently, naively. And after we've disentangled ourselves somewhat—we never fully escape: what was planted there remains, like inextricable shrapnel, or dormant chicken pox viruses waiting to return as shingles—we wonder why we hadn't fully considered the implications of our decisions. And we come to discover that we couldn't, that our needs had gulled us. We went to church, felt a sense of belonging, and were told that because we behaved according to the beliefs of the church our lives were exemplary. Which child doesn't like praise! Who doesn't like the approval of others! We sang hymns whose rhythms and images filled us with rapture, and our ministers told us that the euphoria that filled us was the Holy Spirit, the third component of God. What could be more flattering? And long before we learned that the euphoria we experienced came from our own endorphins, dopamine, and oxytocin—and could be had from running or disco dancing—our psyches were programmed by all that mythology, and we'd already opted for a career that propagated it. And, later, as we wrestle to extricate ourselves and to expunge the beliefs that control us, we are forced to acknowledge that we still crave the pleasure of Belief and abhor the vacuum left by its loss. And when we finally let go, we discover that we were right, that Belief is addictive and deforming and leaves its own brand of delirium tremens.

14

AT TIMES MILLINGTON wonders if he had been drawn to the ministry because of the veneration ordained and even unordained preachers got. Once when one of Havre's ne'er-do-wells was imitating a preacher's gestures and mimicking his statements, Sister Murray called out to him: "Boy, don't mock the Lord's anointed. Boy, stop it! Your hand will wither like Jeroboam own. Stop it!" In that environment he understands why Mem wanted him to become a minister: a clergyman, university-trained, rungs above the self-appointed or bible-school graduates for whom the title pastor was reserved. She was already proud of the fact that he'd won a place in one of St Vincent's elite secondary schools and had held his own there. It gave her status among the mothers whose children had failed the high school entrance exam and therefore didn't go to secondary school or barely passed it and got sent to lesser schools like Esperance Secondary.

She knew that he enjoyed going to church, and after his confirmation she encouraged him to develop close links with the minister. She had her own links with him. Each Friday evening when she was preparing her produce for market day, she packed two baskets, one of fruit and one of vegetables, which he took to the manse. At Christmas they always butchered a goat and gave a hind quarter to Reverend Hennessy.

Shortly after he began to work in the civil service, Millington volunteered to be a Sunday school teacher. Mem was pleased, and reminded him that the doctors had felt that he would die at age five; and because he'd lived, she was sure God had saved his life "for some special purpose." She was, of course, programmed to believe this. Every Methodist *knew* that John Wesley, fifteenth of nineteen children born to the Anglican rector Samuel Wesley and his wife Susanna, had almost died in a fire at age six—Susanna referred to him as "a brand plucked from the fire"—and God had spared Wesley's life so he could found Methodism.

Did he become a minister to please Mem? It's an understatement to say he always wanted to please her. He craved Edward's approval too, but Edward was indifferent to pretty well everything he did. Mem bragged to the neighbours about his school performance; Edward never saw it as anything special, never complimented him or even smiled or nodded.

His preaching began the year after he started teaching Sunday school. He felt that God was calling him to do so. He told Reverend Hennessy about it. They prayed about it in Hennessy's study, after which Hennessy showed him several books that he should read, and said that he needed to be sure that the *call* was genuine. A few church members later told Millington that Hennessy had questioned them about his character, and they'd told him that he was a pious, upright young man. At the time Millington believed the Jonah story and its underlying message: that those whom God chooses to carry out a mission cannot defy him. Moreover, his brain was imbued with biblical stories: the Apostle Paul's conversion, Daniel in the lions' den, Shadrach, Meshach, and Abednego emerging unharmed from a burning furnace.

Of course from age fifteen on, he was in turmoil for another reason that Elijah, Willy, and Neil might have suspected. And possibly Edward. He couldn't tell anyone. By then Jay was far away, in Canada, but there was still the sexual desire he felt for him from the time he was fourteen. For about two years after Jay left, he still dreamed about sex with him. Before Jay left for Canada, Millington asked God each night to cleanse him of "unholy desire." He was sad to see Jay go but glad the object of temptation was gone. But the space his friendship had filled stayed empty. Now he's married to Jay, and that space is still empty.

In 1998, the year he became a Sunday school teacher, he believed in the power of prayer and in guidance by the Holy Spirit. Whenever he could he fasted, hoping that fasting would bring him closer to God, who'd see his piety, and fortify him against evil. But there was the question that gnawed at him and sent his emotions berserk: If God had saved his life for some noble purpose, why had God allowed him to be gay? Eventually his bible reading brought him to St Paul telling the Corinthians that he had a thorn in the flesh and that God had put it there to keep him humble. He saw too that St Paul hadn't been very enthusiastic about marriage, and had likened the human body and human sexuality to dross. A favourite metaphor of Methodists too, drilled into them by Charles Wesley's "Oh, that in me the sacred fire / Might now begin to glow / Burn up the dross of base desire / And make the goodness flow." (Christianity's preoccupation with fire sometimes slips into the bizarre and sadistic. Around the time he began to teach Sunday school, a Pentecostal woman on Main Street burned her teenage daughter with a clothes iron, to "give her a foretaste of hell and put her back on the path to heaven." A couple months later, a delinquent youngster of around twelve was taken to the police station in Esperance where two officers, also evangelical Christians, stippled his body with cigarette burns. They paid the boy's mother not to proceed with a trial. Recently the minister of ecclesiastical affairs in the St Vincent government, also an evangelical pastor, said he would like to toss all gays onto a blazing pyre.)

Millington came to believe that St P and he weren't so different, and felt comforted. He suspected that St P's weakness was same-sex desire. He condemns it with such virulence— reminding the Roman Christians that it was an act punishable by death. (In Judaic law yes; under Roman law, no.) No wonder St P insisted so much on mortifying— killing—his flesh, flesh being euphemism for penis. A pity he left no journals, for, as is the case with Kierkegaard, they'd have probably shown a Paul quite different from the persona in his epistles. Prayer didn't remove St P's weakness. Moreover, he believed that it could be used for God's greater glory. And so Millington too felt that by resisting his sexual orientation he could strengthen his piety.

He even came to revere St P. Amputating his name then would have been sacrilege. Now he sees Paul as a man sizzling with zeal and earnestness, for which, luckily, he found an outlet: establishing Christianity among the gentiles. His ego, compensating for his small stature, is present everywhere in his epistles. What was his testosterone level like? Easy to renounce sex when there's no strong physiological urge. Could be the opposite too. Unfulfilled sexual desire finding relief in zealous religious pursuits. Today's feminists come down hard on him, but his promulgations against women were mild compared to the virulent contempt in which women were then held. "How can he be clean that is of woman born?" meant literally that.

Millington's ordeal attained its acme in 1999. Then Caribbean dancehall musicians were advocating the killing of gays, based, they said, on biblical authority. It was also the year that Britain demanded that its remaining Caribbean territories decriminalize homosexuality and abolish capital punishment in order to become full-fledged British citizens. Caribbean Christians went on a warpath. For several Sundays Hennessy's sermons centred on the evils of homosexuality and his prayers beseeched god to intervene and prevent the inscription of sin into the laws of his people. Those days all sorts of people appeared in Millington's dreams, seduced him, and outed him.

He never suspected—what a marvel of subterfuge the subconscious is!—that his hyper-religiosity was his shield, his mask, against suspicions of being gay. Of course his age-mates and the ne'er-do-wells on the Anglican Church patio waited, waited for his hormones to triumph. Waited for his *fall*.

Today's Methodists ignore Wesley's harangues to lead sinless lives, though they list it on their website as their belief in the doctrine of sanctification. Wesley went up and down England and Scotland quoting Jesus: "Be ye perfect, even as your heavenly father is perfect," and ordered his followers to do likewise. How Wesley could have seen perfection in the Old Testament God—a sadistic, egotistical tyrant—baffles Millington. Not sure how the philanderers in the AMC congregations deal with Wesley's harangue. There was one who, along with his wife and mistress, worshipped in the Havre church every Sunday. At AMC Kingstown the choirmaster's wife was the church's society steward and his mistress was the organist. But the steward of the AMC West Coast Circuit beat all. He was Millington's boss in the Ministry of Labour. A tun of a man whom they called Crapaud-face. Earlier in his career, he chose the young women who went to work as domestics in Canada, and had rejected those who'd refused to have sex with him.

Occasionally, the ne'er-do-wells called out to Millington from the Anglican Church patio: "Boy, love juice go fly up in your brain and send you to the madhouse." One evening Edward came in from work and met him poring over a book Reverend Hennessy had lent him. Standing just inside the main door, his hair and face speckled with sawdust, he stared at Millington sitting with the book open at the dining table and chortled. "Boy, you need a girlfriend to cure you of all this book and church foolishness. I hope you grow out of it. Soon."

Mem was in their bedroom listening. When Edward went outside, she said: "Don't mind your father. Keep doing the Lord's work. Don't follow his advice and dishonour me with no bastard grandpickney." She smiled. "And I don't want no riff-raff of a daughter-in-law neither." She came to sit beside him, held his chin between the fingers and thumb of her right hand, turned his head to face her, stared up into his eyes and said: "Your grandmother, my mother, used to make me go down on my knees, and hold the bible over my head and make me promise never to let a man touch me until he put a ring on my finger in a church. She didn' have to do that. She didn' have to do that at all. I did already figure out that having me was hard on her and I wouldo' never do anything to displease her."

Change girlfriend to boyfriend, and Edward might have been right. It made sense that when he left the ministry, Haverites quickly accepted the rumour that he was crazy, and probably felt he'd been so all along from a semen-saturated brain.

15

HE CAN'T REMEMBER exactly when he resolved to be celibate. It happened insidiously. It was, in any case, the only way he could be unmarried and be an AMC minister. In standard Methodism too.

Millington felt that if Roman Catholic priests could be celibate, so could he. The sexual molestation scandals of the RCs hadn't yet reached the Caribbean, though there were always rumours about local priests whom young boys should avoid. In those days—his late adolescence—talk about girlfriends and sex unnerved him and pushed him further into being a loner. The number of females one had bedded and could boast about was an essential criterion for being a real West Indian he-man. He had no such stories to tell, and, fearful of others finding out why, he kept his distance. By 1999 he'd taken the celibacy vow. For that reason, he did not return Jay's Christmas card that year. Distancing himself from Jay was part of the dross St Paul had ordered him to burn away.

Celibacy. He laughs and shakes his head as he remembers how shocked he was on reading, during his first year at ETC—in Renwick's history of Christianity—that Theodora the elder and her daughters got their lovers and illegitimate children appointed popes, and that a branch of the Gnostics, themselves celibate, believed that the Old Testament God was evil, and his creations inherently so. CW had already been expelled before they parsed these topics. Oh, the fireworks he would have caused in that lecture hall were he still there! *Ah yes, and papal infallibility! Immaculate conception! Transubstantiation. A few of those early and not-so-early Christians could not overlook empirical data, the death and decay confronting us everywhere in nature. They left the church no choice: the Inquisition. Believe what we teach or die.* He shouldn't be so judgemental. His ordination was supposed to mean that he believed in an interventionist God, in the miracles Christ supposedly performed, in the power of the Holy Spirit, and in the centrepiece of it all: that Christ was the son of God, that he rose from the dead, and his death and resurrection guaranteed all Christians an after-death blissful life—in short, in everything stated in the Nicene Creed.

Celibacy. After outing himself to Millington, Horton would call him once, sometimes twice, per week or find excuses to meet with him. Good gaydar. Horton had cisterns of it. Understood Millington's needs better than Millington himself. Criminal lawyer that he was, he'd mastered the art of unravelling his opponent's defence. When they were face to face, as long as no one else was within hearing, Horton talked about sex, loneliness, and companionship, and left long pauses for Millington to fill. He learned how to wait them out, and, as much as possible, he avoided being alone with him.

At one of those meetings in Millington's study, a rainy Saturday—Horton always arranged the meetings for Saturday afternoons or Wednesdays after Millington's regular visiting hours, always when Doris was off—as he was leaving, he grabbed Millington's hand and forcibly placed it on what turned out to be his erect penis. "At your service anytime."

Millington wrestled away his hand, and in backing away hit his head on a bookcase.

"See? Running from sex could kill you. Wow! Rev, your dick is stiffening. Come on. Unzip. Let's get down to business ... Glad to see you're not a eunuch."

"Never mind what I am. Hurry home. Gladys is waiting to put supper on the table, but you might still have time to pull her into the bedroom for a quickie."

Through it all he continued to accept some of Gladys's supper invitations and looked forward to spending time with her, Len, and Alex.

He felt then that he'd love to be a father. Maybe he should talk Jay into adopting a kid or two. Yann, one of Jay's gay colleagues, adopted two brothers from Honduras.

Maybe not. Their marriage is too shaky. Besides, he knows now that Jay once saw himself as bisexual. *It just might set him thinking that he should ditch me for a woman.*

16

IT WAS SHORT-SIGHTED of him not to have read the two letters Gladys had sent him, but he was convinced then that their paths would never cross. He was out walking both times Somerset came to deliver them. Those days he had to burn off a lot of nervous energy and tire himself out so he could sleep. Every day, provided it wasn't raining, he walked, sometimes to the end of the Leeward Highway and back. Twice per week he added a side trip into Esperance. Its steep incline on the way back gave his heart a good workout. He was afraid Gladys's letters would contain statements that Melvin had dictated. Melvin was in damage-control mode and would have used whomever and whatever to persuade him back into the church. He tore up the letters without even opening the envelopes.

His cell's ringing. It's Jay.

"Home already?"

"Yeah. The whole exercise took no more than twenty minutes. I was home before ten."

"It's been a *long* wait. We didn't think it would take this long. We'll celebrate it. We'll invite a few friends by to celebrate with us."

"I didn't meet with Gladys yesterday. She had to put it off to today. We're meeting for coffee at Paragraphe at 5:30."

A couple seconds pass. "Well, today's for celebration. Don't spoil it with maudlin thoughts."

At home when Millington is writing his journal, Jay sometimes says:

"You're recording a lot. Don't make it all negative." At first Millington chafed whenever he said it. Now he lets it drift past him.

"I'll be boarding my flight in half an hour. I should be home around 15:30." He kisses Millington goodbye.

That August meeting with Gladys. "The young women in the Women's League used to wonder if you're gay." She followed it up with: "I've heard that the churches here are quite liberal; some even ordain gay ministers." What was she insinuating? She has definitely linked his resignation to Horton's strange behaviour. What does that mean? Even mentioned how much time he and Horton had spent together that night. Why did Horton make her think he might know the reason for his estrangement? What got into him? Yes, it was a mistake not to have read her letters. But if their purpose was to find out the reason for Horton's bizarre behaviour, he's glad he didn't read them. On the other hand, if he had, he might have been better prepared to deal with her questions. She's under the assumption that he read those letters. What he'd thought highly unlikely then is now reality: they are in touch again. It would be cruel of him to tell the truth—to her, who's the epitome of kindness. She's definitely on a fishing expedition. Well, he can't blame her. Her marriage and her children's well-being are threatened.

Those visits from Horton. Around three one Saturday afternoon, Millington saw the car drive up, heard the doorbell, but decided not to open the door. It wasn't locked. In any case, Millington's car was visible in the carport. Horton pulled open the door, and walked into the living room. Millington said he was about to take a shower and go out.

"Great. Then let's shower together ... Aren't you taking off your clothes?"

"No. Keep yours on. And please leave."

"Millington, stop your foolish games and offer me a seat." He glanced at the sofa.

"I have to go out." He threw back his head and rolled his eyes, his arms gesturing exasperation.

"Rev, cut out the theatre. If I *let* you leave, you'll drive around until you think I'm gone. Save the gas and lessen the pollution, because"—his voice dropped to a whisper—"you'll meet me sitting on your porch. You gave me the same spiel the last time ... Millington, am I a leper? Why don't you like to see *this* parishioner? Afraid of seducing me?" He extended his arms as if to embrace Millington, his eyes big and blazing. "Be my guest. *A-n-y* time." He began unbuckling his belt, but dropped his arms, closed his eyes, and smacked his lips.

After a silence of about ten seconds, Horton said: "I'm here to invite you to join a group of gays I hang out with. Fifteen of us. We meet weekly at a friend's house in St James. Another member of AMC Hastings belongs. You'll never guess who. Of course, if you tell me who you have eyes for in the congregation, and if he's on your list, I could feel him out for you. I'll burn with jealousy but I'll do it ... Oh, by the way, Mr. AMC Hastings suspects that you're one of the brethren. Can't fool everybody, Rev. Another of the brethren belongs to Broad Street and two worship at Oistins. You'll be at home ... in good company ... Rev, those guys, they're *300 percent he-men!* Soon as you see them, your dick will start watering. No hen in them. None o' that waist-winding, sissy shit. You can walk down Broad Street with any o' them and nobody will whistle at you." He squinted and smiled. "You're so handsome when you blush! ... And you know what else is great about those fellows: they're professionals. No leeches among them. The cream of Barbados's gays waiting to embrace you. Now I *know* you're *dying* to meet them. Don't lie."

Millington wondered if Mr. AMC Hastings was Harry.

"Rev, are you telling me that you just let all that love juice collect and overflow when you're asleep? What a waste! I know you're retentive, but this is taking a bad thing too far—too far Rev." He grinned. "Seriously now, which of us churchmen figures—figure—in your wet dreams? When you do your hand jobs? ... No hints? Me? Don't blush like that. Come on. You can tell me. What, afraid Wesley's ghost will haunt you?"

Millington took a long sigh, closed his eyes, and put his hands over his ears. After a long silence, he said: "Horton, now I know the Devil exists: you."

Horton smiled. "As I said, some of our holiest males from Broad Street and Oistins ... are in the tent. I could act as a go-between and get you hooked up ... *Millington*, you're pink as a pig. Are you having a heart attack?" He laughed.

Silence.

Horton resumed. Calm tone. "See, I can come to you naked, but you won't even unbutton your shirt. Wesley urged us to be saints. Hope you don't think he was one. Then again, maybe he was. His wife left him. In those days things had to be damn desperate for a wife to leave her husband. I have a pretty good hunch why. He would have found sex unholy. Just like St Paul."

Wrong. It was because he was dissuaded from marrying Grace Murray, the woman he truly loved. Gladys should leave you. She's too good for you.

"Seriously, Rev, why don't you let me take you to meet the fellows one o' these evenings? I kindo' exaggerated earlier. They're not all he-men." He wiggled his fingers. "A few's kindo' iffy. Some are handsome though. H-A-N-D-S-O-M-E!" He closed his eyes, did an intake whistle, and exhaled slowly. "Sculpted butts, soccer-player thighs, and ripped— yes ripped. Rev, you'll sin and praise God for it, and God will be so pleased to see you're no damn fool, that you're enjoying the sexuality he blessed—or cursed—you with." He smiled. Lips pulled back. Eyes half-shut. "Relax, Rev. Relax. Chill, man. You take your vocation too damn seriously."

You take your lusts too far.

Silence.

"Know something, Rev, if this group was around fifteen years ago, I would o' *never* get married."

They were both still standing. Feeling beaten and foolish, Millington walked to an armchair and motioned for Horton to sit on the sofa, across from him. Horton shook his head.

Millington's skin felt hot. Why didn't someone come? Then he remembered it was Saturday, not Wednesday.

"What's your taste in men anyway?" Horton paused as if expecting an answer. "Tell me. Don't be shy. One of the brethren's an Anglican priest. Ooh!" He did another of his intake whistles and fanned his face.

"What a handsome bugger! If I get into his bed, is Black Rock they going take me afterwards 'cause I won't stop singing the Hallelujah chorus. He'll be just right for you. That's if you like jet-black skin. You're both men of the cloth who'll meet to discuss *holy* matters —with and without the e." He grinned.

Was he referring to Horace? The description fitted him. Horace was one of five, later four, ministers that Millington met with at Silas's manse in St Phillip some Mondays.

"Alright, here's another possibility: I'll get you a wig and a false beard and moustache. That way no one would recognize you. No one would know that Reverend Samuels is in their midst."

At that moment the doorbell sounded. Millington rushed to answer it. It was a lanky fellow who'd come on a bicycle from the Cloister Bookstore with *Godless Morality*, which he'd ordered six weeks earlier.

Upon re-entering the living room, he said: "Horton, I admire your wife, and I love your children—"

"And you love their father too, but won't admit it."

"Yes, as a child of God, a member of my congregation, and my circuit steward. Now please leave. I'm sorry I have to say so to you."

"Okay, I'll go back to my office and cry." He gave a few theatrical gulps, made an eye-wiping gesture, and left.

Millington was so upset, he went to the pharmacy, minutes before it closed, and refilled a prescription for Valium; he'd had to take it for a while to calm his nerves following Melvin's report about the congregation's dissatisfaction with his sermons.

Horton came back at him the following Wednesday just as the 5 p.m. bell was tolling, just as his office hours ended.

Millington met him at the door to his study. "Not you again."

An awkward pause.

"Okay, come in."

He offered him a seat. Horton looked at the chair on the other side of Millington's desk, hesitated, and remained standing.

"How may I help you, Horton?" He tried to sound nonchalant.

"I could answer you honestly, but you don't seem keen to see me. Why aren't you looking at me, Millington?"

Millington shrugged.

"You're *so* transparent. Know something, when you lie, your voice keens like a fiddle and you always turn away your head or stare at the floor."

Silence.

"I think my presence is upsetting you."

"Whatever you imagine, Horton. Why don't you sit down?" He pointed again to the chair in front of his desk.

Horton shook his head. "I'll be too near. I might lean over and kiss you ... and you might call the police ... or I ... an ambulance."

He let that pass.

"Rev, I listen to your sermons. Every Sunday. Sometimes they're good. Other times ..." He gestured so-so. "Now you listen to me. Yours are for my *edification*. Mine is for your *education*."

"Okay, Reverend Bates—or is it Professor Bates? But why preach to me alone? Why not invite Gladys to hear your sermon? Melvin too? You're our circuit steward. He might be impressed and ask you to become a lay preacher."

Horton made a dismissive hand wave. "Melvin lives in the nineteenth century. Let him sip tea with the likes of Mrs. Goddard. I'm trying to bring you into the twentieth. And leave Gladys out of this. She's the innocent victim here." Tone aggressive. "More victim than me. Barbadians say a man must have a woman or else be persecuted. I refuse to be persecuted."

Silence.

"May I proceed?"

"You don't need my permission."

He cleared his throat. "It will be brief, Rev, briefer than your homilies." His tone unctuous: "Consider, my handsome Reverend Samuels, more than the lilies of the field." He winked at Millington. "Consider what makes us sweat and grunt with pleasure and turns us into hogs. Messy, too. *Swilling*." He closed his eyes. "Because, you see, Rev, it's partnered with excrement ..."

Millington growled through his clenched teeth.

"You're coming *already*!"

Millington gestured with palms vertical for Horton to stop.

"Reverend Samuels, I'm talking about the urethra, same conduit for sperm and piss. Think about it. One's excrement—poison; the other the source of life itself and the epitome of pleasure. Both using the same duct. And when they're at war, know who wins? ... Don't know? When your prostate's pissed off you can't piss. That's a powerful fact, Rev ... a fact no religious dogma can alter. More reality in that than in all of John Wesley's sermons and Charles Wesley's hymns ... Probably caused John to hate sex. St Paul too. And now ... you."

"What's your point, Horton? What are you trying to say?"

"*What I'm trying to say!* Are you for real? I did think of bringing along a bit of porn for illustration but didn't want Wesley's ghost to haunt you afterwards. Then again, you might end up soliciting bjs from every man you meet afterwards and scandalize the church. You can never predict how people would react to a new experience." He shook his right index finger.

"Zzzzzz," Millington squirmed and stared at the top of his desk.

Quietly, his tone reflective, Horton continued: "Rev, get out of penance. Loosen up. Live. Enjoy life. Put Wesley's doctrines where they belong." He pointed to the trash basket beside the desk. "You'll soon be wrinkled and warped and then only God will want you." He shook his head slowly and sighed long and loud, put his right fist under his chin, and stared at Millington for a couple of seconds. "And so damn good-looking! ... I feel like tearing off your clothes and grabbing your dick." Now he stared at the floor and grew pensive. "Wanna know something. I'm serious. Okay? I'm serious. I'm not making this up. It's all written down in my diary, which I keep locked away at work ... I have this fantasy ... that you and I ... elope ... Yeah, elope. Elope and leave our fake lives behind; drop them the way snakes drop their skins."

And treat your children the way snakes treat their offspring.

"We'd spend the rest of our days loving and taking care of each other." Horton gulped, and wiped his eyes on his shirt-sleeve. He came closer to the desk then, put a hand on Millington's shoulder, and for a while said nothing. "I didn't want to upset you, Millington. I just had to talk to somebody. All I said earlier was to put off telling you what I really came to talk about ... I have dark thoughts, Millington. Dark ... I'll go now." He squeezed Millington's shoulder. "I wasn't joking about wanting to run away with you, or someone like you: someone beautiful, polished, educated, sophisticated, disciplined."

He left then.

Millington felt foolish. Felt he should have asked him to stay and tell him more. That night he dreamed that he was at Horton's house for supper, and when he sat down at the table, Gladys took a shotgun from the pocket of her apron and said: "I'm going to kill you, Millington, and Batey too, as soon as he comes out of the bathroom. You two are vermin! So much for thinking I'm expendable."

"I never said that."

"Shut up!" She nudged closer to the table, and put the nozzle against his temple.

An explosion, which he mistook for the firing of the shotgun, awakened him. It was a thunder peal, and thick raindrops were striking the window pane. His heart harrumphed and he was bathed in sweat. He got up and changed his pyjamas.

Millington was able to run away. Horton couldn't and shouldn't. Barbadian society might have pushed him into becoming a husband against his will. But he's a father and must care for his children until they're adults. The last time they spoke, Horton said he hadn't wanted children, but had them to please Gladys. *Horton, you will have to resolve your situation with Gladys one way or another. Guess you've begun. Your "uncanny" behaviour is the prelude. And after that what? You say, "Leave Gladys out of this. She's the innocent victim here." Can't be done, Horton. Fate traps us all. We're in her cage even before we leave our mothers' wombs.*

17

ABOUT A WEEK following his first Montreal meeting with Gladys, he dreamed that Stilford and he were sitting under an almond tree on Silver Sands Beach. Probably because Horton mentioned him in his letter. Stilford sang in the choir; that's all Millington would have known about him until one Sunday, fourteen months before he left AMC Hastings, he was at the tympanum shaking the hands of the departing congregation. "Reverend," Stilford said, "I love your sermon this morning. I love all your sermons. They urge us to be good people. I like that." There was a gleam in his eye, and a smile dimpled his smooth, umber round face. He seemed primed to prolong the conversation, but chit-chat at such times was awkward, and those who insisted on it, usually the biggest donors, were exasperating, especially when the minister had to hurry off to preach elsewhere. Millington's bane was Gracie Stone. Melvin's was Mrs. Goddard, a wealthy white widow in her eighties, who gave thousands of dollars to Broad Street annually. Leaning on her cane, she'd hold Melvin up for minutes until people began to steupse and Melvin felt forced to accept her offer to drop by her house for tea.

"You should drop in at the manse to see me," Millington said.

"I will. I will."

He came, toting a grey backpack, around 4 p.m. a Friday two weeks later, directly from the community college he was attending, large wet patches at the armpits of his royal blue short sleeve shirt. He walked into the study swishing his hips. Millington hadn't noted that trait before. His black skin-tight jeans drew attention to his body. He was short—a little over five feet—chubby: roly-poly with large haunches, a biggish behind, and the beginnings of a potbelly. He wore wire-rimmed glasses with circular lenses that made him look nerdy. He seemed to be around twenty. He smiled nervously, shyly, at the beginning.

It was tea time, and Doris brought them a pot and two slices of cassava pone.

"So you like my sermons?"

"'Where evil exists we must combat it, beginning with the evil in ourselves. Search for the good in yourself and nurture it,'" Stilford said, his eyes twinkling.

Millington nodded. Felt flattered.

"Rev, to combat evil, we must have the right weapons and the strength."

Millington pictured Samson wielding the jawbone of an ass while around him Philistines fall.

"You're smiling, Rev. Did I say something stupid?"

"No. I had a silly thought."

They sipped tea and engaged in small talk, during which Millington found out that he was in the sciences, wanted to become a medical doctor, but he was thinking of switching to become a lab technician because his mother wanted him to pursue studies that would lead to instant employment; that his mother was Rebecca Sayers, who was a hotel cook and was famous for the tasty cakes sold at the church fairs held at AMC Hastings and AMC Broad Street; and that Horton was his class leader. His aunt, Hannah Bannister, worshipped at AMC Hastings as well. She had issues with her son Beresford and had already sought Millington's help to resolve them.

"Rev, don't you sometimes doubt your faith?"

Millington was a long time answering, and when he did, he rehashed the standard Authentic Methodist response: God was perfect, so imperfect humanity couldn't fully understand God, and humans have to rely on what's revealed in scripture—beliefs he'd already abandoned. "Do you doubt yours?"

"Sometimes." He flashed Millington a nervous grin, and showed white even teeth. All in all, his face was attractive.

"Is that what you wish to talk over with me?"

His eyes seemed to have grown uncommonly large behind the circular lenses. He tilted his chin toward the ceiling, shook his head slowly, and spoke. "No. I came to ask you to help me overcome my sexuality. Reverend, I'm gay ... Why did God make me this way?"

Millington said nothing right away. He waited for his chin to lower. "How else do you feel about your sexuality?"

"Frightened ... I went onto our church's website to see if there was anything on it, but I didn't find anything. I found something on the American Methodist website. They oppose it." He reached for his backpack, opened an outside pocket, and pulled out some printed sheets. "Here's the info I downloaded." He read a few passages about the United Methodist Church's opposition to gay marriage.

Millington stopped him when he began reading the Leviticus passage that Fundamentalists use to justify persecuting, imprisoning, or executing gays. "Some United Methodist ministers support gay marriage, even though the church dithers over it." He remembered Frank Shaefer but didn't mention his name. "You should go to the British Methodist website. You might need a lawyer to help you understand what it says, but somewhere in the verbiage, they seem to be saying that ministers who are comfortable blessing same-sex unions could do so, but not inside the church. They also say that gays and lesbians are welcome in the church but can't hold office unless they're celibate."

"You think the AMC in Barbados would adopt that position? I mean let ministers bless same-sex unions?"

"No."

A long silence.

Millington broke it. "Have you spoken to your mother about it?"

Stilford straightened his shoulders. His eyes seemed ready to pop. "Reverend, are you *crazy*? When they were stoning the gays that came here on the cruise ships, you know what Ma said? 'If I was there I would o' pelt a few rocks too. Why they don't keep their nastiness up there? We's God-fearing people. Why God don't rain down fire 'pon them like he did do 'pon them sodomites in Sodom and Gomorrah?' Rev, I'd have to be out of mind to tell her."

"You heard your mother say that!"

"Every word, Rev. Every single word."

"Well, God does not rain down fire and brimstone on gays, or on anyone, for that matter. Today homosexuality isn't a crime in Israel. That Sodom and Gomorrah story comes from Jewish, Old Testament, scriptures. Would you like me to talk to your mother? She said those things about strangers. You're her flesh and blood. She might see things differently. I'd tell her that you didn't choose to be gay."

He closed his eyes and shook his head vigorously. "Never! I don't want her to know. I'll sooner kill myself than tell her. If you make the mistake and tell her, she'll condemn you too."

Silence.

"Your father, Stilford. Tell me a little about him."

"I don't have a father, Rev. When he had relations with my mother, I wasn't part o' the bargain. I know who he is, but when I pass he in the street, I look the other way."

Silence.

"No, Rev." He was again shaking his head vigorously. "I can't tell my mother. I can't risk Ma turning her back on me. The friends I used to have done abandon me. Ma's the only anchor I have left. The only one." He shook his arms for emphasis … "Even Alva, who was like my brother. Alva got tired o' people asking him which one of us was the hen and which one was the cock. He said: 'Stilly, I don't want nobody pelting me with eggs …'"

"They pelted you with eggs!"

He nodded, his head bowed. "Sent me home dripping and told me, to thank God we're not in Jamaica." He took a deep breath and held it for a while. "I want to be your friend, Stilly. I want to. But you understand, Stilly, don't you?' That's what Alva said to me. Now he turns his head the other way or crosses to the other side of the street when he sees me." He swallowed and tried to hold back tears.

Silence. A long one.

"Have you prayed about it, Stilford?" He was now bent down putting the pages he'd been holding into his backpack.

"Yes, Rev. I pray all the time. But nothing don't change. When I see a good-looking guy, I still want to have sex with he." An intense stare. "I want to be cured, Rev. Get rid o' this curse in me. I want my mother to be proud o' me. I don't want to disgrace her." He stopped talking. Tears were now running down his cheeks. Millington reached for a box of tissues on the bookshelf to his left and put it in front of him. Stilford took one, dabbed his eyes, swallowed, took a deep breath, and continued. "Rev, I'm tired o' men whistling at me and calling me faggot, bullerman, hen, chi-chi-man, fruit, and whatnot. I want to be cured, Rev. I want to be normal." He shook his balled fists and surrendered fully to his sobbing. "Why God had to go and make me this way? Can you tell me that, Rev?" He brought his clenched fists together violently and shook them. The tears were dripping onto his shirt. "Why, Rev? Why?"

Millington waited for his emotions to cool. His impulse was to put his arms around him, to comfort him, but he remembered Wesley's third rule: *Converse sparingly and cautiously with women, particularly with young women.* The rules, in large print, were posted in a 36" X 24" picture frame on the wall across from his desk.

Stilford wiped his eyes and swallowed.

"Stilford, you are part of the body of Christ and deserving of God's love like every other Christian."

"I am?"

"Of course, you are. You reaffirm it each time you take communion."

"I don't take communion, Rev. I'm unclean."

"Oh no!" Millington closed his eyes, lowered his head, and shook it slowly in exasperation, then took a deep breath and stared Stilford in the eye. "Stilford, Christ died for everyone: Gays, straights and the many in-betweens."

Stilford chuckled.

"You think I can be cured, Reverend?" His body hunched forward, his forearms resting on the desk, his fists now unclenched.

While Millington tried to frame an answer in line with Authentic Methodist theology, Stilford, his face turned away, said: "You know, Rev, I been reading 'bout this group in the States called Exodus: gays who turned straight ..."

"Or think they have."

"You mean ... Rev, you don't think gays can become straight?" He stared, bug-eyed. "You don't think that *I* can change?"

Millington had read somewhere that many Exodus members were leaving the movement and dissing it. He decided to take a different tack. "Human physiology is complex. I think the different branches of the Methodist Church are trying to reconcile their traditional beliefs with current knowledge of sexual diversity."

"Unpack that for me, Rev. Please. You mean they're like ... going to accept it?"

"Not right now. In a few years, maybe. I mean gay marriage is now legal in several countries. Some denominations bless same-sex unions."

"Really, Rev? There are churches that do that?"

Millington nodded. "The Lutheran Church in Scandinavia. Some, like the United Church of Canada, go further: they ordain gay and lesbian ministers. The United Church of Canada incorporates the Methodist Church. But those ministers must be celibate or in committed relationships."

"They ordain gay ministers in committed relationships!"

Millington nodded.

Stilford interlaced his fingers and placed his thumbs under his chin, in rapt concentration. "I don't think I would want one o' them guys to be my minister. It doesn't feel right."

After a short silence: "Do you have a boyfriend, Stilford?"

He shook his head.

"Do you engage in casual sex?"

He lowered his head and mumbled, "Yes, once in a while. Once with one o' my tormentors. Screwed me one night, swore he would kill me if I told anyone, and joined with his friends and pelted me with eggs a week later."

"Safe sex, Stilford?"

His head was still lowered. He didn't answer.

"Stilford, with all that we know about HIV, the campaigns by the Ministry of Health, you're *still* taking chances!"

He gave Millington a quick glance, smiled embarrassedly, and turned his head away. "You don't understand, Rev. You can't understand.

The opportunities don't always come when you're equipped and ..." He stopped talking.

"And you can't resist?"

He nodded and bowed his head, guiltily. "Besides ... Never mind."

"*Never mind* what?" Millington knew he shouldn't be pressing him. He'd been instructed not to do that.

"Can't you see, Reverend?" His arms moved up and down with his thumbs pointing to his body.

Millington frowned.

"Rev, I'm black, fat, and ugly. I get the leftovers—if there are leftovers."

"Stilford, you and I see beauty differently. You must get tested for HIV, Stilford. Stay away from dangerous sex."

"Rev, the only way I can do that is if I get healed. Healed, Rev, so I can marry a woman, and be a real man, and make my mother proud o' me. Understand, Rev? I want to be normal. Normal."

He saw Millington's frown before he could erase it.

"Rev, you don't think it's possible? I want you to pray over me and beg God to heal me."

His request was certainly in line with AMC doctrine. "And what will you do if you pray and aren't healed?"

"Kill myself." He said it matter-of-factly.

Millington breathed deeply to mask the shock, then said as serenely as he could: "In that case we shouldn't pray. It's a mystery why a third of all humans experience some degree of same-sex desire. This conversation would have been different if you and I were in Canada or in Western Europe. I want you to understand that it's not all Christians who think homosexuality is wrong and that gays should be punished or, for that matter, killed."

"But it's not what people think, Rev. It's what the bible says. Rev, I read the passages on a website that's against gay marriage and I verified them for myself in the bible. I have them here." He pointed to his backpack.

Stilford had just said in a long-winded way what Melvin had instructed the ministers to say about the gay issue: that Scripture does not support homosexual practice. Melvin had gone further: "Never enter into discussions on the subject." Told to about thirty of them—ministers, lay readers, and church officials, including Horton—from all four circuits. Minutes before that, Melvin had said that British Methodism was morally bankrupt and that the true guardians of Methodism were now found in Africa and the Caribbean.

"Humans wrote the bible, Stilford. God might have inspired them to do so, but there's a lot in it that couldn't have come from God, if God is indeed a loving God." Millington had long stopped believing that God had anything to do with the writing of the bible—unless God was the name for the system of ethical values governing society, which, clearly, was not what Methodists meant. He thought of asking Stilford how he interpreted the story of the woman taken in adultery, but dismissed it. The admonition, "Go, and sin no more" had become problematic for him. His definition of sin was the mistreatment of others. (He has since added the abuse of nature.) When members of his congregation had nothing of importance to tell him they said: "Reverend, you really love that hymn, 'Oh, brother man, fold to thy heart thy brother.'" Indeed. He loves most of Whittier's hymns for their humanistic appeal. "The wrong of man to man inflicts a deeper pain on thee." He would have needed to know why the woman had committed adultery before labelling her act a sin. And why hadn't they brought the man?

Stilford was frowning, and Millington saw that instead of making him feel better about himself, he was confusing him. He didn't know what to say.

The silence continued for several seconds, then Stilford looked at him directly and said: "Sorry to take up so much of your time, Rev"— and stood up.

It didn't feel right that he should leave while crying. But Millington too stood up, put a hand on Stilford's shoulder, and said: "Remember that the God we Authentic Methodists serve is a God of love. Stay away from the Old Testament. Stick to the four gospels. They'll comfort you ... Remember to go and get that test done, and use your head: a short bout of pleasure, Stilford, is not worth death or a life of suffering." Millington closed his eyes, took a deep breath, then repeated: "Go now and may the peace of God, which passes all understanding, keep your heart and mind in the knowledge and love of God, and of His Son, Jesus Christ our Lord. And the blessing of God Almighty, the Father, the Son, and the Holy Spirit be with you, and remain with you always." When Millington opened his eyes he saw a smile on Stilford's tear-stained face. Millington walked him to the gate. There he told him to call upon him any time he felt stressed or needed to talk.

Dusk was falling. Doris had left thirty minutes earlier and had rapped on the door of the study and said she'd left his supper on the table. He returned to his desk and sat down. He remained there for a long time, disgusted that he'd had to clothe his advice in dogma. All he'd wanted to tell Stilford was to try to find a boyfriend whom he respected and who respected him, and build a relationship, and ignore what the rest of society thought. Of course, Stilford couldn't ignore what the rest of society thought. He was, like Neil, already tagged as being gay, which meant that very few men would have allowed themselves to be seen in public with him. Even those who slept with him in secret felt a need to humiliate him in public. Stilford loathed himself. What a burden! Perhaps he'd come expecting to be castigated.

What if he'd told Stilford that he too was attracted to men, that Horton, his class leader, was on the *down low*? In Wesley's day it was the class leader Stilford would have gone to with his problem. Of course, Millington couldn't discuss his case with Horton.

What if Stilford had said to him: *Rev, want to know the truth? I think you're gay too.* Would he have denied it? Would he have said, as he'd said to Horton: "It's none of your business?"

Millington saw him in church a few Sundays after that, and then he disappeared. When Millington asked Sister Sayers about him, she said: "That hard-ears boy o' mine done gone and join them Wesleyan Holiness. I don't understand what he find there that we Authentic Methodists don't got." Millington could have told her that they offered some sort of ministry purported to make gays straight.

For about a year he hadn't seen Stilford, but two months before his resignation, a rainy afternoon, Millington was walking along Broad Street, and a corpulent young man he didn't instantly recognize ran up to him and said in a familiar-sounding voice: "Rev, share your umbrella with muh nuh. You don' remember muh?"

"Stilford!" He'd gained at least fifteen pounds. He now had a double chin. "Your mother told me you left us and joined the Wesleyan Holiness."

He gave an embarrassed grin. "Wasn' 'cause o' you, Rev."

They walked into Cave and Shepherd to wait out the worst of the rain.

"How's your health?"

"I did what you told me, and everything fine."

"And now?"

He removed his fogged-up glasses and wiped them with the tail of his shirt.

"Rev, I done give muh heart to the Lord and beg he to burn out the Old Adam in muh." He stared at Millington sceptically.

"And did the Lord grant your request?"

There was a long pause in which he stared at the floor. "By the grace o' God, I's trying Rev, I's trying."

Millington appreciated his honesty. "I'm sorry you left us."

"Wasn't 'cause o' you, Rev."

That morning he had just finished re-reading *Godless Morality*, in which Richard Holloway argues convincingly that one does not need religion to live a moral life, an argument that brought his boss Rowan Williams to the brink of apoplexy. Millington was tempted to suggest that Stilford read *Godless Morality*, would have even lent or given him his copy. But Stilford might have taken it to his pastor, who'd have taken it to the media and seized the opportunity to lure tottering Methodists into his fold.

"And your studies, Stilford?"

There was a long silence. He gulped, then wiped his eyes with his shirt-sleeve. "I gi'e them up, Rev. Life been stressful. Too stressful, Rev. Too stressful."

Millington nodded his sympathy and felt his own eyes tearing up.

They waited out the rest of the downpour in silence: a good ten minutes. As they exited the store, Millington told him he could still come to see him if he wished to talk about anything.

Stilford nodded.

Of course when he decided to, Millington had already left.

Withholding the name, he told Silas Stilford's story and the advice he'd wanted to give him but couldn't because of AMC doctrine. Silas was the only colleague he could talk these things over with. On some Mondays Horace would drive to Millington's place in Vauxhall, and, sometimes in his car, other times in Millington's, they drove out to Silas's manse at Six Roads, St Phillip. When Millington joined the group, they were five. Membership was by invitation only. Before Millington's time three members had left: Ezra, a rabbi he'd met briefly—a short man with an olive complexion, squarish build, and uncommonly black and thick eyebrows—had wanted the meetings to be reflections on theology; Bennett—an ash-coloured Moravian, a palm-tree of a man (at least seven feet) with large teeth, an orange-size Adam's apple, and a booming bass voice they all envied, had left because Horace had called Christ's resurrection story a primitive Middle-Eastern myth. Sacrilege for Moravians. Christ's resurrection is the foundation of their theology. Millington never found out why Alex, a Presbyterian, had left. He was a pleasant mixed-race Scotsman with corn-flower-blue eyes, who was, in his own words, "unapologetically fond of a glass or two of fine Glaswegian whiskey." Melvin found out about the group and asked why he hadn't been invited to join. Silas told him that "on Sundays we exhort and castigate our parishioners, and on Mondays we laugh at ourselves and skewer our superiors."

"'You fellows aiming to remove my head?'

"'No. Only to get inside it and alter a thing or two.'"

At Silas's place, they talked about everything except God and church dogma. It didn't take Millington long to see why. The third time he attended, the topic of climate change came up. Millington mentioned its effects on St Vincent's Atlantic coast, where the ocean had already moved several feet inland. Claude, a Living Word Church pastor, said the redeemed had nothing to fear, that the rapture would have occurred "before all that prophesied devastation. If you fellows read Revelations under the guidance of the Holy Spirit, you gon know that. That gon be the period of a thousand years when Satan will rule. A new heaven and a new earth gon come right after." His lips were parted in glee and his bulging eyes gleamed. His colleagues' faces were stricken. Claude saw it and nodded. "Not too late for you all to repent."

Horace made a wow-whistle.

"Man, you sound like a misanthrope," Winston said. He was the standard Methodist minister in St Phillip.

"Misanthrope or no misanthrope, I rely on what my bible says and on the guidance of the Holy Spirit."

Two weeks later Claude launched into a tirade after Horace had said that he wanted the Archbishop of Province of the West Indies to be less fuzzy about decriminalizing homosexuality.

"You're in *favour of gay marriage*?" Claude asked, his eyebrows halfway up his forehead, his normally bulging eyes seemingly poised to leave their sockets, his buck teeth exposed in something resembling a snarl, his voice loud as if he were preaching to all of Barbados.

Horace nodded almost imperceptibly.

"You know what homosexuality entails!" Claude continued to shout.

"Love, sex, companionship, caring. Same as heterosexuality," Silas replied.

"Gays are reprobates, man! Go read your bible. Reprobates worthy of death! Paul—the New Testament, I'm not talking about the Old Testament—is clear about that."

"So what!"

"Come on, Claude," Silas said. "You're reading Paul too literally."

"How else should I read him? Like decadent Methodists? You call yourselves *authentic* followers of Wesley! He must be fuming in his grave."

"Yes, let him fume. Over how he's shackled us," Silas answered. "I want him to fume plenty and then a lot more."

"Wrong! Over holiness. Nowadays it's in your doctrine but completely absent in your lives."

"Claude, don't be such a fundamentalist," Winston said. "Take a break, man. Lighten up."

"Claude, Methodists sin in daylight and Living Word members at night. Unless, of course, you guys are no longer human," Silas said.

"Like, masturbation, onanism, Claude," Winston said, "always behind closed doors."

"With porno to spice it up," Horace added, slapping his thighs.

"Bad joke. You should be ashamed of yourselves. I'll stick to Romans I: 25–32. The Apostle Paul says that when humans change the truth of God into a lie, God gives them up unto vile affections. Women forsake the natural for the unnatural; men burn in their lust for each other and do the unseemly. 'Who knowing the judgement of God, that they which commit such things are worthy of death, not only do the same, but have pleasure in them that do them.'"

Millington rolled his eyes and remembered Hennessy's fevered sermon back in 1999 based on this same text.

"You're a queer fellow," Winston said.

Explosive laughter.

"Demons! Heretics! Apostates!" Claude hissed and got up, almost knocking over his balcony chair. He hurried down the stairs and dashed to his car in the manse's parking lot.

"Now, Brother Claude," Horace called out to him just as he was closing the car door, "don't go walking on water."

Claude never returned.

Millington admires Silas. He defied Melvin's edict that they wear their ministerial collar at all times when out in public. Silas was about five-four, compact, and fit. He cycled to most of his Barbadian destinations. He'd joined the Barbadian teachers on the picket line during one of their strikes and worn a button with the Association's logo and the words "support our teachers." Melvin ordered him to take it off. "You are distorting the true nature of the church."

"And you are paraphrasing Hans Küng. I'll remind you that Jesus chased the money changers out of the temple."

"Silas, you are not Jesus. Don't go starting fires. I have better things to do than to put them out."

"You behave like a circus master."

"Yes. And I will crack the whip when I have to."

Silas couldn't have been the sort of subordinate Melvin had been programmed to manage. "It is the universal conviction of the Methodist people that the office of the Christian Ministry depends upon the call of God who bestows the gifts of the Spirit, the grace and the fruit of which indicate those whom He has chosen." Wesley's Medieval nonsense. But Millington's certain that tractability to authority is one of the traits the assessors look for when determining "those whom He has chosen."

Paternity in the Caribbean was another of the topics the quartet of ministers avoided when they met. The one time they hadn't, the blood vessels in Silas's temple pulsed, his skin darkened (he is part Kalinago), and his nose flared; he shook his fists, and thundered: "Men who go around breeding women and not supporting the children should have forced vasectomies. An end has to be put to all this *wastrelitis* that's been afflicting Caribbean men since the time of slavery." He was the youngest of five children, and when he was two, his father abandoned them and their mother and went to live with a woman in Guadeloupe.

At ordination—investiture—along with their sacerdotal robes, AMC ministers bind themselves to Wesley's contract and don his twelve-rule straitjacket, and it's understood that their years in seminary had pared them for a perfect fit. They shall wear it for as long as Methodism lasts, or until the Second Coming. Safe to say that by the time they're ordained, they are, if not arrant brownnosers, at the very least sheep. Not Silas. He was more like a ram that knew the value of its horns. Melvin had every right to fear them.

So it was not at all surprising that Silas was posted to Grenada that same year. Millington had at times wondered if Silas might be gay. But, just before moving to Grenada, he married Liz, a Kalinago from Dominica. Millington couldn't attend the wedding. He had to go to St Vincent to be with Mem while Edward lay dying in hospital.

He's glad that Stilford is still alive. Maybe joining the Wesleyan Holiness made him confront the delusion that he could change his sexuality. Two years ago, when Millington read that Exodus had disbanded and issued an apology to the gay community, he hoped the Barbadian media reported it and that Stilford was aware of it. Horton's letter implies that he might have. Must be buoyed too by the positive news about gay marriage in France, Britain, Ireland, the U.S. Maybe those changes have caused him to revise his outlook. When he gets around to writing Horton, he'll tell him to pass on the contact info Stilford requested.

18

NOW, WITH HINDSIGHT, Millington feels that ETC didn't train them sufficiently for the counselling they were expected to do. Their tutors told them that some "light counselling" came with their vocation, and, in an unstructured way, gave them a few pointers. Most of it by Dr. Sloan, a burly white-looking Bahamian with a nose that formed a massive ridge in his elliptical, puffy face. His sea-green eyes looked unmerciful. He was a head taller than Millington, who is six-one. Millington recalls his hulk leaning against the side of the lectern as he asked each of them to say what they'd do if a parishioner confessed to them that she had been raped when she was a young girl. Millington's hands began sweating then, and a painful spasm seized his neck and held it in a vise. Sloan made the rounds of the class. No one answered. Millington's head was held down, so Sloan couldn't see his face. Millington heard the sounds of students shifting in their seats. When the vise let go and he was able to look up, those sea-green eyes were fixed on him. He faked a smile and Sloan's gaze went elsewhere.

That day Sloan told them that their role was mostly to listen. "Let your parishioners tell their story their way. It's only when you're satisfied that they've said all that they want to say that you should speak: first, words of consolation, followed by advice to seek professional help. Where such services are available, every minister should have a list of them, complete with telephone numbers, addresses, and contact persons. No matter how dire the situation, don't try to play therapist." Sloan didn't say what ministers should do where such services weren't available. He added that in some instances, they might make suggestions that would help the person gain a better understanding of the problem. But in doing so, they were to move cautiously, and if they felt hesitant, they should refrain. At the end of the lecture he handed out a list of "necessary readings" and invited any who had questions or personal problems to visit him in his office. Again, while saying so, his eyes were fixed on Millington. Millington never went to see him.

Four of Millington's cohorts from different denominations left during the first year. CW (Charles-Wesley Joseph) was the only one he had information on. CW was one of four AMCs in their cohort. He held Marxist views that he knew would "flummox the lecturers." When, in the course on the history of Methodism, they learned that Wesley had "deeded" Methodism to future ministers and put them under contract never to alter his teachings, CW shouted: "What! How can such a contract be valid? The man was a tyrant." For a few seconds, no one, tutor or pupil, spoke. Of course, people before and after CW have called Wesley tyrant, despot, Methodist pope, and perhaps worse, but only after they'd completed their training and passed their probation. (Much of an AMC minister's probation is spent studying Wesley's sermons, journals, and letters. It was a dispute over whether or not to continue honouring "the contract" that caused the schism that resulted in the creation of the Authentic Methodist Church in the Caribbean).

CW's initial outburst might have been overlooked, but in their preliminary discussions on the history of Christianity, he chortled and raised his hand, when the tutor mentioned Constantine's vision of the cross emblazoned with the words "By this symbol conquer" positioned above the sun, and the follow-up dream the same night in which Christ purportedly showed him the same sign and commanded him to conquer in its name. "Dr. Menzies, aren't those the words of a warmonger who found Christianity a convenient tool to further his imperial aims?" Menzies batted his eyes several times before saying he'd contemplate the question.

Not long after, on a late Saturday afternoon, Millington was walking on the grounds and heard CW shouting at him from a few metres away. "Samuels, don't you hear me calling you? You're just like our fluxed-up, constipated tutors." CW got out half of a belly laugh and choked back the other half as Dr. Menzies emerged from around the building and stood less than a metre in front of him. The following week the college told CW that his temperament was unsuitable for a ministerial vocation.

CW switched to history and got a PhD in it. At the time of CW's expulsion, his father was an advisor to the government of Antigua and owned an engineering firm with branches in Trinidad and Jamaica. In other words, CW was from a wealthy family.

Two years before Millington fled Barbados, CW was appointed lecturer in Caribbean colonial history at Cave Hill. When he got in contact with Millington, his first statement was: "So you survived the infantilism"—and the second was: "What doth the church require of thee, Reverend Samuels?"

"That I 'do justice and show mercy,'" Millington replied.

"Wrong! To be a parrot and lick arse ... You are too intelligent, *Reverend* Samuels, not to know that God is a personification of feudal fear and cruelty."

Millington froze, felt he should end the call.

"Are you still there?"

"Dr. Joseph, when are you going to grow up?"

"CW. Call me CW. Never, if growing up means repeating foolishness and licking arse."

Millington said nothing, was still thinking he should end the conversation.

"Your Lord," CW said, interspersed with chuckles, "is ... Never mind. Mine is nature and asks that I live in harmony with it. Reverend, of manure we are constituted and manure we shall become."

Millington said nothing.

"Ah, Reverend, still heeding those buffoons at Etcetera and propagating fairy tales ..." He paused for effect, ever the showman. "Methodist authentic doctrine: M-A-D in every sense ... When are you inviting me for tea?"

Millington took a long time answering.

"I see. You're afraid I'll turn you into an atheist? Naw. I won't try to break your theological carapace and be charged with manslaughter. All right then, *I'll* invite *you* to tea. No phony excuse, please. How about next Monday? You ministers are free on Mondays, and I am too."

Reluctantly he agreed to go. It meant skipping the Monday meeting at Silas's. On the way to CW, he debated turning the car around. It was an address on the St. James coast. He'd thought that all lecturers lived in on-campus housing.

Looking almost as boyish as when he was in college and smelling of Brut aftershave, CW met him at the bottom of the stairs leading up to the second floor of a non-descript three-storey cement edifice with a large condos-for-sale sign at the entrance. Stunted cabbage palms with mostly brown fronds, perhaps recently planted, were scattered on the twenty or so feet of lawn fronting the building. CW was wearing a grey oversize T-shirt, beige pyjama-style three-quarter-length slacks, and sandals. His condo was impeccable and simply furnished: a Morris sofa and an armchair and an ordinary rectangular pine dining table with four chairs in the living area. The books, in the second bedroom, were neatly arranged, in alphabetical order and by subject. Millington complimented him on his neatness; he said a cleaning woman came by once a week.

The tea was hot water poured from a stainless-steel kettle on the stove onto tea bags already in the mugs, and the cake was something orange-flavoured that he'd picked up at a bakery. Millington admired his no-frills simplicity. Wouldn't have worked with Doris. Guests must be served with genuine silverware and bone china.

They took the tea on his balcony and sat on two wooden bucket seats on opposite sides of a round white plastic table just large enough to hold the cups and cake plates. About two hundred metres away the sea battered the shore and cooled the breeze that blew onto the balcony. The day was clear, without the grey haze that envelops Barbados on most sunny days. Up to then, CW had said nothing controversial, and Millington began to relax.

"So, Rev, you're still in the con game. When are you going to stop deceiving gullible people?"

Millington turned his face away, pretended to be staring at the sea, and wondered how Claude would respond. Probably throw the hot tea in CW's face and say he'd been inspired by the Holy Ghost.

"At least you're not doing it to get rich."

When Millington looked at him, there was the mischievous glint in his eye that Millington remembered, and he recalled one of CW's tall tales about a town in Alabama where Blacks were forbidden to wear white and suffered from rickets and goitres because it was illegal for them to drink milk and eat salt. His telling it could have been used to make the case for his expulsion from ETC, if the lecturers had over-heard him or if a student had snitched on him. He'd violated Wesley's second rule for ministers—"Be serious. Let your motto be, 'Holiness to the Lord.' Avoid all lightness, jesting, and foolish talking."

"Beware of the lunatic fringe, Rev." CW interrupted Millington's recall, his tone stripped of levity. "They're forever creating cults that draw the credulous. You must know of Jim Jones and David Koresh."

Millington nodded.

"It has always been so and will be so for as long as humanity lasts. Hope you're a wise shepherd to your flock and, to your superintendent, a well-horned ram. Gore him if you have to." He made a butting gesture.

Millington laughed and shook his head slowly. "No hope of changing you."

A grey grackle flew onto the balcony railing. CW broke a few crumbs from the slice of cake on his plate and threw them to it. It gobbled them up quickly interspersed with glances at Millington. CW broke off a few more crumbs and put them in his left palm. "Come," he said to the grackle, and stretched the palm toward it. It stared at his palm agitated but didn't move. "Not coming? Okay. Then nothing more for you now because you're not coming to get it." He turned to Millington. "See, grackles rightly fear you holy men." To the grackle, he said: "Come back later, he'll be gone." The grackle lingered a while longer then flew off. He dropped the crumbs onto the balcony.

"How did your parents react when you were expelled?"

CW cleared his throat and straightened his shoulders. "You figure. They named me Charles Wesley, my older brother John Wesley, and my sister Susanna. One of my maternal uncles is a Methodist minister in Bermuda, my maternal grandmother was the church organist at Wesley Memorial for close to half a century. When I entered ETC, my paternal grandfather was the steward for the St John's-Parham Circuit. I could go on. My family, paternal and maternal, suffers from *Meth-oditis*. I'm the eccentric—and my siblings aren't sheep: John is a surgeon in Baltimore, Susanna is a lawyer in St. Kitts." He paused. "What was your question?"

"The reaction of your parents."

"Oh, yes. When the news reached Daddy, he told Mommy that if I'd been a trifle younger, he'd have given me the licking of my life. Bollocks! Mommy wouldn't have let him. He ordered me to come home right away. In our first discussion, he asked me if I was planning to lease land in Jamaica to grow ganja. I told him, no, that I wanted to study history. He hemmed and hawed about young people who hadn't yet learned to properly wipe their arses wanting to change the world. But before going home I'd already begged Mommy over the phone to work on him. Daddy's ice in her warm hands. Three days later he said to me: 'Are you sure now?' I said yes." CW smiled broadly. "I guess it all worked out. Don't you think?"

Millington nodded. He wanted to hate him. Such cockiness. "I'm sure they're proud of you and you of them."

"Absolutely. Within a week of the publication of both of my books, Daddy read them and got on the phone to me, to praise what he liked and critique what he didn't. He has the knee-jerk reaction that most West Indians have whenever Karl Marx is mentioned. Can't blame them—can you? They repeat what the colonizers, especially the church, have drilled into them. Even paupers fear losing their penury." He chuckled.

Millington envied him his family's wealth. In his teenage years, when church outings and socials came up, Millington said he was busy with schoolwork. His peers were usually fitted out in new or almost-new clothes. Most of them lived in Havre's wealthier districts, around Main Street and Havre's north side; or were the scions of prosperous banana farmers over in Esperance—and probably had fathers who didn't drink or whore away their earnings.

In elementary school, when Jay and Neil, whose mothers were in Canada, came to school with their backpacks and pencils adorned with pictures of red maple leaves, Millington wished he too had relatives in Canada so he'd have stuff like theirs. Teachers were always gentle with Jay and patient with Neil, who pestered them with questions to get their attention. Neil and Jay had a status no one else enjoyed. Robert Charles, Neil's father, was a land surveyor and owned the biggest and most beautiful house on Pasture Road—two-storeys, a stone façade, a front porch adorned with Greek pillars that ran the entire width of the house. It was painted ochre and was about six metres in from the road. Jay's better treatment came also from being Ma Kirton's grandson. Every August she took him and Paul on trips to the other islands, trips that even the teachers couldn't afford. Now Millington knows that Jay was indifferent to clothes and school supplies with pictures of red maple leaves, and would have preferred to have his mother with him in St Vincent.

CW switched to talking about history, and said he was fortunate to have had Sir Hilary Beckles for his thesis supervisor, that the majority of UWI professors were "still garbed in colonial hand-me-downs. I wish Hilary had refused that damn title. It epitomises feudalism and the colonialism that he brilliantly analyses." He stared at Millington, a glint of mischief in his eyes. "Rev, I have bad news for you. After those young men and women have passed through my hands, they won't come to your church. That collection plate's going to be empty." He winked at Millington. "Just kidding. Naw. You fellows get to them before I can, and you immunize them against reason and common sense."

His face clouded over. "Don't take me too seriously. Tut! Tut! Tut!" He shook his head slowly. "History is not the noble discipline I'm making it out to be. It's still mostly conquerors' tales; capitalist loot funds the publishing houses, even the academic presses. Criticize the master class or the so-called master race, and you're told: your tone is wrong, your facts aren't nuanced, your style is wooden. They won't say, we reject your work because it criticizes the institutions that fund our press and we can't risk losing their funds. It's what happened to my third book. It looks at neocolonialism in the English-speaking Caribbean." He stopped speaking for a long while, seemed to be in deep reflection.

"If I had the choice now, I'd study literature. Man, it takes me into the human psyche as nothing else can. Thought initially religion could do that. But I found out just in time that, apart from the poetry in the hymns and scriptures, religion is dogma and formulae and liturgy which I could repeat even in my sleep—a preventive, not an incentive, to look into the psyche. Literature. Eddy Brathwaite—famous Eddy Brathwaite, now he calls himself Kamau—mastered history and after-wards took up literature. Wish I could do the same, and stop writing fucking boring academic papers. Ever read Kamau's poetry? Man, it's poetry like Wynton Marsalis playing his trumpet. Ever heard Wynton play? Kamau goes into all the nooks where colonizers hid the skeletons, and he drags them out for the literate—alas you have to be literate—to see and touch and feel and, for those with imagination, hear. Kamau Edward Anansi Brathwaite!" His eyes blazed and his dark beige cheeks dimpled. A passionate, handsome man, symmetrical in every way: teeth, bone structure … except temperament. Millington's face grew warm as he remembered that back at ETC, CW had figured in one of his wet dreams. He smiled, wondering what CW would say if he told him so now.

CW got up and went into his study. In the lull, Millington stared at the swaying coconut palms lining the shore and listened to the breaking metre-high waves thrashing the St James coast. Cars zoomed along be-hind the condo complex. CW returned with a manuscript. He handed it to Millington and told him to leaf through it. He remained standing and continued talking—and Millington preferred to listen to him—about a novel he'd been working on for years but couldn't finish "because good fiction comes out of long hours of unstructured reflection, and the host of tedious tasks lecturers do exhaust them and leave little energy and time for the imagination to journey or frolic." Millington was about to contradict him, quoting what he'd said about Brathwaite, when he said: "Poets have it a little easier." Finally, he sat down. Quieted.

CW would be an ideal friend for Paul. He's always talking about literature, and loves having Millington by because he's the only one who truly likes listening to him. When Paul begins his literary discourse, Bernard's lips curl, his head droops sideways, and his eyes glaze over. When Bernard's eyes begin to narrow, Millington finds an excuse to leave. Each time Millington visits, Paul loads him down with "books you should read." It's how Millington discovered Raymond Williams, who helped him understand why the Catholic Church destroyed the liberation theology movement in Latin America, and Matthew Arnold's poetry and essays, especially "Function of Criticism at the Present Time." CW is the kind of scholar that Arnold would champion: one who allows for the free play of the mind and privileges truth over pragmatism and political and class allegiances.

Millington goes into Jay's study for the Arnold volume, sits on the sofa-bed there, and re-reads a few of the passages he highlighted: "In spite of all that is said about the absorbing and brutalising influence of our passionate material progress ... man, after he has made himself perfectly comfortable and has now to determine what to do with himself next, may begin to remember that he has a mind, and that the mind may be made the source of great pleasure." From the tone of "Dover Beach," Millington thinks Arnold lived long enough to see such hopes dashed. Today, he'd despair over the swill that passes for culture and the speed with which humans, in the name of progress, are consuming their habitat. "The mass of mankind will never have any ardent zeal for seeing things as they are; very inadequate ideas will satisfy them ... Whoever sets himself to see things as they are will find himself one of a very small circle; but it is only by this small circle resolutely doing its own work that adequate ideas will ever get current at all." *Adequate ideas becoming current? Not a chance if they threaten the superstructure. Liberation theology in Latin America did.* He turns the pages and the title "The Buried Life" catches his attention. He reads it, then closes the volume, puts it down beside him, and wonders how much of his own life he can unearth. How? And afterwards what?

The life of the mind. Paul and CW could pursue it. Ma Kirton valued it and had the money and vision to send Paul to a school that laid the foundation for it. When Paul became disgusted with the banal public-school curriculum he encountered in Montreal, he turned to Jay's college texts.

He doesn't remember much of what he said for the rest of that afternoon he spent with CW. To avoid driving back through St Michael and eastern Christchurch during rush hour, he stayed longer than he'd wanted. When CW's chatter lapsed, Millington went into his study and perused the books there. There were thousands. But it was his collection of more than 200 books on folklore and mythology that attracted Millington. CW came into the room and saw him staring at them. "They taught me a lot about our psychic needs." He waited for Millington's response. There was none. "Bet you don't know that the Greeks thought the gods created human beings for their entertainment? They did a damn good job. From the Abraham-Isaac story and the book of Job it looks like the Judaeo-Christian God did too." When Millington still said nothing, he continued: "That's the trouble with your pinhole theology. Rev, the only way we expand our external and internal vision is to compare and contrast it with others. Poor Rev. Afraid of becoming unmoored from the Nicene Creed."

"I studied world religions," Millington finally said.

"A good start. Hinduism?"

"Yes."

Millington turned away from him and focused on the books under philosophy. And there he saw the volume by Hume that he had already read. He was tempted to tell CW how his reading of Hume had changed his concept of God and was influencing his sermons. But it would have embroiled him in questions about propagating doctrines he no longer believed in. He became fascinated by another title, *Beyond Good and Evil* from the philosophy section. He remembered Sloan trumpeting: "The likes of men like Nietzsche have proclaimed the death of God, but everywhere he's alive and as powerful as he was yesterday, as he is today, and will be tomorrow." Sloan's use of temporal terms felt odd; he'd already told them that God exists outside of time. CW saw him leafing through the book. "Not a bad place to start re-educating yourself. If you promise me you'll read it, I'll let you keep it. I can always pick up a copy when I travel to Europe or North America."

Millington wanted to say, don't you think you're a trifle condescending? But he was CW's guest, and he never forgot Sloan's advice: "Never assume you know how others will react to what you say. Speak carefully or say nothing"—reinforcing more or less what Mem had already taught him. Besides, those who run roughshod over the feelings of others often complain bitterly when their own feelings are under the boot. Around 5 p.m. Millington excused himself and went walking along the beach.

When he got home that evening, he was convinced that he had wasted his life. Charles Wesley Joseph had gone on to exercise his intellect and published two books on Caribbean history, was seeking a publisher for a third, and working on a novel, while Sunday after Sunday he repeated a liturgy forged since the time of Henry VIII, parts of it since the fourth century, if one includes the Nicene Creed. Never mind the New Testament and before that the Torah, most of it compiled around 600 BCE, at a time when the earth was deemed to be flat and the sun to spin around it, and hell was in the bowels of the earth, and heaven above the clouds. That evening his journal entry was on how human destiny is linked to money, temperament, and social conditioning. He recorded for the first time what he remembered from the lecture on Constantine and added that it was hard to envisage Jesus as a warmonger: the Jesus who told the wealthy man to sell all he had and give it to the poor and then come and follow him, the Jesus who told his disciples that they who live by the sword shall die by the sword, the Jesus who advised his followers to seek the kingdom of heaven within themselves—of course, that's assuming that this Jesus ever existed. Tom Harpur argues in *The Pagan Christ*, that he didn't, that he was an allegorical figure. The early church fathers gave Constantine the status of apostle. Why wouldn't they? What they couldn't achieve through martyrdom, prayer, and fasting, he attained through military conquest and tyranny. Another person, someone with a very different temperament, might have turned to conquering his own war lust in order to create the kingdom of heaven within himself, i.e. a serene psyche with no need to impose its will on others and wade in blood to do so. Now Millington would add: But what would religion be if it did not embody and uphold power? Islam and Christianity would have been long extinct. The boast by Buddhists that they never go to war to spread their religion is duplicitous. They fight their religious wars in the guise of ethnicity—Singhalese Buddhist versus Tamil Hindu, Buddhist Burmese versus Rohingya Muslim.

CW and Millington met a few times after that Monday visit, usually for a meal in a restaurant. He should get in touch with him. Phone him tomorrow and tell him of all that's happened since—except, of course, his marriage.

19

MILLINGTON IGNORED SLOAN'S script when he met with Stilford, but followed it to the letter when he met with Stilford's cousin Beresford. He had run into his mother, Hannah Bannister, one day while she was on her lunch break from the shop where she worked on Roebuck Street. She asked him if he would agree "to talk some sense into that wayward boy o' [hers]." Millington said he'd try. She came to see him the following Wednesday to prepare him for the encounter. Millington learned then that she was married but her husband had immigrated to the U.S. and abandoned her and their two children: Monica and Beresford. Beresford, twenty-two, was the younger. Millington had met him before, briefly, at Easter three years earlier, when Hannah had "forced" him and his sister to come to church. Monica had already completed a B. Ed at Cave Hill and was teaching, Hannah said, her eyes lighting up, when she introduced Monica.

Hannah described Beresford as "wutliss and up to no good. Just like he father. Rev, I want you to talk to that boy and pray with him and see if you can turn him around for muh. He heading for destruction with breakneck speed. He don' listen to nobody. When he been little I could o' get he uncle to come cut he backside for muh. If licks could o' change a body, it should o' change him. But like the beatings only make him worser." *They probably had.* "Now he done gone and give two young girls a girl child each. And he ain't lifting a stroke nowhere. I and Monica is the ones that giving those girls a little something to help out. Imagine that, Rev. On top o' providing a roof and three meals a day for this strapping man. And he does eat like a horse. No matter how I cuss he, he does just look 'pon me and grin. Grin like if I's the joker and he's the king."

One of Sloan's necessary reading texts was Edith Clarke's *My Mother Who Fathered Me,* put on the list to make them reflect on the challenges faced by the large number of single-parent mothers they would meet in their congregations. Some of these women, Sloan said, expected ministers to be surrogate fathers. It wasn't lost on them that Anglicans and Catholics call their priests father, and were looked upon as such.

He met with Hannah and Beresford a late Thursday afternoon. Millington's skin tingled when he saw how handsome Beresford had become: a lean almost six-foot body, very dark glass-smooth skin, angular face, aquiline nose, barely visible lips, and eyes that looked like wells of dark light. He wore a black leather cap that was turned backwards, a black, silk skin-tight V-neck T-shirt, and Hugo Boss jeans that hugged his slender frame. Silver studs shone in both ears. A thick gold chain reached half-way down his chest and glowed against his dark skin and the black fabric of his T-shirt. The links in two gold bracelets on his left wrist jingled whenever he moved his arm. Upon entering the study, he gave Millington a grin that was also a glare, and he took Millington's extended hand forcefully, confidently.

After the initial chit-chat with them, Millington became uncomfortable. Beresford noticed and said: "Ma, get lost. You ain't see the minister want to talk to me private?"

"And what you going to tell the Reverend that you don't want muh to hear?" Beresford smiled at her cynically and waved his hand dismissively in the direction of the door. She left the room then.

To all Millington's questions—about his father, his mother, his future—Beresford shrugged or said he didn't know or care. Asked about school, he said he didn't like studying, that he'd got four subjects in CXC, and couldn't get into community college.

"And work?"

"I ain't find a job that gon pay me what I'm worth."

"For example?"

"A hundred grand."

"Many lawyers don't earn that."

He shrugged.

"You think it's fair that your mother should still be paying for your expenses?"

"I didn' ask she to bring me into the world."

"And supporting your children?"

"I don't ask her to."

"But you're not supporting them."

"I didn' tell their mothers to go and get pregnant." He grinned throughout, seemed to know he was exasperating Millington and was relishing it.

"Do you worry about your future?"

"Naw. That going take care o' itself. What gon happen gon happen. I live in the moment."

"And if your mother passes on?"

"I won't starve."

"How's that?"

He grinned. "Let's just like say the Lord will provide ... Rev, there's like lovely ladies: lawyers, bank workers, even a doctor—know what I mean—begging muh, pleading with muh, to move in." He grinned sardonically. "Sugar mommies, Rev. Got it?"

Rev certainly did. "Why did you agree to come and see me?"

His grin got bigger. His eyes turned cold, cynical. "Rev, Ma said to come, so I am here. I live in her house."

"Would you like us to pray about this?"

"If you want to. Won't make no difference to me. They like pay you to do this. Right?"

Millington hesitated for a few seconds, but he asked Hannah to rejoin them. He asked God to enlighten Beresford and to strengthen and comfort Sister Bannister.

As Millington said goodbye to them at the door, Beresford said to his mother: "You satisfy now, Ma? You satisfy?" Deep pain was etched in Hannah's face, and fear and fatigue had reddened her eyes.

Millington spent a long time afterwards reflecting on and writing about her dilemma. To put Beresford out of her house might push him into illicit activity or into becoming a full-time *sweetman*. He had expensive tastes. But keeping him at home was encouraging him to remain dependent, parasitic. In a journal entry he called him a wastrel, a more urbane version of those who hang out on the Anglican Church patio in Havre.

He laughs now, thinking of his own and his mother's dependence on Jay. Gina calls Laurent a parasite. Behind his back of course. Maybe she calls him one too. And says stupid things like: "Some Haitians make [her] want to say [her] dad's from Martinique." One time when she, Jay, and Millington were together, she berated Laurent for abandoning his common-law wife and their two daughters in Haiti "to come here and live off a white man." Jay told her that Laurent was a victim too, that "a lot of people stumble through life and have little or no control over what happens to them. You don't even know if he had a job in Haiti."

"Jay, children are involved. He should pick his ass up and go get a job and send money to support them and the woman whose future he ruined."

"Maybe Tyrone supports the children."

"No. He doesn't. I asked Laurent about it and he stared at the ground and didn't answer me. I felt like grabbing him by the throat and strangling him."

To Millington's inquiries about Beresford, in the eighteen months following the meeting that he remained at AMC Hastings, Hannah would only say: "Same way, Rev. Same way. No change." The last time he asked her, she bit her lip, but the tears came anyway. In his last month at AMC Hastings, he conducted the funeral of the boys' grand-father, Clifford. The last three months of his life, he lived with Hannah, and Millington had gone to her house once each month to give him communion. According to the tributes, Clifford had been a talented carpenter and a devoted family man. Apart from "ford" in the cousins' names, nothing, in character and appearance, linked them. The irony was that Stilford, decent and hardworking, was the one who was per-secuted, while his parasitic, and perhaps sociopathic, cousin wallowed in social approbation.

20

WHEN MILLINGTON RETURNED to Havre after fleeing Barbados, there were days when he felt like a helium balloon at the mercy of the wind. Days when he thought it was wise to accept the Judaeo-Christian God merely on faith, that without Belief and his career, he had become unballasted. Fortunately, they were few, and the act of recording his feelings in his journal, where he could parse them for truth and falsehood, debarbed them.

> *What do I require of myself? What do others require of me? Hope it's no more than basic decency. What's decency? Your behaviour back in Barbados, how do you explain that? Gladys adopted you into her family in a country where you had no relatives. There's a reason the gods punish those who violate the laws of hospitality.*
>
> *Eleven months of unemployment in St Vincent, the last three in penury; now here living off Jay's charity—punishment alright.*

When he applied to study social work at McGill and was summoned for an interview, he thought of the questions he'd be asked, and knew that it might work in his favour if he were able to show a link between his pastoral vocation and social work. The challenge was how to say it. Jay suggested that he talk with Muriel and Emilia; both are social workers in CLSCs, and both had trained at McGill. Muriel and Emilia didn't tell him anything he couldn't have come up with on his own. They were more concerned about his passing the obligatory French certification exam and finding work afterwards, which indeed was a huge focus of the admissions committee.

Back home after the interview, he reflected on the time he'd watched Isaac, Juanita and Percival's two-year-old, die of leukemia. Isaac had come along when they'd already given up on having children. For that very reason they'd named him Isaac. Juanita was forty-one and Percival was forty-four. In the celebration following the baptism (the first baby Millington baptized at AMC Hastings), Juanita had gushed and gushed over the Lord having answered their prayers for a child. Two years later, she asked Millington repeatedly: "Why, Reverend, why? Why did God give him to us and take him back?" Their experience reminded him of the typhus that almost took his life when he was five.

While Isaac was still alive, he prayed with them a lot, not because he thought it would heal Isaac but because it comforted them. He encouraged them to be hopeful while a search was on for a compatible bone-marrow donor. Isaac died before one was found. When Juanita told him that God had punished her for turning Isaac into an idol, he was dumbfounded. She and Percival were university graduates, and Millington had expected their theology to be more nuanced. "Reverend, I didn't see it as worship. Just love. But now I think it was idolatry." She quoted: "'Lo, all these things worketh God oftentimes with man, to bring back his soul from the pit.'"

"You've been reading the book of Job!"

She nodded. "You don't approve!"

He remembered that he'd been instructed not to enter into theological disputes with members of his congregation—and went into default mode. In any case, it was she who had lost her child, and it would have been wrong for him to prescribe how she should be comforted.

Compared to their case, as well as Beresford's and Stilford's, the others, which were mostly about spousal quarrels, seemed minor. No rape or incest victims ever came for counselling. Melvin had a couple, one of whom had to be admitted to Black Rock after she revealed the info to Melvin. Neither Sloan nor Menzies ever mentioned what to do if the perpetrators came for help. Perhaps they felt that perpetrators didn't need counselling or wouldn't seek it.

The committee of three that assessed him for admission to the social work programme never asked him to make any direct connection between his pastoral work and his desire to become a social worker. They wanted to know why he'd left the ministry. He told them that he discovered he was more of a humanist than a dogmatist. When he couldn't enter in September 2014, they understood his reasons and said they'd keep the acceptance open. He'd hoped to get his residence visa in time for September 2015, but it has come a few months late.

The phone's ringing. He reaches over to the desk and picks it up. Paul's cell. He hopes it isn't to talk politics. Paul's on a campaign to get all his acquaintances to switch their support from Mulcair to Trudeau. He says his late friend Bill showed him the value of voting and why he should be politically active. But the call's to invite Jay and Millington to see a film at Concordia University next week. "And remember, this coming Saturday it's my turn to host Les Friends. Be warned: Guícho will be there."

"He's not in Alberta!"

"Nope. Overstayed his time. The airline said he had to buy a new ticket. Austin refused to give him the money. Guícho cussed him out. 'That fucker owes me. Big time. I got him to go fix his teeth, throw out his fucking rags ... Even get a treadmill. Now he looks half decent and wants to ditch me. Fuck him, man. I'm staying here. He'll come crawling.' Next, Guícho visited his mother and cussed her out too. He must be serious about staying because after cussing her he went to the Thrift shop, bought a dress, borrowed high heels from Gina, and went to audition for a drag show at Maddo's."

Millington chuckles. Guícho, with a waist the width of his shoulders, in a dress!

"He's couch surfing. Might knock at your doors. Right now he's staying at Gina's."

"His monk must be happy."

"What monk!" Paul laughs. "Guícho says whatever comes into his head. In high school, he used to tell us he was a descendant of King Solomon and the Queen of Sheba."

"But, Paul, you were there when Carlos told us that he barged into Guícho's cubicle at the sauna one night, and Guícho was on his back, his legs in the air, moaning, *'¡Bendígame, Padre! ¡Bendígame!'* while his monk was ploughing into him."

"Carlos made that up … Guícho tells invented sauna stories about Carlos too … I have to go."

Millington gets up, goes into the living room, stretches, and tries to touch his toes. Would have gone to the gym this morning if he didn't have the appointment with Citizenship and Immigration. Would go this evening if he didn't have to meet with Gladys. Must go tomorrow morning. Without exercise all this anxiety will blow him apart. He sits on the couch.

He should resume work on a manifesto of faith he began to work on last week. Now that he has cut himself loose from dogma that claims immortality for the human soul, he needs to be clear about what he believes and why. Christ reduced the commandments to two: love of God and love of neighbour. He has chucked the God part, replaced it with the life source—whatever sustains life—in other words nature. CW would be pleased to hear this. But he won't capitalize nature. And he won't pray to it. It would be like praying to his own body, for he's part of nature and wholly dependent on it.

All religions make the golden rule their centrepiece. Even Freud, an atheist, saw the admonition to love one's neighbour as oneself as a fundamental ethical ideal. The story of the Good Samaritan was at the core of all Millington's sermons. He hurled the word altruism at his parishioners constantly, until one morning, while he stood at the tympanum shaking the hands of the departing congregation, Sister Beddows, beaming and nodding vigorously under her yellow, flower-studded, umbrella-wide hat, said: "Parson, I 'gree with everything you say. It is all truism." Later at home, he'd reflect on what he truly believed and what he pretended to believe—the Nicene Creed, for example—and excoriate himself in his journal, and wonder whether one could be a hypocrite and a fraud and remain sane.

There are some days, fortunately not many, when he feels like telling Christians and Muslims to toss out their bibles and korans. That the doctrines they promulgate have been used to promote heinous practices, even genocide. On other days he feels like extracting from the bible and koran their many gems of wisdom and their passages that promote peace, universal social justice, and compassion (what can be more beautiful than "Turn your swords into ploughshares!" Though the wolf lying down with the lamb—carnivores turning vegan—would be something of a stretch—); strip them, so to speak, of their chauvinism and superstitions, similar to what Thomas Jefferson did with the King James Bible, and make them more like the *I Ching*, in substance and in size. The humane urge would be his new name for the Holy Ghost. He knows that minds better than his—Bultmann's, for example—have tried to excise the folklore from the gospels but found that without its supernatural apparel, kerygma is spiky and unappealing.

Richard Holloway's account, in *Leaving Alexandria,* of the crisis he found himself in as he prepared for his first Good Friday and Easter services reminded Millington that at every Good Friday service, the choir demanded to sing "When I Survey the Wondrous Cross." Redemption through the shedding of blood repels him; has bothered him since he was six. To remain in the choir's good graces, he conceded. Paul—his intellectual minister—says that in the publishing world, unless you write the type of book that sells well, literary agents and publishers turn up their noses at you. Saleable books. Saleable sermons. Saleable hymns. Saleable selves. One rises or falls, eats or starves, on the vagaries of the religious and other marketplaces.

At ETC, he on occasion sensed that his tutors were uneasy about Christianity's fairy-tale promises and sought for something solid to root it in. Sloan thought he'd found it in Bonhoeffer's Christocentric ethics. Looking back, Millington thinks that only chauvinistic Christians can claim Christianity to be the only fountain of morality. Jefferson can be forgiven for thinking that the system of belief left by Jesus was "the most perfect and sublime that has ever been taught by man." He lauds it for "gathering all mankind into one family, under the bonds of love, charity, peace, common wants, and common aids." Millington doubts he knew about Buddha and Confucius. But for all Jefferson's proclamations of human brotherhood, the wealth he derived from owning slaves was more important than following Christ's precepts.

The tutors lectured. The seminarians took notes. Memorised them. Gave them back. Sometimes in the tutors' own words. Day after day he ingested dogma calculated to flood every crevice of his being until it flowed out of him and ahead of him to fill and cement the ruts and potholes on those metaphysical paths where he'd otherwise stumble. Whoever devised the curriculum must have calculated that after absorbing all that dogma, he'd be incorrigibly reconfigured, that dogma's hand would vise-grip his intellectual and psychic rudders.

He's not guiltless here. When he prepared youngsters for confirmation, he drilled into them notions of God's omniscience, omnipotence, and omnipresence.

What if he could have told his tutors that there was nothing neighbourly in Christianity's martial and colonizing practices? At the time he didn't know enough about the Crusades, the Inquisition, the Thirty Years' War, or the role of the Dutch Reformed Church in establishing and maintaining apartheid in South Africa—with biblical distortions no less ... Facts CW seemed to know. Menzies made the briefest of mentions to the Thirty Years' War in his lectures on the establishment of Protestantism, and, in discussing Methodist liturgy he couldn't avoid mentioning Methodist descent from the Anglican Church. But he never even hinted that Henry VIII's sexual lust caused his break with the Catholic Church. When Father Henderson, the Anglican priest in Havre and an all-out womanizer and father of two out-of-wedlock daughters, heard from Ma Kirton that Millington was interested in becoming a minister, he told Millington that Methodists were "bastard Anglicans," and that he should consider becoming a priest in "a legitimate church."

21

FROM TIME TO time, Millington feels a need to dis Wesley, for his biblical literalism and his despotism, modeled he's sure, on Yahweh's tyranny and Europe's tyrannical governments in Wesley's epoch and on his nonsensical notions about the Holy Ghost's infallibility. He probably felt that the Holy Ghost inspired the contract he imposed on his followers. In any event he felt that his work had been divinely ordained. He wouldn't have prepared that contract without first praying for God's guidance. Even so, Millington admires him because of his compassion and concern for the poor. That part of Methodism Millington would like to keep. But organized religion is like the packages cable companies offer: you must accept their crap channels to get the few channels you'll occasionally watch. Even the so-called liberal United Church of Canada, for almost a decade now, has been pillorying Gretta Vosper for supplanting Christianity with humanism.

Each time Jay and Millington exit the Atwater metro, on their way to visit Paul and Bernard, they pass the itinerants in Cabot Square. Millington wonders how Wesley would have dealt with them. Paul says he talks with them on occasion and that they're mostly Inuit who've left the Arctic unprepared for the harshness of urban living. Millington sees them squatting or standing with outstretched hands at the entrances to metro stations, gives them whatever toonies or loonies he has. So far from home and destitute on a continent that once belonged to their ancestors. Why did they leave? Where do they sleep? No one chooses to be homeless. And certainly not in a country where the cold kills. Do they get enough from begging to meet their needs? Reduced from owning a continent to beggary, to being the detritus of colonial power and greed. Something similar happened to the Caribbean Kalinago, his parents' ancestors.

On a trip Millington took to Belize in 2009 to visit a Garifuna colleague, he'd had to take a pre-dawn express bus from Belize City to Dangriga. While he waited in the bus station, a young woman, emaciated, visibly flat-chested—at first he mistook her for a man— foul-smelling, and trembling vigorously, asked him for money to buy food. Before she finished her first sentence, two guards flanked her and swung their clubs menacingly at her. He gave her ten Belize dollars and told her the Methodist Church might be able to help her. One guard shouted: "Rev"—Millington was wearing his clerical collar—"I should use this"—he swung his truncheon—"on you. People like you cause trash and this crackhead to collect here." The other guard said: "You mustn't call people trash, man. You have children and you don't know how they will turn out."

Back in Barbados, he recorded the incident in his journal and wondered how Wesley would have handled it. Most likely preach an impromptu sermon … *Take up your cross and follow Christ* … But he'd have fed her, and she might have followed and eventually gone off crack. Wesley died a pauper like the mortal Christ—if such a creature ever existed. Today's multimillionaire evangelists must hate Wesley and see Christ's stories about the poor reposing in heaven while the wealthy are being tormented in hell as tales meant to con the poor. Christ instructed his followers not to lay up "treasures on earth, where moth and rust destroy and where thieves break in and steal." Wesley instructed his to, "earn all you can, save all you can, and give all you can"—and to be holy of course. He gave all he could and died a pauper. Most wealthy Christians steal all they can—in bygone years from pagans, today from the vulnerable and powerless—and call their wealth the fruits of righteous living. Jay says his father's favourite phrase was "Love of gold shrivels the soul," but he believed nevertheless that one day God would make him rich. Wish he'd known that, whether or not scripture supports it, cruelty shrivels the soul and cruelty emanates from shrivelled souls.

On the U.S. Thanksgiving holiday two years ago, Vermont Public Radio broadcast an interview with a bishop who'd disguised himself as an itinerant and begged for alms at the entrance to his church. Several church members told him that itinerants weren't welcome on the church's property and threatened to call the police. Later, inside the church, he removed his disguise while the congregation looked on. In his sermon he didn't castigate his parishioners for their lack of empathy. Initially that puzzled Millington. But he later saw it in the light of his own pastoral experience: there are economic concerns a wise clergyman contemplates before upsetting his congregation.

Methodists love to repeat Trevelyan's statement that because of Wesley, Britain was saved from a revolution similar to France's. Millington envisages CW riposting: so, while the French bourgeoisie and peasantry were battling for liberty, equality, and fraternity, Brits were high on religiosity.

Paul related a story of a Black Honduran couple, Roberto and Anna, in their late twenties, that he'd met near the Mexican-Guatemalan border, in 2006. For almost a minute, they'd scrutinized him standing in front of a *tacaría* a stone's throw from Comitán's main bus terminal, before they approached him, and introduced themselves in English. They perked up when he told them he was born in St Vincent. "Anna and I are Garifuna," Roberto said. "Brother, you're one of us; our ancestors are from St Vincent," Anna said. "Can you help us?" She related that they'd tried to smuggle into the U.S. and had been caught and sent back. By the time they made it as far south as Comitán, they'd been stripped of everything of value. They needed to get back to Honduras; could he loan them the money. "Give us your address. We'll send you back your money." He bought them a meal, walked with them to the bus terminal, paid for their bus tickets to Ceiba, Honduras, and gave them fifty dollars. "Honestly, I felt they were cons, and I was certain I'd never hear from them again. I worried that if their story was true, they might not even make it back to Honduras. Every week there were stories in the Guatemalan media about people like them who were put in prison because they couldn't pay off the border police. But at Christmas 2008, I got a card with a Honduran postage stamp from

Anna. She said that Roberto was working at odd jobs when he could find them, and that was why they hadn't yet repaid the money. I replied that I was glad they'd made it back unharmed, and they were to forget about the loan."

Initially Millington didn't know why he found this story touching, but he understood later that what appealed to him was Anna and Roberto's need to hold on to their dignity. Even in their destitution they wouldn't accept that they were merely beggars.

Justice, mercy, compassion, humility, generosity. Those were the themes of his sermons, which he reinforced with Whittier's hymns. A fool's errand. In his first year thirty-two left. Alarmed by the dwindling membership, Melvin pressured him to "tone it down." In a sermon on the ills of materialism he had quoted: "If any man sues you to take away your coat, let him have your cloak too." At the door a member of the choir said: "Now, Rev, I hope you wasn't telling me it's alright to go 'bout naked."

"No, darling," her husband, also a choir member, said, "Reverend didn't say to give away your petticoat and panty too."

Two days after that sermon Harry dropped by the manse to bring Millington some canna-lily rhizomes. A month or so earlier, Millington was walking past his house on his way down to the boardwalk at Hastings and had met Harry trimming a line of red ixora just inside the chain-link fence separating his property from the road. He'd complimented Harry on the blood-red beauty of his ixora and canna lilies, and Harry had promised to give him some of the canna rhizomes.

Millington invited Harry to sit with him on the porch. Harry's around fifty, mixed-race, about five-eleven, completely bald, trim. Has uncommonly long fingers. He played the organ when the regular organist was absent. He never spoke about himself. His bony hands clasped on his lap, he sat cross-legged facing Millington on one of the green plastic chairs on the manse's porch. His hazel eyes twinkling, he said: "By the way, Rev, if I'd had the chance to on Sunday, I'd have told you that the owners of gold and goldmines are who make the rules. The golden rule has never ruled and never will."

His intense stare and deeply creased forehead implied that he was waiting for a reply. Millington eventually said: "Harry, if those with more than enough give some of the excess to the needy, we'd have a less unjust world."

Harry slapped his thighs and guffawed and leaned forward, his cheeks retracting to form three half-moon clefts on both sides of his face. "Rev, I'm talking about giving my cloak to someone who falsely claims my coat! Next, he'll want my bank card and pin ... Rightly so, if I'm such a damn fool. And if I lend to all who want to borrow, I'll soon be begging and sleeping on the street."

He squinted at Millington, who didn't reply. Logic was on Harry's side.

"And about that other sermon you gave us on charity and forgiveness three Sundays ago, are you aiming to put magistrates, the police, prison wardens, a host of civil servants—the entire justice bureaucracy—out of work? Ah, Rev, you'll have a riot on your hands. Vengeance, Rev, that's what people want. The Ministry of Justice should be renamed the ministry of vengeance." He chuckled. "When I was a boy growing up in Oistins, we had a Church-of-Hope neighbour who spoke in tongues when she was at church and at home would drop to her knees and hurl Psalm 109 at anyone who crossed her. Whenever our chickens grovelled in her garden, she bellowed out at my mother: 'May your days be few, may there be none to extend mercy to you, may your posterity be cut off, may your sins not be blotted out.' Know what her name was? Mercy. I'm not kidding. We added Abundant: Abundant Mercy. Ah, Rev, vengeance—not charity, not forgiveness—gets the human heart pumping." He chuckled. "Rev, here's a fact few people know: twelve million Germans—twelve million—fled Eastern Europe at the end of World War II. *They* were the lucky ones ... What would you say, Millington, to those who insist that compassion for the poor breeds parasites?"

Millington thought of Maggie Thatcher, who was raised a Methodist but later became an Anglican, quoting St Paul out of context to justify her social Darwinist government policies: "If a man doesn't work, neither must he eat." In Wesley's epoch, Anglicans sang "God made the high and lowly and ordered their estate." (In Millington's walks through Spanish Town during his ETC days, he'd glance at the belfry of the Anglican Cathedral and chuckle, remembering that its bell was part of the loot Buccaneers brought to Jamaica. They'd stolen it from the Catholic Cathedral in Panama City.) He wanted to ask Harry what he thought of Thatcher's statement, but feared he might have agreed with her.

Instead, he told Harry about Hosannah, a Jehovah's Witness who sometimes came on a Wednesday afternoon to try to convert him. She insisted that poverty was God's punishment to draw sinners to him. When Millington pressed her for proof, she quoted Psalm 84:11: "No good thing will he withhold from them that walk uprightly."

"And if they walk uprightly but are still poor?"

"Ah, Rev, looks is deceiving. God see what you and me can't."

Harry listened intently and nodded while Millington spoke. "Rev," he said, "if you don't know that many people come to church to curry favour with God in the hope of getting those good things—or not lose them where they already have them—then you're in the wrong profession." He squinted in response to the scepticism showing in Millington's face. "Coming to church is the deal they make with God. They reaffirm it on Covenant Sunday, and they expect God to live up to his part."

"And when God doesn't deliver?"

"They leave and join the evangelicals, because, if the Methodist God isn't listening, maybe the evangelical one would. Life is short. Why waste time waiting?" He chuckled.

What he said fitted Juanita and Percival. Less than a year after Isaac's death, they joined the Nazarenes. Millington never lost the feeling that something he did or didn't do had made them leave.

"Rev, most people don't love God. Most people are terrified of God. They all know the story of Job. When trouble befalls them, what do they say? It's God's will."

Millington itched to ask him why *he* came to church. Once, standing on Harry's porch, Millington glanced at his domestic helper moving about in the living room. Harry never invited him beyond his porch. Whenever Gladys had Melvin, who was a widower, and Millington over for supper, she invited Harry as well. One time Harry had felt the need to reciprocate, but he took them to Scampers. If Millington trusted Horton, he would have questioned him about Harry. His life seemed so circumspect. The sort of person the church wanted to be class leaders. He was the circuit steward before Horton. Once Millington invited him to become a class leader; he shook his head slowly and said: "Millington, I don't fancy telling people how to live their lives or what they should believe." Millington didn't push it. AMC Hastings couldn't risk losing him. After Gracie Stone he was their best donor, not someone Millington could risk alienating.

When Harry left his porch that evening, Millington reflected on Mercy, and his thoughts turned to Elijah and Willy. Did he wish for vengeance? Should he forgive them? He knew then—and he knows now—that forgiveness is complex, that wrongs aren't easily pardoned, that there's no easy access to the psyche's excretory mechanism, that the desire for vengeance is as tenacious as those "demons" that inhabited Jestina.

And the disdainful way he and Jay treated Neil Charles. Does Neil remember? Did he come to hate them? They escaped the harassment Neil endured in the schoolyard daily and in the street from the ne'er-do-wells on the Anglican Church patio. His hip-swishing walk and piping voice gave his persecutors the social licence they needed. Does his sudden compassion for Neil come from the fear that he too will be the target of the ne'er-do-wells—for that matter all of Havre and St Vincent—when they learn about his marriage?

Soon after Millington got to Montreal Paul told him about Christian Reconstructionists. Their long-term aim is to rule the U.S. in order to implement the laws of Leviticus, re-establish slavery, and stone gays and adulterers to death. In the interim, where they hold office, they enact measures to deprive governments of the revenue needed for social programmes and overturn laws that empower women and LGBTQ persons. Hosannah would be very much at home among them.

In his first months in Montreal, while he waited for a work permit, he volunteered at a food bank on Thursdays. He stopped when he began taking courses at Concordia on Mondays and Tuesdays and working on Wednesdays and Thursdays. While in the Caribbean, he never imagined there was material poverty in Canada. Vincentians living in Canada brought back barrels of stuff to give away when they made return visits. Here, the poor—some who were once confidently middle-class (fate can indeed be fickle)—come to the food banks neatly dressed, sometimes bringing along smiling bright-eyed children or grandchildren still unmarked—and, hopefully, will never be marked—by poverty. In his walks along Sherbrooke, he sometimes pauses at the Saint-Laurent intersection to watch the squeegee kids—usually gaunt, frail, and tattooed—weaving in and out of waiting cars and scampering away when the light turns green, and worries that they might get run over. Let me earn your charity, their cleaning your windshield says. Same for the itinerants who stand at the Berri bus terminal and hold open the door for you, a gesture you can't fail to appreciate if you're dragging along a heavy suitcase.

The reflex to help others, not just relatives, is encrypted in Jay's DNA. Paul's less so, although his story about Roberto and Anna suggests that he's more generous than Millington first thought. Jay has an especially soft spot for Adrian, a Haitian who begs in a two-block area around Papineau and Sainte-Catherine. They had attended Dawson College together. At college they weren't friends but were familiar enough for Jay to know that he wrote poetry. Jay had forgotten him. Then one cold blustery day, Jay was crossing Sainte-Catherine at Papineau and heard someone calling his name. He turned and saw the caller standing at the door of the McDonald's, smiling and beckoning to him. Jay had seen him begging there several times and given him the odd loonie but had never connected him with Adrian. Jay crossed the street over to him. Adrian grinned, said he was hungry, asked for ten dollars, and gave Jay a long spiel about why the fortunate should help the unfortunate. Jay took out a five-dollar bill from his wallet, but just before handing it to Adrian an elderly white man came onto the scene and handed Adrian a brown paper bag, which he promptly opened, took out a sandwich, and bit into it. He was genuinely hungry. The man—in his eighties, piercing blue eyes, bony, narrow, face wrinkled like a gizzard, a white pigtail reaching to his middle back: aged hippie-type—said to Jay: "See? That's what they need." He pointed to the fast-disappearing sandwich. "Sonny, put that money back in your wallet; he'll spend it on crack. You give them something to eat: something to eat—you understand? That's what you do."

Now when Jay walks by there, depending on the time of the day, he takes Adrian into McDonald's and pays for a meal for him. Once he took him a slice of cake from one he'd baked. Adrian's always clean, wearing sometimes a grey, sometimes a cobalt blue blazer, bell-bottom trousers, and platform shoes—clothes of another era. Someone, hopefully he himself, ensures that he is clean. Has a clean-shaven beige face, neatly trimmed semi-straight hair. A handsome man overall.

Millington asked Jay if Adrian's poetry was any good. Jay said he never read it.

"Ask him if he still writes poetry."

"I won't. Why?"

"It would show that you remember him at a time when he wasn't an itinerant."

"And if he doesn't want to remember?"

Millington thought about that for a few seconds. "You're right. He might not want to." He would like to read Adrian's poems, though he doubts his French would be good enough for him to understand them. Some might be in English. He went to an English CEGEP. They might offer clues about why he became an itinerant.

He suspects that Jay never wonders what's required of him, that he knows what he requires of himself. Paul disagrees with Millington. He says Jay's a conformist, is "more tractable than a sheep dog." And when Paul introduced Millington to "The Buried Life," he said it was as if Matthew Arnold had been writing about Jay. Millington quietly disagreed. Aloud he said: "It's about all of us." How different, he wonders, would Jay's life be if Anna hadn't left Caleb to put an end to those beatings he administered "to save [Jay's] soul from hell"? And, if Jay had grown up on the edge of poverty and without the benefit of the books in Ma Kirton's house?

There were two books in Millington's childhood home: the bible and the Methodist hymnal. Ma Kirton's was the first home in which he saw shelves of books. In the later years, usually during school holidays, when he went there, he met everyone except Aunt Mercy reading. Jay's favourite reading spot was the back porch, which looked out onto the Caribbean Sea. Jay would take him to the book shelves in the spare room and tell him to choose a book and they would go out back and read together.

At nine, Millington went to the Havre library for a brief period. His teacher Miss Robinson had read them a poem that said there was no frigate like a book and told them that reading was a good way to learn about faraway people and places. The next day she took them to the library and made them take out library cards. He found time to read only on Saturdays after his chores were done. He never finished most of the books because the one-week due date was too short. One Saturday Mem took him to a funeral and he couldn't return the books. The next week when he did, Mrs. Bonnette, the librarian, said he had to pay the late fine before he could get any more books. He stopped going to the library and ignored the fine. Christmas came roughly six months later. It was a time when he got new clothes. On Christmas morning, there was no new shirt to put on. He asked Mem why. She said she'd spent the money paying the overdue library fine and the accrued interest because Mrs. Bonnette brought it up constantly at the Women's League meetings. He was angry with Mem. That money had come from his second cousin Roseanne, who was also his godmother. She lived in Curacao. He was born during the evacuation caused by the volcanic eruption in 1979, and it was with her that Mem and he had stayed, in the single room that she rented in Rose Place, until the volcano quieted. Roseanne went to Curacao when Millington was two, and every Christmas she said that part of the money she sent Mem was for him. He hated Mrs. Bonnette. He never returned to the Havre Library. Apart from school work, the only reading he did was the odd article from the copies of *National Geographic* that Jay brought to school.

After Edward's death, Mem told him that Mrs. Bonnette, who seemed to have been the permanent president of Havre's AMC Women's League, had made his unpaid library fine the subject—a case study— of one of her lectures on Susanna Wesley's rules nine and fourteen for raising children: *Never allow a sinful act to go unpunished*, and *Strictly observe all promises*. "Mill, right there, in the presence o' everybody, that woman embarrass me. She ask me, how I going punish you. I tell her I will pay the library fine. She say: 'Good for a start, Sister Samuels. But you have to go further. You have to punish him so he won't do it again.' I tell her I will talk it over with your father."

"Did you?"

"No."

22

THE SATURDAY BEFORE Labour Day, two weeks after the
meeting with Gladys at Paragraphe, Millington took her to the
Botanical Gardens and the Insectarium. By then Jay knew she
was no ordinary member of Millington's ex-congregation.

"How come you didn't invite me along?" Jay said with an embarrassed grin.

"She might want to discuss personal issues with me."

Jay flinched and was silent for a few seconds. "After the gardens,
take her for a good meal at a half decent restaurant. That one we went
to on Duluth would be fine ... You must invite her by for supper."

Millington gave him an are-you-crazy frown.

"You're sure Mathilda hasn't suspected something and told her?"

"How would she know?"

He shrugged. "Montreal's not as big as it seems. Gina and Lionel
are totally out, and they have lots of friends in the West Indian community. Paul and Bernard are out. I am too."

"Our relationship's off the table in my conversations with her ...
She probably knows her husband's gay and was probably attracted
to me."

Jay nodded slowly. "Then shouldn't you be less chummy with her?
... Sorry. I said that badly."

"Come on. She was good to me. Incredibly good. I knew no one
in Barbados when I first got there. She embraced me like a brother.
Mathilda gave you the impression that she knew me, and you saw that
I couldn't even remember her. Well, when Horton's exposed—no

longer if—I want Gladys to continue to see me as a friend. I could help her understand Horton's dilemma. She's understanding. Forgiving."

Jay's eyes widened. "I guess that's your Christian conditioning—programmed to see good in everyone and heaven at the end of every trial." He turned his head away, meaning that he hadn't said all he wanted.

Twenty minutes later, Millington took the metro to McGill College, walked up University, and met Gladys waiting for him on the sidewalk in front of Pollack Hall. She gave him a perfunctory hug. Her eyes were red and puffy. She seemed sleep deprived. She wore khaki shorts, a flowery blouse, and sandals. A brown purse and a light jacket were slung over her left shoulder. "You won't need that," he said, pointing to the jacket. "It will be scorching today. Water's what we'll need." She turned to go back inside. He called out to her: "Running shoes would be better than those sandals and put on a cap." She returned wearing a dark blue cap and azure sneakers. While they were heading downhill to the metro, he asked her what was wrong. She said nothing but paused her step and stared into his face.

"Are you sure you're up to this outing?"

"It's what I need. I'm sleepless worrying about my kids."

He put an arm around her waist. "Everything will be fine. Horton loves his children."

"Yes, but he has never parented them."

"There's Louisa ..."

"She isn't there in the evening and at night. Horton wasn't present much in the evenings either."

"But your mother's there."

"Mommy has her job running a school during the day and on evenings too sometimes. It's too much to have to look after my kids too. Too much to ask a 64-year-old woman. I didn't think through this decision well enough. We can't have everything. It's either or. Not both."

"Gladys, you're torturing yourself needlessly."

Inside the metro station, he bought two bottles of water and put them in his knapsack. When they were seated in the metro car, she said: "I have a message for you and Jay from Mathilda. She would like to get in touch with you both. She said she gave you all her number but you haven't called her ... Why?"

Why... Why? "She's somebody's wife ..." It sounded lame even to him.

"Come on. You're all from back home, same community; you and she went to the same church back in St Vincent."

"Yes, but Jay and I are *guys*. Her husband's white, right?"

She nodded. "What that has to do with giving her a call?"

Millington sang: "Never leave your woman alone with friends around to steal her," from the Ian Tyson song.

She laughed. "Funny I never thought you would steal me. I'm pretty sure Horton never thought so either."

"Gladys, you must understand how jealousy works. When ignorance about race is mixed in ..."

"Meaning?"

"I don't know what I'm talking about."

Silence.

"Mathilda wants you and Jay to come to a party at her house next Saturday ... You're frowning."

"Oh, I was just remembering that I heard Jay say he had to attend some function or the other at his CEGEP." The lie came effortlessly.

"And what about you? You can come."

"He asked me to go with him." Instantly he regretted saying that.

"Millington ... is that ... the truth?"

He felt embarrassed, he said nothing.

"Sorry. I shouldn't have said that. It's the stress I'm under."

He squeezed her hand to reassure her.

She asked him what he thought about the ongoing election campaign, and he said not much, that all three major political parties seemed to be offering eternal happiness. "I'd sooner believe in Florida's fountain of youth."

She chuckled.

"In any event I can't vote. I'm not even a permanent resident."

She was silent for a long while. When she broke it, she spoke about the terrible time Syrians were having. He told her that Jay and his CEGEP colleagues had put together a group to sponsor a Syrian family.

They said not another word until they exited the metro at Pie-IX.

"This outing is on me, and I'm taking you for supper afterwards."

She shook her head vehemently. "No. No. No." As they approached the ticket booth, she said: "You're not paying for me. You can't afford it. You told me you work two days per week—but not what you do. Think I didn't notice?"

"Let me at least pay for your admission. In any event, I'm paying with a debit card."

"Okay, pay with your card and I'll refund you."

He paid and handed her the ticket. She began opening her purse. He put a hand gently on her wrist and shook his head. "It's my pleasure to do this, and I'll be hurt if you insist."

They visited the regular flower beds, chatted about the various flowers, then went on to the specialised gardens, followed by the greenhouse. Finally, to the Insectarium. They came out from there hungry and exhausted just before 5 p.m. They'd only had ice cream and water.

"My supper offer is still on."

"I haven't changed my mind."

When they were seated in the metro, she tapped his wrist gently, stared into his eyes with a big smile, and said: "Thanks, Millington. I needed this to distract me and clear my head."

"And I think you'll enjoy the food at the restaurant we're going to. It's a bring-your-own-booze kind of place but the food's excellent. Whenever Jay and I go ..." *Oops!* He searched for changes in her face. Saw none. "Whenever my roommate and I go, I always order the lamb. It's excellent."

They got off at Berri, took the Montmorency train, exited at Sherbrooke, and walked up to Duluth.

They were given a table in the restaurant's back patio, walled in on two sides and with an overhead arbour of vines. It felt cool and soothing. There were about a dozen diners sitting back there.

When they sat down, she said: "It's a long time since I've been this hungry. If we'd had another yard to walk, I'd have collapsed. And the heat. Never thought it could be this hot in Canada." She removed her cap and began fanning her face. "So you and your roommate—Jay—come here. Often?"

He gestured once in a while.

"You both must get along very well."

He nodded and searched her face for hidden meaning. He saw none. "Yes. Very well. As I've told you, we've been buddies since elementary school."

"And now?"

"Meaning?"

"Meaning ... the friendship lasted. That's what I mean."

The waitress brought the menus. Gladys decided on beef kebabs, he on lamb from the *table d'hôte*. He thought again about her "and now?" *She has heard something. Maybe she knows the full story.* Her head was turned away. When she turned to face him, he saw that the weight she carried in the morning had returned, so he stayed silent.

"Mathilda's party is next Saturday. You think you could disappoint Jay and accompany me to the party? I would feel silly being there alone. Mathilda will be busy with her guests."

He'd put himself in a pickle. Jay would have no trouble going, would even love it. He couldn't suggest Jay instead of himself; she didn't know him. Besides, he'd already said that Jay had an engagement.

"Mathilda would of course like both of you to be there. Can't Jay beg off going to the other event?"

She's giving me a chance to change my story. "I'll ask him." After a pause, "How's Mathilda adjusting to Canada?"

"Not very well. Come visit me and come live with me are two different things. Poor girl."

Silence.

The waitress came with his salad and Gladys's soup: cream of leek. It was steaming and aromatic. He smelled the rosemary in it.

They ate in silence. While they waited for the main course, Gladys said: "It must be difficult to live here without family and with all your friends elsewhere. You're lucky to have Jay."

Have: what does she mean? "Yes, it is difficult. But Mathilda has her husband."

"Maybe, but Edmond's not enough. When she met him in Barbados, she knew nothing about his parents or his culture. Now she's finding out, and she's not thrilled. Her father-in-law makes jokes about Black people and asks her if she worked juju on Edmond."

"Doesn't Edmond rebuke him?"

She shook her head. "Afraid to. That's what Mathilda says."

"How did she meet Edmond?"

"He's an epidemiologist. He did a stint with the HIV-AIDS team at Cave Hill. She was the administrative secretary for the project."

Silence again.

"Come with me to the party." The girlish charm he loves in her was spread over her face.

"Okay, I'll go with you. I'm sure Jay won't mind."

The waitress—smiling, French-Canadian, chestnut hair in a brush cut, tattoo of a crocodile on her left wrist—brought the main course. He put two pieces of lamb on Gladys's plate.

"Then you have to have half of my kebab."

"Not half. Just a taste: one cube."

They ate in silence for the most part. He saw that the more he kept Jay out of the picture, the more intrigued she'd be about their relationship. She read his body language easily and knew when he was lying or uncomfortable. When the waitress asked about the bill, he said: "*Un seulement.*"

"What did you just say to her?"

"I told her separate bills."

"No, you didn't. It's all over your face. You shouldn't do this." Her tone was scolding.

He took a deep breath and said to her: "Don't worry. I'm managing okay."

She squinted, pushed out her lips, but said nothing for a while. "I appreciate it. But I feel awkward putting you in such expense."

He stretched his arm across the table and tapped her hand reassuringly. "It's alright, Gladys. I can manage."

Back home that evening Jay listened nonchalantly. About Mathilda's party, he said: "If you don't want to go, we won't go. The longer you keep her away from meeting me the more curious she'll be. It's easy to tell when you're lying."

In the end none of them went to the party. Alex was hospitalized with food poisoning that Saturday. Millington went to the residence to be with Gladys while she paced the room and waited for news of his condition. Around midnight she got the news she was hoping for: his blood pressure had stabilized and the fever had dropped. When Millington was leaving, she begged him to go to church with her the next day. He accepted, provided she didn't tell the minister anything about him.

She was in a better mood the next morning. He met her waiting for him outside St James United. Alex had spoken to her that morning. She'd even told him that she and Uncle Millington would be going to church together. Len told her that Horton had undercooked the frankfurters he fed them. "'Mommy, I'm not eating anything, not unless it's Louisa or Granny who cooked it.' Millington, I don't feed my family frankfurters."

The minister welcomed a South-Asian and Caucasian female couple worshipping at the church for the first time. Millington glanced at Gladys to see her reaction. Her face told him nothing. He wanted to ask her about it afterwards, but remembered Mem's advice not to wake sleeping dogs.

23

It's been a long wait for this visa. A long wait to swerve back from the wrong turn my life took. Was it really a wrong turn? Did I have choices? Start-overs aren't always good or practical. One bears the weight—and guilt—of waste. No one likes to fail. You never quite dispel the feeling of ineptitude that failure brings. Proverbs like a rolling stone gathers no moss resonate in your head. And you wonder whether such castigations are there to tether you to jobs or relationships you hate. For me, starting over means years of re-training, by tutors younger than I in some cases. The strain would be less if I didn't have to support Mem. But she supported me—and the binding but unwritten contract in the Caribbean obliges me to support her.

NOW WITH THIS visa he hopes it will be easier to find a full-time well-paying job so he can take some of the financial burden off Jay, at the very least pay for his university credits himself.

Given that Jay lacked nothing in Ma Kirton's household, one would have thought he'd be indifferent to poverty. Five days after Millington arrived, he asked him: "How's your mother faring?"

When Millington hesitated to answer, Jay said: "I mean, how's she paying her bills?"

Millington looked away and said he had to go to the bathroom. The eleven months he'd been home without employment wiped out the small sum he'd saved. The day before he reunited with Jay at Aunt Mercy's funeral, he'd spent his last eighty dollars. With Edward's death, no one was working Hollow. Disease had killed off the bananas that had provided a small but steady income throughout Millington's youth. Besides, it's excruciating labour to cultivate and harvest bananas, more than Mem, already stricken with arthritis in both knees, could handle at sixty-three (now sixty-seven). She still gathers from the land what fruits she can and goes into Kingstown to sell them. But vines are smothering the fruit trees. By the time she gets to the nutmeg trees somebody has already gathered them. About the only cash crop she has left is cocoa from twenty trees Edward had planted. After Edward's death thieves from Esperance and Havre stole her goats one by one. The last time she reported the theft to the police sergeant over in Esperance, he looked up from the pad he was scribbling on, grinned, pointed to a big Pyrex bowl on the counter, and said: "See that bowl there? Is to send back to somebody who bring it for me full o' the best goat water I ever taste. If was your goat, it was damn good."

"You didn't answer me," Jay said when Millington returned to the living room and sat beside him on the couch.

"What was your question?"

Jay snorted. "Listen, if our relationship is going to work, you will have to set aside your false pride. We've committed our lives to each other. That means your mother is family."

Millington nodded, slowly, hesitantly.

"It means as well that we share each other's problems. Now please answer my question."

"Not well. Not so well. As I told you when we spoke in St Vincent, I tried to get a job teaching or working in the civil service. But no one wanted to hire me. St Vincent is a Methodist island. Or used to be: Evangelicals rule there now ... Everyone who interviewed me knew that I'd left the AMC ministry. Some, I feel, were deliberately punishing me. But mostly, it was the rumour that I was insane. One interviewer had the temerity to ask me what drugs I had been prescribed."

"When you were in Barbados, how much money did you send your mother?"

Millington turned his head away. Silent. Humiliated.

Jay clasped him tightly and whispered in his ear: "It's alright,

Millington. Your mother is family now. Don't be embarrassed." They stayed like that for close to a minute. "How did you transmit the money when you were in Barbados?"

"By MoneyGram."

The next day Jay was out when Mem phoned from St Vincent and said thanks for the money. For a few seconds Millington thought she was being ironic. One way West Indians awaken guilt in others is to thank them profusely for doing tasks they'd neglected.

"Mill, you there? I say thanks."

"Yes, yes. I'm here."

"I pay Vinlec for the three months I owe them and ..."

Only then did he understand that she wasn't being ironic. "How much did you get?"

"$710. They say that is what three hundred and fifty Canadian give you. The amount right?"

"Yes, I think so."

"God is really good. I glad you get a job. And so fast. When Jay call and tell me 'bout the money, he hang up before I could o' ask what job you doing."

"Mem, I have to go. I'll call you back."

When Jay got in, he said: "I sent your mother $350 ..."

"Yes. I know. She called to say thanks. I wish you'd told me."

"Well, I got so much resistance from you yesterday, I felt I should just go ahead and do it. Your pride won't prevent Vinlec from cutting off her electricity, won't put food in her fridge—if her fridge is working."

The next week Jay set up a bank account in both of their names. For fourteen months—the eleven months he waited for Canadian Immigration to issue him a work permit and the three months of fruitless job hunting—two days before the end of the month, Jay would ask him, while embracing him in bed, just before they fell off to sleep: "Did you send off your mother's money?" At Christmas and Easter, he insisted that Millington add an additional two hundred dollars.

Employers think there's not a great deal you can do with a bachelor of divinity. Some feel that all it qualifies you for is to talk to God. And you know they're mocking you, but you can't tell them your name isn't Mohammed, Jesus Christ, Moses or for that matter Lonnie. There was no mockery when Lonnie, someone Millington had never heard of or met, called on him at the Manse. Lonnie had told Doris it was urgent. And she'd thought he might have come on behalf of some dying person who needed "the Reverend's prayers." When Millington came out to meet him, Lonnie said: "Reverend, Oi get a call from God to get rid o' all tha' is human in muh. And the Holy sp'rit tell muh you's the' one to help muh." Lonnie was neatly dressed: in a navy-blue blazer with brass buttons, a narrow outmoded tie, discoloured white shirt, and grey flannel trousers. He was half-white and definitely emaciated. His blue eyes, wild and roving, never once looked directly at Millington. As Millington tried to formulate an answer to his request, a gruff voice outside said: "He gone in there." Lonnie tried to hide behind Millington. There was a loud knock, followed by Doris and two attendants coming to the door of the study. One of the attendants—a bespectacled, slender, soft-spoken, ebony-black fellow—said in a gentle, non-threatening voice: "Lonnie, come with us. Whoy you always running away? You don' loike we or what? Come, mon. Le' we go." Lonnie complied but said as he was leaving: "Oi coming back—yuh hear, Reverend?—fuh yuh to help muh." Millington spent a long time that day and the next wondering who Lonnie was and why/how he'd lost his mind. He was still sufficiently grounded in Methodism to repeat Bunyan's "There, but for the grace of God go I." Now fate replaces God—and were the choice his, he'd write it with a capital *F*. Maybe all cataclysmic natural phenomena—hurricanes, tornados, earthquakes, tsunamis, forest fires—should be capitalized.

Talking with or to God. He chuckles. Once when he applied for a job as a human resources clerk, Jean-Marie Bisson, the interviewer—a stocky man around Millington's age, with dark brown hair, dark eyes that peered through thick glasses—was more interested in why Millington had left the church. When he said it was over doctrine, Jean-Marie guffawed and said: "So you were defrocked."

Millington shook his head but Jean-Marie's mind seemed already made up. He muttered something in French, turned to Millington, and grinned. Millington's sure he heard *molester* in the jumble of French words. In the end, Jean-Marie said: "I don't think your knowledge of French will be sufficient for the job." He hadn't asked Millington to speak French or questioned him about his knowledge of French. Maybe he'd said something nasty and Millington's non-reaction showed he didn't understand. He can haltingly say what he wants in French, but he doesn't understand when others speak it. He felt the interview was a capricious exercise on Jean-Marie's part, and he resented being part of a joke.

> *Penniless. Dependent. How will I repay Jay? Spent my life doing what others wanted. College tuition and room and board paid for by the church. Would have had to assume all that if I'd switched disciplines. Somebody's always rescuing me. Aunt Pearl when I went to Kingstown secondary. The church and again Aunt Pearl in order for me to attend ETC. The one time I acted on my beliefs it landed me in penury, and Jay had to come to my rescue.*
>
> *Relax, Millington. Jay loves you. What he does for you is out of love.*
>
> *Relax? Not so easy. What do his friends say about me when I'm absent? What do they say directly to him? I hear what they say about Laurent.*

Still, all things considered, he has been lucky. Mem saw his leaving for Canada as God's blessing. When he told her that Jay had sent him a plane ticket to travel to Canada, she said: "You see how merciful God is; you turn your back on him, and in all of it he didn't turn his back on you … It not too late, you know, Mill. With God, it never too late. When you reach Canada, I hope you see the light and go back to the straight and narrow way that leadeth not to destruction. I tell you, Mill, is then—and only then—this millstone that you put around my neck will fall off." No wonder that in his dreams she accuses him of betrayal.

24

USK HAD ALREADY fallen when he arrived at her home from Barbados. She frowned at the three suitcases the taxi driver unloaded. She wore that frown all evening and remained tense and guarded the following day. Day after day, she said to him, "Something not right, Mill. You not telling me the whole story. Why you bring home all these things? You say you didn' bring them to give away, so what you bring them for? And you refuse to tell me how long you staying. What else you hiding in that mortar underneath the pestle?"

"It doesn't matter, Mem. Even if you knew, you couldn't change it."

"What I can't change, Mill? I want to know. The way you talk is like you do something bad in Barbados and you had to run away. I hope you is not another Neil."

"If you see the police coming up the hill, make sure you warn me." He chuckled, then went to her—they were standing at opposite ends of the porch—and put an arm around her. He stared down into her eyes a foot below him. "No, Mem. Put your mind at ease. Nothing like that will happen."

To further allay her fears, he went to church the first two Sundays, but stopped going after that. By the time the second month rolled around she knew what the problem was—the church's version that is. She'd expressed her fears to Reverend Somerset, Hennessy's replacement, about his coming home.

Before she spoke to Somerset, Millington and he had already met twice in Kingstown. Melvin had contacted him straightway and asked him "to talk some sense into that overly idealistic young man." Somerset prodded Millington to say why he'd left, and what aspects of Methodist doctrine he disagreed with. In a relaxed mood, Millington might have played with him, might have asked him if he believed, as Wesley did, that earthquakes were one of God's ways to punish sinners, and what sin or sins the unleashing of the 2004 Boxing Day earthquake/tsunami and the 2010 Haitian earthquake God had been intent on punishing? Would have been interesting to hear what he'd have stammered out. Authentic Methodist doctrine—its public version at any rate—relies on Wesley's pronouncements. It's in them that ministers are supposed to look first for the answers to life's problems. The church leaders say that theology evolves, that even Wesley changed his mind about some things. *No kidding. The God of the Torah did too. Was sorry he'd created humans and even came close to wiping them out altogether. At first he decreed stoning to death the entire family, even the servants, of any man who broke Levitical law but later limited the stoning to the lawbreakers. But don't try to get the AMC to take a stance against Wesley. They're ever mindful of the way he "deeded" the religion to them. "No person or persons whomever shall ... be permitted to preach ... promulgate, or teach any doctrine or practice contrary to what is contained in certain* Notes on the New Testament, *commonly reputed to be the notes of the said John Wesley, and in the first four volumes of sermons commonly reputed to be written and published by him."* His imperative tone and insistence on absolute obedience were no doubt modelled on, "If any man will [follow] me, let him deny himself and take up his cross and follow me—" found in both Luke and Matthew. The man was nothing if not imperious. And do they ever push student ministers to learn those sermons! There was the Wesley Prize that was designed to foster a deeper understanding of the man and his work—more about the work than the man. Seminarians were encouraged to compete for it. One year Millington won it. A huge part of probation was spending time studying those sermons as a prelude to ordination. Bizarre that Authentic and standard Methodists dis fundamentalists. Their doctrines are identical. True, the leadership of the Methodist church doesn't support the death penalty for gays, and Millington doesn't know of any Methodist counterparts to the late Fred Phelps—he's sure there are some in East and West Africa—but

Caribbean Methodists of both camps are unequivocal, even strident, in their opposition to gay rights. Colton Bennet told the Barbadian press that it was madness. In 2002, during Millington's first semester at ETC, AMC and standard Methodists called for a two-day fast to oppose Guyanese legislation on the matter and the Guyanese parliament buckled.

By the time he met with Somerset, Millington had little patience for the bronze-age answers Somerset would have given to his questions about Methodist doctrine. Now Millington imagines him: triple furrows in his brow, tension in his charcoal acne-scarred face, his deep nasal voice, his Dominican accent—saying: "So, Meleengton, you are gay. Have you prayed about eet?" Wesley had already instructed him, on biblical authority no less, that "Sin cannot reign in any that believeth … and any tendency to an unholy desire, he by the grace of God, stifleth in the birth." Anymore stifling, and Millington would have been asphyxiated. Parts of him are yet to decompress, might never decompress.

He and Somerset held both meetings on a restaurant patio across from Heritage Square. When Millington wasn't distracted by the banter of the taxi drivers and food vendors in the square, he listened to Somerset's nasal Dominican droning on about the ministers' puzzlement over Millington's "reckless refusal to seek therapy. That ees not the Methodeest way, Meleengton—not the Methodeest way at all." Read *Godless Morality*, Millington wanted to say. *There you'll find extensive reflections on the issues that made me leave. Read Hume.* But telling him so would have only led to future encounters in which Somerset would have tried to lure him back with "dressed-up detritus of belief." Except for those days when Millington slipped into a deep funk, doctrine wasn't a pressing issue. A job was.

Somerset convinced Mem that if she tried hard, she could get him to recant. As one month turned into three, six, eight, rumours intensified that he'd returned home mentally deranged. Not difficult: it had already happened to Neil. Sister Murray felt that Neil had probably lied about the call to serve God. "Mem, you can fool man but you can't fool God." She probably felt the same way about him but stayed silent not to damage her friendship with Mem. He would have been in trouble had they known why he'd left. In the Vincentian worldview, sane people don't question the existence of God or call themselves atheists; some of his ex-colleagues felt that way too. And so did Mem. Add homosexuality to agnosticism and hell would have turned upside down.

Eventually he had to tell Mem something. He never told her outright that he'd left the ministry, just that he was wondering whether it was the right vocation for him.

"What can be better, Mill, than a life serving God?" she asked, rubbing her hands, her now liver-spotted face, pleated in a deep frown. *Mem, a life that isn't informed by folkloric theology. A life in which I don't feel dehumanized because of my sexuality.* She revered church ministers and was convinced that their vocation outclassed all others. Edward might have been right in thinking that Millington had studied theology to please her.

She remonstrated with him relentlessly, directly quoting or paraphrasing the pat answers found in Methodist hymns: "We have an anchor that keeps the soul / Steadfast and sure while the billows roll," followed by her question: "Where's your anchor, Mill?" The pain in her voice and face became unbearable for him when she said: "You must pray and pray and pray and ask God to put you back on the right track. You not too educated for Satan to trick you. The bible say a little child shall lead them, and truth does come out of the mouths of babes and sucklings. Humble yourself, Mill. Humble yourself." He could only clench his teeth and listen in silence. When he was a boy, she found solace from whatever was bothering her in the singing of those hymns. One of her favourites was Philip Bliss's "Dare to be a Daniel / Dare to stand alone / Dare to have a purpose formed / And Dare to make it known." When Jay hugged her at Aunt Mercy's funeral, he told her that he remembered her singing "... Many giants, tall and strong / Stalking through the land / Headlong to the earth would fall / If met by Daniel's band ..." She was part of Daniel's band. And a Bliss fan: "Hold the Fort" was another of her favourites. For the first few months, whenever she began to sing it, he left the house. She had to believe that

"Victory was nigh." Eventually she caught on to his feelings and sang something else.

His worst experience was the day she called him to sit inside across from her. Most of their conversing was done on the porch, but that day she sat on the living room sofa and he in an armchair across from her. Her bible was open on her lap, and she proceeded to read to him the thirteenth chapter of First Kings. She stumbled over the words, mispronounced many, and it was painful to listen to her. In the text the disobedient prophet is first warned, and is later killed by a lion. Hard to think she believed she could frighten him into returning to the ministry. He wondered if Miss Collins had put her up to it. That was the level of her theology. Mem must have expected her ploy to work, because she sat there looking confident, staring at him while she awaited his response. He glared at her, got up, and went for a long walk. He wished he could have spoken harshly to her, but pity was what he felt. If he could have afforded the rent, he'd have moved out.

Undoubtedly, she was sincere when she said she was relieved to see him leave for Canada—she repeated it again the morning of his departure. The malicious questions she'd had to answer—questions preceded by: "Me hear somebody say—me not telling you who 'cause me don't want to get inna no comess—that your son ... Is not me that say so, you know ... Me selling it just like how me buy it ... Sekay Bekay say that your son ..."—from those intrigued, titillated, or delighted by his plight. By the third month, speculation had taken on the life of fact: the church had dismissed him because he'd become involved with someone's wife (If he'd looked androgynous, like Neil, it would have been someone's husband). He'd fled Barbados because the woman's husband had come looking for him with a gun, and fear for his life had caused him to crack up. Mem did her best to correct their "facts," but instead of listening, they asked her: "What he going do now, Sister Samuels?" She related it all to him, expecting him, no doubt, to say or do something that would prove them wrong. It seemed that she too had begun to believe the speculation: one time she wondered out loud whether Reverend Somerset had told her the whole story.

"No, he hasn't," Millington replied. "He can't tell what he doesn't know."

"What he don't know, Mill?"

"I'm not willing to discuss it with you or him. And I don't want to hear anymore what people are saying about me. Let them believe what they want to believe," he screamed at her. Two hours later he apologized and said that it was because of the stress they were both under.

No wonder Lonnie had wanted to cleanse himself of all that's human. If he had been sane and the occasion permitted, Millington would have told him the story of King Midas. Christian myths foster illusions. He values myths that shatter them.

25

THE SUN'S RAYS splash slantwise on the parquet floor and give off a glare. Not yet far enough west for its rays to reach him on the couch. He gets up and walks into the kitchen and back. He really should have gone to the gym this morning. This meeting with Gladys.

From outside, a few buildings away, comes the rumble of the Tuesday garbage truck. It reminds him that the small income he has comes from sorting recycled garbage. Unpleasant work but life itself is a process of constant decomposing and recomposing. Even the dead and non-living matter needed to create living tissue. Therein are magic and miracle. Contemplate the life of a tree.

The beeping of the garbage truck gets nearer. Guícho thinks he carries no garbage in his soul, yet felt the need to visit his mother and cuss her out. Trouble comes when garbage—the stuff that should definitely be discarded—and the psyche are so entwined that removing it imperils the psyche. Within a period of three months Melvin twice mentioned the woman in his congregation, an ex-elementary school teacher, who went insane after she told him that at thirteen her father had raped her. Emotional shrapnel. Shaking his head, Melvin said: "I have no explanation for it. How can someone go off to teach every day—from all accounts she was an excellent teacher—come to church every Sunday, seem normal in every way, then confess to having been raped by her father twenty-three years earlier, and two weeks later end up at Black Rock and never recover?" He continued shaking his head for a couple of seconds after he'd stopped speaking. You could never accuse him of being uncaring. Millington wonders if Melvin felt he'd in some way contributed to her insanity.

Remember, Millington? You're not supposed to be dwelling on negative matters today. Think about how good Jay has been to you.

"I want you to take an interest in Jay ..." He laughs. *I have, Ma Kirton. Quite an interest. Not sure it's one you'd have wanted. If you were like most people, you'd want to have great-grandchildren—want your lineage to continue. You'd worry too about the persecution gays endure. On the other hand, you were intelligent and thoughtful and would have accepted the argument that there are already more than seven billion of us on a planet that can only successfully accommodate two or three billion. Rumour had it that you and Mercy were lovers. They also said you'd made a pact with the Devil. Even Edward trafficked that nonsense. "Boy, you sure she ain't after your soul, to sell it to the Devil?" he said after the zinnia and sunflowers he'd helped me plant were in full bloom. Mem told him to stop his foolishness. Of course, Ma Kirton, a lot of people envied your diligence, discipline, wealth, and intelligence, and Vincentians have difficulty under-standing and accommodating independent women.*

And, Mem, what will you say when you find out about my marriage? Will you flay me for not continuing your lineage? When the village women brag about their grands and great-grands and look upon you with pity, what will you say? You certainly ran your mouth off on Job and joined with others who dissed Miss Collins, though I've never heard you call her a mule, or say disparaging stuff to her face. Mem, you and I must paddle the rapids we're in; we'll paddle or drown.

He walks to the balcony door just in time to watch the hoisting and emptying of the three garbage dumpsters. The clanking ends and the truck lumbers off to the adjoining complex. Instantly the crows call out to one another—they must have stayed close by—and are flying toward the empty containers to gobble up what they'd missed earlier, before the janitor comes with his broom.

He returns to the living room and sits on the couch.

26

HE SHOULD HAVE begun as early as his first year in Ecumenical Theological College to take a serious look at how indoctrination works, especially when he learned, in an offhand remark by Menzies, that the Crucifixion and Resurrection narratives resembled the fertility myths omnipresent in Mediterranean and Babylonian world-views. Did Christ's resurrection actually occur? The question arose in his mind and was quickly dismissed. Too many great minds before him had accepted it to be historical truth. He was still, in any case, exulting in his belief that God had chosen him to be a minister. In that first year too he had one objective: impressing his tutors. The poor man who'd starved himself to build a house that turns out to be on hollow ground disbelieves the engineer who tells him so; he might even chase him away with a shotgun. It wasn't until his third year that he began to feel uneasy about John Wesley's sermons being templates for his own.

When he got to Montreal and read Karen Armstrong's *The Bible: A Biography*, he had a clear understanding of how the present-day bible evolved. For sure at ETC they plodded through several exegetical tomes on the books of the New and Old Testament, but they weren't books that questioned the veracity of the content or linked it, except in an offhand way, to the folklore and myths of the day. Their tutors had chosen those tomes because the authors were firm believers in the tenets of the Nicene Creed. The books of the Apocrypha were merely mentioned as something they might read if they had the time. The tutors knew they didn't have time. (Millington read the Gospel of Thomas only after he came to Montreal.) A few figures like Arius, Athanasius,

Jerome, Augustine and, most certainly, Constantine received plenty attention. A lot of time was given to the schisms that resulted in the creation and adoption of the Nicene Creed. It took up roughly a third of all the time they spent discussing the history of the early church; another third was given to Methodist doctrine. The topic of the bible as a political document never arose. Expelling independent-minded students like CW ensured they'd never have to deal with the issues off their lists.

Of course, he knows now that people avoid and oppose—sometimes violently—whatever threatens their sense of security, and find rationalisations for their actions and beliefs. He would have been questioning his tutors' ontology and livelihood. Disseminating their religious beliefs was their livelihood. And he wasn't sufficiently informed to challenge them. And there certainly was nothing in the ETC library that resembled Richard Holloway's *Godless Morality* or Gretta Vosper's *With or Without God*, that would have taken his thinking outside the tunnel of Methodist orthodoxy. Until he came, quite accidentally, upon Hume.

Even so, the miracles Christ purportedly performed obsessed him. The casting out of demons especially. He'd lived next door to Jestina, who'd sown terror on Pasture Road and in Havre in general when she became "possessed by multiple demons." Judging from all the broadcast media, including SVGTV, that descended upon Havre the Sunday when Spiritual Baptists from all over St Vincent surrounded the Murrays' house and sang, prayed, beat the walls and the ground with coconut and sago fronds, and sprayed the yard with Dettol and turpentine, in their attempt to exorcise the demons, everyone on Pasture Road, in Havre, and in all of St Vincent believed she was demon-possessed.

The Sunday after they found out about Jestina's demon possession, Mem asked Reverend Hennessy, while he was engaged in the after-service shaking of the congregation's hands, whether there was any likelihood that the demons could leave Jestina and take up residence inside her family. Hennessy looked away for half a second, seemed to be searching for an answer, then said: "You have nothing to fear, Sister Samuels. The Lord builds a fortress around his own." Even so, Mem nailed a horseshoe onto the front door (there was one on Ma Kirton's door too, put there, Jay said, by Aunt Mercy), got a second bible and an extra pair of scissors, and each night placed a bible open at Psalm 125 with the scissors in the shape of a cross on it outside each bedroom door. She sold four goats and bought three silver chains with cross pendants and insisted that Edward and Millington wear them at all times.

It was easy to believe Jestina was demon-possessed. One morning she stood on their porch, which was three metres in from the road, tore off her clothes, and screamed: "Fuck me! Fuck me!" She scratched her sister Janet's face and arms bloody and ripped off Sister Murray's blouse when they tried but failed to get her off the porch and into the house. That same afternoon, she said in the voice of an infant: "Celestina's a witch and a bitch." Next, in the voice of a crone: "Presley, you're a mother-fucker, a pussy eater, and a cock-sucker." The next day, with cackling laughter, she shoved her hands into her dress pocket, pulled out pellets of feces, tossed them at the crowd in the road, and shouted: "Eat this in remembrance of me." The Murrays called on Mem and Edward to help them immobilize her, while Janet, the older sister, a recent graduate from nursing school, gave her an injection. No one witnessing Jestina's acts and hearing those voices coming out of her would have doubted that she was demon-possessed.

A twig of a girl, tomboyish, ginger-coloured with slanted fiery eyes. A brilliant student. She had taken fifth place in the high school entrance exams and had won the Banana Growers' Association Scholarship. Her "demon possession" began a month before she wrote her Cambridge A level exams. In the end, she managed to untie herself one morning and drown herself in the harbour. He'd like to think that it was done in a moment of lucidity in which she chose to defy fate.

Her suicide left Sister Murray distraught. From her conversations with Mem, usually around the anniversary of Jestina's death, Millington gleaned that Sister Murray had consulted Johnny-the-Obeah-Man, and Johnny had told her that the demons had been sent for her by someone who wanted her husband and her land; but, not finding her at home, they'd entered the person they met there, who happened to be Jestina. "My poor child. Let her rest in peace. Mem, why anybody going want to put demons in me? Imagine that! Some woman who want Presley and the few acres o' rocky land my parents leave me! Why people wicked so? Then, Johnny tell me that in a vision he see the person coming out o' my gate with a handful o' dirt. He ask me where I bury Jestina placenta, and I tell him under the mango tree above the house. 'Go right away and dig up all the dirt there and store it under lock and key 'cause all that person need is a handful o' it to finish off Jestina and release the demon-them so they going enter the right person.' Mem, I run all the way from Esperance to here, and I go to the mango tree, and I see where the same spot did done dig up. And I see that I get the message too late. And so said so done: five days later Jestina start tearing off her clothes and blaspheming, and a week after that she take her own life. One thing I know: God don't sleep. He don't sleep at all. Is a good thing I did have the sense to go back to see Johnny. He sell me a charm to wear, and I get one for Presley and one for Janet, else by now them demons might o' already kill me, and the woman, whoever she is—and I got my suspicions—would o' done kill me and bewitch Presley and get my land. Praise God I act quickly and stop her dead in her tracks. Mind you, Johnny did tell me he could o' put back the self-same demon-them in the wretch that send them, but when he tell me the price: one thousand dollars—where a church mouse like me going get a thousand dollars?—I shake my head, and I say I not damning my soul, and I remember that the bible say: 'Vengeance is mine, sayeth the Lord. I will repay.' I trust God to take care o' the wretch in due time. My head going be pon Jesus bosom while she going be roasting in hell."

When Sister Murray went into her house, Mem said to Millington: "But is under the mango tree their dog does always be, digging up the dirt there. I sure is their dog that dig up the ground."

"Mem, did you ask her how much those charms cost?"

She shook her head.

"Who you think she suspects?"

"Angelita. God know Angelita miserable. But she not so evil. She been only joking when she say she going take Presley from Celestina. You see how *jokify* talk can get people in trouble? And as to that tricky Johnny, I sure he does make up them stories he tell people."

To this day, Angelita's many enemies accuse her of putting demons in Jestina.

Johnny-the-Obeah-Man lived somewhere on the outskirts of Esperance. Rumour had it that he routinely danced naked in the cemetery, that men and women dressed in black held mass at his fenced-in compound every full moon, that animals were sacrificed there. Some felt that humans were too. For a while it was thought that he'd sacrificed a twelve-year-old boy; the police had even taken him in for questioning. Not farfetched: every twenty or so years somebody went to prison for committing human sacrifice. Eight days after the boy went missing, a flock of crows led the villagers to the foot of the cliffs towering above Havre. There they found the boy's decaying body. Granules in a plastic bag beside him turned out to be warfarin. The neighbours said his mother and stepfather flogged him constantly. Some felt Johnny was in some way implicated; he sometimes fed the boy, who was last seen alive coming from his compound.

At ETC Millington questioned Sloan, who was the New Testament tutor, about Christ's casting out of demons. John recounts miracle after miracle as he labours to prove that Christ was God in human form. In Reverend Hennessy's prayers on behalf of the sick members of the congregation, he always evoked Christ as a healer of the sick and lame. "Did Christ cast out demons or did he not?" Sloan said believers were to understand these as metaphors. (He might have been defying Wesley there.) "And the angel who came down to trouble the waters, was that a metaphor too?"

"Sort of. You must understand that the revealed word comes to us in the language and beliefs of the time. Any more questions?"

If Millington's classmates noted his fuzzy answer, they didn't show it. And not wanting to stick out, Millington didn't pursue the question further. Now he wonders what would have happened if he'd thrown in a bit of levity: How come there were pigs for the demons to enter? Wasn't the eating of pork a capital offence in Israel at the time? Were pigs raised to provide homes for cast-out demons? And how many demons could one pig hold? But he was a minister in training on a church scholarship, and to keep the scholarship, he had to choose the tenets of the Nicene Creed over logic, or choose logic and be expelled—all of this occurred subconsciously. Not a week went by without the tutors telling them that "religion's truths surpass human metrics." It could have been the college's motto. Sometimes they quoted St Paul: "We see as through a glass, darkly." Sloan habitually repeated that faith was "the telescope through which we see God." And, of course, all Methodist ministers must "observe" and never "mend" the rules that Wesley laid down.

He laughs aloud, remembering Hume's assertion that "the Christian religion not only was at first attended with miracles, but even at this day, cannot be believed by any reasonable person without one." Suppose he'd said that to Sloan?

For the first couple of years at ETC, it was easy to expunge the awareness that there was skulduggery in the theology he was absorbing. It became difficult to ignore after he studied world religions and discovered his preference for Buddhism. Bultmann's *Kergma and Myth* was in the ETC library. He read it and liked the way it stripped Christianity of its superstitions. They'd already laboured through his exegesis of New Testament theology where he on occasion points to Gnostic and Stoic influences but rarely the folkloric. Millington's aware now, based on the books that were not found in ETC's library, that their reading was restricted to those theologians and philosophers like Tillich and Kierkegaard whose views supported mainline Protestant dogma. Not sure he would have read others, given how little time they had for extra reading. Their days were organised rigidly, around dining, lectures, and study periods; little room remained for anything else.

But in his third year, just before he was sent out to Portland for field experience under the supervision of the AMC superintendent there, the students of United Theological College West Indies invited them to participate in a series of symposia held over two days on the topic of theology today. UTCWI taught a theology that was more liberal than ETC's. Their students also spent two years at the University of the West Indies. It was where standard Methodist ministers were trained. Three minivans transported the ETC students from Spanish town early each morning and returned for them in the evening after the rush-hour traffic had died down. During one of the breaks, Millington visited the bookstore and bought John Allegro's *Dead Sea Scrolls* and Richard Wollheim's *Hume on Religion*.

That August he journeyed back from Portland in turmoil. The impact from reading both books was so destabilising that he began to keep a journal, where he could express his feelings without risking expulsion. Contrary to all he had been led to believe, he discovered that Jesus was not unique, and it was quite likely that the Messianic expectations of the Essenes and the Qumram Sect, among others, had been projected onto Jesus when the synoptic gospels were written. It also answered in part a question that has plagued Christian theologians: Why, apart from what's mentioned by Josephus, is there no historical record of Jesus? (And the authenticity of the Josephus document is considered by some to be wholly fraudulent and by most to be partly fraudulent. Sloan had conceded that there might have been some "minor tampering.") The answer: If Jesus existed, he was just another of the crackpots of the day who were executed when they challenged Jewish orthodoxy or threatened Roman rule. A man is crucified, then buried and comes back to life after three days and this feat eludes the chroniclers of the day! Not possible. Moreover, with the thirst and hunger for a messiah that afflicted Israel under Rome's tutelage, how could this man who'd conquered death, thus proving that he was divine, go unnoticed in a society whose single hope was the coming of a messiah? Why did only a handful of Jews buy the story? (The fact of course is that Christianity, which began as merely another ascetic sect, triumphed when the Roman emperor Constantine became a Christian and imposed it on the empire. Seven years after Millington left ETC, in one of his rare conversations with Melvin on the topic of doctrine, he raised the question with him. Melvin's answer: "The Jews were hankering for a warrior messiah, somebody who would conquer the Mediterranean and the near east and make them glow with imperial power. Jesus was what young people nowadays call a wimp.")

At the time of Millington's ordination, he accepted Hume's assertion, which Hume himself, in the persona of Philo sometimes wavered about, that the existence of the universe was the only proof that some sort of divine intelligence existed—the doctrine of the first mover, the understanding that nothing comes from nothing. Pretty much the same argument used by today's theorists of intelligent design. Hume, however, doubted the skilfulness of the maker of the universe, and readily convinced Millington that the artisan's work was seriously flawed. Christians had, of course, already coded a response to that argument in their hymn: "God moves in a mysterious way / His wonders to perform / He plants his footsteps in the sea / and rides upon the storm."

The month before he'd left for Portland, they'd concluded their study of Pauline theology, which is founded in faith, Christ's resurrection, and the incorporation of all Christians into the body of Christ, "which is and shall forever remain the tenets of our gospel," Sloan said. "Reason, which is the atheist's tool, inheres in imperfect humanity and cannot measure God, who is perfection. We come to know God through the faith given to us by the Holy Spirit and divinely ordained scripture." Millington had his doubts. When he learned the word casuistry from Hume, he felt it aptly described what Sloan had said.

Already taciturn, upon his return from Portland, he plunged more deeply into silence. The tutors noticed and were alarmed. They questioned him about it. He told them he was fine. They weren't convinced and tasked Wilbur Spring, his roommate and the only person in college with whom he had a relationship resembling a friendship, with finding out what was bothering him.

After months of agonizing reflection, he concluded that, rationally, no more could be claimed for Christianity beyond its ethical message. He examined his options and saw that there was no point abandoning ETC. He had gone too far. He focused on his one remaining hurdle: completing his trial sermons successfully. Convincing himself that, after ordination, he would structure his ministry along Unitarian lines: following the example of Christ-the-man, humans should cultivate what's good and just in themselves. He was able to pull through in spite of nightmares in which the tutors told him that they knew he was leagued with the Antichrist.

Now he laughs at his naiveté. It's wise—and also foolish—not to know what's lurking on the road ahead. He chuckles remembering a line from Wilbur's trial sermon: "The paths of the flesh are deceptively crooked, and many there be who fall in them and never rise." The sermon was based on a direct citation from Bultmann's *Theology of the New Testament* (which they'd nodded and yawned their way through): "The man who is concerned for himself factually lives in fear, shutting himself up against the future, which is not at his disposal. The man of faith is relieved because in faith he has let anxiety about himself go."

Wilbur's sermon had set Millington thinking of the fellows in Havre, sometimes as many as fifteen, who sat—and still sit—on the Anglican Church patio, playing cards, draughts, and dominoes; flirting with all the women passing by; and castigating those men who were letting down the patriarchy. In 2010, he saw them as wastrels; in 2011, dropouts who understood the illusions hidden in ambition and avoided it. They ate three meals each day, from the labour of their mothers and sisters and those brothers who hadn't given up on toil, and clothed themselves with whatever they bummed from Vincentians visiting from the U.K., the U.S., and Canada. He wonders how Maggie Thatcher would have dealt with them.

Two days after Wilbur, in Millington's own trial sermon, based on Matthew 25, he deliberately veered away from the Pauline scriptures. His text was: "I was hungry and you gave me food, I was thirsty and you gave me something to drink, I was a stranger and you welcomed me, I was naked and you gave me clothing, I was sick and you took care of me, I was in prison and you visited me ..." Years later when he gave a similar sermon, he incorporated James' insistence on works as a correlative of faith and Paul's admonition to the various Christian communities to let their behaviour reflect Christian ideals. What could he have done otherwise? When a person is hungry and must sing for his supper, he sings. And now he wonders if hunger might not have forced him to resume singing had Jay not intervened when he did.

The evening of his ordination, he pledged adherence to Methodist creed and living an ethical life worthy of his calling, then went to his room and dropped heavily onto the armchair at the foot of his bed. Wilbur, who'd been ordained as well, was out celebrating with relatives and friends. Millington had turned down Wilbur's invitation to join them. For a few seconds, he listened to the breeze trilling the leaves of a eucalyptus tree outside his window, to the chirping crickets and a pack of dogs barking in Independence Square, and wished his life were as simple. Visions of careworn Jamaicans followed. Women carrying their bodies like burdens to and from their slum dwellings. And he wished he'd pursued studies that could have benefitted them. Eventually he told himself that many—perhaps most people—labour day after day and year after year in jobs they hate. And so he commanded himself to hoist his boulder and begin the ascent.

Around one a.m.—Wilbur was still out, he sat up in bed, listened to the crickets chirping away, and called out loud to the tree, "They toil not neither do they spin." An owl hooted. He remembered that Haverites believe the hooting of owls, jumbie-birds, foretells death. This time his own living death. He turned on his bedside lamp, took his journal out from his night table, and wrote: *I am trapped.* He couldn't continue writing. His chest heaved and he began to sob.

Wilbur came in about fifteen minutes after he turned off the light. When Millington did fall asleep, somewhere around 3 a.m., he dreamt that he was on the pulpit of Lyndhurst Methodist Church about to deliver a sermon, and cackling laughter exploded from the back of the nave. The laughter grew more and more thunderous while the congregation fled as if the church were on fire. Next, he was at Hollow and Edward, Elijah, and Willy were shouting "Liar! Liar, Liar" and moving slowly toward him. He awakened then and found that he was trembling. The dream resumed when he again fell asleep. This time it was Elijah telling him in the presence of Reverend Hennessy: "What I did to you was done to me. Bet you never thought of that."

27

ONCE, WHILE HE was walking down Pasture Road to Main Street, a bitty fellow with a swollen tummy and unusually bright eyes, aged around eight, stood on a low bank bordering the road and called out to him: "Mr. Reverend, you is a crazy-man for true?" He replied: "Sonny, I don't know, but others think so." Neil rarely came beyond the gate of his father's house whenever he accosted Millington. He'd run from the porch to the gate as soon as he spied him descending Pasture Road. If Flora, Neil's stepmother, saw him, she'd yell to him to return to the porch and he'd obey.

It pained Millington that his godchildren, ten- and eleven-year-olds, avoided him. The year before, when he'd come for Edward's funeral, all six had come to visit him.

Mem got the harassment he was spared. Got it raw. He wished it could have been otherwise. She has her own private burdens, which he learned about when he was sixteen. From the time he was nine it had puzzled him that no one spoke of his other maternal grandfather. He and Mem were in the outdoor kitchen—the indoor one was five years away—and a heavy rain was pounding the kitchen's tin roof. She was fanning the smoking fire with breadfruit leaves, trying to create a blaze under the pot; her eyes were tearing. He asked her what was her father's name. Staring fixedly at the kitchen floor, she said: "I don' know. Mammy never tell me who he is. I couldn' question her 'bout him 'cause she would start to tremble and her eyes would get wild. The last time I bring it up was early one morning. She shout at me: 'I already tell you I don' want to talk 'bout it. Stop questioning me!' And she clam

213

up for the whole day. Millington, I suspect a lot o' things and they is not nice."

"And you didn't think about asking your uncle, Roseanne's father?"

"Fred. Uncle Fred." She shook her head slowly. "In the end I been 'fraid to find out. And Uncle Fred die young before I couldo' ask him. One thing I know, it ain't Gramps who is my father 'cause he been in Aruba, and I too white-looking to be his child. The one thing I can say is that some white man been my father, 'cause if you remember, your Grama Emma been a black-skin woman."

A long silence followed. She broke it. "My family didn' have a easy life. Not easy at all. Was like if God sentence we to grow arrowroot 'pon rockstone without rain. When Gramps come home from Aruba and buy this house spot and the land at Hollow, we moved down here from Sandy Bay. I been six years old. This road was a dirt track at the time and most of the land round here been empty. Our first house had two rooms, but the same year Gramps die, he put on the addition. It finish just before he die. One month before I get married to Edward, Mammy find out she had cancer o' the womb. Is that what kill her when it come back in her liver nine years later ... Edward did plan to take me to Sandy Bay to live after he marry me. I tell him: 'Edward I not marrying you if I have to leave Mammy alone here sick.' I was already twenty-eight, past me prime, but I didn' care. We compromise. He agree to stay here and so I marry him ... It been a hard life, Mill, a hard life, but like the hymn say: 'We will understand it better by and by.'"

Throughout childhood, he'd always felt there was something missing in his parents' marriage, though at the time he couldn't express it. Following his father's death, he realized that his conversation with Mem about her father had taken place some nine or ten years after she and Edward had stopped having sex. It occurs to him now that he'd never once heard Edward compliment or thank her for anything.

He has contemplated various ways of telling Mem that he's married to Jay: over the phone, writing to her about it ... There's no good way to deliver bad news. And this will be beyond bad. *Jay would be angry with me if he knows I'm calling our marriage bad news. Well, if he looks at it objectively, it's bad for him too—for different reasons.* He wonders if the result of the gay-marriage referendum in Ireland has had any impact on Vincentians or on Mem. Does she even know about it? *Mem, you'll be at the centre of a firestorm if the news about Jay and me trickles into Havre.* He envisages Miss Collins calling out to her from the road, loud, so all of Pasture Road could hear: "Sister Samuels, I hear from good sources that Millington and Jay get married. You know anything 'bout it? ... Surely the coming of the Lord is at hand." Somebody like Ma Kirton could handle that. Not Mem.

Yes, he must return to Havre and tell her himself; it mustn't get there before him. Borrow the money from Jay and go. Get Mem to dispel all that demonizing foolishness she has absorbed. How will he do that? She too heard Hennessy's excoriations of gays back in 1999. Can he face her alone? Would Aunt Pearl go with him? Aunt Pearl would have sway in areas where he wouldn't. Would he be able to make Mem understand that parents don't own their children? West Indians have trouble understanding that. Pearl could educate Mem about same-sex reality in the U.S. and elsewhere and offer comfort and support in the first few days when the blow would be most painful. He hopes she can accompany him. He'll offer to pay her fare. Borrow the money from Jay.

At least he won't have to deal with Edward. One less burden. How would Edward have reacted? Maybe he'd value Felix more. His rum-drinking cronies would have teased or pitied him for being the father of ... What word would they have used? Millington envisages Edward blaming Mem, putting it all on church-going. Elijah, and Willy had gleefully savoured—or pretended to savour—the details of the beating Jack and Brady got and the burning down of Brady's house. Elijah said: "No surprise them boys turn out bullers. Boy children that grow up without fathers, you can never tell how they going turn out." What if Millington had said to him then, in Mem's, Presley's and Edward's presence: *"Godfather, what caused you and Willy to become bullermen?"*

Edward was silent during that discussion about Brady and Jack. What did his silence mean? Then again, he was for the most part always silent. *Why did he say a year later that I needed a girlfriend to cure me of religion?* "Train up a child in the way in which he ought to grow, and when he's old he won't depart from it." He imagines the fingers wagged in the faces of the poor Old Testament mothers whose sons had just been stoned to death. He visualizes Miss Collins doing the same to Mem while lamenting that killing Millington is no longer lawful.

Elijah and Willy. He shouldn't hate them. They're already dead. Did somebody abuse them too? Willy was a member of the Wesleyan Holiness Church and was often singing, praying, and testifying with them up at the crossroad. He himself lived alone two houses above the crossroad. His left thumb was missing. It was rumoured that in his early twenties he'd worked in Florida as a cane cutter and had deliberately chopped it off to get the insurance money, which he used to buy twelve acres of Laird's unwanted rock-strewn land. He lived off the produce from that land. Edward, Willy, Presley, and Joey Brown (Zeppie's older brother) formed a mutual-aid farming group, called a compere partnership; they along with Mem, Sister Murray, and Joey's wife Zelda took turns working on one another's farms.

Everyone in Havre knew that long before Willy abandoned the Anglicans to join the Pilgrim Holiness (the name before it changed to Wesleyan Holiness), his wife Lydia, a woman of South Asian ancestry, who lived in Barrouallie, had left him. She'd become a Jehovah's Witness, and had expected him to become one too; when he refused, she told him she wouldn't be "yoked to an unbeliever," and quoted Luke 14:26: "If any man come to me, and hate not his father, and mother, and wife and children, and brethren, and sisters, and his own life also, he cannot be my disciple." Lydia and he had no children. During Millington's childhood and adolescence she was often in Havre, in people's yards and on their porches, urging them to become Jehovah's Witnesses. Now he wonders if Lydia's conversion was a subconscious decision to resolve a conscious problem.

Miss Collins hurled Luke 14:26 at the ne'er-do-wells who offered constantly to rescue her from spinsterhood, so she wouldn't "go back to God the way she'd been born." They told her: "The scripture you quoting say *man*. It don't say woman. You is a man, Miss Collins?" And she'd reply: "Man or no man, it going take a real man, not no half-man or quarter-man like you all, to find out."

Mem and Sister Murray had many a belly laugh at her expense, and offered many opinions on her nephew, Godfrey, and his wife, Josephine. Like Miss Collins, they were Adventists. Josephine's parents had forced her to marry Godfrey. He had a "good job" with Vinlec, was an only child, and his parents owned several acres of good land and one of the best houses in Havre's North side. But Josephine refused to have sex with Godfrey. Guffawing, the ne'er-do-wells shouted at Godfrey from the Anglican Church patio: "Godfrey, man, is true Josephine not giving you any? Man, she is your wife. Hold her down and take it." To Josephine, they said: "Girl, why you don' like to fuck? It sweet, you know. Try it. It sweet can't done."

One Saturday while Sister Murray and Mem were picking peas from the pigeon-pea shrubs they'd planted along the fence separating both properties, Josephine walked past on her way to the Adventist Church over in Esperance. As soon as she was out of earshot, Sister Murray said: "Mem, is not only the ways o' God that pass human understanding, the ways o' people too. Now take that one that just walk by here. Mem, you remember that woman over in Chateaubelair that did have a voice like a man, and used to swing axe like a man—stronger than plenty man too? Mem, you don't remember her? … She did get married. They say her parents force her to, just like this one that just gone by here. But within months she leave her husband, and everybody been puzzled. And then when she in she fifties, she had a operation for fibroids and the doctors find a *tolo* and balls inside her."

Mem said nothing.

Josephine taught at Father Crowley's. She had a roundish face, ebony skin, a trim, well-proportioned body, and a pleasant contralto voice. Nothing in her physical appearance hinted of sexual ambiguity.

Sister Murray continued: "Then again it got women that only go with women. I hear plenty o' them live in town."

"Celestina, that not the same. The bible say in plain language: 'Choose ye this day whom ye will serve.' Them woman choose to serve Satan."

"I not certain 'bout that, Mem. I not certain 'bout that at all. The trouble Jestina had with them demons open my eyes. God know we did beat that child; we beat that girl—my heart hurt me just to think 'bout it—to drive them demons out. But was Jestina who been feeling the blows, not the demons-them ... After Jestina dead, I say, Celestina, don't you pass judgement 'pon nobody."

"Celestina, lemme ask you this—you sound like you know every-thing—how the lesbian-them does do it? I hear some o' them women got *tolo*."

"Don't ask me, Mem. Go ask them."

"You remember George from Troumaca? ... He tell me that one time he had a girlfriend up in Georgetown that he had to run from. He could o' never get her to sleep at his house. One night he get her drunk, and when she fall asleep, he find out that she have a tolo nearly the size o' he own. George say to me: 'Mem, when the girl wake, nothing there. Nothing at all! It normal-normal. Is the strangest thing I ever see. She beg me not to tell anybody. And I promise she. Afterward she go way to Trinidad and turn lesbian.'"

Sister Murray didn't answer.

"Have to be that them-woman got tolo, 'cause me have eyes and me have common sense, and me know a mortar ain't no use without a pestle."

Josephine eventually went to live in Tortola.

He crosses his fingers and hopes Sister Murray would help Mem see reason when she finds out about Jay and him. Wouldn't surprise him if Mem were to think that Jay has a vagina that comes out at night.

"If any man come to me, and hate not his father, and mother, and wife and children, and brethren, and sisters, and his own life also, he cannot be my disciple." His own life too! Is there a cause that's worth someone's life? Martin Luther King, Mahatma Gandhi, and Nelson Mandela would say yes: living in freedom and dignity. Mem would probably say her faith. She often sang: "Faith of our fathers living still ... How sweet would be their children's faith, if they like them could die for thee."

One time, Jay showed him a thin collection of poems that he'd picked up at a yard sale. The author, Rueben François, had set himself on fire on a downtown street sometime back in the 1970s. That Tunisian fellow who self-immolated and sparked the Arab Spring did it, the media said, to highlight the plight of unemployed and underemployed young people like himself. At ETC, Menzies mentioned Tibetan and Vietnamese Buddhists who self-immolated to protest injustice, along with Dietrich Bonhoeffer, who justified setting aside his ethical beliefs for a greater good: the assassination of Hitler.

Less than a month after Jay had shown him Rueben's poems, he read about Charles Moore, the United Methodist minister who set himself on fire to draw attention to the mistreatment of African Americans, LGBTQ folk, and capital punishment in the U.S. For a few minutes the image of a human figure ablaze left Millington frozen. In the end he saw that, through Christ's crucifixion, Christianity was linked to excruciating suffering, and that martyrdom was a feature of all religions, but couldn't see how Moore's ending his life so excruciatingly would bring about the changes he wanted. To justify his act, he cited Bonhoeffer's execution for his role in a failed plot to assassinate Hitler.

Why did Rueben set himself on fire? Millington goes into the study and takes the thin volume from the bookshelf and goes to sit at the dining table. Did Rueben encounter injustice here, the sort that drove him to self-hate and suicide? The poems are certainly full of disillusionment: politicians are liars and hypocrites; businessmen are lying racist capitalists, murderers and vipers; clergymen are beasts that support the wealthy and powerful; orgasms are empty. Perhaps he was insane. The poems are rife with paranoia. Perhaps existential protest drove him to immolate: that *to-live-or-not-to-live* question that tortures so many. And he chose Schopenhauer's answer over Camus'. But setting himself ablaze!

A searing pain in his gut. He glances at his watch. 2:17. Apart from toast and peanut butter and a cup of tea he had this morning, he hasn't eaten since. He heads to the kitchen. Regarding funerals, Melvin used to say: "Eat before you bawl." You bawl better with a full belly.

There's food in the fridge from Friday, including quinoa, which Jay loves. Paul says Jay was a better cook than their mother. He marinades his chicken in a melange of lemon juice, ginger, cardamom, rosemary, and fennel. He cooks his rice with vegetables, enough so that he never has to add water. Millington puts some of the food onto a plate and into the microwave, takes a few sprigs of coriander—Jay introduced him to it—and watercress and a tomato from the fridge and prepares a salad.

He eats standing at the kitchen counter, washes the plate and cutlery, and goes to lie on the couch. He hopes Jay's flight is on time and he resists the temptation to call his cell.

28

A CLICK IN the lock awakens him. He gets up and meets Jay removing his backpack and windbreaker at the door. Jay looks tired. His frown lines are deep. They hug.

"Congratulations, Mr. Newly-minted Immigrant." Jay squeezes Millington's body tightly to his. "This was a *long* wait. When Ma applied for us to come here, it took her six months, but that was 1997, under a government with a friendlier immigration policy ... We should celebrate this. Do something you really like."

"We have tickets to see the play that's on at Centaur next Saturday. That's enough."

"Are you sure?" He releases Millington and stares into his eyes.

Millington nods.

"I'm *hungry*. I should have texted you when I got to the airport and told you to reheat some food for me. Rushed to board the plane. Didn't eat anything on it." Recently he had a flare-up of his irritable bowel syndrome and had to take prednisone. The doctors don't know what's causing it.

From the kitchen, where Millington's dishing quinoa, chicken, and vegetables onto a plate, he asks how the conference went.

"Half and half. There were some good presentations, but our panel was a flop. The first panelist went over by ten minutes, the second by almost as much. There wasn't even time for me to finish."

"No wonder you came in frowning and exhausted."

Millington opens the microwave to put the food in and discovers a cup of tea he doesn't remember putting in it. While putting a place mat and cutlery on the table, he notices Jay seated on the couch and staring into space.

Jay gets up and comes to the table, still with his preoccupied look. Millington puts the food on the table and returns to the kitchen and puts the tea to reheat before joining Jay at the table. Jay's lips are pursed and he still has that faraway look.

"The behaviour of those panelists seems to have upset you."

He shakes his head, picks up the cutlery, and begins to slice the chicken breast. "No. It's not that. Paul texted me just as I was boarding the plane to tell me that Laurent spent last night in police custody and Tyrone's right arm's in a cast. It happened last night."

"How come?"

"Seems Laurent caught Gao, the janitor in the condo complex, in bed with Tyrone. Gina got Laurent out on bail this morning. For the time being he's staying at the Y."

A long silence.

"Lionel would have joined them," Millington says.

Jay frowns disapprovingly at him.

"How come Tyrone called the police this time?"

"He didn't. Gao did. Laurent blocked the door with his body and beat them with the pole of a floor lamp ... You've seen Gao ... in his janitor overalls milling around in the foyer of their building: a squat, muscular, bow-legged fellow, around thirty. Togolese."

Millington stares at the food getting cold. He taps the table. Jay shudders as if awakened suddenly, looks down at the plate, and picks up the cutlery.

"Another thing: Jonathan was at the conference. He came to my session and waited outside the door afterwards to talk to me. I didn't expect to meet him there; his name wasn't on the conference programme ... He's on the editorial board of the journal that the association publishes. Meeting him like that ... I told you how he vomited in the bathroom when I told him that you and I were getting married. The way he stormed out of here ... This is the first time I've seen or spoken to him since. Around the time of our fallout he'd submitted his application for tenure at UQAM, so I asked him how that went. He said he got it, and I congratulated him. I told him to give me a call. He said he would. Then he dashed off to a meeting and I to a session that had already started."

Millington says nothing but feels his palms moistening. He gets up and reaches for the plate to reheat the food, but Jay stays his hand and resumes eating. Millington goes for his tea and sits again. About Jonathan he knows only what Jay and Paul have told him ... Jay probably sees their marriage now as a case of, "What can't be cured must be endured." The enduring might well be what's causing his irritable bowel syndrome. July 1997 to February 2012, fourteen years and nine months, that's how long they hadn't seen each other. And then they meet briefly at Aunt Mercy's funeral, and things move along at cosmic speed. A life-altering decision made too quickly.

Jay says: "We have to find out if Laurent needs help. Gina will do her best, though she's angry with him, but we can't put it all on her. I'll call Lionel and see what we can do."

"I hope he's already taken out citizenship."

"No. He failed the exam."

Jay finishes his meal, washes the dishes, plugs the kettle in, and makes a cup of tea, which he takes into the study and says he has a class to prepare for.

While Jay works in his study, Millington sits at the dining table for the hour or so remaining before he heads off to meet Gladys. He mulls over a statement by one of Paul's characters: "Even when food looks like trash, hunger obliges you to eat it." If he were Bernard, that would make him nervous. Bernard's Tutsi nose, that marked him for death in 1994, and the piercing stare in his deep-sunk eyes were what grabbed Millington's attention the first time he saw him. It was quickly followed by his skeletal frame and birdlike neck. How can anyone be so skinny? Probably burns up his calories dealing with the aftermath of the Rwanda genocide, and loses his appetite when it overwhelms him. Paul says that when the memories overwhelm, he isolates himself in the room he uses as a studio and listens to Corneille.

Jay said that Paul met Bernard at a party at Lionel's house at a time when Paul was still dealing with his meningioma; Paul had gone to the party hoping to seduce Lionel. Jay thinks Paul still wants to. Probably true. He can't keep his eyes off Lionel when Les Friends meet. A case maybe of like attracting like. There's a transparency to Paul that Millington admires and envies. Lionel's transparent too. Loathsomely so. They're both curious with a sort of blithe nonchalance—in contrast to Bernard's glumness. Paul calls himself an Epicurean and goes to excessive lengths to explain that being Epicurean doesn't mean a promiscuous abandonment to pleasure. Lionel's a *coureur de bobettes*. Gina's term. "Men," he says ad nauseam, "are there to be sampled, a whole world of them," his arms spread wide as if to enclose all men. "A rich banquet. *Riche en hostie.*" A smack of the lips. "Join the feast, guys. Dine." And he shakes his arms emphatically to emphasize the point. "Show me a truly monogamous man, and I'll show you a liar. Africans are wrong about a lot of things, but not on this one. Guys, Puritans chain themselves with monogamy to please God, not their wives, and certainly not themselves. But even they unlock the chain when they think no one's watching. Remember Eliot Spitzer?" In a half-drunken moment, he told Tyrone: "You're lucky we're not elephants. You wouldn't stand a chance with Laurent."

"Naw," Paul said. "With those muscles Marc-André would be the winner."

"*Je veux pas moi.* Leave me out of this," Marc-André answered, his eyes a flaming blue, his face a deep pink.

"Ya! Ya! Who're you kidding?" Lionel said.

Jay's somewhat taciturn—Millington completely so—when they're with Les Friends. Carlos thinks their marriage is *lo más aburrido del mundo* (the most boring in the world). It probably is. In this latest episode of the Laurent-Tyrone saga, Lionel must be calling Laurent a fool.

Millington visualizes Hennessy—in his white soutane and purple surplice, his dark eyes flashing, perched on the altar that's awash in the tinted light coming in through the panes of stained glass windows on all three sides—incorporating Lionel's statements into his sermons, and shaking his fists. "They're hedonists. Their only goal is pleasure. We cannot—we will not—let Europe and America turn our sons and daughters into sodomites and put our children in the snares of pedophiles." A boiler-plate sermon they'd all been ordered to preach. Silas told him that in 2002, when the Barbadian legislature was debating whether or not to repeal anti-same-sex legislation, the circuit superintendents sent out a directive for all the ministers to preach against altering the law.

What would Millington say to Hennessy today? What would Hennessy say to him? *I became a minister in that church. Incredible! If that's not a case of selling your soul, what is? "He that hateth his life shall find it."* Bull! How could he have been so confused? What if Jay had remained in St Vincent and showed that he desired him? Would he have had a reason to lust after holiness? In Horton's attempts to bed him, would the outcome have been different if Horton had been single?

Mem and Edward. Bernard and Paul. Laurent and Tyrone. Gladys and Horton. Gina and Emilia. Carlos and Marc-André. He and Jay. Couples. Behind their façades all couples have their problems. Enormous ones sometimes. And you don't tamper with the façade. You know too that relationships fizzle when the pain partners cause exceeds the pleasure they offer. Even so you're puzzled that some couples endure what sometimes seems unbearable. Lynette and Twine. And, until now, Tyrone and Laurent. No surprise if those two get back together. Ginette, a work colleague, constantly tells the six of them who work in sorting that her relationships have a maximum shelf-life of five years. "After that I get tired o' looking at the same stale body, the same *quéquette,* the predictable sex play. I need freshness, surprise, and thrills to make me wriggle. This body: it's a garden. Needs fresh manure. *Régulièrement. Oui messiers.*" She's the only woman on the team, a wisp of a woman with chestnut hair and sad-looking brown eyes. Jean-Guy, another team member, is always trying to bed her. "I'm under contract," she tells him, grinning. "And you're the type who'll jump off a bridge if your woman tells you she's tired of cream cheese and wants to taste the neighbour's chocolate cake." He wonders if what she says is true, whether she's another Guícho. Mem used to say: "Unless you see it with your own eyes, don't believe it." Sometimes you shouldn't, even when you see it, as was the case with Jestina.

Jay and he got each other. Maybe they shouldn't have. Jonathan didn't get Jay and probably saw all the time he'd invested in him as a waste. Is he angry that Jay didn't *put out* when he expected him to? Was this a case of friendship without the hoped-for benefits? In this materialistic society everyone's conditioned to think *quid pro quo.* Pro for my quid.

Marriage. The night before he boarded the Air Canada plane in Barbados, he recorded the excitement and fear he was feeling at the thought that in thirty-two hours he would be in Jay's arms. He was apprehensive about Canada's cold and finding employment. He sat on his bed and recalled the moment when he first became aware that he was sexually attracted to Jay. Jay was thirteen. He was fourteen. Kingstown Secondary had organized a hike to the volcano from the windward side. An Easter Monday. The bus took them through the broadest expanse of flat lands he'd ever seen in St Vincent to about two kilometres from the foothills of the volcanic crater. They walked along a road lined by bamboo and cluttered with roots until they got to Riverbed, a bowl-like formation in a gorge of grey rock issuing from the summit lodging the crater. From there they scaled an almost perpendicular slope. The day was cloudy. The summit was buried in damp mist, and they couldn't see the volcanic crater. It was cold up there. Ma Kirton made Jay carry a thick beige sweater. She was from that part of the island and knew it would be cold on the summit. When they were sure the mist wouldn't lift, they returned to Riverbed. Hundreds of people were there sitting around their picnic baskets. There was music, but he couldn't get into the holiday spirit.

On their way back to Havre, they stopped at Georgetown. Mr. Squires and Mrs. Morrison, the teachers chaperoning them, gave them three hours to wander around. Jay and he went to a fair on the Anglican Church grounds. Jay bought pound cake, sorrel, and *toulum* for both of them. He asked Jay to show him where his father lived. Jay said it was too far to walk, but he pointed out the building where they'd once lived upstairs and his father had conducted church services downstairs. They walked along the beach bordering the cricket ground. Millington was spellbound by the roughness of the Atlantic; its three-metre waves struck the shore with the sound of exploding dynamite. In the quick after-tow pebbles rattled menacingly. When the breeze gusted, he felt the ocean spray on his face, neck, and arms, which were already white in spots where the spray had dried. Jay said that people swam in the Atlantic, and fishermen went out into it in just their canoes. While Jay spoke his back was turned to the ocean, and the beams coming from the sun perched above the mountains to the west turned his eyes into pools of amber. A warm feeling filled Millington and he got an erection and became afraid and embarrassed. Twenty-two years ago. Of course a year later … *Not that. Not now.*

As regards their marriage he was over-optimistic and, in matters of psychology and trauma, naïve, even though in his last year as a minister, following what Mem had told him about her and Edward's marriage, he'd begun to see marriage differently. Also, in his role as minister, he'd observe the frolicking on the wedding day and wonder whether the marriage would last, whether each partner would have unrealistic expectations of the other, whether each would or could accommodate the other's flaws and needs. Especially after children came. From the women who came to him to be comforted, before or after separation, he knew that some of the earlier marriages hadn't survived. In one case it was because of the burden of caring for a child with spina bifida; the husband hadn't counted on "wasting" his youth that way. Some twenty or more women consulted him about their problems, but apart from Horton and Stilford (he doesn't include Beresford; he was coerced into coming), only one man came. He'd come, he said, because of a sermon Millington had preached about the perils of dishonesty. He related that his parents had forced him to marry a mixed-race woman whom he'd impregnated, but she'd lost the pregnancy after they got married. He was twenty-eight and his wife twenty-seven, and he'd held off having children because in truth he didn't love his wife. The woman he loved was still unmarried and would marry him if he left his wife. "What should I do about it, Rev?" Millington told him he should resolve the situation one way or the other as soon as possible. Two weeks later his wife came to see Millington and the story was, as he suspected, more complex. The other woman was in fact his mistress and she was pregnant for him. His wife was contemplating ending the marriage and wanted Millington's opinion. He told her she should, provided that she felt certain it was the right decision, and she should discuss the matter frankly with her husband. Their marriage ended.

Will my marriage last? More important: should it last? Doesn't Jay deserve more than I can offer? When he told Jay he wasn't sure Ma Kirton would want them to be together, did Jay understand that he meant more than class? From her journals, it's clear that she wouldn't have put up with an inadequate husband any longer than her economic circumstances forced her to. She'd predicted that Caleb's fundamentalist beliefs would turn Anna's marriage into a nightmare, had advised against marrying him, and had later intervened to end it. Does Jay regret turning down Jonathan's marriage proposal? From what he's said, Jonathan's a decent fellow. Over-possessive and earnest but decent. *He wouldn't be the burden that I am, that's for sure. He grew up in liberal Canada where homosexuality was legal before he was born. He even discussed his love for Jay with his mother. Imagine me trying to do that with Mem. Paul's sure Ma Kirton would have approved of Jay and me being married. Can't blame him for being gullible. Came here when he was eleven. Never experienced the wounding homophobia that West Indians dispense mindlessly.*

On days when these thoughts are heaviest, he longs for a simpler life, and his childhood wish to be Catholic returns. He could have been a monk. Guícho's monk is fantasy, but Millington used to wonder if he flagellated himself after his nights at the sauna and whether the rest of the monastic community knew about his bawdy encounters, or whether they too gratified the flesh. There's a Boccaccio story, which Paul, with glowing eyes, recounted to him, about a group of nuns who turned their gardener into a sexual handyman and paid him handsomely for his services. Now there's an author who knew a thing or two about public masks, private practices, and the body's tyrannical imperatives. All of a piece with the Gnostics, ascetics who sometimes tumbled into outrageous debauchery.

29

JAY'S IN DEEP concentration in front of his computer screen when Millington goes to tell him he's heading off to meet Gladys. The screensaver is on, so his concentration isn't on his work.

He meets Gladys standing at the bookstore entrance. Her head is covered by the hood of a royal blue sweater the front of which is visible beneath her partially buttoned winter coat. She smiles when she sees him, but it doesn't hide the dark circles under her eyes, probably from the six hours of classes she has on Tuesdays. She orders coffee for both of them. He declines her offer of something to munch on. For herself she orders rusk like the last time.

They sit at the front, quite near to the door. He asks how Alex and Len are doing, and she says alright.

"Has Horton's cooking improved?"

She chuckles. "I'll have to see the result to believe it."

They spend the next fifteen minutes chatting about her professors, her classmates, and bland cafeteria food. The pauses are long, and she fills them with fidgeting. He tells her that he got his permanent resident visa today. A glow comes into her eyes, and the look of fatigue briefly disappears.

"I'm so happy for you. The weight must have taken its toll."

"My roommate has been quite supportive. Jay's as good a friend to me as you were back in Barbados."

"Thanks. No need to exaggerate what I did."

The conversation lapses, and for several seconds she frowns and seems to be staring at the table top. He's tempted to ask what's bothering her and why she needs to see him so urgently, but his ministerial conditioning warns him not to.

Frowning, she looks up at him. "Millington, I'm worried. Looks like I'll have to give up my studies and go back home." She looks away and puts her hands on her lap. "Mommy has been trying to tell me something." She stops talking and glances at a group of loud-talking McGill students waiting to place their orders. "It's like Mommy's preparing me for bad news. 'Things will change when you return home.'

"'What things?'

"'Not in my place to say.'

"She always beats around the bush. 'Should I come home?' I ask her.

"'No, it's not at that point yet.'

"'Then why all these insinuations? Do they have anything to do with Len and Alex?'

"'No,' she says.

"'With you and Daddy?'

"'No.'

"'Well that only leaves Horton.'

"'And you.'

"'Why don't you just come out and tell me?'

"'I can't because it's only a hunch, and I might be wrong. I'm sometimes wrong and you enjoy letting me know.'

"Millington, what you think? Should I go home?"

"I'll trust your mother. If it were something disastrous, she or one of your friends would have told you. Bad news travels fast. I don't think your Batey's misbehaving."

"How would *you* know?"

He affects a blank stare and hopes his face isn't betraying him. "Intuition. That's all. Horton loves you and his children too much to do anything stupid."

She smiles, tight-lipped, before answering. "You're saying that Barbadian men who take up mistresses don't love their wives and children! Come with another explanation, Millington."

He takes a deep breath; his attempt at reassurance isn't working.

She sips her coffee and stares into the space ahead of her for a few seconds. "You've heard of the seven-year itch, right?"

"Yeah."

"Horton and I are into our eleventh year—of marriage, that is. We dated twelve years before that. I was slim and trim then. Don't you see how matronly I look now? If he's been holding back that itch for four years it would be driving him crazy now."

He remembers Ginette's statement and suppresses a chuckle. "Gladys. Please."

"It's true, Millington. For men these things are important. I've been promising to remove some of this weight from the time I began putting it on, but instead I keep adding."

He wants to say that she's exaggerating, that if her assertions were true most overweight wives would lose their husbands and most chubby women would never find partners. "Your imagination is running out of control."

"Today, I did something terrible. I'm ashamed of myself."

He waits for her to say what.

"You don't want me to tell you?"

"Only if you feel comfortable sharing it."

"First, you have to promise you won't judge me."

"Found yourself a beau?"

She chuckles, takes a deep breath, and lets it out slowly. "I phoned Louisa on her cell ... I asked her if she saw anything unusual going on in the house. Louisa asked me what I meant. I tried to beat around the bush. She got annoyed. 'Mrs. Bates, if you is asking me to spy on your husband, you is asking the wrong body. No, I ain't see nothing out o' order in your home, and if I did see something I wasn' going tell you. I think you forget I is only the maid.' Millington, I felt so foolish afterwards. Louisa certainly put me in my place. What do you think of my action, Millington?"

"I can understand why you did it." *Yes, it was poor judgement. Why's your mother feeding you this information, if she doesn't think it's important? Maybe she finds being with the grandchildren onerous and wants out. On the other hand, Horton does his "thing on the sly." Has she found out?*

"I felt that as a woman Louisa would want to look out for my interest. I understand now. I didn't take into consideration that Horton is her boss, and it would be bad form to inform on him. I'm daft at times. In the end I felt stupid when I had to beg her not to tell Horton about the phone call … And if it's she he's sleeping with?"

He laughs and shakes his head. Louisa *is* matronly, portly, and a good ten years older than Gladys, not the sort of women men with the seven-year itch run after. Maybe if Louisa had a fine-looking brother who came by the house … He puts his hand on hers. "I'm pretty certain there's no one. Horton told me the night we last spoke that he loves you and his children very much."

"What made him tell you that?"

Her tone is accusatory. Her eyes are fixed on his face, the stare is burning. He dares not turn his head away or lower his gaze.

"He didn't just tell you that out of the blue. Come on. He had to tell you something before that. Or you had to tell him something that made him say that. Something he was tempted to do, or something he did that could endanger our marriage."

Wow. You are sharp. "If he did, I don't remember."

"Of course, you remember. The last time I raised the subject with you, you gave confidentiality as your reason. You're no longer a minister, Millington. You're no longer in charge of AMC Hastings. You can tell me."

Wesley's rule number six echoes in his head: *Speak evil of no one, else your word would eat as doth a canker; keep your thoughts within your own breast till you come to the person concerned.* "That's not all that I told you, Gladys. You've trimmed away what I said before I mentioned confidentiality." Now there's fear in her eyes.

Silence. A long one.

"This afternoon I had more control when I spoke to Len and Alex. I clenched my teeth each time I felt tempted to ask if their daddy had brought any new friends to the house. If he had, I think Alex would have told me. Len wouldn't … I'm tempted to ask Garfield to help me."

"Who's he?"

"My brother."

"You *have* a brother! ... Sorry."

"Yes. The apple of Daddy's eye until ... Forget it."

"What sort of help?"

"He's a man, isn't he? He'd be up to the tricks you men have. Just like how men talk about certain things *only when they're with other men.*"

Touché. "What exactly do you want Garfield to do?"

"Find out if Horton has another woman. What else? Remember the late nights out, the drinking, the swearing, the personality change? You refuse to tell me why." She swallows loud. "Those things men talk about between themselves. Right?"

"How would your brother do that?"

"Oh, he has street smarts. He has dirt on lots of people in high places that he can use to wheedle information out of them." Her eyes bulge. "Oh, yes. He does."

Am I hearing right? She has metamorphosed. For a few seconds he's speechless and his right arm twitches.

"Millington, you're blushing."

"And suppose Horton finds out? You know that if your brother starts snooping around, his colleagues would tell him?"

"I'll ask Garfield to shadow him. Find out who he hangs out with."

"And you're sure Garfield will want to?"

"He owes me. Big time. Since Daddy and, to a lesser extent, Mommy turned their backs on him, I've been the only one in constant touch with him."

"Why did they do that?"

She frowns.

"Sorry, you don't have to answer. I'm being indiscreet."

"Garfield was to be the lawyer that Daddy couldn't be because he married young and had us soon after. Every evening Daddy schooled him at home. Every single evening. Millington, I'm not exaggerating. Garfield sailed through Harrison College, aced his A levels and seemed set to do the same at university. It all crashed in his second year: the police followed a cocaine dealer onto the Cave Hill campus and arrested the dealer and Garfield in the middle of a transaction.

"He didn't go to jail then. Daddy paid the fine—$500. Insignificant. I think it was because the magistrate had been Daddy's college mate. He told Garfield: 'I'm not sending you to prison. You are from a good upstanding family. I am giving you the chance to turn your life around.' Until Garfield's arrest Daddy was president of the Lions' Club. He resigned after Garfield's arrest.

"The evening after the trial, Daddy cursed him out, went on and on about how Garfield had dragged us in mud and soiled our good name, about all the time he'd invested in him, and how it had come to nought. When Garfield couldn't take it any longer, he shouted at Daddy to stop. Daddy ignored him. Garfield got up from his chair, walked up to within a foot of Daddy's chair, gave him a burning stare, and shook a finger in his face. 'When you leave here on evenings to go visit Uncle Alistair, whose house you ending up in?' Uncle Alistair was my godfather and a close family friend. He was a widower and had become a quadriplegic following a car accident.

"'At Alistair's place. Where else.'"

"'Just listen to this bare-faced liar!' Garfield said, staring at Mommy and pointing his finger at Daddy.

"'Get out! Out! This minute. This in my house. No child o' mine speaks to me like this in my own house.'

"'I will. Mommy should put you out too. Then you can go live with Loretta Weekes. Uncle Alistair, huh.' ... He got deeper into drugs and has been in and out of prison. Horton doesn't want the kids to know him. They don't know they have an uncle. They know Horton's sister, Liz. She teaches at the Montessori school and babysits them sometimes."

Another long silence. Millington's too stunned to speak. Eventually he says: "At least your parents' marriage held."

She shrugs. "Isn't that how it is? One day we West Indian women wake up and discover our husbands have other women. We get angry and afterwards we grin and bear it. Most of the time we can't grin, we just bear it. We're too lazy to start over. What's the guarantee we'll find a better man? Better the devil you know."

Not altogether true. My mother fought back. Quixotically, I'll admit.

"Tell me if I'm wrong, Millington."

He doesn't answer.

"Garfield told me that Horton's colleagues are some of his best clients. He sells them whatever they want ... He could put their backs against the wall." She looks at him with raised eyebrows and nods.

"Extortion is a crime, Gladys."

"You mean blackmail?"

"Yes."

"But I want to save my marriage."

"Getting your brother to extort information out of your husband's colleagues is probably worse than not finding out the truth. If Horton finds out he might not forgive you."

"He'll know I did it out of love."

"Okay, so you ask Garfield and he agrees, and he finds out that Horton has another woman, what would you do?"

"Shame her into leaving my husband."

"And if she doesn't have any shame?"

"You haven't seen me in action."

He suppresses a chuckle. *And if he prefers* him *over you?*

"There's something ... I didn't tell you in August." She looks away. Her coffee cup is still full. The rusk is untouched.

"That night when I stayed up and confronted Horton, I did it over something else. That afternoon, as soon as I got in from Combermere, the phone rang. A male voice at the other end asked if I was Mrs. Bates. I said yes. 'Then tell your husband if he don't honour the deal, all hell going break loose.' He hung up before I could ask him his name. The day before that the bank had called me at work to tell me that a cheque I'd written couldn't be put through. When I looked over the debits, I saw that Horton had withdrawn $3,000 from the account without telling me. That night I asked him about it. He didn't answer, but the next day, along with the apology, he dismissed the phone call as a crank call and said the $3,000 was an emergency loan to somebody or other from his Eagle Hall days who'd fallen on his luck, and he'd forgotten to transfer the equivalent amount from his savings account."

Silence.

"I shouldn't be burdening you with my problems."

"It's alright." He looks at his hands to be sure they aren't sweating, and puts a hand on hers.

"I don't know what to think, Millington. I want to chuck my studies and go home. And I want to stay here and do something for myself. But if I stay, will I relax enough to complete the programme successfully? I don't think so. And if I stay, I might return to traumatized children. What should I do, Millington?"

"Do exactly what you feel is right." He suspects that she has already made up her mind to go home.

Her cell rings. By the time she gets it out of her bag it stops. "It's Mommy," she says ... "There's a message." She takes the message, and her shoulders slump. The phone falls onto the table. She is clearly in shock.

"What happened?"

Her eyes are closed, a hand over her mouth, her head shakes hysterically.

"Gladys, calm down. Calm down. Calm down," he whispers, tapping her hand. "What's wrong?"

Her body gives a contorting shiver, and sobs come. "Horton's ... in hospital."

She gets up and totters slightly. They get out of the café as quickly as they can. Outside he takes her arm, and they walk toward the university residence. Half way there, her cell rings again. "It's Mommy again," she says before answering. She listens then lets him hold the phone while she searches for pen and paper in her bag. "I need to write down the number of a plane ticket." While she writes the conversation continues.

"*The Advocate!*"

She listens in silence for about two minutes.

She hands him the phone and sways. He holds onto her. She breaks into hiccupping sobs.

"He ... overdosed. The story's ... already ... on the *Advocate's* website." The words break through her sobbing.

He gets her to sit on the sidewalk bordering the McGill campus.

He dials Jay's number. And as he pauses to find the appropriate words, Jay says that Jonathan is there visiting him. Not sure he wanted to hear that. He tells Jay that Gladys is having a serious crisis and he doesn't want to leave her alone.

"Bring her over. I'll prepare the sofa-bed."

He stops the first cab that comes by. They meet Jay waiting at the elevator. Her hiccupping sobs are gone but she's wobbly, and her face is tear-stained.

As soon as she gets into the apartment she asks for the bathroom, and they hear her vomiting. About twenty minutes go by and she doesn't come out. Millington calls out to her. He raps on the door. No response.

He meets her sitting on the toilet seat staring vacantly ahead of her. He coaxes her to come with him, and she follows as if sleep-walking. He pulls back the covers of the sofa-bed and gently eases her onto the bed. "Now, lie down and rest."

Jay comes to the door of the study. Millington waves him away.

She mumbles, then laughs.

He remembers that he has Ambien that he'd been given for insomnia. He goes to the bathroom and sees that the expiry date is December 2015. He takes the pills and a glass of water to the study.

She mumbles, "I'm lost."

"No, you're not lost."

He puts the water and the bottle of pills on a corner of Jay's desk, and sits on the armrest of the sofa-bed.

"Where am I?"

"In Canada, Gladys. In Montreal."

"Oh, yes. I remember now. What time's it?"

"A quarter to seven."

"It's coming back to me now. We were at Paragraphe for coffee. How did I get here?"

"You had bad news, and I didn't want to leave you alone."

"Bad news? I had a nightmare. A terrible nightmare." She pauses. "No. It wasn't a nightmare. Batey's in hospital. In a coma. Took an over-dose of pills. Blackmail. That's what Mommy said. Yes. It's coming back to me. Was home and didn't come for supper. Len went to get him.

Found him in bed and couldn't wake him. He screamed for Louisa. She came, read the suicide note, shouted for the neighbours to come, and called an ambulance. The journalists and police got there at the same time."

He puts a hand on hers and remembers that in their last conversation Horton told him that he'd attempted suicide twice during his teenage years.

She stares blank-eyed at the ceiling. "A journalist at *The Advocate* had already tipped off Mommy that they were sitting on an explosive story about him. That's what she wouldn't come out and tell me ... Say something, Millington. Tell me it's a nightmare."

He squeezes her wrist gently.

"No. Not a nightmare. I must get to my children. I was warned. There was that $3,000 withdrawal and that lie about helping a friend. And the phone call from that man." She stops talking.

"He used to get these calls and go into the spare bedroom to talk. His clients, I thought, and only got suspicious after his behaviour changed ... Millington, you think ..." She turns her head to look at him ... "I came here to run away from what my unconscious knew would happen?"

He taps her on the shoulder. "No, I don't think so."

"I'm too trusting. Mommy used to always say so."

"You need to sleep."

"Not too much. I have to be at the airport by 7:30. I need to be with my children. Poor Len. Why did I come away and leave them? Why? ... What time's it?"

"Just past seven. I have something here that will help you fall sleep."

She doesn't answer.

Silence.

"Millington, do you know that Horton is gay?"

He hesitates answering, fearing where the question might lead.

"You don't have to hide it from me anymore." Her head shakes slowly. "He said so in his suicide note."

"O-k-a-a-y."

"Okay, what?"

"Yes, he told me."

"That night he drove you home?"

"No. Before."

"Told you anything else?"

He hesitates.

"I want to know, Millington."

"He told me he loves you very much. That your love for him gave him a reason to want to live." He stretches the facts a little to help soften the feelings of betrayal.

"Are you ... gay too?"

"Yes." He holds his breath.

"Jay's your boyfriend?"

"My spouse."

"Does Horton know you're gay?"

"Yes. But I never told him outright." He waits for the next question. She doesn't voice it. He hears her swallowing and sees the light reflected in her tears.

"There were rumours about him, you know. Even before we got married ... Mommy told me about them, but I felt it was because she didn't like him. And Bruce, this gay history teacher at Combermere, used to drop hints. Bruce. Wears black blazers. A black handkerchief with white polka dots in the right pocket and green ties. The male teachers tease him, and he tells them they don't have what it takes to satisfy him. One time I begged him to tone it down, and he said I should go find the fleas in my own blanket ... There were hints, Millington. There were." She falls silent. It lasts several seconds.

She sits up. "I have to get back to residence. I can't lie here in these clothes."

"I'll go with you, but you must come back and sleep here. I would stay with you in residence, but I don't think it's allowed."

She squeezes his hand. "Thanks."

He calls a cab. They sit in silence on the way to the campus and on the way back. Back at home, she accepts the Ambien he offers her.

30

H E REMAINS IN the room for a good forty minutes after she falls asleep, during which he relives his last encounter with Horton. That Friday he'd got back home at 5:15 p.m., irritable and disgusted with himself after conducting a funeral in which he'd solemnly repeated words he no longer believed ... "Whosoever believeth in me shall never die ..." The man's wife had requested the recital of the Apostle's Creed: *conceived by the Holy Ghost, born of the Virgin Mary ... the resurrection of the body and life everlasting.* It got under his skin. It was already a couple of years since he'd felt humans should accept their place in nature and accede to its laws. Telling his parishioners that they can conquer death was treating them like cretins.

Around 6:30 p.m., when he turned the ignition key in the car to head off to Horton and Gladys's, the car sputtered and didn't start. He phoned to let them know he might be late, and before he could say he would take a taxi, he heard Gladys telling Horton to go pick him up.

During the drive from Vauxhall to Regency Park, Horton was circumspect. It was the first time Millington was alone with him in a car since his attempts to seduce him. Millington enjoyed the meal that evening: roasted chicken, rice, fried ripe plantain, sweet potato, carrots, christophine, salad, and for dessert, coconut-jelly ice cream. Simple, tasty Caribbean food, beautifully arranged. Never alcohol.

When taking him back to the manse, instead of driving towards Vauxhall, Horton drove south towards Worthing.

"Where are you taking me?"

"For a drive. Then into the bushes to rape you. Relax ... Just need to chat with you a little. Couldn't do that with Gladys present." He drove in silence, past Dover and turned onto the Maxwell Coast Road, drove a short distance, pulled up to the side of the road, and got out of the car. A strong breeze blew, the trees whistled, and higher than usual waves crashed heavily against the offshore reef. The light from an almost full moon glimmered on the water visible through a set of randomly spaced casuarina and fig trees, and a faint smell of jasmine was in the air. Horton fished something from his shirt pocket, then struck a match. Millington didn't know he smoked. Through the open window came the smell of marijuana.

Horton finished his joint and re-entered the car. "Now I must take my saintly minister home." But he didn't turn the engine on. Instead he pulled Millington's head toward him in an attempt to kiss him. Millington resisted and slapped Horton's free hand that had begun to fondle his groin. "Stop it and take me home."

Horton laughed, straightened, and returned his hands to his lap. Next, he smoothed his thighs. They remained uncomfortably silent for about ten seconds.

"Ever thought of ending your life, Millington?"

"No." That wasn't altogether true. At fifteen he had given it a passing thought, but his belief then in a just God and a literal hell had kept him from pursuing it any further.

"I tried a couple o' times, but people got to me before the poison took effect."

Millington heard him gulp. He put a hand on Horton's shoulder. The moonlight reflected in the tears filling Horton's eyes. He gulped again and swallowed. "When I found out I was gay and no matter how hard I prayed and nothing changed, I tried to kill myself. My first attempt was at sixteen. I swallowed a bottle of aspirins behind our house. Sister Brown, Doris's mother, saw me, and yelled to my parents: 'Miss Bates, Horton swallow a whole bottle o' pills. Gorblimey if Oi is lyin' pon he.' My mother pushed her fingers down my throat and made me throw them up, then rushed me in a neighbour's taxi to the Queen E, where they were already waiting to pump my stomach." He paused for a few seconds. "Daddy was asleep when the hullabaloo broke. It woke him up. He was a night watchman and slept during the day. When I got back from hospital, he wanted to beat me, but Mother intervened." He fell silent for a short while. A car drove by slowly.

"Luck rescued me the second time. A Saturday morning around eleven." He fished for something in his left shirt pocket, probably another joint, but retrieved nothing. "My parents had the only bedroom in our two-room chattel house. My sister Liz slept on a settee in the bedroom. I slept on another settee in the living room. I drank a tumbler of Clorox and lay down on the settee with my face turned to the wall. Mother had left for the market fifteen minutes before. Fate had it that Mother remembered that she had a letter to drop in the mailbox, and she came back to get it. 'Why in here reekin' o' Clorox? ... Horton, Why you ha' put Clorox in this glass? Horton! Horton!' By then she was standing over me. 'Help!' she screamed and yanked me up, and out gushed the Clorox. 'Help!' She shouted again, and I heard footsteps running toward our house. She sent Brother Abe, Doris's father, two houses down to telephone for an ambulance that rushed me to hospital." Horton was silent for several seconds. He fished in his right shirt pocket again but came up with nothing.

"Funny, I remember nothing more about the actual incidents. What I remember are my thoughts about what it was and still is to be gay in Barbados. Miss Simmons, who lived four houses down from us, had a son called George. When he was nineteen—I was twelve at the time—she came in from church one evening and met him naked with a man. All the neighbours knew about the relationship long before she did. You know how cramped Eagle Hall is. Everybody knows what's going on in everybody's house. It was one of them who went and got her from the Church of God where she'd gone for bible study, and 'opened [her] eyes to the abomination taking place under [her] roof.' She threw George out that same night and never spoke to him again. Four years later he died of AIDS. She didn't go to the funeral. Most of us went, but she, his mother—his mother!—didn't. She told my mother she wished George had died in infancy ... before he could disgrace her. Wished he'd died in infancy. His mother said that.

"My father threatened to put me in the street if I brought disgrace on him a third time." He swallowed, paused. "After the second attempt I decided to live—sort of. Since I'd failed twice, I felt it wasn't supposed to happen. Gladys and I were in the same history and English A level classes. I saw that she was in love with me, and I liked her. Now I can say I love her. Her parents weren't keen on our relationship, but we stayed together all through university and got married in our late twenties after I'd established my law practice. I didn't want children—I felt too insecure—and urged her to go on the pill. But that wasn't going to work with Gladys. As you've seen, Gladys is happiest when she has people to fuss over." He stopped talking—for quite a while. The odd car passed by on the narrow road. The wind whistled through the trees. The waves crashed. Millington wanted him to move on, felt that Gladys would be worried.

"It's been difficult, Millington. Difficult. Sometimes I wish I could make it disappear." He swallowed. "And expensive. Expensive in all the meanings o' that word. I did ... been doing ... my thing on the sly, always taking care not to take anything home to Gladys. She's so devoted ... Why me, God? Why me?" He began to sob.

Millington patted his left shoulder.

"I'm all right now," he said after about a minute and turned the ignition key.

They drove in silence all the way to the manse. At the door, before Millington got out of the car, Horton said: "Can I ask you a little favour? ... Can I ... can I come in?"

Millington hesitated. He wanted to say no, that Gladys was probably worrying. But he said yes.

They entered the living room. Horton sat on the couch and motioned to Millington to sit beside him. He did. They sat in silence for several seconds.

"You know, Millington, some days I'm ashamed to look Gladys in the face." He smoothed his thighs, frantically.

"You're okay?"

"The dam's about to break ... Any day now ... It's going to end badly. Poor Gladys. Why did I ruin her life? She never had a boyfriend before me. My children. Len and Alex. What will happen to them?"

"*End badly.* What do you mean?"

"Can't talk about it ... Move over." Horton pointed to the far end of the couch.

Millington moved over.

Horton slipped off his shoes, then lay down with his head on Millington's lap, his knees bent, his feet on the couch. "Put your arms around me." He raised his torso slightly. "Hold me. For just a little while. We won't do anything. I promise. Just want to feel your arms around me. I have to pull myself together before I go home."

Millington complied.

After a couple of minutes, he undid Millington's arms, got up, and went to the bathroom. He re-entered the living room naked.

Millington panicked.

Horton raised his arms. "You don't have to do anything about it ... Not unless you want to." He sat beside Millington for about ten seconds, all the while fidgeting, then got up and pulled him toward the bedroom. Millington followed as if hypnotized. He pushed Millington onto the bed and began to kiss him wildly. Then the spell broke. A chain of issues collided in Millington's head: adultery, his vow of celibacy—a veritable avalanche. As if he heard Melvin's stentorian voice bombarding him from inside his head: *Reverend Samuels, you vowed to uphold the precepts of Authentic Methodism and to inculcate them in others, to be a light to those stumbling in darkness, to be a model of holiness to all, to follow the path set out by John Wesley. Reverend Samuels, why are you in bed with your circuit steward, your church treasurer's husband?*

A tremor went through him, and he shook as if having a seizure. When he regained control, he pushed Horton away, sat up, and said: "Put on your clothes, Brother Horton." Horton stood up, gave him a bewildered look, and went into the bathroom where he'd left his clothes. Two minutes later Millington heard his footfalls heading toward the main door and, seconds later, his car drive away.

It was a hot, humid night, but his body felt cold. Panic filled him as he wondered if he'd ever be able to look into Gladys's face again. Talk about violating the laws of hospitality!

Sleepless the rest of the night, he wondered whether he could ever again mount a pulpit. He was already alienated from his vocation. His primary congregation at AMC Hasting and the others where he guest-preached would have thought him mad had he told them that the salvation he had sought in Methodism could be found only inside himself; that Christian rituals had ceased to be soul-sustaining, had become empty, sere, and false; that he was more at home with Buddhism than with Christianity—Buddhism minus reincarnation. It was what he'd written in his journal a few months before that fatal night.

He thought about all those who'd feel betrayed if he left the ministry: Aunt Pearl, Mem, Havre's AMC members, Reverend Hennessy, everyone who'd rallied to get him the bursary that paid for his studies ... The many mothers who'd flocked to have him be godfather to their children. And he feared the uprooting, the uncertainty, that would follow. What would he do for a living? A bachelor of divinity prepared him for one thing only: shepherding his congregation through this difficult life that Methodists once called a vale of tears—by nurturing their belief in the next. He was pretty sure there wasn't a next life, at least not in the way Christians—or Buddhists for that matter—proclaim it.

31

H E SPENT A miserable day all that Saturday. He was to preach at his own church and at AMC Speightstown the next day. Winston Gomes, the AMC Speightstown regular minister, had to rush off to Antigua. His mother had died suddenly. Melvin had called Millington on his cell while he was at Gladys and Horton's place to tell him about the death and to request that he fill in for Winston. He should have spent part of the day preparing a sermon, but settled on using one he'd given as a guest preacher at AMC Broad Street a few months earlier. In his distraught state, he'd made no attempt to get the car repaired, and he panicked when at 8 p.m. he realized he hadn't arranged transportation to Speightstown. He phoned Richard, Doris's older brother, a taxi driver, and asked him to take him there for 7 a.m. and to return for him an hour and a half later.

"Reverend Samuels," Brother Holder, the sexton, said to him as he got to the door of the vestry, "you looks like you been setten up all night."

"Had trouble sleeping. Stomach problems." Indeed. His stomach's where anxiety strikes. At ETC for a while he'd had to take cimetidine to combat what the doctors had thought was a gastric ulcer. On Saturday night bicarbonate of soda hadn't helped, and his stool was black that Sunday morning.

The second hymn, chosen by Gomes, was: "How firm a foundation, ye saints of the Lord." ...

When through fiery trials thy pathway shall lie,
My grace, all-sufficient, shall be thy supply;
The flame shall not harm thee; I only design
Thy dross to consume and thy gold to refine.

The soul that on Jesus doth lean for repose,
I will not, I will not, desert to his foes;
That soul, though all hell should endeavour to shake,
I'll never, no never, no never forsake.

Every line screamed, traitor! When it came time for him to preach, he couldn't. He was trembling. He told the congregation that he was feeling faint and suggested they sing a few more hymns to fill in the time. The choir obliged. Before the service ended, while they were singing "Awake, My Soul and With the Sun," he walked into the vestry, removed his ministerial robes, and exited the church, and in that moment he knew it would be the last time he would preach in one. Richard was already waiting for him.

In the car on the way home, he regretted his brashness. He could have toughed it out, and ended the service at the end of the hymn. Then again, it would have been too painful to stand or sit there shaking the hands of the congregation and exchanging bits of conversation, and he wouldn't have been able to keep his hands dry. That departing handshake is as important as every other part of morning worship. The congregation went home without hearing: "May the God of peace who brought again from the dead our Lord Jesus, the great shepherd of the sheep, by the blood of the eternal covenant, and may the Holy Spirit guide and protect you now and forever more"—and they probably blamed him for whatever went wrong in their lives that week.

Back at the manse he phoned Gladys and asked her to tell the Hastings congregation that he wouldn't be able to make it to church and to ask one of the lay readers to take charge. Next, he made oatmeal porridge to soothe the fire in his gut. He returned to bed and lay there considering his options. The phone rang at least a dozen times. He did not pick it up. Around four he unplugged it and went back to lie down.

Around 8 p.m., he got up, went to his desk, and wrote his resignation letter to Dr. Speedwell—Melvin. He made the resignation effective immediately, because his behaviour and beliefs were "now at variance with Methodist doctrine." He was on the roster to preach at Oistins AMC Wesleyan and his own church the upcoming Sunday. He advised Melvin to find a replacement.

Next morning, he mailed the letter and packed his clothes, journals, and the books he cared to keep, and air-freighted them to St Vincent that same afternoon. Two days later, Melvin phoned several times. From the Sunday onward, Gladys phoned many times as well. Her mother was in the Speightstown congregation that Sunday. He did not pick up the receiver.

On Friday Melvin showed up unannounced at the manse three hours before Millington's departure for St Vincent.

"Reverend Samuels! Reverend Samuels." His smile disarming. "Your behaviour is most peculiar. The congregation at Speightstown thinks that you've had a nervous breakdown. Without giving a credible explanation you didn't show up to conduct services at your own church. Are you well? What is your letter all about? You *cannot* leave the church like this. You're abandoning your vocation on a whim! What aspects of Methodist theology are you in conflict with?" He was (he died from a massive heart attack last month) a portly, very African-looking man, with an avuncular air, and a voice that boomed like a drum. Millington almost expected him to pat him on the shoulder and call him Sonny.

"I don't want to discuss it."

Melvin loosened his clerical collar and sat down.

Millington hadn't offered him a seat. He looked at his watch.

"Do you have to go somewhere?"

"Yes, to St Vincent in less than three hours."

Melvin frowned. "We have to get to the bottom of this. No one impulsively renounces holy orders in such a summary manner. When are you coming back?"

"I'm not coming back."

Melvin twisted his lips to the left, to the right, pushed them out, then pulled them in. He said nothing for a few seconds. "You've been planning this for a while, haven't you?"

Millington shook his head. "The leaving, no. But I've had doubts about the doctrines since I was in training."

"Why didn't you leave then? Why didn't you voice them then? Your tutors would have settled your doubts."

"I don't think so." *They'd have said: "Faith is the spiritual telescope. through which we behold God"* ... *that "the doctrines of the evangelical faith which Methodism has held from the beginning and still holds are based upon the divine revelation recorded in the Holy Scriptures."*

"So, this has been festering for a long time?"

"I won't use the term fester. There are other issues too. Non-theological."

"Reverend Samuels, let's get down to basics ... Have you impregnated a member of your congregation? Is that what your cryptic statement: 'my ... behaviour that is at variance with... means?'" He pulled the letter from his jacket pocket.

Millington began to laugh, tried to stop, but would break out laughing all over again, as if someone—an unholy spirit—were tickling him. Mr. Circuit Superintendent stared at him with furrowed forehead, bunched-up cheeks, and bulging eyes. The more Millington laughed the higher Mr. Superintendent's eyebrows rose.

"Reverend Samuels! You are hysterical! Get a hold on yourself! Stop it!" His voice was like a thunderclap.

And just like that the laughter stopped. When Millington's breath settled, he said: "Were that to happen, Mr. Circuit Superintendent—I mean getting a member of the congregation pregnant, I would have to be God and the woman's name would have to be Mary. Oh yes, and she would still be a virgin after she'd given birth. And down the road would come a new religion that would supplant Christianity. Don't look so sceptical. Mohammed did it some six hundred years after Christ. The Mormons less than two hundred years ago. Revealed scriptures, conversations with God, the whole kit."

There was silence, and for a moment Millington thought Mr. Circuit

Superintendent had turned into stone. *He must be convinced now that I'm truly mad.*

Millington looked at his watch. "Now, Mr. Circuit Superintendent ..."

"Don't be insolent. My name is Melvin Speedwell. You've always called me Melvin. You seem to have taken leave of your senses; have you lost your good manners too?"

Millington let that pass. "Unless you're planning to give me a ride to the airport, I have to ask you to leave."

"I'll drop you at the airport. What time's your flight?"

"A quarter to six. It's already ten to four, and you know how traffic is at this hour. Thanks for the offer." He picked up his take-on case—everything heavy had already been air-freighted—and headed toward the door. Outside, he locked the door and gave Melvin the keys. That morning he'd sent Doris home with two month's pay and told her he'd be away for a month or two, but that she should begin looking for work, in case he didn't return. She'd probably alerted someone, who in turn had alerted Melvin.

As he entered the car, thick raindrops began to fall. It had been cloudy and blustery all day and threatening to rain. A desirable rain for everyone but the tourists. The dry season was on.

"Millington, after the hiccups at the beginning, there are now only good reports about you." Melvin was now exiting the gate.

That surprised Millington. And in lieu of a response, he thought about the complaints Melvin had received—that his sermons were abstract, intellectual, and even heretical. One of his statements in particular seemed to have bothered some members of the congregation: "We redeem ourselves in the service we render to our fellow human beings." They said it was heresy and insisted that it was by Christ's blood only that humans could be redeemed: "the doctrine of the eternal covenant." Wesley would have agreed with them, but Melvin wouldn't have disagreed with Millington. Melvin's problem was with the declining church membership. "Millington, bring it down to their level. Make it good old-rugged-cross-that-they-will-one-day-exchange-for-a-crown theology. Liturgical tracks and doctrinal paths have been laid in their brains since infancy. Put new vehicles on them and they will crash;

take them off those rails and soon they'll be tangled in thorns and assailed by hornets." He had paused after, perhaps expecting Millington
to compliment him on his eloquence, but Millington said nothing. He
resumed. "They come to hear you repeat what they've been hearing
since childhood. You alter it at your peril. They want to be reassured
like you and me when we wake up and see the sun rise. Speak to them
as Jesus did in the Sermon on the Mount. It was for his comforting
words that thousands had flocked to listen to him."

Loaves and fishes too.

"Remember that our parishioners spend their lives struggling to
feed, house, and educate themselves and their children. They delegate
the care of their souls to us, and we should be comforting and inspir-
ing: urging them to go on, to fight the good fight. Life is hellish
enough. No need to make it worse. Those who want to be scourged for
their sins leave us and join the fundamentalists. Don't give the others
reasons to leave."

Millington had replied, sincerely, that he thought his assessment
was astute; however, he preferred to deliver sermons on ethical themes
and he saw no reason to change that. To which Melvin said that a
woman in his Broad Street congregation had asked him to preach a
sermon on adultery because her husband was having an affair with a
woman in the congregation. "And, parson, I want you to look at them
two while you is delivering that sermon. I want you to hit them hard.
You must make their conscience boil. Parson, if you don't do it, you
will end up burying them and visiting me in Glendairy. Take my word
for it this bright able morning."

"Did you?"

Melvin smiled. "A little bit. Yes. We have to meet them partway."

Because they pay our salaries. Millington didn't comment further.
It was enough that at every service he had to say the Nicene Creed,
sometimes with clenched teeth, sometimes with a sigh. Christmas,
Good Friday, and Easter services were difficult. He felt dirty after.

On another occasion he'd told Millington: "Intelligence is distrib-
uted in a way that obliges the few to think for the many; and if the few
fail in their duty, the many would thrash about in a moral void. Look

at what Jesus accomplished with allegories as he ministered to simple people. The masses will drift and drown if we don't provide the rafts and clear the snags and steer them away from rapids and dangerous currents. To the drowning ones we throw a lifeline." He was from Guyana, had grown up in an isolated village where his father managed a sawmill on a bank of the Essequibo River, and his only means of travel had been by boat.

Millington had mentioned his parishioners' complaints to William "Bill" Johnson, who'd replaced Silas in the South East Circuit. Bill was craven in Melvin's presence but mocked him behind his back. Bill advised him to focus on rhythm and rhetoric—style—when preaching and to forget about message. "I heard of one who got thunderous amens after proclaiming, 'I will chew the unchewable, invite the inevitable, and screw the inscrutable!' Your church will be packed Sunday after Sunday."

Millington laughed. "Have you tried it?"

"Not yet. It's a long apprenticeship."

Melvin and he were about a mile from the airport. Millington felt desolate and afraid. The rain was coming down heavily, the windshield wipers were swiping away at their fastest, the horizon was a dark grey, reminding him of a burial he'd conducted a month earlier under pouring rain. Since then it hadn't rained.

A man goes far to find out what he is. He'd read that somewhere, and knew that it meant drilling into the core of the soul to learn about and engage with the controlling forces there. Something every serious Buddhist knows. Something he hadn't done. Something he hadn't urged his congregants to do enough of. Instead he'd been told to bedazzle them with saviours, paradise, eternal life, crowns of thorns, and crosses —to be like he had been before going to ETC. He felt like shouting, Melvin, you and I are fakes. We encourage ignorance. I am tired and disgusted with this hoax. We are parasites. We prey on people's fears. I can't do it anymore. It's why I'm leaving. Instead he stared at the sweeping motion of the windshield wipers, then at Melvin's hands, small compared to his bulky body, manipulating the steering wheel.

"Why are you being so drastic?" Melvin broke the silence. "I tell you what: we all have patches in our lives when our faith is tested. God's enemies are busy. I'll keep our conversation confidential and accord you two weeks of stress leave. Something—I wish you would say what it is—is affecting you inordinately. Your behaviour is out of character. You have always been sedate and accommodating, always sensitive to the needs and feelings of others. This is not you, Millington. This is not you at all. I'm sorry that you won't be here. I would have arranged for you to consult a psychiatrist."

He would have. His pompousness aside, he was a deeply caring person. Millington remembers sitting across from him in his living room and hearing the compassion in his voice as he spoke about the parishioner who'd been raped by her drunk father. His laced fingers were behind his wattled neck and he stared directly across from him, the usual boom in his voice muted. "We see people taking drugs and wonder why they're destroying themselves. She's etched in my memory —her freckled honey-coloured face heavy with agony, pinched nose, sad light-brown eyes, and quivering lips. 'From then to now Rev,' she said, 'I've seen myself as a sack of filth ... A year ago when Papa died, I thought I would be free, that I would begin loving myself. It didn't happen.'

"'Did you tell anyone about it?'

"'Never. I couldn't live with the thought that others might know.'"

Melvin paused and tried to hold back his tears. "A week later her mother called and begged me to come by. Rose (that's not her real name) had locked herself in her bedroom for two days. She was an elementary school teacher and should have been at work. She laughed at me when I knocked on the door and pleaded with her to come out. Eventually, her mother called Rose's brother; he came and broke down the door. She stopped answering to her real name. Two days later when her mother stepped out of the house, Rose locked the door and set the house on fire with herself in it ... Since then she has been an inmate at Black Rock. Now when I go to see her I don't offer her communion. The first time I offered it, she knocked it out of my hand and called it poison." He stopped talking. This time he made no attempt to hold back the tears. He dried his eyes and said: "Sometimes confessing is like removing the scab from a wound ... More like she'd been caging a minotaur inside her and it grew too big for the cage ... In a single bout of drunkenness, that man ... that man ..." He did not finish.

As Millington was exiting his car, Melvin said: "I want you to spend the next two weeks in prayer and fasting and let the Holy Spirit guide you into making the right decision."

"I ..." *don't believe in the Holy Spirit.* "I'll pray about it." He gave him that, pretended to be in his snag-free current—he deserved something for his visit.

32

H E LOOKS AT Gladys lying on her back in the sofa-bed. Her breath is loud. A deep anguish fills him. This should not happen to such a decent person. Tears come.

Before rejoining Jay in the bedroom, he sits on the couch in the living room for a few minutes, to breathe deeply and compose himself. Flashes of the meeting with Jay in the Kingstown bar three and a half years ago fill his mind but quickly leave as he remembers that Jonathan was visiting Jay earlier. What was that about? He said his love for Jonathan was strictly Platonic. *Was that to placate me? Said too that his first gay experience was with me. Paul said so too. I want to believe them. But I'm not Gladys. Jay's agnostic, so religion didn't push him into abstinence, and he's indifferent to the black community's homophobia. First relationship with me at age thirty-two! In this liberated country where homosexuality has been legal before he was born! Come with another one, Jay. And so relaxed in bed—until my problems frustrate him. He must be angry—has to be angry—that he didn't marry Jonathan. I'm a pig in a sack, a pig that's afraid of mud.*

I should be forthright and ask him.

And if he says yes?

The earlier image of him sitting pensively in front of the blank computer screen comes to Millington. There's probably more to that Emory University meeting with Jonathan than Jay told him. Maybe he told Jonathan he would be out and invited him to come by. The other day Paul said something that stayed with Millington: that literature is full of works in which beautiful maidens turn out to be repulsive hags.

And Millington grew up hearing Elijah's stories about mermaids and *Jablesses*. And there's Josephine and Godfrey's story, a real story, not folklore inspired by men's fear of women.

His hands are sweating. He waits a couple minutes more for his feelings to settle before going into the bedroom. He meets Jay sitting pensively in the armchair that's in a nook on the right side of the bed. The reading lamp behind the armchair is turned off. The only light in the room comes in through the bedroom door that Millington has left ajar. He sits on the edge of the bed, almost at the foot, on a slant from Jay.

"How's Gladys doing?"

"She's asleep."

"That's good. Sleep helps."

"She has to be at the airport by 7:30. Her mother got Maggie, Doris' sister, to stay with the kids, so someone will be there when Louisa is away. Remember who Doris is?"

"Wasn't she your domestic helper?"

"Right."

Jay gets up and comes to sit beside him, enfolds him with both arms, and rocks him gently. "You must go help her pack in the morning. She's likely to wake up distraught. And you should go with her to the airport. Tell your boss you can't come in. You'll be too tired after all this ... Trouble comes without appointments."

"What was Jonathan's visit all about?"

Jay's a while answering.

"You mean it's confidential? You looked so preoccupied before I left to meet with Gladys."

"I was thinking about Laurent. Wondering what would happen to him now. He's not a Canadian citizen. Not sure if assault is a serious enough crime for him to be deported."

"Let's hope it's not. And Jonathan?"

"He came to tell me what happened—bring me up to speed, I guess—since he stormed out of here some three years ago and ignored my emails and phone messages. He said that for the moment he's 'a born-again virgin' but will reconsider if he finds 'a good fuck friend.' Said his last two relationships were disasters. One with a Haitian and one with a Senegalese. The Haitian's in the closet and has three children and expected Jonathan to be his *angel*."

"Where's the children's mother?"

"Here. They have joint custody."

"And the Senegalese?"

"Amadou. I've forgotten the Haitian's name. Amadou is doing a PhD in political science at l'Université de Montréal. He moved in with Jonathan. Stayed at his place ten months, then announced that his girlfriend was coming to join him and would live with them; they'd make a few minor adjustments, like having sex when she wasn't there. Anyhow, it turns out that Aminata—that's her name—wasn't his girlfriend, she was his wife. Up to then Amadou hadn't even hinted that she existed. And guess what? He told Jonathan: 'I give you great sex, and I don't even make you pay. Men like you who play woman, you have to pay plenty money to get fucked.'"

"What!"

"Jonathan told him to pack his things and leave immediately. Amadou threatened to trash the apartment. Jonathan called the police."

For a few seconds they're silent. "Jay ... I told Gladys that we're married."

He feels Jay's chest convulsing. Sobs follow and Jay's arms tighten around him. Jay swallows, releases his right arm, and dabs his eyes on the sleeve of his dressing gown. "I'd begun to think that you saw our marriage as something dirty that should be kept a secret."

Millington rests his cheek against Jay's and says: "You can't understand. You came here at seventeen. You haven't had to live any of your adult life worrying that one day your disguise might slip and you move from parson to pervert, from revered to reviled. So, yes, I'm here now, but my deception, my masks, they're not easy to remove. I know you see through my excuses not to accompany you to West Indian events."

Jay's silent.

"Say something."

"You do the talking."

"Know what I was thinking before I entered this room ... ?"

"What?"

"Forget it."

"Are you trying to get me angry?" He pulls away from Millington and puts his hands in his lap.

"No."

"Then say what's on your mind."

"Aren't you sorry you turned down Jonathan's marriage proposal?"

An eerie silence.

"Why should I be sorry?"

"Well, you know … You know the reason."

He's shaking his head.

"Jay, Jonathan's a university professor. I work two days per week sorting garbage. I'm a burden to you, another Amadou, another Laurent." *And the sex I offer is less than mediocre.*

Jay tilts his head back and puts his thumbs under his chin, then stands facing Millington. "It was a mistake to tell you about Jonathan, but Paul's free mouth left me no choice … Millington, please. You insult me every time you talk like this."

"Look at it this way. If I go to events with you, everyone knows you're a history professor. When they ask what I do … Do I tell them I sort garbage?"

"No, you tell them you're an unemployed theologian, and ask if they know of employers who need your skills." He moves closer to Millington and drops his arms onto his back. "I want you to stop your silliness. You think you can do that?"

"Another thing," Millington says, his head now leaning on Jay's chest, "when you came to St Vincent and found me distraught and destitute and proposed marriage, why did you do it?"

Jay snorts. "If you insist … Let's start with your sorting garbage. I wanted you to begin retraining. You turned down my offer to pay your tuition. I even got Paul to try to persuade you. It didn't work. Grudgingly, you accepted to let me pay for a few university credits. That's your choice, and I respect it … And what's wrong with sorting products to be recycled? … About my proposing marriage: I did it because I came to realize that I was in love with you and that together we might have a meaningful life. Should there be better reasons?"

"Not because you felt sorry for me?"

Jay backs away a little but doesn't remove his arms. "This is exhausting. You're tired. It's been a long day for me, and a devastating one for you. Let's go to bed."

"Not yet. I have another question. Why did Lionel propose a threesome with us?"

He snorts again. "You'll have to ask Lionel about that yourself ... Did you want the answer to be yes?"

"Don't be absurd."

"Absurd questions elicit absurd answers." He backs away a metre.

"Well, I felt you'd told Paul about my sexual difficulties ... And perhaps he'd told Lionel. And ..."

"Understand this, Millington. What happens in our bedroom stays in our bedroom. Grama instructed us to hope for the best from people but to expect the worst, to talk a lot about world affairs but not about our personal lives." He sighs. "She was right. Wise people keep their private affairs to themselves. I hope you know that."

"Come closer," Millington says.

Jay does and Millington reaches for his waist, pulls him to him, puts his head on his chest and listens to his heart pulsing away. He feels vulnerable. *Jay, I don't want to lose you.*

"Let's go to bed," Jay says. "It's been a long day for both of us."

Millington stands. Jay pulls back the covers, then goes to the bathroom to brush his teeth. Millington follows. They return, undress, and get under the covers. Jay turns onto his side, puts his arms around Millington's neck, and whispers in his ears: "Get rid of your silly thoughts. I love you and want to spend the rest of my life with you. I don't love you for your academic qualifications or the income you bring in or don't bring in. In time we'll work around the sex thing. You're still the beautiful person I admired back in St Vincent. You told me your sermons were on ethical issues. I want you to relax and love me as much as I love you. You think you can promise me that?"

"Yes. But ..."

"There are no buts."

Is this how it is in all love relations, Millington wonders. Can't be.

Then again almost half of all marriages end in divorce, many in the first few years. On the other hand, some bizarre couples, like the Huxleys, survive just fine.

He should put a night light in the corridor in case Gladys gets up to go to the bathroom and becomes disoriented; and, while he's at it, he should look in on her to make sure she's alright. He tells Jay this while slipping on his bathrobe.

Gladys is lying on her back and mumbling in her sleep.

He re-enters the bedroom and leaves the door open a crack, to hear her if she awakens confused.

He rejoins Jay under the covers. He knows he won't be falling asleep soon. His thoughts turn to Horton: the secret life he has led, its cost. Will he come out of the coma? Will it disable him? Will he be able to practise law if he recovers? And Len and Alex, how will they be impacted? Len especially? Discovering your father's inert body. Knowing he'd tried to kill himself. One day a family seems happy and whole, the next it breaks apart. Horton had sent out distress signals. The Saturday that he bullshitted about excrement and sperm, he said he was full of dark thoughts. That was six months before Millington learned that he was suicidal. He hopes Gladys is strong enough to handle all this. She loves him, might even want to stay with him, assuming he gets better. Requires an iron will to do that. Will Horton want to stay with her? Guess he could say he's bisexual, and she could say she's a liberated woman. She could point to Hillary Clinton who didn't abandon Bill in spite of the Monica Lewinsky affair. *The two aren't equivalent, Millington. For certain, not in Barbados.*

He listens for Jay's breathing pattern when he's asleep. He doesn't hear it. As if on cue, Jay turns onto his left side, moves closer to Millington, puts his arms around him, and kisses his neck. "I won't be able to sleep," Millington says. "I think I'll go read in the dining room. That's okay with you?"

"Yes," but it's followed by a loud breath intake that Millington interprets as protest.

He doesn't get up. They lie there quietly. He feels Jay's arm going limp but knows he's not yet asleep. His thoughts return to Jonathan. He'd like to see what he looks like. Wish he were still here when he and Gladys arrived.

He hears footsteps in the corridor, gets up, and puts on his bathrobe.

"Gosh, I woke you. I'm dying of thirst," Gladys whispers. "I don't want to wake Jay."

"He's awake. Don't worry. His class is at one tomorrow."

"I feel so guilty."

"Please, Gladys, please."

By now they're in the dining area. He pulls a chair out from the table, motions for her to sit, turns on the kitchen light, and goes to the fridge to get the water. She drinks it. He sits at a right angle to her.

Silence.

She breaks it. "Go back to bed, Millington. I won't fall asleep again. I'll just sit here quietly."

He shakes his head.

"Go back to bed. I'll be alright. I have to stay strong for Len and Alex. I won't have a nervous breakdown." She turns her head away. "Sorry. I shouldn't have said that."

"It's alright. I'll repeat again: Gladys, I didn't have a nervous breakdown." *We'd better clear this up once-and-for all. Everything's in the open now anyway.* "Gladys, I became disgusted with myself for attempting to bury my homosexuality in religion." He decides not to tell her about his disagreements with AMC doctrines. "I know now that I was waiting for something to trigger my departure. When Horton left to take me home that evening, he wanted to talk about his double life and the agony and guilt he was carrying because of it. It's quite likely that he went home overwhelmed by all that he'd told me. He made a veiled reference to the extortion, that leading a double life was expensive. His exact words were: 'Expensive in all the meanings of that word.' I didn't read extortion into any of those meanings, although I should have because I'd read in the Vincentian press of cases where extortion had resulted in the murder of one man and the suicide of another. Men who'd been paying former lovers not to expose them."

He stops talking. She shifts her head slightly, and the light from the kitchen shows that she's silently crying.

"After listening to Horton, the heaviness of my own secret became overwhelming, and I decided to leave the church ... I'm sorry. I failed you and I failed Horton. I wish I could have warned you, Gladys, but the rules of confidentiality prevented me. Forgive me. I wish the situation were otherwise ..." He begins to cry.

She stretches both arms across to him and takes his hand in hers. "I understand. I understand. Millington, I do. Your duties as a minister limited what you could say or do." She swallows loudly, a couple times.

He's relieved when she doesn't say anything about his ending up in bed with Horton that night. If she'd known, this would be the moment to say it.

His mind turns to wondering what his reaction would be if Jay were unfaithful to him, and he remembers that initially Jay had identified as bisexual. One time, Paul teased him about it; mentioned some girl he'd had an affair with while studying at McGill. He becomes fearful.

They fall into a long silence, during which her tears stop. Her swallowing too.

She breaks it. "Why don't you go back to bed? Jay's probably wondering ..."

"Don't worry. He's glad I'm out here with you. He's goodness itself. Compared to him, I'm a crook."

"You're not a crook." She yawns. "You're sure you don't want to get some sleep? ... Thanks for the Ambien. I can't take anymore; I have to be alert tomorrow. Don't want to get lost in these large airports."

"I'll come and help you pack."

"That's too much trouble."

"And I'm coming with you to the airport."

"No. You and Jay have done more than enough. Thanks."

"You're welcome. Always."

She squeezes his hand. "God promised never to forsake us in times of trouble." ... She begins to sing softly:

We have an anchor that keeps the soul
Steadfast and sure while the billows roll,
Fastened to the Rock which cannot move,
Grounded firm and deep in the Saviour's love.

He squirms, then remembers that those beliefs were his refuge and comfort during his lonely teenage years, especially after Jay left for Canada. "Let me just look in on Jay." He hears Jay's breathing when he gets to the bedroom door. He pulls it closed and returns to sit with Gladys.

33

AT 8.10 A.M., WHEN he goes downstairs to catch the airport bus back into town, he meets a man standing in the bus line who looks every bit like Elijah—scrawny, hunched shoulders, narrow, molasses-coloured face, beady eyes; he even wears the same type of grey felt hat that Elijah did—and it takes his mind back to this year's Vincy Unity Picnic, which he'd refused to attend. When Jay returned from it, he told Millington, while they were in bed waiting for sleep to come, about all the Vincentians he'd met there, mostly former class-mates and villagers. Millington had asked him to inquire about Alan. In a group that came from Connecticut, Jay met Elijah's daughters. A cousin of his Aunt Mercy introduced them.

That night when Jay's breathing indicated that he was asleep, Mil-lington went into the study and sat there poring over how he'd dealt with Elijah. Was it right to have remained silent? From the time he became a Sunday school teacher up to the time he left to prepare for the ministry in 2002, he'd come close to telling Reverend Hennessy a few times. How would Hennessy have handled it? Elijah would have denied it. Would Hennessy have pursued it and subjected the church to scandal? Millington thinks not. He wouldn't have had the strength or the support to deal with the fallout. But it has never been a sleeping-dog matter, for someone is always talking about rape and pedophilia on the radio or on television. And when he's asleep, he has no defences against Willy and Elijah.

They both died within months of Edward: Elijah two months later, Willy five. Since their deaths, there have been moments when he has felt like denouncing them. But they're dead; their relatives would deny it; he would bear the opprobrium. Mem said that Elijah got a grand funeral. When AMC members paraded up and down Main Street belting out "Onward Christian Soldiers" to the music of the police band, Elijah held one end of the banner, Mrs. Bonnette—another hypocrite —the other, as if he were the cross and she the flame. Elijah founded Havre's branch of the AMC Men's Fellowship. Mem said that busloads of them came from all over St Vincent to attend his funeral. Hennessy flew in from Trinidad to deliver the eulogy.

"I hope you coming for the funeral," Mem told him.

"I can't come."

"I wish you could o' come. He been very good to you."

They're dead; he lives with the nightmares in which they accuse him of luring them, and wakes up in a cold sweat, relieved that it was a dream, and wonders if there had been anything in his behaviour that had enticed them. Since coming here and reading about sex and the supernatural, he has wondered if more than lust was involved in Elijah's case. Was that why he'd wanted to masturbate him and get the semen? Did he need it for some occult purpose? Did he have mystical beliefs that required homosexual sex with adolescents? Why did his wife leave him for another man? What was Willy Green's role in this? Shouldn't put anything beyond someone who sacrifices a thumb for money. *Stop it, Millington. They're dead. Besides you've been attracted to men since you were fourteen. Elijah probably saw it in you and decided he would be first.*

The 747 bus pulls up. He boards it. The man who resembles Elijah goes to the back. Millington sits up front, directly behind the driver.

As the bus moves through Lachine, he wonders again if he should tell Jay about Elijah and Willy. Jay used to frown at his sweating hands whenever they made love. He doesn't now and is convinced that with time they'll overcome such hurdles. "We'll grow into each other; sex is only one part of marriage."

A vital part.

Why's he afraid to tell Jay? In many cultures around the world, rape victims are outcasts. Conquering armies turn it into a ghoulish carnival.

The ultimate proof of conquest. *See? I can violate your wives, sisters, mothers, daughters, you too, for that matter ... in any way I wish, and you cannot retaliate. Yes, it's a horror we want to hide, a horror we're ashamed of, a horror others would rather not hear about. Then again, a quick detour into history—pace Rwanda—reveals that today's violated were yesterday's violators. Even Bernard, a victim of the Rwanda genocide, admits this.*

Why would Horton resort to suicide? Alright, so he has a suicidal personality. He said he'd had the children to please Gladys; but, whatever the reason, a devoted father—Millington doesn't mean fathers like Edward and Twine, who've been damaged by slavery and colonialism—wants to be there to help nurture his children to adulthood. *Expensive in all the meanings of that word.* Did the payments exceed his income? Did self-disgust cloud his judgement? Did he feel that his children would be better off with him dead? Or was he just a coward? *Compassion, Millington. You haven't the right to judge him.*

Yes, Horton, lying is a costly affair. My homosexuality hidden from the church authorities. My masks. Not telling Jay what Elijah did to me. Keeping my marriage hidden from my mother and the general public. Lies! Lies!

In Barbados he'd written in his journal that *the urge to classify those who're different as witches and burn them at the stake is still with us. No longer able to execute "eccentrics," we cast around for other ways to punish them.* Seen today in Putin's Russia and pretty well everywhere else in Eastern Europe ... Uganda's anti-gay laws and the persecution from the religious right. And he was a minister in a church that promotes anti-gay discrimination, that joined the suit against abolishing Belize's anti-gay laws. A church that in 2002 called for a two-day fast in Guyana to oppose the decriminalization of homosexuality and to uphold discrimination against gays—they were especially determined to keep gays from becoming teachers. He entered ETC in the midst of this, to train to become a minister in that church! Unbelievable! He guesses that if one has been told over and over that he's guilty, he begins to think he is and might well fall into the trap the Central Park Five found themselves in and accept culpability for crimes others say they've committed.

How is Stilford faring? How's he reacting to Horton's dramatic outing? Is he shocked to discover that his class leader is gay? Maybe his gaydar had already picked it up. He too had threatened to commit suicide if he couldn't be "healed" of his homosexuality. From Horton's letter, Stilford seems to have moved away from wanting to commit suicide. In any event he believes in a literal hell where he could be tortured by fire eternally. Dissuasion enough.

When the bus is one block from entering the Berri Bus Terminal, Millington resolves that today's the day he should tell all. But walking home from the terminal, with the wind threatening to tear off his clothing, he's no longer sure. They've just come through a difficult night. No point getting into a situation that might cause another.

34

H E MEETS JAY coming from the garbage chute when he exits
the elevator.

"Back so soon?"

"Gladys got processed quickly. I had no reason to hang around
the airport."

"Go get some sleep. Your eyes are puffy ... Worrying about Gladys,
aren't you?"

He shrugs. *Shouldn't I?*

"Is something else bothering you?"

"Know what? Yes ... I'm tired. Let's go sit." They're standing in front
of the coat closet. Millington points down the hallway to the dining
table. They walk there.

Millington sits and points to the chair across from him.

Jay sits. "So? I'm waiting."

Millington raises his arm, gesturing patience. "I know—believe me,
Jay, I know—why victims kill their aggressors."

Jay frowns and glances at his watch. "Okaay."

"I'll make it short. While I was in seminary, I heard about a boy
in the U.S. who killed his adopted father who'd been sexually abusing
him. I remember asking myself: why should that monster go his merry
way, perhaps doing the same thing to others?"

Jay frowns and rapidly opens and closes his eyes.

"Raping a son, killing a father ... That's stuff you expect to find
only in a Greek tragedy."

"And this is a prelude to ... ?" He glances again at his watch.

Millington's a while answering.

"This is the intro to ... Who would you like to kill? Me?"

"You're funny. You're not to repeat any of this. Not even to Paul. You understand?"

"Okay. I think I do."

Silence.

"What am I not to repeat?"

Only one can keep a secret ... The first dry heave comes, followed by others.

Jay gets up from his side of the table, comes to stand behind Millington, and kneads his shoulders, then goes to the kitchen and returns with a glass of water.

It takes a while for Millington's breathing to normalize and his stomach to settle. He feels cold even though sweat is on his forehead and trickling from his hands and armpits.

"Remember, Jay, that I always wanted you to accompany me to Hollow?" His teeth are chattering.

"Yes." Jay sits on his left and puts an arm around him.

"Ever wondered why?"

"No. You accompanied me to my grandmother's land sometimes."

"Well, it was because ..." Millington stops.

"Because?"

"From the time I was fifteen I was afraid to go there alone ... Afraid I might meet Elijah Bowman on the road or Willy Green working on my parents' farm. You knew them?"

Jay purses his lips pensively, shakes his head questioningly, and says: "Paul would, if they shopped at Grama's store. What about them?"

Again, the roiling in Millington's stomach. He presses his elbows against the table and takes three deep breaths. "You remember when I sprained my ankle?"

Jay nods. "Yes, it was in August, not certain which year. Grama, Paul, and I had gone to Bequia. When we got back, your mother told Grama about it."

"I turned fifteen that August ... One late afternoon ... our Boys Brigade troupe was on Father Crowley's grounds playing soccer. A player collided with me while I was kicking the ball away from the goalpost. I fell sideways and sprained my left ankle. Kelson—he was already over twenty—helped me to sit up. You must know Kelson. He became a police officer."

Jay nods.

"Holding on to Kelson I hop-climbed Pasture Road to my parents' house. By the time I got home, my left ankle was swollen to almost twice the size of my right. Daddy felt that Elijah would be able to help me ...You sure you don't know Elijah? Folk healer, storyteller? The man who made potions?"

"Oh him. We sometimes smelled his brews when the breeze was blowing downhill."

"He played dominoes on our porch with Daddy ... He was my god-father. Leaning on Daddy's arm, I hopped to his house, five downhill from ours. Elijah twisted my ankle this way and that and massaged it. He said it was just a bad sprain. By the time he finished smearing it with a lot of yukky stuff and bandaging it, my foot and my entire leg were on fire, and I couldn't put any weight on it. He said that most of the pain and some of the swelling would be gone by morning. My mother came by, and he explained the situation to her and asked if it was alright for me to spend the night at his house. She left and returned about fifteen minutes later with my supper and my pyjamas. Our families were close; he was a pillar in our church.

"He had a settee in the living room. He made up a bed there for me, and around eight o'clock, he gave me a tumblerful of one of his concoctions and said it would lessen the pain and let me sleep soundly. I don't remember being awake much after that until ... I awakened flat on my belly, a searing pain up my rectum and Elijah's body on top of me ... As soon as he realized that I was awake, his thrusts became rapid and violent, followed by his trembling body and groans as he ejaculated ... I was too frozen to cry. It was early dawn.

"'Turn over and lemme jerk you off. I want your cum,' he said, and tried to turn me onto my back.

"I resisted. 'I will tell my father. I'm going to tell Daddy,' I said, when my voice came.

"'And if you so foolish to do that, you will disgrace me for true, but I will tell all the secret bullerman-them that you beg me for bull you, and all o' them will have a go at you and threaten to expose you if you refuse. And afterwards everybody going know, and treat you like Job. You want people for treat you like Job?' He spoke quickly, calmly, as if he'd rehearsed it. Next, he pulled open a drawer, picked up his wallet, extracted a $20 bill, and shoved it at me. I shook my head and folded my arms. He tried to force it into my hand. It dropped onto the floor ... He said: 'You remember the gun I have?'"

"He had a gun?"

Millington nods. "'You tell anybody 'bout this and I will blow out your brains first and blow out mine afterwards. I will. As God is my witness, I will. You not going destroy me and get away with it.' ... Jay, it happened two days before my birthday ... I don't remember anything more about that August, not even when my ankle healed or how long it took ... I worried that he might have infected me with HIV, a worry I carried for years. Whenever a pimple appeared on my skin, I thought that was it.

"He tried many times to bribe me after that. A yellow shirt one Christmas. I never wore it. I had it spread out on my bed and was hold-ing a pair of scissors to cut it up, when it occurred to me that I could give it to Alan, which I did. He sent me money in an envelope another Christmas. I never knew how much because I never opened it. He'd sent the shirt and the money via Mem. At some point she noted that I'd never worn the shirt and asked me about it. I told her I hated yellow and had given it to a friend. Anger showed in her face, but she stifled it. If she'd asked me about the money, I'm sure I would have lied. A few days after he'd sent it, I was at our gate and saw him holding a machete and heading down Pasture Road in his wellingtons; on his way to look after livestock he kept on land he rented in the valley behind ours. I waited for about fifteen minutes, then went to his place and put the envelope with the money onto his porch. Before he raped me, he'd give me sweets—a small bag of toffees—usually on my birthday, pens and pencils at Christmas, and when I ran errands in the shop for him and the change wasn't much, he'd let me keep it."

Jay hands him a napkin from the holder on the table, and Millington dabs his eyes and blows his nose.

"Whenever I met him in the street, I quickened my pace to put distance between us. One time Mem noticed that I was avoiding him and asked me why. I shrugged. She frowned but didn't question me further. Every morning on my way down to Main Street to catch the bus for school and every afternoon returning from school, I crossed over to the other side of the road until I got past his house. Like us, he had a hibiscus fence at the front of his property and a gate that Daddy had built. One day, a couple of months after the incident, Mem and I were walking down the hill together, and I instinctively crossed to the other side. When I rejoined her she was frowning ... 'Why you trembling, Mill?'

"'I'm not trembling,' I said and forced a smile. She wouldn't have wanted to know that Brother Elijah—our church usher, close family friend, my godfather—was a pedophile-rapist. She was convinced that good, if carefully nurtured, could triumph in every human being, that prayer could work miracles. Twine, the alcoholic wife-and-child-batterer who lived down the slope opposite us, was often in her prayers. To discover that Brother Elijah—as we all called him—had raped me, I'm not sure what it would have done to her faith."

Jay's breathing is audible, his face is taut, his elbows are pressed to his sides, his knuckles on the table are closed tightly and pushed against each other. He breathes deeply, then leans into Millington, and puts his arms around him.

"For a long time I feared for my life."

"And Willy Green?" Jay asks, as he reaches toward the napkin holder in the centre of the table for a napkin. He dabs his eyes, wipes his nose, and resumes holding him.

"About three months after the incident with Elijah, I walked by Willy creating rows of earth mounds to plant sweet potatoes on our land. He was part of a farming group that my parents belonged to. I greeted him and continued over a low hill into a valley where I had tied the goats that morning. As I was untying the second goat, I heard thudding footsteps a few metres below me. I turned and saw Willy approaching, his fly open, his penis in his hand. He licked his lips at me, stuck his tongue out, one hand pointing to his penis, the other beckoning me.

"'I will tell my father. I'm going to tell Daddy. Leave me alone,' I screamed.

"'Don't try for play innocent. Elijah tell me you loves to do it. I will pay you.'

"'I'm going to tell Daddy! Leave me alone!' I screamed even louder.

"He pushed his penis back into his trousers and hurried away. For about a month, he stayed away from playing dominoes on our porch, and when he returned he was on tenterhooks every time I crossed the porch. Of course, I never told anyone."

He listens to Jay's swallowing and loud breathing. For several seconds they sit in silence, Jay's arms tight around him.

"So, you see, it's why, apart from wanting to be with you, I needed you, whenever you could, to go with me to Hollow ... Remember that film that Madonna made, in which the little Malawian boy's testes are cut out to be used in sorcery? Try to imagine how that boy feels, and you'll have an idea of the feelings I've been living with all these years ... You boarded in town during the school year, so you could only accompany me in July and August. After the encounter with Willy I bought a penknife and always had it on me whenever I went to Hollow ... I've never heard anyone call them bullermen or child molesters. But I doubt my situation was unique. The gun gave him an advantage. Fear of being killed probably kept his victims silent. Fear of becoming pariahs too."

Silence.

"I've never felt clean or safe after that. In St Vincent, whenever a man looked at me, I would feel my body tensing. I was afraid too that Willy would tell others what Elijah had done, that the news would spread, and Elijah would think that the info came from me, and kill us both."

Jay sighs and reaches for another napkin. "And you never told anyone! Not even me! Incredible." He holds Millington tighter than before. "You've carried this secret for ..."

"Twenty-one years. For a few years I believed that God would one day punish them. Believe me, it helped—until I stopped believing in hell and a final judgement."

"You couldn't tell me then. That I understand. But three—more than three years—it took you all this time after our marriage for you to tell me!"

Millington doesn't know how to reply. How could he tell him that each time they make love he's assailed by images and emotions from that experience twenty-one years ago?

Jay shakes his head slowly and says: "You shouldn't have suffered alone like this after we got married. You shouldn't have. Besides, Willy and Elijah have been dead for ..."

"Five years ... I wasn't sure you'd understand. Are you ...?"

"Of course, I understand! I get it. That's why you're anxious and tense when we make love ... I wish you'd told me when we reconnected in St. Vincent. I wish you had."

"Why?"

"I'd have had a better idea of the trauma affecting you."

"And?"

Jay's silent.

"You're not thinking I hid this, fearing that you would reject me?"

"Do you really know me, Millington? I would have pushed you to see a psychologist three years ago ... as soon as you got here. We'd have had a three-year head start. That's what I mean."

"And the cost? I'm already a freeloader."

Jay takes a deep breath, lets it out noisily, removes his arms and gives a long sigh. "Don't use that word in connection with our relationship! Don't! My work insurance would have paid for most of it. And if it didn't, I have enough to cover it." He sighs again. "So many callous, predatory people in this world. So many!" He pulls Millington close to him with one arm. With the other he lifts his chin, kisses him, and resumes clasping him. "We'll do what's necessary to heal you."

"Jay ... don't you feel cheated?"

Jay begins to answer but Millington shushes him. "Let me finish. I shouldn't have married you. Remember that first time we had sex, I told you we shouldn't go through with the marriage? I should have been more insistent."

Jay unclasps his arms and pulls Millington's head around to face him. "Why do you say such things? ... You know, Millington, at age nine ... ten, I felt ashamed of my father and wanted to stay away from him. I'm glad I didn't. On her deathbed, Ma told me that the year she came home to see us—I was ten, Paul was four—Daddy told her that, but for the pain it would have caused me, he'd have drowned himself in the Atlantic. I'm glad that in all that horrific brutality, I somehow knew that my father loved me, and that I made an effort not to reject him. Maybe about killing himself, he didn't mean it. Though if he'd continued drinking at the rate he was, he just might have. Ma told him then that she wouldn't let him see Paul unless he gave up drinking. You know what? He gave up drinking. I watched my father turn his life around, and I became proud of him."

"So?"

With his raised right arm, Jay gestures patience. "Millington, my father doesn't have your intellect, your education, your sophistication, yet he was able to turn his life around. Are you implying that you don't deserve to be loved, that you are no longer entitled to enjoyable sex, because someone abused your innocence? How are you responsible for what Elijah and Willy did? Besides, they're both dead."

"That's not how psychological trauma works. I once dreamed that my mother found out and told me it was my fault, that I had no right being gay. I was raised in a church that condemns homosexuality."

"And you became a minister in that church." He raises his arms, defensively. "Okay. Okay. Don't get me wrong. You've left it and have assumed your sexuality."

"*Trying* to assume my sexuality." What he should really say is that he has been thinking Jay would be better off if they separated, that the price he was paying to stay married to him was too high, that Jonathan was still single. At least they'd resumed contact.

"And I used to think I had problems ... We Caribbean kids rarely grow up with affection. Paul's an exception. Many of us are made to feel that we are burdens to our parents. Our parents hold us only when they're raining down blows on us ... when they're wounding us—before my father became an alcoholic, he never hugged or complimented me—and we have trouble handling affection when we partner up. Perhaps it's why there's so much cruelty in Caribbean marriages; why so many children of Caribbean origin here are in the care of child protection services." He falls silent.

"Do you love me, Jay?"

"Of course, I love you, Millington. Of course, I love you ... Is there anything else that you are hiding from me?" He puts his arms on the table.

"Like what?"

"I don't know. Anything else you feel too ashamed to talk about, that you want to keep hidden. That dirtied you. Anything that's on your conscience. I don't mean ending up in bed with Horton. Hope you're not blaming yourself for his attempted suicide."

Silence.

"Are you?"

"No. I told Gladys the entire story last night. Almost the entire story—all except being in bed with her husband. I felt she was too vulnerable to handle that part. Horton's story's in the *Barbados Advocate*. The reasons too."

"How was she at the airport?"

"Outwardly calm. Her children are her priority."

"You haven't answered my other question."

"No, there's nothing. Are you angry with me?"

"Millington." His right hand moves to Millington's chin and caresses it while he speaks. "Not angry. Frustrated. Frustrated that you hadn't told me this before ... I'm seeing more clearly now. Horton's attempted suicide is the blow that broke open the vault you kept those secrets in."

Silence, a long one. Millington listens to Jay's agitated breathing. His is too.

Jay puts his hands in his lap, swallows loudly, then says: "I remember how much I didn't want people to know about my father, how ashamed I was of the bribes he paid ... his alcoholism. In Montreal it was Paul's delinquency... Hearing your story, you've set me thinking about Paul and me staying in Kingstown during the week. What if Cousin Alice's boyfriend were like Elijah and Willy and he'd abused Paul or me?"

They stay silent for a long time. Jay puts his elbows on the table and rubs his hands.

"Jay." Millington takes a deep breath and lets it out slowly. "There's something else I want to tell you. This is hard to say. Bear with me. Don't get angry. Aren't you dissatisfied with your sex life?" Jay does not answer. "You should be ... If you'd known I was such a psychological mess would you have married me? ... That went through my mind when you told me yesterday that you met up with Jonathan at the conference." Jay's silence makes him nervous. "And he followed it up with a visit here right after. Was that to test the waters?"

Jay glares at him but says nothing.

"See? I'm right. He brought you up to speed. Did you bring *him* up to speed?"

"Meaning?"

"You know what I mean."

"You mean, tell him what goes on in our bedroom?"

"Yes."

"Stop it, Millington. Stop it. Stop reducing our relationship to sex. You think you can do that?"

Millington begins to sob. Jay holds him tight against himself with both arms.

When the sobs end, Millington says: "Yes, what happened to Horton helped me open up. You're right."

Jay sits up straight and pulls Millington's head around and stares into his eyes. "Today, while I'm at work, I want you to make an appointment with our doctor and have him refer you to a psychiatrist."

Millington nods.

"Go get some sleep. You didn't sleep last night. I should be getting ready to head off to work."

35

MILLINGTON LIES IN bed unable to sleep. His mind is fixed on last night's events and his earlier conversation with Jay. It took him fifteen years, until he was thirty and already a minister, to understand why he hadn't told his parents about Elijah and Willy. After the gun threat lessened, it was the fear that if his parents found out, they'd have confronted Elijah; and all of Havre, and eventually many Vincentians, would have known; everywhere he went afterwards people would have whispered behind his back. Some to his face. A frightening scenario. Certainly, Elijah didn't think he should keep the story to himself, for he'd told Willy. Perhaps they trolled for each other. Willy probably felt Millington would feel degraded enough to yield to his advances ... Low self-esteem resulting from childhood rape and incest is one of the main reasons young women—young men too he's sure—give for going into prostitution. Elijah and Willy probably told others. Neil Charles? Did they make a go at him? Or was Neil merely able to see behind his mask? No, if Neil knew he would have hurled it at him. How many knowing eyes stared at him moving through Havre? How many men thought they might lure him into some secluded area and empty their semen in him? What would have happened if he'd accepted Elijah's gifts? Would others have tempted him with gifts too?

Gladys should be in Miami now. He hopes she's bearing up well. She appeared more in control this morning. Around 4 a.m., he watched her struggling to eat the breakfast Jay had prepared for them—oatmeal porridge, toast, eggs, fruit salad and coffee—pausing her chewing and staring ahead of her, her forehead deeply wrinkled. A couple of times Millington tapped the table in front of her to make her snap out of it. In her room in residence she showed him three dresses: a dark green satiny one, a royal blue, and a yellow, and asked which one she should wear. He suggested the green. She wore it with black coral earrings, a black belt, and black flat-heel shoes. She said nothing about last night's events. Not here. Not while they sat on the airport bus or in the airport before she cleared security. He waited until the last minute, while he was hugging her goodbye, to tell her to hug the kids for him, and to give her $50 to buy trinkets for them in the departure lounge. She objected but he stuck it into her coat pocket and told her not to forget. He made her promise she would call him when she got home, regardless of the hour. And then she was gone. To what only fate knows.

Jay glances into the bedroom and is leaving silently. "I'm awake," Millington says. Jay comes, half lies on top of him, and kisses him. Millington begins to cry and feels foolish. "You'll be late for work." Jay kisses him again and gets up. When Jay's at the bedroom door, Millington calls to him: "Come home early. There's a lot more to talk about and decide."

"I will. And we still have to plan something to celebrate your permanent residency."

"Something quiet. Just the two of us. I told you already the play at Centaur would be enough."

Now's the time to inform Mem of his marriage. Horton's neighbour wished that her gay son George had died in infancy. What did she say when AIDS took him four years later? She didn't attend his funeral. What if Mem tells him: I wished you'd died that time you were sick and in hospital? Stilford was adamant about hiding his sexuality from his mother: *"Reverend, are you crazy? She'll disown me."* Millington felt he was exaggerating, but George's fate said otherwise. Paul told him that it was probably a father-son confrontation over hidden homosexuality that caused Marvin Gaye's father to kill him. Telling Mem won't be easy. Her comments about Job are seared in his memory.

He decides that he'll take Aunt Pearl up on her offer to help him. Just in case ... The day after the e-ticket from Jay arrived, she and Mem spoke while Millington was out on his walk routine, and Mem gave her the news. When he got in, Mem said: "Make sure you phone Pearl when you get to Canada. You owe her plenty." She stared at him and twisted her lips a few times before saying: "For the education you have ... the useless education you have ... Anyway, you owe her a lot." The pauses meant more than the words.

Three or so months earlier, he'd overheard her asking Pearl to plead with him to return to the ministry. In those days Mem repeated to him almost daily what Somerset had told her: "Reverend Somerset say your superintendent didn' find nothing wrong, and is your stubbornness that holding you back. Humble, yourself, Mill. 'Pride cometh before destruction and a haughty spirit before a fall.'"

But Aunt Pearl was more interested in his health. "Nephew, maybe it's a little loving you need. Boy, that is good medicine. The best there is. Aretha Franklin has a song about it. And isn't it the gospel truth!"

Edward considered her to be his only surviving sibling. He insisted that Lilian, a half sister, wasn't his father's child and never spoke about her. Pearl was thirty-two when she moved to New York, after living in Trinidad for eleven years. For a few years she worked as a maid on weekends and went to school during the week until she qualified as an LPN. Immediately afterwards she began a degree in social work, and got her BSW a few months before Millington began studying at ETC.

Two days after Jay and he got married Millington phoned her. After exchanging banalities, she said: "So you in Canada on a holiday or what?"

"No. It's ..."

"You got a permanent visa for Canada!"

"No. Not yet."

"You met somebody from Canada in St Vincent and he gave you a job?"

"No."

"You got married to somebody?"

He paused a long time before saying: "I got married two days ago."

"And you couldn't tell me? My only nephew that I care about get married and I only a bus ride away and he didn't invite me! ... You love the woman? You know what I mean."

Of course, he knew what she meant: Was he paying this woman to marry him in order to become a Canadian resident or was he pretending to love her until he got his resident visa and ditch her afterwards?—a phenomenon so common everyone knew of it. A few of his parishioners had done it.

"Yes. There's lots of love between us. Lots of love."

"Sounds like you smitten bad, nephew."

A long pause.

"So where's she from?"

"She's ... She's ..." He couldn't continue.

"Millington, what you hiding from me? What is it, Millington? Don't be afraid to tell me. She's handicapped? ... Millington?"

His throat constricted. Jay came out of the study and was passing by. Millington grabbed his hand and gave him the receiver, now coated with sweat. Millington went into the bathroom and splashed cold water on his face. He doesn't remember how long he remained in the bathroom. He heard Jay calling to him, saying that his aunt wanted to talk to him.

He went to the dining area where Jay was and took the phone from him.

"Millington, I'm happy for you. I'm glad you have the courage to do what you know is right for you. Is not everybody can do that. I worked with a St Lucian doctor that killed himself and his wife with AIDS because he used to lead a double life ... So, Jay is Ma Kirton's grandson. I met her at her store that time I came to St Vincent. 1979. The Soufrière erupted the week after I left. Your mother was pregnant with you." Millington knew the story. Mem had told him.

"So you married a teacher. Now I hope you all don't do like some o' the gay fellows I work with. I hope the both o' you will take care o' one another and don't fall into temptation. I see too many happy gay couples break up because one or the other didn't know when to keep his zipper closed. I am eager to meet this Jay. He sounds so nice over the phone. I'm happy for you, Millington. I am."

"Aunt Pearl, can I beg you a favour?"

"What, child?"

He hesitated

"You need money?"

"No, not that."

"Well, you know if you need it and I have it I will give you."

"Not money. Another kind of favour. Can I ask you to keep this a secret? I'm not ready to face the world with this. It happened too fast. I'm not ready."

"What you mean *you not ready to face the world*? Don't tell me you shamed o' the way God made you? Don't tell me that, Millington. And you were *a minister*!"

"No. It's because I don't know how to break the news to Mem. Mem hates gays. I don't. want her to hear it from anybody else before I've told her myself."

"Okay. I will keep my mouth shut. Yes, that will be tough for your mother. You can't blame her, you know. You can't. I might o' been just like her, if I didn't come away and broaden my understanding. Well, not quite like her. It had a gay fellow, Jiggle, in the tenement building where I used to live in Laventille. Was the tenants gave him the name Jiggle. He had a big bumsie that used to jiggle when he walked. One bumsie jiggled up and the other bumsie jiggled down. Something to watch. I wasn't one of the ones that called him names or ridiculed him. Deep down I did know that Jiggle didn't make himself so, and nobody could o' convince me otherwise. Millington, if you want my help when you get around to telling Mem, let me know."

How will Mem respond when she hears the news? Hopefully not say she wished he'd died or she'd died before he could shame her. She'll definitely run to see Somerset. And he'll pray with her, and ask God to give her strength to bear it, and he'll advise her to keep it a secret. But as soon as she leaves he'll be on his computer emailing the news to Bill

Johnson, Melvin's replacement, Bill in turn relaying it to all and sundry and asking: did you suspect he was one?

We don't, not even the humblest among us, want to be turned into pariahs. It's why Horton tries to kill himself. His third attempt. I suspect he'll fail this time too.

36

SOMETHING COLD TOUCHES his cheek. He opens his eyes just as Jay is lifting his head. It's dark in the room.

"Slept well?"

"Yes. Fell asleep about an hour after you left. What time's it?"

"7:25." He turns on the light.

His mind turns to Gladys. He wonders how her day's been going. He remembers then that she'd given him a phone number of someone to contact at McGill to advise the university that she had an urgent problem to attend to in Barbados. He feels bad that he forgot. He'll do it first thing tomorrow.

Jay sits on the edge of the bed. "On the metro going and coming, I wondered what you were waiting to discuss with me; but, first, did you call to make that appointment?"

"No, I fell asleep and never woke up until you got in. I'll do it to-morrow. Don't look so sceptical. I will. I want to."

"So what are we supposed to be discussing?"

Millington stares at the wall ahead.

"Having second thoughts, huh?"

"No. I want to be the first person to tell my mother that you and I are married." His bladder is full to bursting. He gets up and goes to the bathroom.

Jay is still sitting on the edge of the bed when he returns. He looks into Millington's eyes and says: "So your mind's made up?"

He nods. "I can't delay it forever."

"And you won't change your mind—tomorrow ... next week?"

He shakes his head and sits down on Jay's right.

"You shouldn't do it over the phone."

"That's what I think too ... I was hoping that Aunt Pearl could be with me when I tell Mem."

"Well, she did offer to help you break the news ... See if you can arrange it ... All three of us could go to St Vincent. It would have to be at Christmas though."

"You know that we'll have to be out of St Vincent before the news spreads? If we hang around we'd be harassed."

He nods. "You could ask your mother to keep it a secret until after we leave."

"It wouldn't be fair to ask her to bottle up her anguish."

"She might surprise you."

Millington shakes his head. "Her pride got a huge blow when I left the ministry. You won't understand how deeply Caribbean Methodists revere their ministers, and she was the mother of a minister. Alas, one who forsook the ministry. This blow will be several times worse. The belief that I'd had a nervous breakdown cushioned the first blow somewhat. There'll be nothing to cushion this one. For her and all of Havre, I'm a pervert. Besides, Caribbean mothers with gay sons are told they didn't raise their children right, and they believe it."

"I know all that, Millington. My mother blamed herself for our sexuality. I'm from St Vincent. Paul knows it even better than I. He remembers everything the shoppers said about Jack and Brady and their mothers. You better prepare yourself. For argument sake, if your mother gets sick after you tell her and blames the news for her sickness, will you be able to live with a clear conscience afterwards?"

He's a long time thinking about this. "Jay, if I don't tell her, she'll hear eventually and complain that people are spreading lies about me. After which I'll have to tell her. You know what she'll think then? That I pretended to be gay and forced myself into a relationship with you in order to come to Canada."

"Okay." He sounds weary. "Speak to your Aunt. Find out if she can go to St. Vincent at Christmas. Tell her we'll pay for her plane ticket and her accommodation. If she can't go then, we'll have to delay it until the spring break or June."

"June will be too late. By then there'd be gossip about us in Havre. It would be unfair to expect Gladys to keep our marriage a secret. Melvin's dead but there are at least half a dozen ex-colleagues of mine that she knows. She'll tell one or two of them. Soon the ministers of the entire district will know. By June Miss Collins would have already gone to comfort 'Sister Samuels in this her time of affliction and help ease this burden that the Devil done saddle her with ... All you see the disgrace what pickney does bring?'"

Jay laughs. "Not bad."

"Behind Mem's back—maybe even to her face—Miss Collins would talk about the beatings I should have got and say I turned gay because Mem and Edward spared the rod and spoiled the child. Oh, the pleasure she would have in what she and other Haverites would call 'Sister Samuels' affliction'—when Mem's present—'Sister Samuels' downfall,' when she's not. No, Jay. I have to prepare my mother beforehand. If Aunt Pearl can't go, both of us or I alone should go."

He shakes his head. "Not you alone. I want to be with you."

"Do I seem so fragile?"

"It's not a question of fragility. It's a question of being there for you. We're on this journey together. Besides, you're likely to get anxious after telling her about Elijah and Willy."

"I won't touch that."

"Why not?"

"It would be too much all at once. Don't forget that Elijah was my godfather ... She might choose not to believe, but if she does, she might think that the rape made me gay, and might even tell others so in an attempt to exculpate herself ... You are the only person I've told about the Elijah-Willy incidents, and you must never tell it to anyone, even if I predecease you."

"You've certainly thought that part through. So, you will never tell her?"

"Never!"

Jay frowns and shakes his head sceptically. "It's almost half past eight. Phone your aunt."

Millington feels his neck muscles tightening as he reaches over to pick up the phone on the night table. He hopes she's out, but she answers on the third ring, "Yes, my dear nephew."

They get over the polite greetings, and Millington falls silent.

"You're so quiet. Like you have bad news for me?"

"No. It's a favour I call to ask you, a big one, and I feel foolish asking it."

"Anything honest I can do for you, Millington, I will do. Just ask."

He takes a deep breath, then tells her what he wants from her.

It's a while before she says: "Why you all didn't plan this before? Lemme see. I can have Christmas off if I choose to work New Year's ... I tell you what, you all work out the travel plans, and tell me what the ticket cost. I pay for my own ticket, you understand?"

"Jay offered to pay ..."

"*Stop interrupting me, Millington.* Tell Jay I want to spend two weeks ... You can't go all that distance for only one week. I will ask for two weeks' vacation ... Lemme check the calendar ... Tell him December 15–29. They will want me to be available on December 31. And as soon as you get your papers, you and Jay have to come down here and visit me. That's an order, Millington, my price for going to St Vincent with you. You understand?"

"Perfectly."

They talk on about this and that for about five minutes. He's tempted to tell her that he got his permanent resident visa yesterday, but decides not to.

Jay gets up and goes to his computer to look for flights.

It's almost midnight when Jay comes to bed. "I've managed to book your aunt from New York to St. Vincent on December 15 and from St. Vincent to New York on December 29. But you and I will be on standby when we get to Barbados on December 15 and on standby again from St Vincent for our return on December 29. We might have to spend a day or two in Barbados, going, returning, or both. I'll try LIAT again tomorrow."

It's an hour later. Jay is snoring away. Millington's earlier sleep leaves him awake and alert. Didn't Horton have a friend he could have confided in, who would have discouraged him from attempting suicide, somebody in that group of gays that met in St James? He saw the storm clouds before they broke. Couldn't someone tell him to go get a visa at the American consulate or just buy a plane ticket and come to Canada? Once here, he could have asked for refugee status. He remembers: *"Dark thoughts, Millington, dark thoughts."* Horton might have confided in him if he hadn't left the ministry and he might have been able to dissuade him. *Too late now, Millington. Too late.*

Millington rests his head on Jay's chest and listens to his heart ticking away. What will time do to their relationship? Where would it take them? He sits up and stares at the outline of Jay's body in the dim light, and he becomes intensely aware of the present, the present that becomes the past as soon as it's perceived. He recalls himself at twenty-one-twenty-two with his dreams of becoming a Methodist minister, the elation he felt when his candidacy was accepted: the zenith before the descent to sunset and night. He stares at Jay's heaving chest, thinks of all the love it holds for him now, and wonders when this moment is remembered decades from now, when their bodies have become decrepit, will they have grown tired of or sated with each other? One of Paul's characters says: "Intelligent humans discover quite soon that the road whose destination promises bliss is full of detours that take a lifetime to sort out, and we die before we finish sorting. If we're lucky we come to know early that our real destination is death." Paul is too young to be so wise. Guess with cancer in his brain, he has an incentive to be.

He feels afraid. He has promised Jay he'll undergo therapy. And if therapy doesn't work? Can the effects of trauma be erased? What if their problematic sexuality is because they aren't sexually meant for each other? When they watched *Kinsey*, it was what he'd wondered, but he'd quickly dismissed it. He still wonders what would come to the fore if both of them were to get drunk. Parts of their buried selves for sure. *"A man goes far to find out what he is." How far will I—can I—go? And if I'm repelled by what I find? A few of Mother Bernice's pilgrims returned crazed by their encounters in the nether world. Taken apart, some things can't be reassembled.* He wipes his sweating hands on the sheets and wonders if thoughts like these assail Tyrone, Lionel, Gina, Carlos, Marc-André, Emilia, Muriel, Guícho. Paul certainly. Jay maybe less so.

It's 2.05 a.m. Gladys hasn't called. Probably afraid of waking them. Perhaps overwhelmed by being with her children. Maybe she sent an email. He gets out of bed as quietly as he can, goes to the study, and turns on his laptop. There it is, from gbates.

> *My dear Millington,*
> *I'm home. The flights were on time. When I got to the immigration desk, the officer looked at my passport, offered me his condolences and said that arrangements had been made for me to leave the airport secretly—to get away from the journalists outside—and they would take care of my luggage and bring it to my home in the morning.*
> *An airport vehicle drove me a few miles from the airport to a location, where Mommy, Daddy, Len, Alex, and Garfield were waiting for me.*
> *Before boarding the flight in Miami, I received a text from Mommy telling me that the worse had happened. With God's help I'm holding myself together. I'm still numb. Don't expect to hear from me for the next few days.*
> *Thanks for all your help. Say thanks to Jay for me. Will be in touch when things settle down.*
> *Gladys*

Sadness and a feeling of helplessness overpower him. Then tears. Then anger. So much injustice. So much pain. So much waste. Why? Why? What the hell are we? He remembers a journal entry: *Even with playthings to distract us, life's a trap until the deliverer comes; some won't wait that long and commit suicide.* Easy to write. Easy to damn well write! He leaves the desk and sits on the sofa-bed. He's tempted to remain there until Jay wakes up. After a while he remembers that he didn't reply to

Gladys's email. What will he say to her? He dislikes the clichéd phrases that express grief, but for now they'll have to do. He returns to the computer and writes that he's sorry the situation resolved itself that way, that she should dig deep in herself to find the strength to carry this burden through the mourning period and beyond. It seems hollow, insufficient. He adds that he hopes she knows she can call upon him at any time. He wonders about that last statement. How would he be able to help her? He clicks send anyway.

At some point in the future, depending on her willingness to listen, he'll discuss with her the situation in Barbados that led to Horton's tragedy. Let her know that similar persecution in St Vincent had pushed him to become an AMC minister. Unless she understands the depth of Horton's problems, she might become hateful and angry—no one likes to feel used—and waste energy that would be better spent imbuing her sons with the confidence they'll need to successfully negotiate their way through life.

He rejoins Jay in bed.

"What's wrong?" he asks.

"Nothing."

"You're trembling."

"Horton is dead. Gladys sent an email."

Jay turns onto his side and clasps his body to Millington's. He too is trembling. "Poor Gladys."

They're silent for a long while. Millington breaks it. "Suffering. Too much of it."

Silence.

"You should go to the funeral. She'd appreciate it."

"I don't think so. I'm not ready to face my ex-colleagues and parishioners. With Gladys I've rectified what can be rectified ... Maybe when you and I change planes in Barbados in December, I could try to see her and the children ... Go back to sleep. You have an early morning class. I'll lie quietly beside you. We'll talk more about this when we have time."

Acknowledgements

I offer my thanks to the several people who have directly or indirectly aided in bringing this novel to fruition: Clayton Bailey and Olive Senior read the manuscript and offered comments. Ilona Martonfi's Reading Group, of which I'm a member, offered valuable advice on the excerpts I read. Audiences at Argo Bookstore, Montreal expressed their appreciation for the excerpts I read there. Julie Roorda and Michael Mirolla skilfully edited the manuscript. David Moratto bore with me as we brainstormed about designing a visually-relevant cover. My late uncle, Rev. Dr Cyril Dickson, was an invaluable resource for the theology that informs *Easily Fooled*. Carlyle Williams and I spent many hours discussing the central themes of *Easily Fooled*. Benoit's love, patience, and emotional support made the writing possible. A final thanks to Guernica (Connie McParland, Michael Mirolla) for making the publication of this novel possible. Excerpts from an earlier incarnation of the novel were published as follows: "Break-out," *Transition* 124. 2017; "Unusual Gardening," *Montreal Serai*, https://montrealserai.com/article/unusual-gardening/; and "A Hefty Cost" *ArtsEtc, https://artsetcbarbados.com/fiction/hefty-cost.*

About the Author

H[ubert] Nigel Thomas grew up in St Vincent and the Grenadines but moved to Montreal in 1968. He is the author of 11 books and dozens of essays. His novels *Spirits in the Dark* and *No Safeguards* were shortlisted for the Quebec Writers Federation Hugh MacLennan Fiction Prize. *Des vies Cassées* (the translation of *Lives: Whole and Otherwise*) was shortlisted for le Prix Carbet des Lycéens. He holds the 2000 Professional of the Year Jackie Robinson Award, the 2013 Université Laval's Hommage aux créateurs, and the 2020 Black Theatre Workshop's Martin Luther King Jr. Achievement Award. The Canadian High Commission to Barbados and the Eastern Caribbean States deems him to be one of Canada's outstanding immigrants from St Vincent and the Grenadines. His books *Behind the Face of Winter* and *Lives: Whole and Otherwise* have been translated into French.